PILGRIMS REST

Michael Nicholson is a well-known British television correspondent, the author of several novels and the winner of many international awards for his coverage of foreign affairs for ITN. In 1981, after four years as their news correspondent in South Africa, he drove home to Europe overland with his wife and two small sons – a five-month trip which took them across Africa from Cape Town to Cairo.

Also by Michael Nicholson

Fiction

THE PARTRIDGE KITE
RED JOKER
DECEMBER ULTIMATUM
PILGRIMS REST

Non-fiction

ACROSS THE LIMPOPO

PILGRIMS REST

Michael Nicholson

FONTANA/Collins

First published by William Collins 1987
First issued in Fontana Paperbacks 1988

Photoset in Linotron Old Style by
Rowland Phototypesetting Ltd
Bury St Edmunds, Suffolk

Made and printed in Great Britain by
William Collins Sons & Co. Ltd, Glasgow

To my wife Diana,
my sons Tom and William,
and the Africa we all love.

Author's Note

Most of the characters in this story are based upon real people who lived in Bethesda, Pilgrims Rest and Pretoria. Most names I have not changed, and likewise most of the major events described are historically correct. However, those readers who know the time and places better than I, will recognize a few liberties I have taken. I hope they will forgive me.

Acknowledgements

My thanks to Michael Sissons for encouragement, to Topsy Levan for her tireless typing and editing, to Angus McDermid for his help with Welsh, to R. Merfyn-Jones for his history of the North Wales quarrymen which inspired the opening chapter, to George Chadwick from Durban and his knowledge of the Zulus, to Persis Tozer, to the Lowveld Diggers and Transport Riders Society in White River, to Peter Coston and Andrew Hall of Pilgrims Rest Museum, to all the early chroniclers of this story's time and place, and especially to all those dead and buried diggers whose unmarked graves line the hillside overlooking Pilgrims Rest.

MN

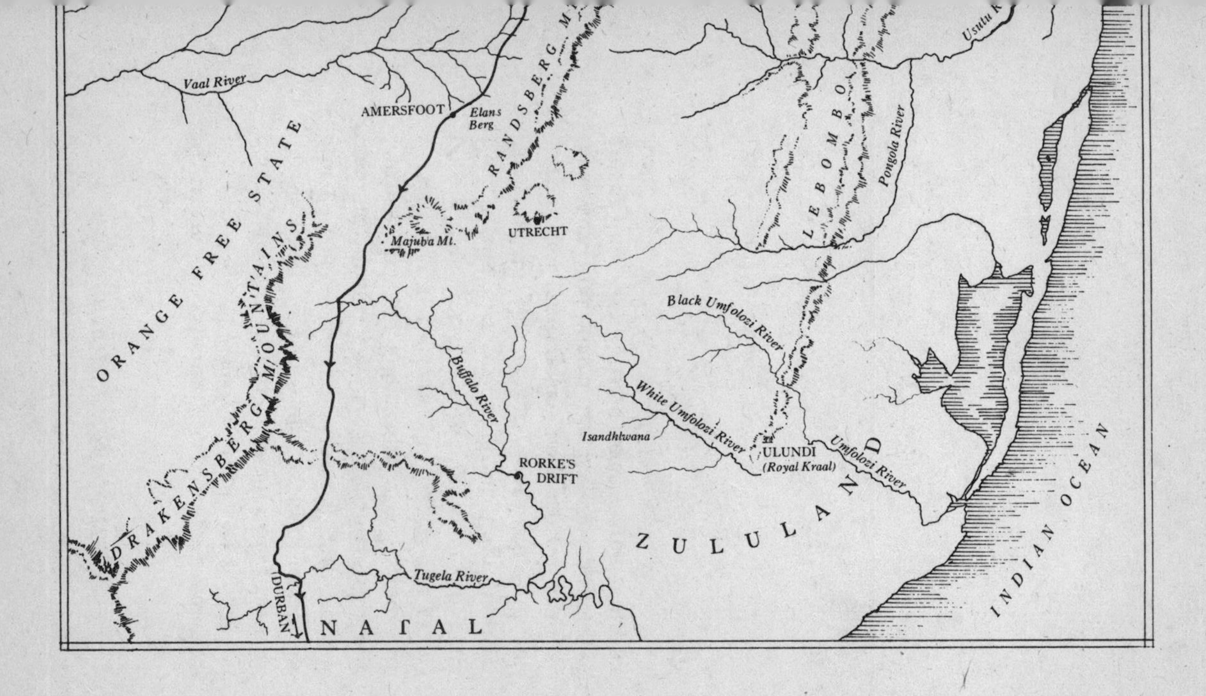

ORANGE FREE STATE
DRAKENSBERG MOUNTAINS
Vaal River
AMERSFOOT
Elans Berg
RANDSBERG M
Majuba Mt.
UTRECHT
LEBOMBO
Pongola River
Usutu R
Black Umfolozi River
Buffalo River
White Umfolozi River
Isandhlwana
RORKE'S DRIFT
ULUNDI
(Royal Kraal)
Umfolozi River
ZULULAND
Tugela River
DURBAN
NATAL
INDIAN OCEAN

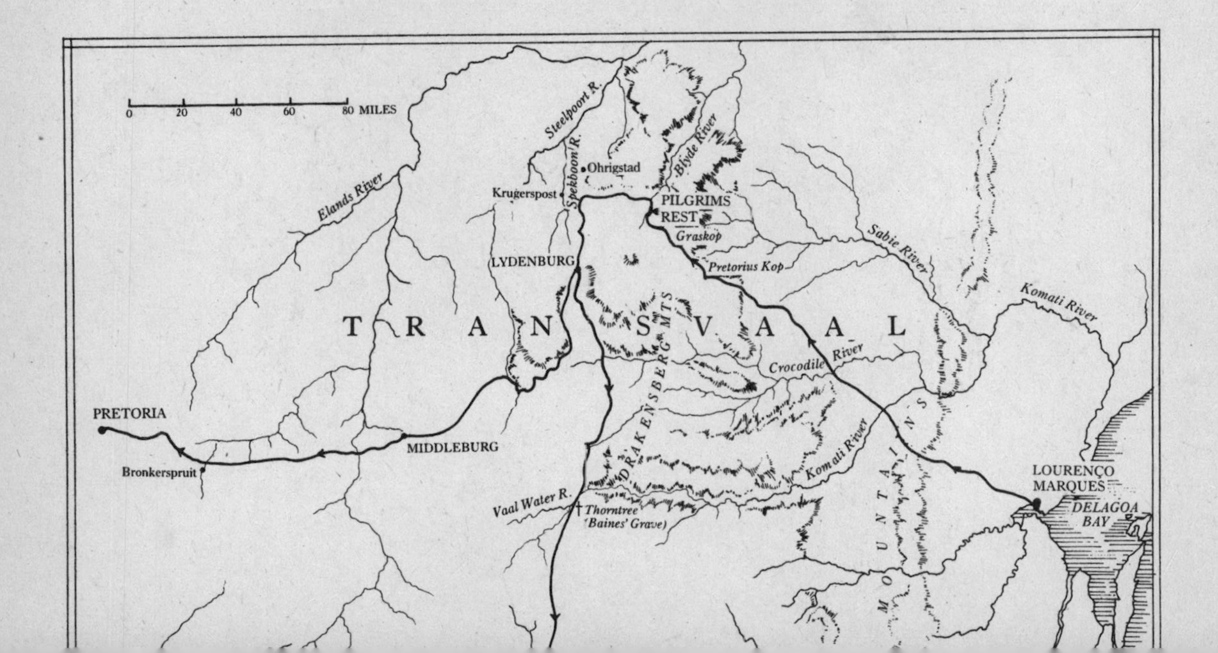
0
20
40
60
80 MILES
TRANSVAAL
PRETORIA
Bronkerspruit
MIDDLEBURG
LYDENBURG
Krugerspost
Ohrigstad
PILGRIMS REST
Graskop
Pretorius Kop
Elands River
Steelpoort R.
Spekboon R.
Blyde River
Sabie River
Komati River
Crocodile River
Kom ati River
Vaal Water R.
Thorntree
'Baines' Grave)
DRAKENSBERG MTS
MOUNTAINS
LOURENÇO MARQUES
DELAGOA BAY

CHAPTER ONE

Since they had sailed from Dartmouth she could not look at the sea and the grey tricks it played. But now, as they rounded the Cape of Good Hope, she felt settled for the first time. She saw the sky and sea were the same blue, joining each other on a cloudless horizon and she gripped the handrail tight with both hands and held her face up to the large evening sun to smell the spray better. It was no hazard now and it did not threaten but tasted sweet on her lips, sweet, when for so many painful weeks it had tasted only of salt and bitter bile. She filled her chest with air and was surprised. They said there was no land for at least a hundred miles and yet the air was heavy with the perfume of flowers.

The sea had not been easy but whatever her sickness, she had felt safe because it was the Atlantic. It had touched Wales, washed Wales, she had seen its surf on the rocks at Bangor when she was a child. It was the water of home, and as long as she could see it, smell it and taste it, she was in some small, diminishing way still tied to Wales. But not now. This, they said, was the Indian Ocean and she prayed to herself aloud in the breeze, surrounded by this strange calm scented sea. The bells rang forward, sharp shrill familiar sounds now, and she could hear her boys shouting, 'Bombay!' and 'China!' and she knew Wales was no longer with the ship. This was the water of a new world and she cupped her hands over her forehead to shield her eyes from the biggest, reddest sun she had ever seen. And they said the shadow under it was Africa.

* * *

How short is a year, but how her life had changed in less than one! In that first week of January, Owen had sat in their front parlour, dressed in his best suit and shirt, and they had all eaten cake. She had knitted him a woollen tie and Ianto had spent a halfpenny to buy him a new paper collar so that he would look smarter than all the quarrymen who came to shake his hand and wish him happy birthday. Later, Huw had stoked the fire and Ianto and William had poured out the red bottle of ruby wine they had hidden until everyone had gone. Then, when the children were upstairs asleep and the bottle had turned an empty green and the cinders only warm in the grate, she had sunk under Owen in love.

Next morning they went to chapel with the Sunday bell ringing, the snow crisp and sparkling in the sun, men in their bowlers and the women with their black shiny umbrellas. She had knelt and prayed to God that this time it would be a girl because she could call her Kate, though, she told him, she would not mind another boy because she could call him Tom.

And then by the late autumn, heavy and waiting, Bethesda was a village dying, Owen was already dead, and she left her new baby in his cot for the funeral.

Mary Llewellyn was thirty-six years and a few months old, but the quarries had not aged her like the other women. Although the sun was seldom seen, her skin had the colour of honey and Owen had often said God had meant her for another place. She was a handsome woman with many curves; round full lips and round brown eyes in a round full face, and all the roundness neatly capped by the bun of shiny chestnut brown hair. The quarry had not scarred her nor made her wretched, though other women were old before they were thirty and, more often than not, widows before they were five years older. Only the very young men were strong in Bethesda for it was not long after manhood that the dust began to eat at their chests and wither them away.

She remembered how Doctor Williams had held Tom, only minutes old, and said, 'God turns out a very even lot of babies, Mary. But look at them as they pour out of the quarry thirty years on, and ask what changed them so? Why they die so young and how frequently they die, when a well-fed man, breathing good air, might have lasted so much longer? Our men die too soon,' he said, 'while our English masters go off with gout and apoplexy, white-haired in their beds.'

Even now she could hear, in those early wet and wringing foggy mornings, men spit up the slate dust in their parlours before they went in the dark to work, slamming doors on their wives still asleep.

But it was not the dust that had killed Owen, nor the dampness. Nor was he wrong to have left her alone with the children. She simply felt angry sometimes that she should have lost him, a good man who had loved her, when there were so many others in Bethesda whom God might have chosen and who would not have been missed, even by their own.

There was nobody there to miss her now, no one to leave, nothing left, nothing to be missed. Not the tiny cottage squeezed with others into Douglas Terrace: little houses built for one family that sometimes housed four, and the beds never empty. Nor would she miss the chapel that sat like a squat grey throne, sending out ugly shadows, always judging and always finding guilty.

It had not really been a valley when she and Owen had first moved in, she seventeen and already pregnant with Ianto. But long before her first son was a man, mountains of slate slurry had risen each side of them, right up from the fence in the back yard, and as she watched the sky grow smaller she felt she was sinking into the middle of the earth.

For nineteen years she had lived in a parlour, a front room and two bedrooms, a tiny house full of big men. Huw, her second, was no trouble and Will, her youngest before Tom came, was everybody's darling. Only Ianto was on the outside. Much later, and now too late, she recognized how deep was his love of Owen, who should have been his father. The other children took Owen so easily but Ianto grabbed his love as if something inside told him it did not belong to him to have and only she knew why all these years. She had not left the secret behind in Bethesda. She had brought it with her and it would travel everywhere she and Ianto went together. Once she had thought she might tell him, carefully pick a time, but not now, not since Owen died.

When Ianto was thirteen and at the end of his school, he had wanted to join the railways, but that would have meant him going south to Cardiff or even across to Bristol and Owen would not have it. Above all things, he said, he would keep his family together. She remembered the evening, with Owen naked in his bath by the fire, talking in his quiet and gentle way about the quarry and how Ianto should come in with him.

'It's hard work but not heavy for a boy like you. You'll not notice the labour. Even a lad half your size would not break himself, for a man is slowly brought up to work the slate. The rock, you see, has been there since God first placed it and you need to coax it gently. You could do it, Ianto, you have the eyes and the hands to bring it out. It's like an art, you see – like poetry and singing. Did you know that quarrymen go to the Eisteddfod every year where poetry and music and slate-splitting rival each other for the Crown? If you come in I'll teach you how to spit and dress, I'll show you how to trace the posts and the beds and the spring veins, and one day, I promise you, they'll sing to Ianto Llewellyn, proud on his Eisteddfod throne. You'll not get that, shovelling coal for steam; any Englishman could do that. But they won't touch the slate, you see, Ianto, because it's Welsh and it talks only to us. You must be Welsh to break the rock, because it speaks no English.'

His pale body had glistened red in the glow of the bright cinders. But it was not the fire that made Ianto's eyes sparkle. It was his father's words and the love he had of him. So he never spoke again about going south to steam. How different it would have been if he had! How different.

* * *

Everyone blamed the English; they should not have messed with the system. Lord Penrhyn was not content to own the land and the quarries, the railway lines, the ports, the tolls and machines and all the village and houses around. It was not enough for him to know that every Welshman and his family there depended on him for everything they earned and owned. He wanted their souls as well, every one of them. George Sholto Douglas, Lord Penrhyn, they said, wanted to be an emperor. He had come from the linen mills of Manchester to take his father's title, and thought he would rule the quarrymen like his factory workers. But Wales is not Lancashire, and Owen was not the only one to see the wrong, nor the first.

After nearly thirty years working the slate, Owen was his own and so was every man like him. They were proud of themselves and would polish their bowlers for work every morning and brush them smart again for the walk home at night. They were honest fellows with furniture at home and some small savings with the building society.

From the start, Owen said they should never have been tested that way. The English, he said, had brought hatred to Bethesda when they should have left it at home.

In the months before Christmas, the men worried about Lord Penrhyn and Mr Young, the new manager he had brought with him. Mr Young had gone about with pen and paper, ever consulting his pocket watch, and on Christmas Eve he nailed up on the doors of the dressing sheds and on the line of elms along the top of the quarry, a notice headed RULES OF WORK. Nothing was done about it on Christmas Day or Boxing Day but when the men started their shifts on the Tuesday they spent a long time drinking their tea at the midday break. Before it was dark that afternoon Owen had taken five of them to see Mr Young in his office to tell him the rules were not necessary, that the quarry had always worked well before they were posted up and it would work well again once they were taken down. Owen had said to him: 'We do not complain of our money or our hours. The burden of complaint is the spirit of our treatment. Let us be treated and respected like men.' Owen was not used to it and had not meant his words to be taken as an ultimatum, but that was how Mr Young reported it back to Lord Penrhyn that afternoon.

For the rest of that week the men worked normally as best they could, and might have managed until their tempers went away but on the Saturday afternoon Robert Roberts' boy David died from consumption. He had worked in the quarry for two years since his schooling, and it was customary for the men to attend his funeral the following Monday. But on the morning another rule had been nailed to the elms and dressing shed doors: men could not take time off unless the loss were made up.

Owen and his committee, for that was what they now called themselves, went again to Mr Young's office but the manager would not move from his chair to speak civilly to them.

'What can it matter?' he had said. 'The boy was only fifteen.'

Owen had replied, 'You are a heathen, Mr Young. There are many here who do not forgive you for being English but you are the bigger fool to stop this boy having his friends at his funeral.'

Mr Young had tried to close his door, saying that Lord Penrhyn's own Doctor Harrison blamed many of the men's days off on their habit of attending funerals in the rain. Nonsense! Owen had said. Doctor Harrison had a blue face and wheezed. There were tiny flecks of blood on his handkerchief whenever he spat, just like Robert Roberts' son, and Doctor Harrison had never stood wet at a Bethesda funeral.

There was no further negotiation. Mr Young had simply said that any man who walked out of the quarry that afternoon would not walk back in again and his door was shut before anyone could answer.

A handful did not work their contracts normally that morning but moved out among the men, and from his office window Mr Young watched them on their errands and when the whistle went at midday he quickly sent his own runner to Lord Penrhyn.

Before the men had finished their lunch of boiled tea and bread-and-lard it began to rain hard and thunder could be heard towards Snowdonia. The sky went so dark they could hardly make out the horses and hearse as they came along the top. Nor could they see much of the women under their umbrellas walking behind. But by the time the whistle blew again the quarry was empty and the procession of men was already halfway up the slope, following young David Roberts to his grave.

It was nine months before they went back, and in those long and hateful days their world was turned around. New English words were heard in Bethesda – lockout, strike, blacklegs, union. Every Monday morning fresh notices were pinned to the elms, stating that the men would work to the rules or not at all. Throughout January they met every evening on the steps behind the chapel and sang hymns which always started with their favourite, 'Lord God of Providence' to the tune 'Pembroke'. Then they made speeches so fierce and so loud the women wept and the chapel elders shook their heads and went indoors, saying it was the Devil dressed up. It was, they said, as if men had saved up their hatred all these years.

'We are slaves, perfect slaves to the English,' Moses Hughes had shouted. 'Each year we slip into servility to the last grain and I think we will have to be squeezed near to death before we shout.'

Emrys Price said that if Lord Penrhyn's quarries had been in Rhondda his castle would have been burnt about his ears. And Glyn Davies, who was always such a quiet man, said, 'We have been too easy with them. We are singing hymns when we should be learning how to box.'

And Robert Roberts, wearing a black armband on his shirt, said, 'We workers must come to own our work because without it our lives and our honour are left to the mercy of others.'

Mr Young paid informers to listen and remember the names of those who spoke that way and they went down in his notebook as men who, for all their shouting, would never have a job in the quarry again.

In February, with the winds bringing snow off the mountains, Lord Penrhyn connived with the other landowners and called in his loans and ended tenancies in such a way that English law had nothing to do with Welsh justice. Farmers and merchants who had helped the quarrymen with food and clothing found themselves reduced to labourers with nothing to sell. Then Penrhyn sent an agent to Douglas Terrace to remind everyone that it was built on his lordship's land. The agent, a Scot, first came to Owen and stood at the door, shouting loudly so that everyone on the terrace would hear.

'You are paying a mortgage for this house, Llewellyn, but it does not belong to you. Part of it already belongs to his lordship and that part will grow year by year and when you are dead it will pass to his son, not yours. Remember that. The longer you are in this house, the less of it is yours.'

Owen had not spoken before at the evening meetings. He said he thought it was wrong of men to deafen good sense with their shoutings and he believed that Lord Penrhyn would soon choose his time to be reasonable. But after the agent had gone he took his place that evening on the steps with the other speakers, tall among so many, his face shining white against his dark cap and the black cloth of men around him. When it was his turn, the chapel elders came to the windows and listened behind their curtains.

'We have not changed, so pray God Almighty tell us what made them change so. But if change will give us work and honour again, then change we will too. There are those who would deny us our rights as workmen, deny us our voices as men. They say it is the master's privilege because it is his quarry, his money and his capital. But what are our labour and our lives but our capital, and how many men have lost their lives in this quarry, and how many orphans and widows are there here who have seen their capital brought home in pieces upon a bier?

'There is no chance of work again if we continue to shout on these steps like drunkards, for we are too far away and Penrhyn will not hear us in his castle. Let just one voice speak for all of us – one voice from many come together like a choir. Let's have a union. We must have a union of men. We may have to wait a long time for justice and I believe it's certain the English lawmakers will make our places so hot and intolerable that a union will be our only refuge. So let us organize ourselves now and make this the first day of our union. We must stand together like men, or fall lower than men.'

The chapel windows gently closed and the men cheered so loud that it was said later they could be heard in Bangor. Mary saw Ianto on the steps, taller and blacker, with his powerful arm under Owen like a prop.

In March recruiting sergeants from the Royal Welch Fusiliers came to Bethesda offering a shilling and a contract to sign, but the women threw mud over their scarlet uniforms and one sergeant was taken away in a wagon, bleeding from a piece of flying slate. A cold wet April passed, a cold wet May became June and men still wore their scarves and topcoats.

'Strike in the warm weather,' they had said, 'so no one suffers. Strike for the summer, the time when the bosses have their busiest trade.' Yet the summer did not come until it was almost time for autumn and Lord Penrhyn seemed not to care whether he sold his slate or not. Winter had a long, bitter tail. Mary remembered God leaving them in Bethesda and the men gradually drifting away from Him.

In August they earned sevenpence a day in the hayfields around Blaenau Ffestiniog but the money was shared and there was little enough to go round. At first farmers had sent sacks of potatoes and kale and strike funds had been launched by printers in Manchester and dockers in Liverpool. Silver bands from the south had sent a banker's draft in the post but that was in the spring and it would soon be September. There was precious little money, and homes had been emptied until the pawnbrokers shut their doors to everyone except buyers, and there were precious few of them either.

The men remained strong and every time manager Young had fresh copies of his rules nailed up they were quickly torn down again and rolled tightly together with string for the men to play football with.

It was in the middle of September, a Friday, that David Morgan came running to the terrace and told Owen that Lord Penrhyn was transporting Cornish tin miners to work in the quarry.

'He's bringing them by special train to Port Dinorwic. There are thirty or more wagons to bring them here, and he's got the police from Caernarfon to see them through. We must stop them, Owen. The union must stop them!'

But they did not, even though they lay down in the road and frightened the horses with flaming rags and threw tar at the Cornishmen. The policemen had their orders from the chief constable and he from the county magistrate and he from Lord Penrhyn direct, and so they used their truncheons brutally, knocking even children and women to the ground. There was commotion and screaming and more bloody faces and broken bones than Bethesda had ever seen. But it was not until all the wagons were through and the injured men were dragged to the grass for the women to wipe them clean that they saw Owen's body, crumpled and torn. The men stopped their groaning and the women their crying and Ianto knelt and with such a sigh lifted Owen like a baby in his arms and carried him to the quarry's edge. Then the policemen from Caernarfon and the blacklegs from Cornwall stopped and turned and looked up as the echoes bounced across the quarry's walls, making ten men of one and Ianto's curses seem like thunder. Mary did not hear them nor see his tears. Only Owen's beautiful face, crimson and still, with no pain or blame in his eyes.

She buried him within the week but Ianto was not there. Men came from as far away as Llandudno and Harlech and there was even a wreath from the printers in Manchester. A newspaper man from the south said there were over five hundred people and only half, she knew, were from Bethesda.

Mary watched the men pass the grave and she knew it was all over. They would go back, there was no stuffing in them now. The following morning when Lord Penrhyn's rules were nailed afresh to the elms, no one tore them down. By mid-week the Cornishmen had left and those in Bethesda who were not in Mr Young's notebook went back to work. A week later the newspaper man sent Mary a cutting of his story, just as he had promised to do, and after she had read it she folded it neatly and put it in her Bible under Canaan:

> 'Terrible times have overtaken us, trials pour like a flood upon us to test our fidelity to God and to each other. The path to Canaan in all ages leads through desert, chaos and pain.'

The man had also sent a second cutting from his newspaper and for a long time she looked at that. Then she put it on the mantelpiece next to Owen's silver pocket watch, to make certain the boys would see it too.

It took no time at all to leave. There was no work for the boys whose names were in the book, especially Ianto who had not spoken a dozen words since Owen's death: not since he had cursed the English, the English who governed Wales, who ate it up and who would leave nothing. They were Owen's words.

'One day, the English will be gone. The men and their machinery will be gone, the slate will be gone, and all that's left will be a hole in the ground to show where we have been.'

They travelled down Wales in the rain but sailed from Devon in bright warm sunshine, and people on the decks were laughing and saying it would always be so. The gun was fired as they passed out by Dartmouth Castle and the sea was as smooth as oil and flat as a pond. Twenty-four days they said it would take, past France and Spain, past Madeira and Puerto Santo and Saint Helena. That evening as she felt the ship's first roll she kissed the boys goodnight and suckled Tom before his time so that she might go to sleep early. She picked out the pins and brushed her long brown hair and wound Owen's silver watch and polished the shining wood of the lovespoon he had made for her. Then she brought the candle closer to her bunk, and in red crayon she wrote on the inside of her Bible,

'November the First, 1874.
Today we all left Wales.
For Pilgrims Rest.'

CHAPTER TWO

'Use the leather, Rodriguez . . . Give it to them hard. Let them feel the sting. Give it again, man!'

The small Portuguese looked up and waved back, then swung his whip again, catching the black shoulders, mixing sweat with blood as they pulled at the ropes bringing the bow and stern to the quayside. Captain Jeppe walked from his wheelhouse to the ship's side to see that it was properly fastened fore and aft.

Mary turned her head away. She had never expected this, not the heat, not the stench, not this parade of misery. She had never seen blacks before but spread out below her across the wharf were thousands, standing, squatting, men and women, young and miserable. Fifty yards away she could see a hundred or more chained together, hand and foot, all men and much bigger than the rest, slowly walking in line one behind the other, each carrying an elephant's tusk.

Captain Jeppe came along the deck and stopped her. He smelt of gin, tobacco and dirt. 'Dhows, missus, Arab slavers and the longest line I've seen in ten years. King Tippoo himself must be here. Keep out of his way, though,' he laughed. 'A handsome woman like yourself might well take his fancy and you'd be the first white wife in Zanzibar.' He showed his yellow teeth and took off his cap and wiped the sweat off his bald head with a red handkerchief. He said he was a Boer, but Huw had heard from the crew that he was from Lincolnshire and had spent time in a Cape prison, though no one would say why.

'There must be three thousand kaffirs ready for the boats,' he said. 'Lucky, though, if half of them get to the market. I've seen boats leave here so heavy they're a yard below the line. But when they sail into Zanzibar they're a foot above, they throw so many dead overboard. Best fed sharks anywhere off Africa, I reckon!' He pointed to the ivory slaves. 'You could do with a few of those big fellows yourself where you're going, missus.'

Mary did not answer. She tried to move away but he held her arm. 'Now why are you off there, anyway? Handsome and without a man, and with a baby, going to join diggers and drunkards? Haven't you heard what's at the end of the Delagoa Road?'

She pulled her arm away and faced him. 'Pilgrims Rest is where we're off to, Captain Jeppe,' she said defiantly. 'That's where we're going, my baby and all.'

He laughed, then coughed and spat into the narrow strip of water between the hull and the quay. Then he wiped his nose and his forehead again with the red rag. 'You're a joker, missus, but someone's had the bigger joke on you.' He stopped smiling and leaned forward. 'Shall I tell you how many jokers I've seen here, how many I've dropped off in this hell with their picks and shovels and new hats on their heads and great grinning faces, paying the odds for a wagon so as to be first to the Valley of Gold? And do you know how many ever get there?'

Mary did not want to hear but she did not move away. 'You listen, missus, and save yourself and your baby. You're not the first white woman I've landed here but I hope they'll not send me any more. Twenty-seven diggers left three months ago, women and children with them, off along the road and singing as if they were going to church on a Sunday morning. A month or so later one came back, one, mark you, and already half animal so she couldn't tell where the rest had ended it. But end it they did, by the kaffirs, hyena, lion, leopard, one or all of them or just the fever. It makes no odds. Their bones are scattered and bleached by now, the only white things in the whole of this filthy black country. They never made it to the end of the road, the Valley of Gold, that's what they call it, Pilgrims Rest. I call it the Valley of Death. You die going, or you die there or you die trying to get back out again.

'You mark me, missus. If you leave Lourenço Marques you'll not live to see Christmas, nor will any of those men of yours.' He waited but she did not answer, so he spat again into the water and watched small fish attack the phlegm. Then he walked back to his wheelhouse to supervise the unloading, wiping the sweat from the back of his neck with the red rag.

They had spent two days and two nights on the grimy little coaster Captain Jeppe had named *Ladywood*, but did not leave it until after midday, waiting on deck despite the flies and the heat, until the nets had landed their luggage and equipment.

They had left Bethesda more than a month before with four trunks and Mary's sewing-machine carefully wrapped in sacking smeared with wax. But now on the quayside were a dozen or more different packages, items they had bought in the one-day stop in Durban as they had transferred from their ocean ship to the *Ladywood*. They had been met in Durban by a man who said he represented the government, but he represented nothing of the kind. He worked for the local merchants and was paid commission for the people he brought to their shops but his advice was good, and helped and advised by him the boys bought picks and shovels, long and short handled, tin basins, pounds of flat-topped nails, buckets, claw hammers and long- and short-handled axes. Mary did her own shopping to add to the things she had packed so carefully in her trunk: candle wicks, lighting- and cooking-oil, squares of arsenical soap, maize flour at four pounds a sack, small tins of yeast at a shilling, tins of condensed milk at half a crown each and sealed buckets of Cape butter at seven and sixpence. She also bought a roll of blue flannel and, on the store manager's advice, two stone jars, one of rosemary, the other of turpentine which he said would keep the mosquitoes away. For the fever he sold her little round boxes of rhubarb pills and bottles of Doctor Livingstone's Remedy made up of jalap, calomel and quinine. The label said the dose was ten grains at the first attack but the merchant told her that if the fever was not gone within the first twenty-four hours she should consider herself dying and beyond help. Lastly, she bought herself a bag made from carpet with bamboo handles and a wide-brimmed straw hat with a ribbon to tie under her chin for the journey. The storekeeper said she looked so pretty, he gave her a gift, a brightly coloured tin of Keating's Persian Insect Powder. It killed all fleas, he said!

Lourenço Marques was smaller than she had expected and more wretched than ever she could have imagined in a hundred nightmares. When the ship had turned into Delagoa Bay that morning, the port looked wide and spread out but once they had neared it she saw that the sprawl was African mud and thatched huts. The Portuguese lived side by side in wooden shacks which they had built in a semi-circle around the harbour so they could see every ship, every boat, however small, come in and out.

The port was surrounded by a crescent of swamps and when the breeze turned to the sea it brought with it the stench of rottenness, sweet and sickly. It also swept before it clouds of mosquitoes, whose bites quickly erupted into swollen yellow sores, soon covered in flies that swarmed on the pus. Captain Jeppe said it was the wind that brought the swamp fever. There was death in the smell, he said. People breathed it in and then caught fire and their bodies seemed to burn until they died in pools of their own sweat. Some, he said, thought the mosquito killed with its bite, just like the tsetse fly, but he laughed at that. Nothing so small, he said, could kill a man so quickly. It was the rottenness of the swamps in the air.

Captain Jeppe came to the gangplank to see them off but kept his distance from Mary now that she was with the boys.

He shouted to her instead. 'If you must go, missus, go only with Baines, don't dare chance the road without him. He's the only transport rider who'll take you through and keep you from the blacks and Portuguese. That's him, beyond the ivory kaffirs, the tall old fellow with the grey beard. That's Walrus Baines. Stay with him. He's the only honest man in the whole of East Africa. And be careful with that baby of yours. He deserves better than this.'

She came down the plank slowly with baby Tom close to her breast, and kept one eye on the man with the long grey beard. He was pushing his way through the mass of bodies towards the quay in such a hurry that by the time she stepped onto Africa he was waiting at the bottom of the gangplank with the first words of greeting:

'Good day, ma'am. Walrus Baines. Welcome to Lourenço Marques, the most wretched place on God's earth, but smiling for the first time in its life at the sight of such a pretty woman.'

Walrus Baines was so tall he stooped as he walked and talked. It was as if he felt too far from people and wanted to be closer. Everything about him was long: his face, his beard, his moustache, his eyelashes, ears, hat, and his hands which touched his knees. He wore moleskin breeches and black leather kneeboots and his shirt, dyed brown, had been patched with so many colours that Mary thought it could well have been cut from a patchwork quilt. But his waistcoat was magnificent, made of black sable and stitched together with strands of leather as thick as a quarryman's bootlaces. A sheep's bladder stuffed with tobacco hung from his belt so that the thorn-wood pipe in his mouth was never empty. Grey hair covered his ears and there was little of his face to be seen, except for his nose which was brown and wrinkled and also long.

Like baby Tom, he had been brought to Africa in the first few months of his life, though he had never been able to find out when or where he began it. He thought it might have been in Walvis Bay on the Skeleton Coast of German South-West

Africa, because that was where he was found by the family that took him from his dead mother and gave him a surname. Father Baines feared the baby might already have been christened, and rather than upset the church, the baby was simply called Boy Baines. But as he grew into a man and the long drooping eyes and the long drooping nose were joined by the long drooping moustache, he became famous as Walrus. For those first years he trekked with the Baineses from South-West Africa due east to Windhoek, then dropped south to Fish River Canyon, trading as they went – blankets, printed calicos, knives and tobacco, snuff, beads, bangles, looking-glasses, mouth-organs and lotions until finally they crossed the Orange River into the Cape. Sometimes they farmed, until Africa's sun and Africa's floods forced them to move on; sometimes they trapped and shot for skins but Father Baines could not match the traders' dishonesty.

So they drifted further south, sidestepping the tribes who would not give them any part of their time or their lands, until they settled in what seemed a paradise: the grape farms of the Paarl Valley. But then Mother Baines died of sleeping sickness the day Victoria became Queen of Great Britain and Father Baines closed all the shutters on all the windows of the tiny farmhouse and would not let them take his wife from her bed for a week. He sat at her side, combing her hair and washing her face, trying to talk her back to life. The apples were not picked and the vines were not watered, and when they finally came for her, Father Baines had lost his voice. Soon he lost his mind and finally his adopted son.

On the day of the funeral he told Boy Baines the story of Walvis Bay and a baby in a dead mother's arms, and the fourteen-year-old was sad to be told it and did not forgive Father Baines for the telling and before the earth had settled on the dead old woman, he had gone, leaving the old man, sitting in the darkness of his kitchen, giggling to himself and talking to the empty chair on the other side of the fireplace, to the ghost of his wife sitting there darning.

Boy Baines packed his saddlebag and rode away from the vineyards and orchards, north towards the Karoo Desert, and for the next half a century cursed himself for doing it.

All these things he told Mary that afternoon after he had taken her, baby Tom and the boys to his stables a quarter of a mile from the quay. The stables would serve as their lodging-house for the two nights they would have to wait for the wagon-train to leave.

That evening, after he had cooked them a stew of antelope meat and corn husks, Mary sat with her back to the door and suckled Tom and laughed as Walrus Baines tickled the baby's tiny feet with the stem of his pipe. The evening air was cool and the breeze made the candle flame twirl like a cobra, and Walrus Baines took off his sable waistcoat and draped it around Mary's shoulders as she pressed the baby to her breast.

'I reckon my father must have been a whaler,' he said. 'There's no other reason to land at Walvis Bay. That's the Dutch name for whale. They never did find my father and it seems my mother only spoke a few words before she died. Father Baines thought it was German, though it might have been Dutch. Anyhow, the Baineses were English, so that's the pedigree I go by. They were shipwrecked off the Skeleton Coast, from the *Sea Nymph* bound for the Cape. It's the strangest story I've ever heard in Africa, and I've heard a few. Father Baines said the ship was rammed by whales. Line abreast they were, barged in until they broke open the timbers, then held off and watched people jump into the sea, waiting for the ship to turn over. Then they swam away as peaceful as you like. Nobody's ever known it before or since. I reckon it was revenge, the great things must have thought the ship was a whaler. Anyhow, Mother and Father Baines came safely ashore and do you know how, little one?' He prodded baby Tom again with his pipe. 'They came ashore riding a horse! Well, not exactly riding, but it was a horse. There were a dozen of them aboard, New Forest mares out of Portsmouth coming for breeding in the Cape. One of them broke loose before the ship capsized and the Baineses, man and wife, held on to her tail and she towed them to the shore. It's hard to believe, but it's the truth. Mother Baines told that story a hundred times, and in fourteen years I never knew her to lie. Except just the once.'

'And they kept the horse?' asked Mary.

'Yes, they did. They kept her and they called her Saviour and she lived until the day Mother Baines died, then she died too. When I rode away from Paarl that afternoon it was on one of Saviour's own foals. That's the way life is, little man,' he said, peering at baby Tom. 'It's all put together like a well-made wagon that rolls along for years until an axle breaks. But I had a happy life there in Paarl, just the three of us, and I would happily have died there an old farmer. But the axle broke when Mother Baines was bitten by the tsetse fly and when she went the old man thought we'd live better together if he told me who I was not. I didn't like to hear it. So I left with nothing except Saviour's mare and with nowhere to go. And all the good things God had put so nicely together just fell apart.'

For a while Mary said nothing. Across the street she could see Ianto, carrying her sewing-machine under his arm, coming towards the stable, deliberately kicking up the black sand as he walked.

'Did you leave,' she asked, 'just because he told you he was not your father?'

'That was a skinny little boy a half-century ago, and if I said I could remember why, it would be a lie. Perhaps I thought if I didn't belong to Father Baines I didn't belong anywhere. Anyhow, I've been travelling ever since, and there's not a day goes by that I don't curse that young lad's cussedness.'

Ianto came into the stable and placed the sewing-machine by her, and she pulled him close enough to kiss his ear, the great big son who did not belong and would never know why.

* * *

The next day was spent packing and repacking the trunks and tying the tools and things together in readiness for the trek. Walrus Baines said that everything had to be in neat order, everything in its place, and when he saw how the boys had trussed the picks and shovels together in a heap he told them to untie them and start again.

'They have to go into a square box, so make them the same shape.'

Later in the day, after much hammering he emerged from the back of the stable with a table and a three-legged stool and Mary sat the afternoon cutting patterns from the roll of blue flannel and made three shirts, each with large pockets at the front and with large collars that turned up to protect the neck from the sun. When she had finished them she began a fourth for Walrus Baines, a present, once they had safely arrived.

Once Ianto heard the old man had English foster-parents, he did not speak much to him again. More and more, the mention of England or anything English sent him into a black mood, and that evening Mary had to stand between him and three diggers who had been in Lourenço Marques a month waiting for a wagon, and who were singing English sea songs, squatting on the dirty ground, drunk on palm gin. Ianto did not leave the stable again but sat sentry over the trunks and equipment, speaking only to Mary and his brothers when he was called for food.

But Walrus Baines did not seem put out by Ianto's black mood. Instead, he took a liking to William and spent much of the second day showing him the wagons, the teams of oxen and his five ponies. He made William repeat all the names of all the parts of the wagon and the pulling harness. He drew pictures with a stick in the sand to show how the axles and wheels were built, how to repair broken ones, and how to take them off with a wooden jackpole and pack the hub with fat. William was shown the lead ox and made to repeat its African name a dozen times before he got it right, and using pebbles in the sand, Walrus showed him how to bring the wagons round in a circle and unharness the oxen in their proper order.

'On the journey, Billy boy, you start at first light to get as far as you can in the cool air. Then you stop for breakfast as soon as the sun is high, let the oxen off their yokes to graze, and let them eat all they want. When they begin to lie down they've had enough, so bring them in fast or you'll not get them in at all.'

For an hour or more he sat cross-legged on the sand, talking with William, and at midday he shouted to one of his blacks to bring bread and meat. After they had eaten, Walrus stood up, stretched and kicked at the pebbles. 'Can you shoot, Billy?' he asked.

William laughed. 'No, Mr Baines, there's not much call for it in Wales, at least not that I know of. Men don't as a rule carry rifles there and only the farmers and gamekeepers have shotguns.'

'What did you do there, boy?'

'I was a quarryman.'

'Digging for stone?'

'No, sir, slate, the best in the world, and ours was the best in Wales.'

Walrus snorted. 'I can't think of a more fool way of spending a life, digging for stone or digging for gold. Either way, you end up broken and poor.'

'Is that what you think will happen to us? My mother is certain you'll get us there.'

'Oh, I'll get you there, boy. Your mother, your baby brother, even the one who hasn't a kind word for any soul around.'

William stood up too. Then he said, 'But there is gold there, isn't there, Mr Baines? The advertisement in the newspaper at home said so.'

'Yes, boy,' said Walrus. 'There's gold there but it's well hidden and it doesn't give itself up easily. I must have taken a couple of hundred diggers there since the rush began a few years back, and except for a half dozen, none have made enough even to live on.' He spat at a lizard and watched it scamper under the stable door. Then he walked across to William and held him by the shoulders. 'Billy, I've known you for all of forty hours. You belong to a fine family and that's why I wish you'd all go back aboard a coaster to Durban. There's one in now. It leaves in the morning. It's a better life there with plenty of work for young fellows like you, and it's not hard either. You end the day before it's dark and you have supper in a house, and that's more than you'll ever get up in Pilgrims Rest. There you burn in the day and freeze at night, with not enough oil to cook your food. Not a night will pass when you won't dread the coming day, and you'll be so busy digging gold, you'll never have enough time to build your mother a home. I've been there and back all this year, taking my wagons across some of the worst country I've seen in fifty years of trekking, but believe me, I've an easier life than you'll ever have up there on top of those mountains. It's not for you, Billy, not for your mother and not for your baby brother especially. I don't as a rule shove my long nose into other people's business but none of you know what's ahead. I haven't told you what it can be like along the Delagoa Road, but I've a good mind to if it'll put you off going. Tell your mother that, Billy, tell her to take you all back to Natal. I'll buy your gear at the price you paid and give a little extra above it to help pay your passage. Hunting gold is not for you. You go now and tell her that, Billy boy!'

William did not speak. He looked down at Walrus Baines' boots and for the first time saw how they shone. He could see his own movements in the toecaps. Then he walked away, but slowly, hoping the old man would speak again but he did not and William had lifted the catch on the stable door before he turned to see Walrus Baines already thirty yards away, striding towards the quay. William opened the door and looked into the stable. In the dim light he could see the family asleep, sheltering from the hot afternoon sun, Ianto sprawled out with his trunk as his bed, Huw face down on the straw and his mother in the corner manger with one arm over the baby's cot. There was not a sound. Even the flies were resting.

The equipment was now stacked ever so neatly in the middle, picks and shovels, pails and basins, axe-heads, the small sacks of nails, the flour, the butter, the jars of oil. William thought they looked like a parade of soldiers, ready for the long march to the mountains. It had seemed such an adventure, reading that slip of newspaper in the parlour at Bethesda. Such a thing, to sail and make a fortune in the new world and find a nugget so large that one hand would not lift it, not even Ianto's. Mother had been so anxious to leave, with father in the ground and faces that would not lift to you as they passed. She so desperately wanted a new life, not just outside Wales, not just across the border in Chester or Bristol. Even London was too near to his grave, because they would go back and see it at anniversaries and they did not want ever to go back there again, not even for him.

The ponies were quite still, and he stroked their flanks, smooth and shining like a polished table. The air was so cool inside and sweet with the perfumes of fresh straw and the dried cut grass and the crushed maize in the bins. Surely it could not all be bad in a country so big. There must be somewhere that would give them a proper chance to start, whatever Walrus Baines said. Why not? Why shouldn't God help them, just this once, and let them find a piece of gold that even Ianto could not pick up? William closed his eyes and rested his head against the wooden rail post and prayed.

'Dear God,' he said softly, 'I think it's time you helped, now that you've taken Dad. We've come all this way and we only need a little bit of help. Please give us a chance. Just this once. I won't ask again. Let us find a nugget. Amen.'

He waited, but there was no sign, no answer, only the blast of a ship's horn out in the bay. Quickly he opened the door again and sprinted away down the street towards the quay, dodging the lines of slaves, jumping the piles of ivory, just in time to grab Walrus Baines by the hand as he stepped onto the gangplank of a Cape coaster newly arrived.

'Mr Baines,' he said breathlessly.

'It's Walrus, boy.'

'Mr Walrus, will you teach me to shoot? You see, we are determined to go. We've come all the way from Caernarfonshire and they must never know there that we didn't do what we said we would. Whatever you say, we will find gold and we will build mother a house, even if we have to take time off from the digging.' Then, with a pause and a deep breath he asked, 'And will you teach me to be a transport rider like you?'

For a moment Walrus Baines said nothing, just stood there, looking at the boy beneath him. Then he bellowed: 'A transport rider like me, boy? A nipper like you? D'you know what it is to be one? Course you don't. D'you think it's all downhill on a sunny day? Well, it ain't, lad. It ain't ever downhill and the sun burns you and shrivels your face like a prune so you pray for the rain and then you curse yourself for doing so, 'cos it rains, rains, rains, and the veld becomes a mass of mud, clinging to the wheels like mortar, and no sooner do you dig one out than the other goes in. I've gone on tracks to Pietersburg and Lydenburg where I've not made a dozen miles in as many days. And can you take the cold, lad, 'cos it's colder on a midwinter night up on those mountains than you'll ever have had where you're from. So cold, men's fingers fall off and oxen freeze solid in their yokes. Your blood runs cold and you pray to the Devil to help you, you pray for his fires and the heat of Hell and before you know it a season's past and by the end of another the veld is as bare and as dry as a bone. No rain for five, six months and you and your oxen are choking with dust, mile after mile, week on week, nothing but grey dust and yellow dust, and red dust, and every water-hole dry and around them are the white white skeletons of men and beasts picked clean by the vultures. Is that the life you want, boy? Tripping from one corner of this cussed country at the mercy of nature's whims, counting every birthday as a blessing and not expecting to see the next and most times not wanting to. Is that what you'd pick for? Is it?'

William looked up at the tall man, red-faced and pouting, and he nodded. 'Yes, sir. If that's what it means!'

Walrus saw how bright the boy's eyes were, wide and sparkling blue. He slowly began to laugh. He laughed until William thought he was crying. Tears drenched the grey moustache, and dripped onto his beard. He wiped his eyes and his hair dry with a handkerchief. Then he shook William hard by the shoulders and boomed, 'You're a brave, stupid boy, Billy, but I will, I will! I'll teach you to shoot a tick off an ox's back at a hundred yards and you'll ride better and faster than any man in East Africa. I'll show you how to trap and skin antelope and how to outwit even a buffalo and I'll have you learn this land better even than the kaffirs themselves. And I'll teach you how to cross it so silent you'll be behind them while they're waiting to put a spear through your liver. Consider yourself my apprentice, Billy boy, the first Walrus Baines has ever had and the first the Delagoa Road has ever seen. I'll make you a transport rider, Billy. At least that way you'll live to be an old man and not die waiting for God in Pilgrims Rest!'

Walrus Baines picked the strands of meat out of his back teeth with the skinning knife and shifted closer to the stove. 'That's the first time in near on fifty years that a woman cooked me such a supper, and I might easily get used to it,' he said, nodding to Mary. The sun had been down an hour and the sky was quickly filling with clouds low off the silver sea, bringing a chill with them. Walrus had lit his small patterned cast-iron stove in the yard behind the stable, away from the Africans who found Mary such a curiosity. All afternoon they had come to sit around her, talking to each other and giggling, the children brave very quickly. One, wide-eyed, had stroked her long brown hair and then run away screaming with excitement. Their mothers fingered the bottom of Mary's petticoat and then put their fingers to their lips and shook their heads at each other, marvelling at the smell and softness of the pretty linen.

At first Mary was amused by them and showed them the stitching and the embroidery and had unrolled her bun so that the children might see how she combed and pinned it up. But eventually Walrus took her by the hand and brought her into the stableyard, for soon, he said, stories of the new entertainment would spread twenty miles each way along the coast and by evening there could be three hundred or more Africans come to see the show!

When the family had eaten, Walrus sent Ianto, Huw and William to the port's only carpenter to spend the evening with him learning how wagons were built and how to repair a broken spoke or a seized hub. The carpenter was an old Portuguese who had jumped ship forty years previous. That would not have mattered much except that it was a Portuguese navy brigantine on its way to a skirmish in the Arabian Gulf, so he had to remain in Lourenço Marques under sentence of death should he ever return to Lisbon. He had taught a dozen Africans his trade and together they serviced the ships that came into the port, and in between times they built and repaired wagons for Walrus.

The breeze hissed through the palms overhanging the mud walls enclosing the yard and Mary shifted her stool closer to the pretty little stove. 'Walrus,' she said, 'Captain Jeppe told me a white family came through here some months ago.'

'That's right, ma'am. Through, but not much beyond.'

She went on. 'He said they all died except a woman.'

'He's right there too.'

'Did the woman die in the end?' Mary asked.

Walrus did not answer but opened the top of the stove to let the flames jump out. Then he took a small leather bottle from inside his waistcoat and turned out the cork with his thumb and sipped from it. 'Best gin,' he said, 'saved for special times like this!'

'Tell me about the woman,' said Mary. Still he said nothing. 'Walrus,' she said and touched his arm, 'tell me what's ahead.

I am afraid, as you might expect. But I think I would be less so if I knew.'

He corked the leather bottle again and put it back inside his waistcoat. He relit his pipe from a fireband then stood up and leant against the wall, his face hidden in blue smoke. 'I should have waited,' he said. 'But I had my wagons near full of supplies for the goldfields and wanted to be on my way. The *Ladywood* was due but no one knew when or if there were any more diggers aboard, so I went on. Those people would still be alive if I had stopped a while longer.'

'Could you have stopped them being killed?' asked Mary.

'Yes,' he answered. 'Portuguese don't go for my wagons. They know better and they're the ones behind it all, the scum who live here. They send people off along the road but send runners ahead of them to tell the kaffir chiefs they're coming.'

'The Portuguese?' asked Mary.

'Yes, the Dagos. The blacks attack the wagons and strip the bodies too. Then they sell it all back to the Portuguese here for a few bags of flour and salt. There are cellars in this port full of gold and silver and clothes taken from the poor devils who've been speared on the Delagoa Road. There was one blackguard here who wore a chain with gold teeth strung to it, until the blacks sliced him up as well!

'Anyhow, I found them on my way back, midway between the Komati and Crocodile rivers. The poor beggars had stopped for the night but hadn't known how to do it properly and by morning they were dead and the wagons burnt out. They must have been dead for a week by the time I came across them but the wagons were still smouldering and the ground was covered in vultures, gorging themselves. Some of the men must have survived long enough to bury the dead but the graves were too shallow and the lion and hyena had pulled the bodies out. I've never known such a stench! The ground was littered with bones and skulls and torn-up clothes. I was just about to ride on when I saw shapes crawling out from under a large thorn tree a hundred yards off. The light was too strong and at first I thought they might be leopard. Then my blacks shouted, "Muntu!" and as we came closer I saw they were men, though not as God made them. Three of them. They tried to stand, but their bodies were in shreds and they'd gone mad, and screamed and tore at the loose skin on their chests. Their lips were black with fever. I could have given them water but you don't give such precious stuff to dying men. Probably they had run out of their own and had started to drink from the gin barrel. That's what people do. Gin's cheaper than water and when they run out of one they drink themselves to death on the other. So I took my gun and shot each one through the head. Then I got my boys to bury them deep into the ground and prayed God to forgive me.'

He pushed his hat back and rubbed the red sweat-line across his forehead. A long way off there was thunder. He said, 'We'll have rain tonight, just enough to keep the dust on the ground tomorrow, which will suit us fine.'

'Tell me about the girl, Walrus.'

'We found her an hour further on. Must have tried to follow the wagon's tracks, though how she got so far I'll never know. She was near naked and her face was caked in dried blood so you couldn't tell what was face and what wasn't. My blacks expected me to shoot her as well, but I'd never killed white men before and I couldn't kill a white woman. We wrapped her in a blanket, but before we'd even moved off she was wet with the fever's sweat so I gave her quinine and thought she'd be dead by the morning. But she wasn't, and when we got to the Komati we put her in it and washed her clean. Couldn't do much with her face, though. Looked as if a lion had bitten half of it away. We got her back here and we kept her from the sun and the flies and she began to heal. Then a month later I had to go south to pick up some timber and I left her with some diggers, but by the time I got back they'd shipped themselves off and a Portuguese had taken her as his property for the debts they'd left behind.'

'Is she dead now?' asked Mary.

'No, but she might just as well be. The Portuguese use her for their filthy ways whenever they can get away from their black wives. Better she dies. God only knows why He saved her for this!'

'Where is she, Walrus?'

'No need to ask, Mrs Mary, you'll not be able to see her.'

'But I do want to see her,' said Mary quietly. 'And I will!'

He shook his head. She stood up and faced him. 'Walrus, I want to see her. Please take me.'

'No, Mrs Mary,' he said. 'There's nothing you can do. Better let her die, and she must do it soon. God can't be so cruel to such a young thing.'

'Young?' asked Mary.

'Ay! That's the rub. She can't be more than twenty years, though you'd not think so with that wretched face of hers.'

Mary grabbed his hand. 'Take me! Please! Show me where she lives. You don't ever have to see her again. Just show me where to look.'

Walrus took his hand away. 'Mrs Mary, you don't understand. The Portuguese would never let you near her.'

Mary pulled her shawl around her shoulders and shook her head. 'You take me, Walrus Baines! Take me now or I'll take myself onto these streets and I'll walk them until I find her, even if it takes all night and all tomorrow. And if I don't come back you can send my sons to find me. I mean it, Walrus!'

For a moment he hesitated, then he turned and picked up his rifle. She watched him open the gun and finger the end of the cartridge. Then without another word he led the way out of the yard and she had to run to catch him up as the sky broke above them and the rain came down like pins, hard and sharp on her face. Within minutes they had left the wharf and followed the line of black wooden shacks on the seaward side. Orange lightning streaked across the sky and the rain quickly turned the black sand into mud and brought the stench of rotting vegetation and human filth out of the ground. She cupped her hand over her mouth and breathed through her fingers and for five minutes ran at his side. Suddenly he turned left into a narrow alley of shacks, sturdier than the ones facing the quay. He reached out for her hand and held it tight and pulled her with him. After fifty paces he stopped, and waited for the next flash of lightning to light up the alley so he could be certain they were alone.

He had stopped outside a shack much taller than the rest with shutters over the windows, each secured by an iron bar and lock. He banged on the door with his fist. There was a moan inside and the sound of something falling over, a chair or a table, and the door was opened. A lantern was held high by a large fat black woman, bare-breasted and with her head close-shaven and dyed copper red. Her teeth and lips were made a brighter red by betel nuts she chewed. She held the lantern closer to Walrus Baines' face and then shook her head.

'Not here, baas, Manuel not here.' She tried to close the door but Walrus quickly lowered the gun from his shoulder and pushed it between the door and the post. Then he forced the woman aside with it and took the lantern from her hand.

The light hardly filled the room. A blanket was strung from bamboo at one end and the mud floor was slimy from the rain that dripped through the plaited grass roof. There was a table, made from packing-cases, and a stool on its side in the corner where the woman had been plucking a chicken hooked by its neck to the wall but still half-alive and struggling.

Walrus stood there until his eyes found their proper sight. Then he shouted, 'Manuel!'

'*Filha da puta!*' the Portuguese shouted back from behind the blanket screen. '*Cai fora . . . Eu nao estou aqui . . .*'

The black woman edged past the gun-barrel and shouted, '*Manuel! E O Inglesi!*' Then she righted the stool and went back to the chicken.

The Portuguese pushed through the curtain and came into the room, tying string around his trousers.

'My pardon, Senhor. I did not know. The black cow makes me stupid. Ah, you have a friend, and a beautiful one! Senhorita, my great pleasure. You are the first I have seen in this rat-hole my government calls Lourenço Marques.' He showed his teeth, as red as his black wife's, and held out his hand to Mary but Walrus pushed it away with the gun-barrel and the Portuguese stopped smiling.

He was small and very thin and his skin was yellow and pitted with tiny scars. Around his face were wisps of grey hair where a beard and moustache might once have been. He had no shirt and the skin hung loose on his breasts like an old woman's long empty of milk. He looked at Mary with wide unblinking eyes, not seeming to care for Walrus or his gun. He pulled a red handkerchief from his trouser pocket, exactly like Captain Jeppe's, and wiped his armpits and then his face.

Walrus said, 'My friend wishes to see the girl, Manuel.'

The Portuguese did not take his eyes from Mary. 'Not possible, Senhor,' he said. 'She's mine, not yours. No!'

'She wishes to see the girl for a few moments,' Walrus said again as if the other man had not spoken.

'Englishman, it is not possible. Please, you leave before I call my friends. Senhor, you go now!'

'Manuel,' said Walrus, 'my friend wants to travel the Delagoa Road but I have told her not to and I want her to see the girl so that she knows what can happen to a woman who tries.'

'I think you want to take the girl, Senhor, like you did before. But now she's mine and she makes me many favours.'

'Favours?' Mary spoke for the first time and stepped further into the room. 'What do you mean, favours?'

'Favours, Senhorita! I give her to my friends, many friends, and then they owe me many favours.' He laughed and spat betel juice into the palm of his hand, which he examined and then wiped onto his trousers.

Mary pulled her hand away from Walrus, grabbed the lantern on the table, and pushing past the Portuguese, tore down the blanket and the bamboo. Then she cried out and turned back into the room, holding her hand across her mouth, contorting her face.

'Oh, Walrus,' she whispered through her fingers. Her eyes filled with tears.

The girl lay on a canvas sheet that was stretched and pegged across a litter of dried grass. She was naked as the Portuguese had left her with scratches and little bruises showing up on her white body. She stared unblinking at the ceiling.

Walrus moved towards Mary, but as he did the Portuguese tried to grab him, so he swung the gun-barrel and hit the man full in the face. He screamed in pain and fell back over the table, splitting it in two. The black woman grabbed the chicken, but before Walrus could stop her she had run out of the open door and into the rain and night outside. Walrus picked the blanket off the floor and laid it gently over the still body.

'Is she dead?' asked Mary.

He took the lantern from her hand and held the light nearer the girl's face to see her eyes better. 'No,' he said, 'but barely living.'

Mary looked closer. 'The Portuguese did this?' she asked.

'The road did this, Mrs Mary,' he answered, 'though we'll never know how. Wild dogs, maybe a lion, perhaps hyena. The wagons were near to charcoal when I found them so she might have been burnt.'

Mary knelt by him and tucked the blanket under the girl's scarred chin. 'And yet she was pretty, once,' she said. 'Her hair is pretty and her hands. Do you see her hands, how small and pretty they are? Oh, Walrus, why did God do this to such a pretty thing?'

He stood up and stepped back from the bed. 'I would not have had you see this, Mrs Mary. I should never have told you she lived. But now maybe it's better to see what Africa is and what Africa does. It won't happen to you, not while you're with me, but you've come to a cruel place that was not meant for white people. God would have put us here if He had meant it that way, but He didn't and sometimes He reminds us of it. Go back to Durban, Mrs Mary, settle yourself there and let your boys hunt for gold later if they wish to.'

But Mary did not hear him, nor did she hear the groaning of the Portuguese on the floor. She looked only at the girl and at the grey-green eyes, wanting to touch her but afraid to, just as it had been with Owen that moment before the funeral men closed the lid and took the light from his face forever.

'Why doesn't she move or cry?' she asked. 'Why does she lie so still, as if she didn't hear us?'

'She can't speak or cry, Mary,' said Walrus. 'She has a tongue but something's taken away its power. She can see but she does not want to speak again after what she has seen and what's been done to her.'

Mary leant closed to her and stroked the long fair hair so unlike her own. 'Can you hear me, child?' she whispered. 'If I thought you could hear, and there was hope, I would take you with me – away from them.'

The Portuguese stirred on the floor as the wind slammed the door shut. The lantern candle flickered and a thousand shadows danced on the walls. Walrus touched Mary's shoulder. 'Come now,' he said. 'We must go before the black woman brings back his friends. We'll not leave at all if they find us here.'

Mary looked up at him. 'Let's take her, Walrus. Help me take her!'

'Don't be a fool,' he said. 'This place has taken her already. She is broken. You can see it. She's dying. She'll go the way they all do off the ships, wrapped in her blanket and thrown into the swamps. She'll be dead by the morning or tomorrow morning or the morning after that. Now, come, or I'll pick you up and carry you back!'

The Portuguese tried to sit up but Walrus turned and kicked him hard in the back and he rolled over again, coughing blood. Mary let go the girl's hair. Then she put her hands together, closed her eyes and whispered the hymn in Welsh that she and Owen had sung so often together every Sunday chapel morning.

Yng ngwyneb pob caledi
Y sydd new eto ddan
Dod gadarn gymorth imi
Lechu yn dy law.

'Mary . . .' said Walrus quietly, touching her shoulder, 'look at her! Look at her! She understands you, she knows what you're saying!'

Mary opened her eyes. The girl had turned her head and was looking at her and her lips were silently mouthing the words and her eyes were full of tears.

'In the face of all suffering that is or is yet to come . . .'

And Mary cupped the scarred and twisted face in her hands. 'Oh God! Dear, dear God!' she said. 'She's from Wales!' And the tears ran down her fingers.

'It was marvellous! Marvellous! Walrus cantered along with her in his arms as if she were a tiny child and me with his gun on my shoulder like a trooper! And still we outran them!'

Mary stood in front of her sons, clapping her hands and laughing as she spoke. 'Running at us they were, shouting in their language and the black woman spitting the colour of blood, her great breasts bouncing. But we ran. My! How we ran, with Walrus pulling so hard I was off my feet half the time. And at his age, too! What a man, what a man! And an Englishman too, eh, Ianto?'

She laughed again and clapped her hands loudly. But her men were not happy. It was Huw who spoke first.

'Mother,' he said, in his quiet voice, 'isn't it better she goes straight to Durban? We cannot take her with us, not the way she is. And we cannot wait here with her and miss the wagons tomorrow.'

'Oh, really, Huw?' she answered him. 'And who will take her on the ship? And who will she go to in Durban?'

'But such a girl . . .' said Huw. 'And all that way. And we have baby Tom to think of, too. What if she dies?'

'If she dies,' said Mary, sharply, 'she'll do it with us, among friends and not here, in this filthy place. And don't worry about baby Tom, he's been game since we left Bethesda. Don't be a fool, Huw. She's with us now and she'll stay with us until God decides to take her away.'

'Then let it be soon,' said Ianto. 'And better tonight if she's to go at all.'

Mary stepped forward and slapped him hard across the face, something she had not done in many years. She took the lantern from its hook on the post-rail and went across to the manger where they had made a bed for the girl with dried grass and a blanket and a clean pillow stuffed with moss. Mary turned to them, her face on fire.

'There she is!' she shouted. 'Look at her, a tiny thing, and pretty once, who came from Wales and lost everything in Africa. Look at that face! Everything but her life she's lost. Damn your men's talk, prattling and complaining. She's helpless and wretched and you would have me leave her here to die? Never! She's one of us, and we're going along that road – whatever they call it – her, baby Tom and myself. You come as well if you're pleased to. Or you can go and join the English in Natal if that suits you better. But hold your tongues now, whatever you fancy, because my mind's made up and you all know well enough by now not to try and change it!'

Her shouting had woken baby Tom, and he began crying. With her temper quickly over, she sat down and fed him before his usual time. Minutes later, exhausted by the night's adventure, she fell asleep with him still at her breast. When she woke some few hours later the boys had tucked extra blankets around her and the baby. Moonbeams lit the stable, and it was as light as day. Huw and William were asleep each side of her, but Ianto was not in his usual place at her feet. She raised her head and looked across to the manger where the girl lay, and saw him by her. Then she heard him.

He had cradled her head in his arm and was swabbing her face from a basin of water and speaking to her softly in Welsh.

Walrus Baines woke them at four o'clock, an hour before the sun rose from the Indian Ocean. The early-morning air was fresh and as they stood in the stable doorway they could see lights a mile or so out to sea where the fishermen were already at work. And beyond them the first hint of dawn. Four wagons had been pulled out of their sheds and lined up in the main street and they watched as the teams of oxen were brought up. The lead wagon was taken by three English diggers who had been waiting in Lourenço Marques for nearly a month. Walrus said they had told him they'd dug for gold along the Yukon River in North America. Early in the year they had tried the long way to Pilgrims Rest, skirting the Natal border with Zululand, but they had been attacked by Zulus north of Ladysmith and they were the only survivors to find their way back to Durban two months later. But still, lured by the smell of gold and the stories of the huge nuggets to be found high up in the mountains, they had worked the summer in the sugar plantations and saved their money for the steamer fare to Lourenço Marques. A bad sea had held them up and they had just missed the wagon train that Walrus found burning near the Komati River. When they had heard of this they drank to their good luck and they had been drinking ever since.

Walrus Baines said they had already paid for their wagon places and had bought food, but, he said, they would arrive in Pilgrims Rest penniless and much weaker than was safe for them.

Mary felt the chill and kept baby Tom well wrapped as she fed him. Then she settled him into the travelling cot that Huw had spent all the previous evening making from an old plank he had found on the quay. It was smooth and as hard as oak, and he'd fitted crescent-shaped rockers at each end and had given an African woman a handful of maize flour to plait marram grass for a hood. Then he'd used the blacksmith's iron to burn Tom's name into the end panel.

Ianto and Huw humped the trunks, equipment and the sewing-machine outside into the street, and William went off in the half light to find their wagon and help Walrus Baines harness the ox-team. Walrus had told him their wagon was the third in line but when he came to it Walrus was not there. Instead, laying the wooden yokes by the feet of the oxen was a tiny black boy. He was naked except for a thin strip of cloth around his middle, and as soon as he saw William he stood to attention and saluted as smartly as a trooper. Then he smiled.

'Morning, baas. I am Tongogara.'

'Is this Llewellyn's wagon?' asked William.

'Yes, baas. This Lellin's wagon. I'm your wagon-boy.'

'Where is Mr Baines?'

'Catch chickens.'

'For breakfast?'

The boy laughed again, high and shrill. 'No, baas. Not eat. To stop us sleep.' And before William could question him again he began to harness up and he beckoned William to help.

The sixteen oxen were standing in pairs and together the two boys lifted the heavy yokes onto their shoulders and laid the leather reins around their horns. A second rein was fastened under their throats and when all was ready they wheeled the lead ox around on itself so as to loosen the main chain, which William laid along the others' backs, ready for the start. A rope was looped over the lead ox's horns so that Tongo could lead him.

Ianto and Huw brought the trunks to the wagon and William and Tongogara heaved them aboard. Everything was packed square under the triple canvas tent stitched to bent bamboo hoops, just as Walrus Baines had said, and wedged tightly together so that nothing might move and break open the floor or side planks. Mary's sewing-machine, her jars of rosemary and turpentine, the sack of flour and the little carpet bag with all her private belongings were put in the wagon box up front, under the driver's seat. Finally, they hauled up the bed, a hard wood frame with straps of ox-leather tightly criss-crossed and on top of that was a straw-filled palliasse. When the bed was secured, Ianto went back into the manger and brought out the girl in his arms and they helped him lay her gently onto the bed. He covered her in a blanket and placed a thin muslin cloth over her face, to keep off the flies and mosquitoes.

All this was done before daybreak and they were already drinking their first beaker of tea, sitting around the fire, when the first orange-and-yellow light streaked across the sky on the eastern horizon. But still Walrus Baines had not arrived and Mary began to worry.

'Do you think the Portuguese have harmed him?' she asked.

'William says he's gone to get chickens,' said Huw.

'At this hour?'

'Maybe for breakfast.'

'No, mother,' said William. 'Tongo says they're to keep us from sleeping.'

'Then they're best left behind,' said Mary. She tried to smile to hide her anxiety. Walrus had told her they must be on their way before the sun was seen, out beyond the swamps before the smell and the biting mosquitoes rose with the warm air. They had to be way up on high dry ground, he said, before the sun was hot. Those were his last words before he had said goodnight. Yet soon they would feel the sun and Walrus was nowhere to be seen. Maybe the Portuguese came back to try to take the girl? Maybe they had taken Walrus in revenge? Maybe even now he was lying injured and dying, perhaps dead? Suddenly the commotion made her look up.

Coming down the road was Walrus Baines covered hat to boots in black mud, and in each hand were two red-and-white cockerels, screeching, twisting and flapping as if they were only seconds from the chopping-block. With every stride he held one up in front of him and cursed it loudly with words that Mary, in all her life among men, had never heard before. They smelt him many yards before he reached them – the sickly-sweet stench of the swamps.

'Devils!' he roared. 'Damn them for it! I'll cut out their livers myself as soon as we've done. God stop me from wringing their cussed necks now!'

The cocks clucked as he eyed them. He moved towards Tongogara but the boy ran backwards from him.

'You black dwarfed scoundrel!' he shouted. 'Take them and tie them to the wagon and I'll have the skin off your back if you let them free again. Take them! And keep your distance from me, or you'll not sit for a month!'

The boy took the cocks and ran as fast as he could to the wagon and jumped inside to hide.

'Good morning, Mr Baines,' said Mary in her sweetest way. 'Would you care for some tea?'

He turned slowly and looked at her. She thought his moustache might have bristled, had it not been so damp. 'No tea, thank you, ma'am,' he said, 'and my good morning will begin once I've shifted this filthy swamp off me into the sea.'

'Did you find the cockerels in the swamp?' she asked.

'No, I chased them there, right into the deepest, stinking middle.'

'Mr Baines,' she asked again with a smile, 'why are you so dirty and they so clean?'

Walrus scowled at her. He pulled his moustache from the corners of his mouth and squeezed the water from the ends. 'I am dirty, ma'am, because they can hop, skip and fly and I cannot.'

'But why did you chase them?'

'Because I wouldn't travel the road without them, that's why! And if I hadn't caught them today we would have waited for tomorrow until I had!'

'Why are you so fond of them, Mr Baines?' asked William, taking the wink from his mother.

'Fool boy!' the old man growled. 'I ain't fond of them. I'd cut their throats now, but they're our night guards and our alarms, the best safety we could have against the kaffir killers.

The cocks will crow if a black comes within a hundred yards of us in the night. You'll get the fondness of them, boy, when you know you can sleep safe just as long as they stay quiet. But you'll not be so fond of them when they crow just before sunrise to tell you it's time to start the day again! Now drink your blessed tea, and be ready to move when I get back.'

With that he strode off towards the shore on the near side of the quay and with a second, hot beaker of tea in their hands they followed and saw him sit down in the surf, still shouting his curses, then watched as he washed himself without even taking off his hat.

He came back clean, dripping brine, with steam already rising from his clothes. He was on his horse – the one he called Flansman – and behind him, held by a halter, were two mares. He found the family obediently waiting at the wagon, Mary with baby Tom in her arms, Ianto and Huw sitting abreast on the front wagon box and William with Tongogara by the front oxen, reins in hands. The two cockerels kept silent in a wicker cage that hung between the rear wheels. He pulled his horses round in a tight circle, showing them off, and then raised his hat to show his balding head for the very first time.

'Walrus Baines, ma'am, sweet-smelling again and bone-dry by breakfast time.' He edged Flansman closer to them. 'Now, I've told the English diggers up front what's in store for them, so now I'll tell you. Only the geography, mind you, 'cos that's the one thing I can talk of, it being the only thing that's constant. The rest can change, even as you're looking at it. Africa does that all the time.

'The first problem is always the kaffirs. Tongo here is mine, so he'll do like me. He's a good boy and you'll like him, except he has numb fingers with chickens. The rest of the kaffirs that's coming would do better as shark food. They've agreed a price with me for the trek but in a few days they'll likely sidle up by you and try to double it. Tell me when they do and I'll make them work twice as hard for half as much. And watch if they get red-eyed and swagger. Don't know where they keep it but they're bound to be carrying brandy and the hurricane gin they make from the palms.

'Now, the first thing we do this morning is to cross the swamp, so keep yourself inside the wagon. I've put a stove in there and I'll burn some damp wood so there's plenty of smoke. You might choke a bit but it'll keep out the smell and the flies and mosquitoes. Some believe it's the mosquitoes that carry the fever, though I've yet to hear a doctor say it.'

Ianto said something to Huw that Walrus could not hear. He took it to be a protest. He went on, 'Of course the choice is your own. You can sweat yourself dead in a blanket with the fever if you choose.

'Anyhow, after twenty miles, once we're on higher ground the road sets hard and your spine will be like jelly. Far off you'll see the Lebombo Mountains, which is always a good sight and by then you'll have forgotten you ever smelt the stench of this hole. In about three to four days, if we don't have rain, we come to the end of Portuguese territory, which is when I give a yelp and take a mouthful of my best gin to celebrate. Mind you, I don't drink more than a mouthful 'cos there's not that much to celebrate. From there on is what I call the Tsetse Run. The tsetse is a little black fly that does business for the Devil. Anyway, in three weeks or thereabouts if we dodge the tsetse and lion, hyena and crocodile and given no one has brought the fever with him, we begin our climb towards Pretorius Kop with gulleys and streams and green woods and where the air is clean and the breezes cool. It's a comfort just to think of it as you sweat yourself across the lowveld. You might even see, in the far off, diggers already working the slopes, like little ants on a molehill, and just as crazy!

'Then we trek on up to Beacon Hill, near a farm called Orphir on a sharp stony crag. It's easy going from then on, down the slopes into the valley and maybe your fortune. At least, that's the dream that'll keep you all going!'

No one spoke for a while. Such a way across Africa and the day's ride from Bethesda to Dartmouth had seemed a long adventure. Then there had been trains and stations and porters to ask the way. Now there was only themselves and baby Tom, a sick girl who could not move and would not talk, and three Englishmen who could not properly stand for drink! But Mary looked at Walrus Baines, old and strong. 'Go only with Baines,' Captain Jeppe had said. 'He'll see you through. The only honest man in the whole of East Africa.'

'How long will it take to get there, Walrus?' she asked. 'Captain Jeppe said a month.'

The old man answered, laughing, 'And he was never known to tell a lie! A month without trouble, though, is true enough. But with it – and you won't see Christmas there.'

'Oh yes we will!' said Mary quickly back, pushing out her chin to him. 'We'll be there in good time for that. I have my plans for Christmas Day. They include you, and I won't let any silly thing upset them!'

Walrus Baines clapped his hands, stood up in his saddle and roared again. 'Then so be it, Mrs Mary, so be it! You've the look of a lucky woman and wise enough to carry it in your purse. So spend it carefully on us and see us through and I'll catch you a guinea-fowl for that Christmas dinner.' He dug his heels into the horse's ribs and as it reared he cracked his whip a foot above Tongogara's head. 'Let them go, Tongo!' he shouted. 'Speed them away! Wao – away! Wao – away! There's a month's trek ahead and a long, long way to go but I'll bet my boots that come lion, tsetse, goblins and all we'll be there for Christmas Day!'

William at the front, flushed red with the nearness of the whipcrack and the excitement of Walrus' words, waved and cheered and his cheers were taken up by the three Englishmen ahead. Then the ox-teams leant forward with the strain and took up the trek chains, and with a crack and a creak the great wheels turned and the wagons rumbled off, out of the black sand of Lourenço Marques, away from the Portuguese merchants peering from behind the doors at the first light of day, away from the quay empty of Arab dhows and of the slaves and their misery, out onto the track known only as the Delagoa Road that would lead them to the Transvaal and high up into the mountains men called the Drakensbergs and to the Valley of Gold they had christened Pilgrims Rest.

CHAPTER THREE

The bird stood in the pool of dark water staring at its reflection in the moonlight, white and still, a very special bird, the one who knows the unknown, the one whose eyes can follow things that vanish when you look at them, the bird that always stands on its own and has conversations with wizards and who, once in its lifetime, in the hour before the cocks crow, turns into a man. And because wherever it goes the wind and rain follow, it is known as the rainmaker, the herald of thunderstorms. The Africans call it *impandulu* – the lightning bird.

Twelve paces back from the pool, sitting in a semi-circle, were Walrus Baines' boys, among them Tongogara, all watching the lightning bird and waiting for an omen, waiting for its chest to swell and its legs to grow and its head to change shape and colour; waiting for one of a thousand ancestors to come and show himself and speak his wisdom to them before the cocks called.

Mary woke and saw them there kneeling, with their hands in their laps and their heads slightly bowed as if they were listening to a preacher. The night was nearly over. Stars were scattered around the moon like diamond dust, but the faint orange glow she was now used to seeing every morning, an hour or so before the sun rose, was beginning to show itself on the horizon and she heard the chickens shuffling in their cage beneath the wagon.

Carefully, so as not to wake baby Tom in his cot, she lifted herself up and edged onto the wagon box, pulling the blanket with her, wrapping it around her shoulders and tucking the ends between her knees. They had been on the Delagoa Road now for a week, but still she could not sleep the whole night. The day was taken up with work and worry, feeding and pleasing her baby, caring for the girl and worrying for William as he darted in and out of the oxen with Tongogara, when Walrus Baines bellowed out orders from the saddle. And when the day's trek was over and they outspanned, there was the washing and sewing, and spooning the flies and spiders out of the stews and tea brews over the fire. Her body was exhausted, but her head was too full of things that would not sleep.

For those first few nights it had been the excitement that had kept her awake. At last on the road, on the move, away from the filth of Lourenço Marques. They had spluttered and coughed with the smoke as they had sat huddled inside the wagon tent, moving through the fevered swamplands. And then, as Walrus had halted on hard firm earth, the marvel as they had come out into the sunlight to see how high they were above the sea with the dry open veld all around them.

And then in these past few nights, her dreams had played unkind tricks, putting up pictures for her to watch and weep over. Perhaps they would not have come had it not been for William.

On the morning of the fourth day, one of the wooden yokes across the neck of the second ox snapped and Tongogara had darted in between them to pick up the reins and the broken pieces before they trapped and twisted the animal's legs. William followed, but he was only half as nimble and he stumbled and fell, and would have been trampled and squashed by the wagon's wheels if Ianto had not jumped off the driver's box into the middle of them and lifted him clear. In her dreams that night, and all the next too, that moment was repeated again and again, the images dissolving and then coming back as something else: Ianto standing large and strong with William in his arms like a baby, his young face and arms scratched and bleeding. And then Ianto standing at the quarry's edge carrying

Owen, whose breath had been squeezed out of his body by a wagon from Caernarfon.

The first cockerel crowed as the first shaft of red light fanned from the east and then the second joined his chorus. Mary gripped the sides of the wagon box, surprised by the sudden start of a new day. She looked across to the pool, but the lightning bird had flown and the boys were already back rekindling their fires for breakfast. She felt the wagon rock a little as Huw and Ianto turned over in their blankets, not anxious to leave them. The oxen were hunched shadows in the long tambootie grass, but one by one they stirred and heaved themselves up with a groan and wandered off separately to graze. The sharp shrill cock calls had pierced the veld, but now it was still again as if everyone had decided to sleep on and wait for a second call. Huddled like this in her blanket, Mary remembered her parlour, sitting alone by the hob waiting for the kettle to boil. Owen would not get out of bed until he heard the tea being made, and nor would the boys move until they heard his steps on the landing. For an instant the parlour seemed so real she could smell the fire and hear the lid of the kettle jumping with the steam, and the sound of Owen's boots on the stairs. What was real? And what was not? Why was her mind tumbling so freely? Was it finding its way, trying to cope and come to terms with all the real and unlikely things that were now happening around her?

Was it because nothing was how she had imagined it? Why had she pictured jungles, with trees touching the clouds, when there was nothing but dry grass between one horizon and the next? Why was everything the colour of sand when she had expected a thousand greens? And why, when she had looked for lion and leopard and pink flamingos, was the first wild thing she saw a solitary black spiralling vulture, a single speck in the cloudless blue? She had seen it on their third day, when one of the trailing oxen had dropped a calf stillborn and Walrus had ordered the boys to bury it. But they had dallied and before they could drop it in the pit the one vulture had become a dozen, all suddenly appearing like magic from the sky and dropping on the dead calf the way Mary had seen crows fall on dead lambs at home.

The ugly birds tore the frail carcase apart and clawed and pecked each other for a bigger helping, pulling at the entrails, gorging themselves. Walrus said they were the birds of death, never killing but always its witness, the butchers of the wild.

Mary also saw the honeybird. At first she thought it was dying. It flapped its wings, and staggered and screeched as if it was caught in a trap, but as soon as Tongogara and the other boys gathered beneath it, it rose and flew off, hovering every few yards to make sure they were following. William went with them and two hours later he returned, hot and excited. He told how they had chased the bird as it squawked its way from tree to tree until it finally perched at the very top of a tall Msasa, three feet from a bee's nest. The boys clambered to the top and despite the angry swarms and their stings, pulled out handfuls of honeycomb, and stuffed it into their mouths, bees and all. The honeybird watched it all from its perch, waiting patiently for a reward, and this, Tongogara told William, had to be paid. So a large piece of honeycomb was hooked onto a bough just below it as payment. 'If we forgot,' said Tongogara, 'the honeybird would have its revenge and the next time lure us to a lion's den.'

They outspanned early that morning long before the sun was really warm, because Walrus said the trek to the next water-hole was across dry and rocky veld where there was never enough rain for the grass and therefore never enough grass for the oxen. While they ate a breakfast of chicken and potato stew, he fed the oxen on maize husks to fill out their stomachs, and help them pretend over the next few days they were full.

Mary had now begun to bake bread. On the morning outspan she mixed her dough, then left it in a basin to rise in time for baking on the afternoon stop. On the fifth morning she had seen the boy called Jacob, who cooked for the English diggers, baking in a makeshift oven scooped out of an anthill. Seeing her interest, Jacob brought her a plateful of his 'cookies' which tasted very much like the scones Mary had baked at home, except that instead of currants, Jacob had mixed in various seeds. Mary asked what they were, so Jacob ran back to his kitchen and returned with dozens of little bundles all wrapped together in a large blue spotted cotton square. He spread them out in front of her, more spices, herbs and perfumed seeds than Mary had ever seen before. She recognized cinnamon and sage, rosemary and peppercorns, roots of ginger and leaves of thyme. He had drilled holes through nutmegs and held them like a necklace and had done the same with a string of cloves. He dabbed her finger into bright red powder that tasted hot and yet sweet, and then into bright yellow powder that burnt her tongue quicker than any pepper.

He had sticks of hard wood that might have been liquorice but were not, and sheaves of different coloured dried leaves as brittle as a flake of slate. And all of it, he said, had come from the slave traders in Lourenço Marques. He told her he carved figures of men and animals from tiny bits of broken ivory left scattered on the quayside and then exchanged them for the spices the Arabs brought in from Zanzibar.

Mary unpacked a tin of yeast from the wagon box and, with Jacob's help, kneaded her first dough. He explained it was not always possible to find an anthill for an oven, so he showed her how to build one. First he scooped a hole in the earth a foot deep and placed a japanned tin plate at the bottom. Nearby he lit a fire and an hour later, when it was charcoal and ashes, Mary's dough, risen in the warm sun, was laid on the plate and covered by a cast-iron cooking-pot turned upside down. The hot ashes and charcoal were then heaped over it all. When the ashes were scattered and the pot lifted, the smell of new-baked bread brought Walrus Baines running.

The next afternoon Mary baked again, but there was a crisis. Walrus and Tongogara had come to her with armfuls of what looked like peat, but Walrus explained it was dried ox manure. It burnt, he said, with a fury. Mary said she certainly would not bake with cow dung and refused to touch it! But her temper did not last long. When she saw Walrus and Tongo kneel and gather up the discs, she relented and went to the wagon box and searched through her carpet bag until she found a pair of white linen gloves trimmed with cotton lace that she had worn only with her Sunday chapel best. Without further fuss she put them on and picked up the manure and from then on she wore them whenever she baked and Jacob soaked them in salted water to bleach them fresh and white again for the next day.

It was on Sunday, the seventh day, that Tongogara was attacked by a snake. Mary had been kneading her dough on a boulder during the morning's first outspan and had come away from the wagons because of the flies swarming over the sweating oxen. Tongogara followed her to watch, but was soon fast asleep in the long grass. Suddenly he screamed and began rolling in the grass, kicking his legs and pounding the earth with his hands. Then he stopped and very slowly stood up a few feet from her, his face contorted in fear, his mouth and eyes wide open in terror. The snake hung from his head, its fangs buried in his scalp, curling its glistening speckled body under his arms and around his neck. The boy did not move but stared at Mary, waiting to die. She could not move, even though the snake's tail whipped across her breasts. Her hands and her feet no longer felt part of her and she wanted to scream but it could find no way out.

Then she felt hands on her arms, strong brown hands that led her some paces away, and she could hear Walrus telling her to be still and brave. In the same calming voice, he spoke to the boy in his own tongue. He stepped closer little by little until the snake's tail was slapping his face. And just as carefully he raised his revolver, rested the barrel on his left arm, two feet from the boy's scalp and an inch above it, and pulled the trigger. The snake's head exploded into pulp and for an instant it rained blood, splattering their faces. But still Tongogara did not move. He could not. In the last spasm the headless thing clasped him tighter around his chest until its muscles died. Then it uncurled and fell to the ground at his feet. Tongogara watched it fall and then his eyes filled with tears and Walrus caught him before he fell. The old man picked him up gently in his arms and carried him away, pressing the shivering body close to him and whispering comfort in the child's ears.

For an hour they waited for Tongogara to die, his little body wrapped in a blanket. Walrus told them it would be a painful death and said they should go far away from the wagon so they would not hear the child's last torments. But they would not and instead Mary sat bathing the tiny sweating face, waiting for the contortions to start. An hour passed but the boy's body did not swell, nor did his chest heave for air, nor the muscles tighten. He did not spit blood or claw at his skin and when Walrus lifted his eyelids the whites of his eyes had not turned red. The boy was sleeping peacefully and Walrus was puzzled. But he had to wait another half hour before he had the explanation, and it was William who provided it. He was washing the blood and snake skin from the boy's head when he stopped and peered closer. Then he tugged at Walrus' arm and when the old man saw what was caught in the thick wiry hair he pulled the skinning knife from his boot and carefully shaved the hair in a circle about two inches across. Holding his breath, he lifted up a patch of the black wool, the size of his thumbnail, and in it were white fangs, as thin and as sharp as needles. The snake had tried to bite, but the fangs had been trapped in the mesh of coarse hair and unable to puncture the skin. The poison had ejected harmlessly a fraction from it.

The other boys began dancing and singing when they heard because to have such an escape could only have been done with the help of the spirits. It meant that Tongogara was favoured by his ancestors and was therefore very special. All the same, Walrus said, the boys were angry with him for destroying the snake. 'Africans believe it has medicine magic, *mootie* they call it. Eat its brain and a man will inherit its cunning. Eat its eyes and he will see into another's mind. Stretch and dry its tongue and wear it as a necklace, and no young girl would ever pass him by.'

Tongogara did not stay in his sick-bed long. That afternoon he was at the head of the oxen again, striding with them and shouting their names as if the terror of the morning had not happened. And only Walrus knew why. The boy believed that the snake had indeed been trapped by his ancestors. He had waited for the spirits to rise from *impandulu*, the lightning bird, but they had not chosen to. Instead they had come with the snake, and once visited, they would not go away. They would stay at his shoulder, guiding him, protecting him, making him much more than a man. As long as he was good and true to them and to all mortal men, he would live long and well. And when he died, he would join them.

Tongogara urged his oxen forward with a new strong voice, digging his heels into the earth, breathing the warm air deep into his lungs to give his muscles more power. And Walrus, on his horse, smiled and spoke aloud the only two lines he could remember of the only prayer he had ever learnt.

They travelled hard, moving slowly out of the lowveld towards the lower slopes of the Lebombo Mountains. The trek was only slightly uphill, but without the grass around them and knowing well enough the barren prospect ahead, the oxen became sluggish and obstinate, the lazy ones refusing to pull their weight despite the whips. For hours they trudged to the top of a hill and then dropped steeply down again, with the wagons bouncing from rock to rock. It was like a giant staircase with the steps a yard deep so that the wagons fell and shuddered and Mary thought they would explode and the spokes fly out from the wheel hubs.

Behind and below, the land swept down to a shadow that was the sea and she was astonished that she could trace so much of their week's travel. How vast it was, this land, where she could see the sun rise and set from one horizon to the next, uninterrupted.

Now though, the evening sun was hidden by a haze and the air felt wet and heavy and enormous black clouds were filling the sky from the sea. She felt a breeze on her cheeks and Walrus called out that they should expect a storm and he ordered the boys to put out the cooking-pots and pans to catch the rain as soon as they outspanned. The clouds broke as they were about to cross a narrow ravine, a dry river bed about fifty yards across with a high wall of rock on both sides. Walrus said a cloudburst would turn it into a river quicker than they could cross it, so he stopped the wagons early and said they would camp the night, wait for the storm to move on, and cross the next morning when the earth had dried out. The timing of the storm made him angry, believing it was the Lord's cussedness.

The lightning followed the thunder so quickly, Mary had no time to count the seconds in between. It was almost directly above them, as near as she had ever been to a storm's centre. She sat with the others, huddled inside the tent, watching the canvas shine yellow with every lightning strike and the wheels vibrate with every thunderclap.

She leant forward and held the girl's hand. Sometimes, in the days since Lourenço Marques, Mary thought the twisted face had moved to a smile as one or the other had talked with her. The lips had parted, but then her eyes had clouded and glistened again as if all she was trying to forget came suddenly flooding back. Or maybe the things she was trying to remember. But even now, in the middle of all the storm's commotion, there was no longer fear in the grey-green eyes. She could not speak and her face could never again express itself, but her eyes let everyone around her know the pain was leaving. She was growing strong again, not just in her limbs, but in her heart too, taking strength from the family who washed her, fed her, brushed her hair and spoke to her in the language of home.

Now, every evening, with the family around the fire, Ianto carried his plate of food and ate it with her in the wagon. He sat her up against a pillow and talked to her in whispers, and always in Welsh. Mary had forbidden Huw and William to follow and listen, but she did herself, just once, eavesdropping by the backboards with only the tent's canvas between them.

Ianto spoke of Bethesda and the quarries. He told her how he had split slate and dressed it and how one day he might have been crowned at the Eisteddfod, if the troubles had not come. His words were Owen's, spoken from the bathtub by the fire in the back parlour. 'It's an art, like poetry and singing. Did you know that quarrymen go to the Eisteddfod every year, where pretty words and music and slate dressing rival each other for the Crown? It's better than shovelling coal. Any Englishman could do that. But they won't touch slate because it's Welsh and it only talks to us. You must be Welsh to break the rock because, you see, it speaks no English.'

He told her about the village and the chapel and the chapel elders, vicious men with faces the colour of shadows and even blacker hearts. He told her of their war with the English, of how the men had been betrayed, of how they had finally betrayed themselves and with his father hardly cold in the graveyard. And he told her in whispers that became hoarse and angry, how he and his mother and brothers had been sent out of Wales because their own folk had outlawed them, blaming them for what had happened, when they had not the courage to blame themselves. How foreign Mary thought it all seemed now, the places and names he spoke of. Even the mention of Owen seemed to belong to another time, almost as if he had belonged to another woman and had never been hers at all.

Africa was taking hold and pushing things away from her faster than she realized. How quickly its miles seemed to have distanced her from half a lifetime, the years growing dimmer and smaller with every African day. It was strange, that even though she was so new to Africa, she was already beginning to feel old in it, as if she was simply following some part of her that had gone before. And odd that ever since she had known Owen, ever since he had first stroked and caressed her naked skin, calling it the colour of honey, he had said that God had not meant her for Wales, that He had meant her for someplace else, a place in the sun. And here she was. She did not feel she belonged, at least not yet. Only she had the strangest feeling that she was returning.

For nearly an hour that evening Mary listened to Ianto and the agonies he poured out to the silent girl who could not give him one word of consolation back, and was still too shy to allow her eyes to show their sympathy. Mary walked away from the wagon and sat alone in the darkness, but she could still hear his whispers, reminding her of the son who could no longer talk to her, who had not the mind to come and kneel and ask her comfort. And she too full of guilt to go to him.

The storm blew itself out quickly and the sun shone bright and warm a good hour before it was due to set, so Walrus bellowed out his change of mind and the spans were harnessed and the water pots gathered and twenty minutes later they were trundling their way across the ravine, with the wheels squelching their channels through the shallow red mud.

Soon it was dark and Mary wondered why there was no twilight in Africa. The sun set with hardly a shadow of warning and the light quickly drained away. There was no gentle coming of the night; the sun was gone, and there was the moon. The day's thousand colours were suddenly a flat moonscape of black and white, where daytime things had no meaning, where everything that moved appeared an enemy and everything that was still threatened to move. The low moon was so bright Walrus said they would trek on and make the most of the night light and catch up on the time lost in the storm. Mary could not sleep so she sat up on the wagon box with the heavy blanket wrapped around her, warm and snug. She shuddered, though she could not think why. Maybe it was the sudden emptiness, as if the sun had taken all living things away with it. Every sound, the rumble of the wheels, a cooking-pot hitting the tailboard, the rustle of the harness across the oxen's backs and the thud of their hooves across the stony ground, all echoed like voices in a room without a carpet. She had never been up so long after dark, even in Wales, and never before had she accepted the arrival of night so casually. Since she could remember, the end of the day had always been treated with some ceremony and it had never altered, summer or winter. The doors, back and front, had been bolted and the curtains drawn across them to keep out the draught whether there was one or not. The shutters were closed and the curtains pulled tightly together even if there were still some last shafts of sunlight left. Finally the chairs were pulled closer to the hearth, no matter how warm it was. It was such a ritual, stopping the night coming in, barricading themselves against it. It had always been that way. Maybe that was why, from her childhood, the night had always threatened.

A little after midnight and with the moon still white and large, Walrus rode up and pulled the lead oxen around in a half circle and the other wagons followed until they had formed a complete circle. The animals were unharnessed, but Mary noticed they were tied to each other to keep them close as they ate their ration of corn husks. She saw how the boys scampered about quicker than usual, gathering wood, pulling up dead and withered bush for the fire. And there were more fires than usual and bigger. There seemed altogether an urgency. Huw sensed it too, and jumped down to speak to Tongogara.

'*Inconyama*,' the boy whispered to him. '*Inconyama*. Many lion,' and then he too ran off to find wood.

The stew was soon hot on the fire and ready. It never took long to cook because it was never fresh. Cuts of meat and bags of potato and onion were thrown into it at the end of every meal, so they were soaked in the juices and half cooked in time for the next. Sometimes Walrus would contribute a dozen or more small birds he'd shot and all of them, except the feathers, went in to add to the flavour.

Walrus had eaten more than his usual extra-large helping and was picking his teeth with his skinning knife. Tongogara squatted at his feet. Huw held baby Tom in his lap and Mary had tucked her knees under her chin with the blanket well wrapped around her so that only her face and the tips of her toes showed. Ianto had finished his supper quickly and had mashed up a helping of meat and potato to take to the girl.

The night air was cold but the fire gave off such a wonderful heat and such a glow, Mary said she felt they were all inside a bubble, warm enough to keep out a frost and strong enough to keep out the hungriest lion.

Walrus laughed and reached out with the ladle for another sip from the pot. 'You'll hear them tonight,' he said, 'but I don't expect you'll see them. If it's any comfort, Mrs Mary, they only roar when they're full, so as long as you can hear them you can be sure they'll not come near. Anyway, the *inconyama* prefer the kaffirs to the white man's meat, isn't that right, Tongo? Tastier than ours, eh?'

He pushed the boy with his foot then growled at him and reached out with his long fingers curled like claws. The little boy turned his head away and edged closer to the fire, ignoring everyone's laughter.

The fire crackled as Walrus pulled out a burning ember and puffed at his pipe. He stretched himself and rested his shoulders against his saddle. This was the time he enjoyed most, a long day's trek over, a stomach full of good food, a well-stocked fire, a well-stacked pipe, and a sip from his flask of 'celebration gin'. It was the time, whenever he was with good company, when he would remember his life and dwell on the favourite parts of it. Tongogara, knowing the signs well, turned over with his back to the fire and curled up to sleep, his head on his master's boots.

Walrus began: 'I lost a wagon and a full span of oxen to a lion once, and all because of a sticky boot.' Mary looked at Huw and raised her eyebrows and Huw winked back. William, suddenly alert to the old man's adventures, sat up and crossed his legs.

'Yes sir,' said Walrus, 'sixteen oxen, good and strong, for a boot that wouldn't budge. It was less than a half day's trek from this very spot, used to be a spring there, though it's long dried up now. We'd stopped to fill our water barrels and we were not being too careful with it, slopping it here and there, so there was mud where none should have been. I was casual then – well, I'm going back now forty years – it didn't happen again. Anyhow, I didn't notice the boys had forgotten to stake the ox reins to the ground; they were so busy watering themselves, not that I blame them, we were all careless that day. Best blame me 'cos when the lion did come I hadn't got my rifle on me. I could see it only a couple of paces away, but just as I went to fetch it I found I was stuck ankle deep in the mud of my own making. Well, that lion jumped into the back of the wagon to grab a buck I had shot early that day and thrown in to skin later. But instead of leaving the way he went in, he left by the front with the buck in his jaws, and when the oxen saw him they were off like a bat out of hell, with the lion up there on the wagon box trying to work out whether to jump with the buck, jump without it, or not jump at all. Well, I shouted loud enough to skin my throat and managed to pull my foot out of one boot, but I'm damned if I could move the other, and by the time I reached the rifle they were dots in the dust. The more that lion roared the faster the oxen ran, until they went right over the edge of Soutspan Kop. Wagon, lion, ox and a year's profit five hundred feet down. That was the most expensive buck I ever shot!'

He sucked at his pipe and the grey smoke mingled in the red glow like swirling paint. He nudged a piece of burning wood back into the fire with his boot, but gently, so as not to wake Tongo.

'Yes sir,' he said, nodding to no one in particular, 'this is a terrible country for extracting the strength and resolution out of a man. It takes a lot of life to succeed here. And more luck than you're due for! Fact is that in fifty years and more, the only successful men I've ever known have been the luckiest, too. One of them was a man in Kimberley, name of Hardy, who worked his diamond stake for five years, and no one worked harder, he was so certain he had a good one. He was up before sunrise and still at it when it went down. First four years he was doing comfortable, picking up one here and there, not enough, mind you, to make him wealthy, but enough to keep him looking for the big one. That's what keeps them all going, the thought of the big one. He was a happy man, saving his stones so that he could send for his wife and children back in England. Well, at the end of that fourth year he reckoned he was going so well he took on some kaffirs to do the digging for him. It was getting too much for one man but as the months went by instead of things getting better, they got worse. From finding a couple of stones a week he was now only getting two a month even with five extra shovels, so by mid-year he was selling off his store of stones to pay his boys and feed himself and, little by little, the spirit left him. He fed himself less, got up later in the mornings and went to bed drunk while the sun was still hot.

'One evening, it was meant to be his last, he sat in his shack with a gin bottle at one elbow and a revolver at the other. All day he'd been there trying to write his family a letter of goodbye. That was the only reason he was still sober, first time the whole winter. Anyhow, he wrote his last lines and sealed the envelope and rested it against the lamp so as nobody should miss it. Then he picked up his gun, pulled back the hammer, put the barrel in his mouth, and pulled the trigger.'

Walrus Baines puffed at his pipe, but it was dead and he tapped the ash out on the knuckle of his thumb. The only other sound was the hiss of wood sap burning. He waited. He had told his story many, many times and knew well enough the best places to pause.

'Well, the hammer hit the pin but the pin didn't hit the shell. It jammed. Gun hadn't been out of his trunk in years and must have been rusty. He was just about to try again when he remembered he hadn't paid his boys off. Odd thing to bother with, you might say, just as you're about to meet your Maker, though maybe that's why he did. Didn't fancy standing judgement with debts left behind, even if it was only kaffir money.

'So, he went off to find them. He knew their hut was on the slope, and coming up quietly, he spotted them sitting around their fire jabbering and pushing and shoving the way they always do when they've been smoking their dagga pipes. As I say, he came up on them quietly, soberly you might say, something he couldn't have done on any other night that year. But then he stopped when he saw what he saw, and dropped down on his knees and crawled on all fours, as clever as a cat so's not a twig cracked or a leaf moved, his muscles working just as he told them to. What he'd seen by the fire concentrated his mind wonderfully well. He got closer and closer until he was only five yards from the biggest of them and the clay bowl he was holding on his lap.

'Then, suddenly, the big fellow stood up, alerted by a sound or just a sense that someone was near. He picked up his digging pick and raked the fire to give more light and as the flames rose he looked and saw Hardy beneath him. Well, that kaffir was so surprised and angry, he gave a great roar. Then he dropped the clay bowl, raised the pick high above his head and, with a scream like a jackal, plunged it down just as Hardy's bullet hit him full in the chest. And the pick split the earth a foot deep and a flea's width from Hardy's head.

'The others ran off and Hardy never saw them again. But if they weren't caught for what they did to him, they'll have been hanged for something else by now. Not that Hardy was in a mood to worry about them then, or ever again, because in the light of that bright fire he knelt by the broken clay bowl and picked out of the sand more diamonds than he'd ever seen before, so many, no decent living man could spend their worth in his lifetime. You see, he had found one of the best stakes in the whole diamond field, but he'd also found himself five of the biggest rogues to dig it for him. At first they had kept one stone and given him one, then they kept two to his one, and then three and four, until in the end they were so greedy, they gave him none at all.

'So you see, if it hadn't been for a revolver that wouldn't fire first time, those kaffirs would have been the wealthiest in all Africa. Mind you, if it hadn't fired the second time they'd still be. That's what I mean about being lucky. You see, old Hardy had only put one bullet in the gun!'

There was a minute and more of silence. It was Huw who spoke first. 'You might call it luck, Mr Baines. Others might say it's the work of the Lord.'

'That's always possible, boy,' said Walrus.

'Divine intervention.'

'And hallelujah to that, boy,' said Walrus, laughing. He reached for the sheep's stomach to refill his pipe.

'Do you not believe in God, then?' asked Huw.

'That's enough, Huw,' said Mary. She did not like him bringing his chapel manners here. 'Whether a man does or not is a private thing.'

'No matter, Mrs Mary,' said the old man. 'You can ask Walrus Baines anything at any time, though he may not always give an answer. Anyhow I don't know, boy, whether I do or I don't. Must say, though, if there is a God, He has the strangest habit of keeping the worst people on earth and taking away the best.'

'God works His own way,' Huw said. 'He isn't obliged to tell us His reasons.'

'No, boy, He ain't. But if He loves us the way the Bible says He does, then I reckon He ought to make more effort to explain things better. And He ought to show Himself a bit more often 'cos I don't think you'll see much of Him down here, son. He's never found the time to come down here.'

For a while Huw said nothing. Then he leant over and

tucked the bundle of baby Tom inside Mary's blanket, and kissed her on the cheek. Then with a nod and a smile to Walrus he took William's hand and they left for the wagon together.

'I spoke badly, Mrs Mary,' Walrus said once they had gone. 'I shouldn't have said those things, knowing the way he feels.'

'No, Walrus,' she answered. 'Huw loved his chapel and he's brought it with him to Africa but that doesn't make us all his congregation.' She pulled her blanket tighter around her and felt baby Tom warm in her lap. Then Walrus sat up and lifted his nose to the night air like a dog picking a scent. A long way off Mary heard a sound like the soft roll of drums.

'Lion!' said Walrus. 'Up in the hills, letting the others know where he is and what he's got. Long way off. He'll not come mucking with us.'

Pipe smoke hung above his head like a crown. 'Your older boy, Mrs Mary, Ianto,' he said. 'He seems to have nothing but trouble in his pockets.' She did not answer.

'Seems apart from the rest of you, as if he was chipped from a different block. That's how old Mother Baines used to say it.'

'He's a bit like his father,' said Mary. 'Very Welsh, very brooding. Always worrying over things he can't live with but can't see any way of changing. There's a lot like him at home. People who only seem to remember the days when it rains. Mind you, it was a grey place and I've always thought places make people.'

Walrus nodded. 'Sounds like a place where there's no decent tomorrows.'

Mary looked up from the fire. 'That's exactly how it was,' she said. 'Just like that. There was never ever anything to look forward to. Nothing beyond supper time.'

'That's why you left?'

'No. I wouldn't have come this far if it hadn't been for the boys. I left because I wanted them to follow. I wanted them as far away from Wales as I could get them and they wouldn't have done it on their own. Like all the men there they'd ambition as long as their noses. They might have drifted south eventually, of course, to dig coal. Then end up buried under heaps of it in the Rhondda.

'After their father's funeral there was the oddest thing. A newspaper man who was there sent me a cutting about the goldfields, though I can't think why he did. He couldn't have known so much about us just standing by the grave, could he? I've still got it tucked into my Bible. It was only a little story, but it was so nicely written, about people from Wales starting a new life in Africa. And such a pretty name, Pilgrims Rest, he made it sound like a little bit of Wales only with sunshine and a thousand times better. He said there were valleys and steep mountains and clear streams running over black rock, and mists in the morning. Is it like that, Walrus? I've been so worried you'd say it's not.'

Walrus nodded to her. 'Oh, yes. It's just as you say. But there's none of the comforts you had in that village of yours. There's no gas lamps and no water pipes and no grocers that open at eight with their shelves full. Dammit,' he said, biting into the stem of his pipe. 'I still don't understand how a woman like yourself, and with a baby still taking your milk, should come halfway round the world just to get away from home?'

'Oh, Walrus,' she said, 'maybe it's the same reason you put that saddle on Saviour's mare and rode off from your farm. I'd lived in that place all my life, but when my Owen died there was nothing left to care about. Nothing I cared for. Death was all that ever changed things. Nothing ever changed for the good. Mondays were always the same as Tuesdays and Tuesdays were like Fridays. And Sundays were devoted to chapel, just like the Sunday before and the Sunday to come. I remember something would happen and I'd say, "Well, now we might see a change." But I never did. Except that once and they killed him for it. People were afraid to be happy, as if they thought they'd be punished for it, as if it was more right than wrong to be unhappy. That's how they were, most of them. Do you know, when I was a young woman, they said I'd never go to Heaven because I danced too much! But you know, I danced and sang and flirted because I wanted to stir them up a bit and myself, just to see if things couldn't be better, even living there, living with them.

'It was like dropping a pebble on your reflection in the water and seeing all those lovely interesting things happening to your face. Then, when the water settles, there you are, the same old face again, as if there had been no commotion at all. That's how it was in Bethesda, Walrus, little ripples but nothing ever changing. I would like to say I was happy there, but I was not. I had the feeling of being loved, of being needed, but that's not enough to make you happy, is it? Terrible, really. I had to wait for my Owen to die before I had the courage to be myself and go away.'

'Forgive me,' said Walrus, 'but you're a very handsome woman for someone who's been unhappy for so long.'

'Not unhappy, Walrus. But not happy. There's such a lot in between, isn't there? And I'm only beginning to know how much. It's so hard.'

She looked up at him again and smiled. 'Do you know I can't ever remember speaking for so long at once.'

'It's my age,' said Walrus. 'Reminds people of their grandfather. I'm told it's always easy to talk to your grandfather, though goodness knows who mine was.'

'That's a shame,' said Mary. 'It's good to have roots even if you're not too proud or fond of them. Perhaps your grandfather lived in a house like mine, and lived as well as we did. Do you know, there was nothing we needed that we couldn't afford to save for. And the chapel looked after our souls for sixpence a week in the bowl. We had a clean bottom sheet on the bed every Friday, a new pair of shoes every birthday, and I bought paper patterns for a new frock every Christmas.'

She paused and poked the fire with a stick. 'But there were so many times I wanted to get away. Owen would not leave, though. He had no life outside the quarry and our little house. He once said he was as near the world as he ever wanted to be. I asked him to take us and settle in England, but he said that getting to know new people and new places was like learning a new language and he only wanted to speak his own. But not me. I was so greedy to do things.

'I remember when I was a little girl my father took me to the Bangor Fair Day. We went on his pony and halfway there we stopped at an inn, and he bought hot meat pies and I drank from his beer mug, and we threw the stale bread and cheese mother had given us to the geese. He lost all the money he had that day, betting on a wrestling match, so for the rest of the afternoon we took the pony down to the beach. Do you know, I had never seen the sea until then. Can you believe it? So near the coast we were at Bethesda and there I was, a girl of ten, standing in the surf for the first time. And when I asked my father why we'd never been before, he said the seaside was only for special times!

'Well, anyway, I got terrible sunburn that day, dancing about in my knickers. When I got home my mother punished me for it. I thought I ought to have been cuddled, but she whipped me instead where it burnt. I cried because I hurt all over, but I was so happy. On the inside, you see, it was special times.

'I never went to the sea again. But I've never forgotten it. All these years the memory has been nagging me, knowing there was something so big and so beautiful so near. That's what hurt. Living in that black valley all that time with so many things to see and do outside it.'

'And now you're doing them, Mrs Mary.'

'Yes, Walrus. And so are my boys and so will my baby Tom.'

'And the girl too,' he said.

'Yes, and that's why I wanted her so much. She had come so far and must have dreams like mine. I know she has. I just couldn't leave her.'

'She may not thank you for it,' said Walrus. 'Not the day she sees herself.'

'No,' said Mary. 'Maybe she won't. But I'll look after her until then and not regret it.'

In the distance, across the plateau, they heard the half roar of a lion, and the call answered seconds later.

'Still moving away,' said Walrus. 'Jacob told me he'd seen some buck higher up. The lion will have had their fill and with full stomachs they'll be looking for their beds. Anyhow, it's off to yours, Mrs Mary. The cocks will be calling in a few hours' time and we have to be on our way again soon after sun up.'

He stood up and stretched. Then he lifted the sleeping Tongogara in his arms.

'Walrus,' said Mary, 'how did it get its name – Pilgrims Rest?'

He paused, and tidied the ashes with his boot.

'There are lots of stories,' he said, 'but the one I hear most is of a digger called Wheelbarrow Patterson. He got the name wheeling his barrow halfway across the Transvaal to get to the goldfields. He used to watch new people coming in over the hills, with their new trousers and their new boots, new picks in their hands, and a hatful of dreams, and he'd say, "Here come more pilgrims to their rest. God give them a little gold and let them die happy."'

'Amen to that, Walrus,' said Mary.

'And Amen again, ma'am,' he said and walked slowly away. Then he turned and grinned through his beard. 'And plenty of those special times, Mrs Mary. Let's hope the Lord will be generous with those special times!'

On the slopes above them, where the land quickly climbed away, there came another call, even fainter now, as the lion gave their last roar at the moon before sinking into their den beneath the yellow mimosa trees.

Mary slept soundly in those few hours to dawn and might easily have missed breakfast had it not been for baby Tom noisily demanding his feed. And yet as she lay lazily beneath her blankets, feeling the warmth of the sun through the canvas, he did not seem frantic. He was gurgling, not fretting, and she was almost ready to fall back happily to sleep again when she felt a tug at her blanket, and then another. She turned and opened her eyes. Then she sat bolt upright. Across from her, with baby Tom nestling in her lap, was the girl holding a tiny piece of corn husk to his mouth like a teat.

'Sweet heaven,' Mary said. 'Up and strong and as fine as the day.' She called out, 'Ianto, Huw, William, quickly! Come and see what we have here this morning. Ianto . . .' she called again in Welsh. Mary undid the buttons of her petticoat and held her breast to baby Tom. The girl held him out to her, but Mary said, 'No, you hold him still. Just lean him towards me, a special treat for the two of us to pamper him!' The three men peeped through the front flaps to see their baby brother happily suckling. 'Look at her, Ianto,' said Mary, nodding to the girl. 'She's feeling better. Look how well she is!'

Her face scars had healed and had hardened into pale red ridges criss-crossing from ear to ear, bridging the nose and jumping from cheek to forehead. Only her lips and eyes had escaped, as if she had shut them tight when whatever it was had torn her. Her ears too had not been touched. They were long and almost pointed at the tips like a pixie's. How different she looked, Mary thought, from that terrible night lying naked and bruised on the Portuguese's bed. Her hair shone and her grey-green eyes sparkled at the faces watching her.

'Anything wrong, Mrs Mary? I heard you calling.' It was Walrus outside.

'Come in, Walrus, come and see our patient.' Seconds later the wagon shook as the old man jumped from his horse and poked his head in.

'My goodness,' he said, looking first at baby Tom and then at the girl. 'That's the two prettiest sights I've seen all year. She's looking so sturdy, maybe it's time your lad here lifted her down and she can sit in the air and we'll get Jacob to cook her some eggs for a celebration breakfast.' His long nose was so near, Mary wanted to kiss it but she hesitated and then he was gone.

Ianto returned carrying a small bowl of water for the girl to wash herself, and Mary helped brush her hair. She cut off some inches from the ribbon on her straw hat to tie it up, then held open the front flaps as Ianto lifted her down to Huw and William waiting below. She stood there, her arms round their shoulders, her face now drained of colour so that the ridges stood out like tiny bloated veins.

'Carry her over here, boys,' shouted Walrus, 'here in the shade. She hasn't seen the sun in three months and it'll do her no good to have too much of it at once.' Huw and William crossed hands and lifted her to an old fig tree with only enough leaves on its twisted boughs to shelter her. Jacob brought her scrambled eggs and two of his cookies and Ianto sat on the ground a yard from her, ignoring the heat, watching every movement she made.

Mary drank tea with Walrus by the breakfast fire. 'Isn't it strange,' she said, 'that she should be so strong so suddenly?'

'Stranger than you know,' said Walrus. He turned and pointed ahead of them. 'The Komati River is five miles on, so this is about near where I found her. Look!' He put his arm over Mary's shoulder and pointed. 'Follow my finger. See where it ends, a little to the right of a tree that's split in two? Well, that's where I saw her the day we came along this track from the Komati. Her family's buried ahead.'

Mary paled and put her hand to her mouth. 'Walrus, but that's not possible! How could she have known, how could she tell it was here? She couldn't have done, not stuck inside the wagon.' She looked beyond him to the girl. Then she said, 'Must we tell her?'

'That's for you to say.'

But Mary did not have to. The girl did not need to be told. She did not need the sun or the stars or any other navigation to know where she was. The Africans would say it was the spirits of her dead family waiting to remind her. Others, that the terror of that day had lingered on, unable to hide in the open desolate bush.

But then an even stranger thing happened. As soon as she had finished her eggs she pointed to Huw's walking-stick, the one he had carved from a thorn tree. He gave it to her, and as he and Ianto watched, she leant forward and drew a pattern in the earth, and when they saw what she had done, Huw knelt and prayed and Ianto ran off to bring Mary. What she saw scratched an inch deep in the soil was a line of five crosses, one for each of the girl's family. And under them she had written her name: Jollie Thomas.

'Jollie?' whispered Mary and the girl nodded and mouthed the name again. Then she let the stick fall and her tears dampened a tiny patch between her feet.

Jollie Thomas sat close to Mary inside the wagon just behind the driver's box with the front flaps open so that she could see the passing country. As they neared the graves Walrus rode up alongside but before he could speak Jollie shook her head. She would not go. She did not want to see the mounds of earth and the five crosses Walrus had hammered together so recently. And as Walrus rode off again to his position ahead, Jollie reached for Mary's hand and held it tight and Mary whispered something into her ear. It was something she already knew. She had lost a family and now belonged to another.

All afternoon Walrus rode a hundred yards ahead, his rifle across his saddle and a second cartridge belt over his shoulder. Jacob had seen them and so had Tongogara but they would not speak of it to the others unless Walrus told them.

Along the ridge of blue rock five hundred feet above them and keeping pace with the wagons was a line of black warriors. Walrus counted forty though there were probably as many again on the far side, out of sight. Their heads were shaved and strips of coloured cloth hung from their spears and Walrus knew them as the Sekekune, who three months before in exactly this place had plunged their spears into the chests of helpless women and panicking men and who had thrown the bodies, stripped of clothes, into the wagons to burn and their children in after them.

For an hour and more they moved along the skyline, keeping pace. They were still there when Walrus held up his hand to stop that evening with the sun turning red and the Komati River less than a mile away.

As the others ate their supper, Walrus, Jacob and Tongogara patrolled the camp's perimeter. There was no movement in the hills but the Sekekune had not lit their fires: they had either gone back to their kraal or were still waiting. Walrus doubted the first and feared the second. The night was clear and although the moon was on the wane it was still bright and that pleased him because nothing could move around them for four hundred yards or more without being seen. The oxen were grazing by the fires within the circle of the wagons and Walrus had told Mary to keep herself and Jollie inside but to make sure all the men and boys kept on the move around the fires so the camp looked busy. Two hours passed and still there was no sound from the hills or from the open bare veld around them. Then Jacob held Walrus by the arm and pointed towards the south-east, to an area of the sky where the stars abruptly stopped. There was cloud on the way and soon, in an hour, maybe less, the moon would be covered and the night become abruptly black and they would be sightless beyond the firelight.

Walrus pulled the skinning knife from its sheath in the top of his boot and handed it to Jacob. 'Go together,' he said. 'Four hundred paces. But come running as soon as you hear. You understand? As soon as you hear them.'

They nodded and then they were gone, shadows across the grey luminous earth.

Walrus returned to the camp fire and called Ianto, Huw and William to him and told them what to expect and what he expected of them should the Sekekune come down.

'The English diggers are drunk again and sleeping, which is just as well. I'll take their guns – safer in your hands than theirs even if you haven't fired before. My boys will keep you stacked with shells and show you how to work them but remember, don't wait until you see them. If you do it'll be the last thing you'll ever see. Shoot at the sound of them. We've plenty of rounds and it'll do no harm to fire wild. What we've got to do is to let them know we're busy and ready. Don't look so worried, Huw. I doubt if you'll even smell powder, but it's just as well to be prepared. Now off you go and listen for them, and remember they can stick you to the ground with their spears from fifty yards and take your pipe out of your mouth and be away before you know it. Just preparations, boys, and a bit of a show too. And if it's any comfort, I've seen a lot of nights like this but only once has a Sekekune spear done me any harm. Just let them hear that breech open and let them hear it slam again.'

Three times Walrus noisily loaded and unloaded his rifle to show them how, and then sent one of his boys off to the English diggers' wagons to bring back their guns. By the time the boy had returned, and with a quickening of the wind, the clouds had covered the moon and the land around them was suddenly curtained off.

Ianto took his position beneath the second supply wagon. Twelve times he opened the breech and pulled out the cartridge and twelve times he reloaded it, noisily slamming the breech shut. The black sat by him showing him what to do, how to cover the trigger, how to knock the trigger-guard down with his little finger to open the breech, how to sight, and how to pull the wooden butt hard into his shoulder to cushion the recoil. Finally, when he felt easy with it, he lowered the barrel through the wheel spokes, resting the stock on the hub.

It was the first time he had ever touched a gun. The only ones he had ever seen before were carried by Lord Penrhyn's gamekeepers. But suddenly he liked the feel of it and the smell of oily metal, its shine, the sharpness at its edge and the smooth running of the breech. The sight was not made of metal but from a piece of ivory and finely carved and he remembered Walrus saying that game hunters cut their own sights from bone or ivory because they didn't reflect the glare of the sun.

They had been waiting for what seemed to Ianto half the night when the boy tapped him gently, cupped his hand over his ear and pointed through the spokes. Ianto understood. For a minute he listened. He could hear nothing, but he brought the gun-barrel down level with the ground and curled his finger around the trigger. Then he heard it too, a swish, like the sound of a broom sweeping sand. He felt his pulse beating in the pressure of his finger on the trigger. Then he heard it again, moving to his right, and his heart beat faster. He tried to follow it but the gun would not move. The barrel was wedged between the spokes and could fire only in the smallest arc. Whoever was out there was moving across him and he could not follow. Panic hit him like a fist in the chest. Quickly he leant back to pull it free when there was a scream, and then another louder, nearer and more dreadful. Ianto pulled the trigger and the night exploded. He was flung back and before he could sit up again Walrus had slid in beside him.

'Did you see them, boy?'

'I saw nothing. Nothing. I just heard it and then I . . .'

'Doesn't matter what you did or didn't,' the old man said. 'They've taken him.'

Ianto turned. 'Taken who? Who have they taken?'

'One of the diggers, the drunken fool. Left his wagon and wandered off – must have passed by you close here. The other two want to go after but they can hardly stand and I'll whip them if they try. It's what those murderous kaffirs want. They'll be out there waiting for one of us to follow. Anyhow, he's dead by now and gone a bad way, too. By morning there'll only be his bones to bury and we won't wait for that. Now load your gun again, boy, and do it quick. And sit at the side of the wheel; you'll not do much damage through it.'

Ianto was dazed and his shoulder hurt. Across the camp he could hear Walrus shouting at the diggers and their drunken obscenities back. Then the crack of a whip and nothing more. Very carefully, and keeping his eyes on the night, he opened the breech and the dead cartridge case came sliding out. He breathed the smell of the cordite deep into his lungs and held out his hand and the boy dropped a new cartridge into it. Still doing it by feel, he thumbed it into the breech and slammed it shut again. Then he sat there hoping, praying almost, that he might be allowed to pull the trigger again and enjoy the ecstatic moment of pandemonium that followed.

Jacob and Tongogara came back when they heard the guns but confirmed that the main Sekekune force were still on the ridge. So Walrus assumed that a small raiding party had come down the long way, skirting along the river, darting in to prod the camp's defences. And the English digger had decided on his night's ablutions just as they passed.

Mary stayed all night inside the wagon as Walrus insisted, with baby Tom on her lap and Jollie Thomas in her blanket but awake by her side. On the floor and held firmly between Mary's ankles was the large wide-bladed panga that Jacob kept to cut up his meat.

Walrus did not send anyone out again. There would be no more raiding parties now, he said. If the Sekekune were coming they would now come off the ridge together. But Walrus wagered they would not, now they had heard the guns. And he was right. When the long night was over and the cocks crowed and the morning sun broke open the grey clouds, they looked up to the ridge and saw it was bare. And just below it, strung up by the arms between two thorn trees, was the digger's headless corpse. Walrus said they had taken their trophy back to their chief, and they would not be back again.

They inspanned and were away as soon as they had drunk their mugs of tea and eaten their chicken stew and corn. Within an hour they reached the Komati and it was just as Walrus had described it to them, broad and brown and slow-flowing with shallow banks. The oxen crossed with hardly a falter, the water lapping their bellies.

Ianto asked Walrus' permission – it was, he said, only the second time the boy had spoken to him directly – to walk a hundred yards away from the wagons so that he could practise with the dead digger's gun. Walrus said yes but sent Tongo with him and the rest of the morning's trek was punctuated by shots as Ianto fired at birds, trees, boulders and bushes, anything that presented a target. Mary had never seen him so absorbed before, and she did not know whether to be pleased or not. That afternoon Ianto continued the practice with Tongogara throwing stones in the air and later, when they returned, Tongo told Walrus that the quiet white man had hit many more stones than he missed.

During the following day's journey to the Crocodile River, Walrus kept his early promise to William and taught him how to saddle a horse and then how to ride it and William took his instruction quickly. It seemed there was nothing he did not want to know and little he could not remember once he had been told. Walrus showed him how to trap birds by chewing birdlime from mistletoe berries and laying it like glue across branches. He told him of a tribe across the Limpopo River on the far side of the Drakensberg Mountains, who caught hundreds of birds this way. He said they skinned them very carefully so as not to disturb the feathers, then stuffed them with dried grass and sewed them to their headdress. Sometimes, Walrus said, a young warrior might have thirty or more small birds strapped around his head.

William learnt how to trap rabbits with snares made from the hair of a pony's tail and on the third evening, as they outspanned on the banks of the Crocodile River, the old man showed him how to catch fish with gunpowder.

He emptied the powder from three cartridges into a small flask made of dried clay. Then a fuse was fed into it and the neck of the flask sealed with candle-wax. The fuse was lit and as it touched the wax, Walrus threw it into the river. It exploded seconds later and when the fountain of water had settled William counted sixteen stunned fish floating on the surface.

They stayed by the river longer than Walrus had intended, which made him strut about cursing because when Tongogara had brought the oxen together from their grazing one of them refused to stand. Its eyes were bloodshot and swollen and there were sores around its udder.

'There's a lot wrong with it,' said Walrus. 'It's the tsetse that's brought it down. Taken it fast, too – usually it's six weeks or more.' He looked at the other oxen. 'If one goes there'll be others that follow.'

The two English diggers, who were drinking more nowadays, shouted that he should move it 'the Boer way' and Mary asked what they meant. Walrus explained.

'When an ox goes down, a Boer will consider no tortures too severe to get it up again. They'll whip it until its body's wet with blood. They'll fill its nostrils with sand and stuff burning grass in its mouth and stick hot embers up its rear. They're a cruel people, Mrs Mary, kind *and* cruel. You'll see.'

The Boers' way was not Walrus' way. First he tried to pour his own concocted medicine down the beast's throat, but it kicked so much that they had to tie its forelegs to the front wheels and its back legs to the rear. Then he levered open its mouth and emptied half a bucket of soap and salt water down its gullet and spread an ointment of zinc and lard over its sores. But by the afternoon the beast's stomach had distended, its eyes were glazed, so Walrus shot it dead with a single bullet through its ear. Then Jacob, helped by two others, set to work to butcher it. First they skinned it and rubbed the hide with saltpetre and stretched it with pegs in the sand to dry. Then they cut the meat into joints, putting aside the heart, liver and kidneys. Every part of it was kept to be boiled or dried or smoked. Even the stomach was pulled out full. The boys dragged it to the river and emptied the contents into the water, which infuriated Walrus and he slapped their heads, shouting that the blood and bile would attract crocodiles and he had a good mind to make them walk waist-high across the river as punishment. By sunset Jacob had finished and the camp looked like a butcher's shop with meat hanging from every tree and bush. The smell and the flies were awful and Mary, for the first time, doubted Walrus' judgement. She asked him if the smell would not bring the lion and hyena and every other hateful hunter. Surely he should not let them eat meat from a diseased animal? Yes, he said, he would let them eat it, and yes, there was the risk of hyena, lion and wild dog. But he said that if he had ordered them to bury the ox there would be revolution. They lived on corn, and meat, wherever it came from, was a gift from heaven. 'If I'd had them bury it,' he said, 'they'd have left us and gone back and dug it up again. This way they keep their meat and we keep them.'

That night the boys cooked and gorged and talked and sang and cooked and gorged again. They ate so much that by the morning none of them could move and many lay on their backs groaning and stroking their stomachs, pretending not to hear Walrus when he shouted to them to inspan. But he threatened to shift them the way the Boers did their lazy oxen and began mixing a bucket of soap and salt medicine, and soon they were on their feet and the wagons were away rolling down towards the river within the half hour.

Walrus led the diggers' wagon down the bank, cracking his whip and pulling the lead ox with his pony. The two supply wagons followed. But then, with Ianto and Huw at the reins and William and Tongogara sitting astride the leading pair, their last wagon began to slide sideways, tugging at the harness and jerking the yokes on the oxen's necks. Suddenly, there was a crack and the tear of timber and Walrus pulled his horse back as the oxspan strode on towards the far bank, the reins trailing behind them, leaving the wagon stranded in the middle, sinking deeper into the mud.

The dusselboom, the pole that anchored the trek chain, had snapped in two. Walrus rode alongside, the water over his pony's back. 'Stay up there, boys,' he shouted to Ianto and Huw. 'And don't worry, Mrs Mary, we'll have you out soon enough. I'll bring the span back and Tongo will go under and tie the chain to the front axle. I'll bring a second span in if I have to.'

Tongogara and William had already whipped the oxen around and Walrus pushed through the water to reach them. Then he picked Tongo off and held him under his arm like a sack of mealie, brought him back to the wagon and dropped him into the water where he worked blind in the muddy river, wrapping the trek chain around the axle, coming up briefly for air, then disappearing again. He was looping the leather reins through it to hold it tight when Jacob came running along the far bank, shouting excitedly '*Umgwenya—Bwena . . . Bwena.*'

'Damn them!' said Walrus, looking upstream. 'Crocodiles! They've heard the fuss and they're coming to see us. They'll go for the oxen and horses . . . try and drag us down.'

Tongogara surfaced, pulled the knife out of Walrus' boot and dived again. Walrus looked at Ianto. 'Got your gun, boy?' Ianto reached behind him and pulled out the rifle, polished and gleaming clean.

'Right!' said Walrus. 'You stand up there on the box, get yourself comfortable and take them as they come across those reeds, see, just on the near side of the bend? Water's shallow there so they'll rise. It's the only time you'll see them clear but it's eighty yards or more.'

'I'll hit them!' said Ianto and climbed up, resting his elbows on the tent frame.

'Shoot for their eyes or their bellies, boy,' said Walrus. 'You won't hurt them anywhere else that shows. Just go for their eyes and bellies.'

He jumped from his horse and stood shoulder-high in the swirling brown water heaving at the reins, taking the strain so that Tongogara could finish his work quicker.

Mary leant out and shouted an inch from Huw's ear, 'Get down there, boy. Don't sit here helpless and praying, get in there and pull!' And she pushed him full in the back and he went tumbling over into the water. Above them Ianto lowered the rifle to his shoulder and set the ivory sight on the dark green bank of matted reeds.

They came slowly into view, one at their head, the others trailing in a narrow column. The sun was behind Ianto but, just as Walrus had said, the ivory did not dazzle and the leader was sharp and clear in the tiny white wedge. Ianto felt the trigger and he could count his heartbeat against the finger of metal, quick and quickening. How large they were, green and glistening, the water spinning off their backs.

The river's flow was carrying them fast but still Ianto could not see their eyes and they were too low in the water to show their green and yellow stomachs. All he could see were their snouts. Jacob was calling again and waving his arms and Walrus shouted at Ianto, 'Fire, boy! Don't wait any longer. Take the front one. For God's sake don't let them leave the reeds!'

But Ianto did not answer and held his fire, his barrel steady despite the buffeting of the water against the wheels, watching the ivory, waiting for the snout to rise. Then, at last, the long green body lifted and slid across the reeds and there was an eye, unblinking and wide. He squeezed the trigger and saw the eye turn bright red an instant before the bullet smashed into the brain behind. The long body turned on its back, exposing the soft greenish-yellow belly, but there was no need to fire again and he watched it tip over the far side of the reeds, the brown water trailing crimson behind it.

The second and third crocodiles, close behind, seemed not to notice or care and swam on but as they too rose to mount the reeds their heads exploded as two shots quickly echoed each other. Then abruptly the rest turned away and submerged, surfacing again on the mud banks twenty yards back. Ianto watched them slither their way to the protection of tall rushes and the fallen branches of a tree. Only when they were out of sight did he lower his gun.

Jacob was jumping up and down and clapping his hands

and Walrus raised his hat and gave a cheer. 'That's to you, boy!' he shouted. 'That's miracle shooting – miracle! You hadn't touched a trigger a week ago and now you've three crocs to your hat and straight hits every one of them!' Then he turned to Mary, laughing. 'You just make sure,' he said, 'that boy of yours keeps that little bit of ivory on the beasts and birds. Wouldn't do for a man to find himself at the end of it.' And he roared again with laughter and relief and lifted the dripping Tongogara onto his shoulders. But Mary did not smile and Ianto had already turned away to watch the green and bloodied bodies tumble downstream. For a while she watched him, the rifle like a toy in his large hand, and knew he was now moving even further away, from her and from everyone, and she prayed she would know in what direction in time.

With the trek chains holding and with Walrus, Huw and William turning the wheels, the wagon was slowly eased out of its ruts and twenty aching minutes later, with the oxen wheezing and Walrus' whip nicking their ears, they reached the far bank. Huw and William fell into the grass exhausted, not caring about the Mopani flies that buzzed around them. Ianto came down from his perch to clean his gun again. Mary and Jollie began to unload the kitchen and cut more meat for the supper stew as Jacob continued shouting at the top of his voice, telling the boys of Ianto's expert slaughter.

Only Walrus, cross-legged under the wagon, winding more strips of leather around the axle, saw in the brief parting of the billowing white clouds the tips of the mountains dark and pointed against the blue sky. Tomorrow he would cut a new dusselboom and they would be skirting the mountains' sides by the evening's outspan. And a few days after that they would rumble and slide and drift their way down the slopes on the other side of them and into the Valley of Gold.

'When I retire,' said Walrus, 'I shall buy a bed above Rathfelders restaurant in Cape Town and eat roast leg of lamb and hot custard pudding one day and boiled leg of mutton and cold custard pie the next. I will have hot water in my bath every Friday and pay a penny to have my toenails cut, too. I reckon that's due to a man of my superannuation,' and he laughed. And as no one knew quite what he meant they all laughed with him.

For the first time since they had left Lourenço Marques, Jollie Thomas had joined them by the fire for her supper. As usual, Ianto had not. He sat on his own, his back against the wagon wheel, the gun across his lap, alone and withdrawn as if there were no one within a night's travel of him. They had left the Crocodile River that morning and the day's trek had been their longest yet. Walrus had cut down a young bluegum tree and cleaned it and shaped it and fitted it to the front axle. Their stops had been short, hardly long enough for the oxen to even half-fill their stomachs, but for Mary it was the happiest day yet because at the morning call Walrus had told them they were nearing their journey's end.

They were higher now than they had ever been. The light was sharper and the air smelt of woods and everything about the mountains was cleaner and fresher because it was swept and rinsed every morning by the clouds.

Mary felt they had crossed a border unannounced, so much had suddenly changed about them. The yellow and brown low-veld was turning green with every revolution of the wheels, trees threw out slender boughs that sprouted dark green leaves, and bushes were filled with flowers. The water courses they crossed were bordered by a dozen different ferns and she counted twenty shapes and colours of cactus in almost as many minutes. There were scarlet creepers and purple lilies and yellow mimosa beneath the hanging mauve tree blossoms that Walrus called jacarandas, and she saw what at home she had called red pokers. As they climbed, more and more tiny streams trickled down the black rock, sparkling and flashing in the sunlight, joining each other one by one, working their way down to the great wide rivers below.

They outspanned that evening by a ruin of stones and broken

and charred timbers which Walrus said was once called Hart's Cabin and over supper, sitting close to the fire, he told its story.

'Hart was the kindest man I ever knew. Yet – and it may seem a bit unnatural to you – he didn't seek the company of other men, especially those who reckon a white skin is a warrant for any behaviour. He did not consider a white man a friend or a brother simply because he was surrounded by blacks. On the contrary, he found them more often than not a certain nuisance and an aggravation to be avoided at all costs, which just about sums me up, too. That's maybe why he spent his life stuck in the middle of nowhere and I've spent most of mine on the move everywhere. Both ways you can avoid what you don't want.

'Anyway, I was saying how good he was to birds and beasts. Wouldn't kill a thing, let alone step on an ant. I've even seen him pick up a beetle and put it aside in case a wagon wheel crushed it. Problem was, he kept things alive that by nature ought to have been dead. Place was full of cages and pens and stalls and things. I once heard someone call it an orphanage of lost causes. There was a three-legged leopard that had lost its fourth to a wild dog; there were thrown-out lion cubs, a blind antelope, a crippled zebra, an old bad-tempered baboon and enough monkeys to fill Noah's Ark ten times over. He'd brought them in to save them from the hyenas 'cos that's how they'd have finished up.

'He ran a trading post and because he was the only one between here and the sea he did good business. There ought to have been a lot more traders like him, say every couple of outspans, but the Sekekune killed or frightened off all who tried, all, that is, except old man Hart. Maybe he had too many friends among the local kaffirs, maybe they were scared of a man who could tame a lion or get a bad-tempered old baboon to eat from his hand. Anyhow, they let him be and he lived well. There was plenty of good spring water here, he grew his own fruit and vegetables, and he could be certain of passing company every now and again as the diggers' wagons came through. So he had a pleasant life, until that afternoon – it's six years ago now – when half a dozen Sekekune, full of drink and dagga, came onto his verandah and demanded his gun. Well, the old man spoke to them for a while. He had a nice way with him and he probably would have sent them off peaceably, but another one had already been sent round to the back door and he came through the shop with Hart's rifle in his hand and shot the old man in the back. Whether it was the dagga or the fact that kaffirs go wild at the sight of blood, but with old Hart dying at his own front door they set fire to the cabin and pens and cages with the animals still trapped in them.

'I saw the smoke, but I was still five or more miles off and by the time I reached here there was nothing but charcoal and bones. Hart had tried to crawl to the nearest pens and he probably lived long enough to let some of them get free because, for a few years after, people passing here would see a three-legged leopard and an old baboon sitting where the cages used to be. I never could vouch for the story myself, 'cos I never did see them.

'Anyhow, some diggers came running up and we buried what we could of Hart though there wasn't a lot left.' Walrus pointed beyond the fire. 'We put him over there, just beyond the outcrop of rock, that pile of stones. I painted them white but it's worn off now. We went after the kaffirs. Took us three days and three nights tracking them but we found them in the end.'

He looked across to William. 'Don't let anyone ever tell you the white man can't beat the black at his own game; he can and always will and you remember that, boy.' He paused.

'Well, we found them sitting by their fire smoking their pipes, hadn't gone back to their chief, probably afraid to after what they'd done. Chief Sekekune didn't have the appetite for murder then the way he does today. We didn't wait, went straight in and took them before they had a chance to go for their spears. All except one, that is, and I took his blade through my side just about the time my shot took his head away. Anyhow, it didn't do me much damage and I rode away when it was all over. Funny thing, though.' He rubbed his right side. 'That scar never bothers me for months on end, but every time I camp here at Hart's Cabin it begins to pain. How d'you explain that, Huw, boy? God's punishment? Or old Hart's ghost poking me in the ribs for coming to help him too late?' Again he laughed, but not long. For a while he was silent. Then with a long sigh he stood up and stretched himself. He turned again to Huw. 'God had a pretty long arm that day to reach all the way down here and take old Hart. I only hope He had the good kindness to take some of the old man's animals along with him. He was very fond of them. Very fond. He was a kind fellow, who did me a lot of favours. And then he goes off before I could pay him back for any of them.'

He walked off slowly into the darkness, towards the small pile of stones he had once painted white.

It was now twenty-eight days since they had left Lourenço Marques and the morning was bright with expectation. That night, Walrus told them, they would eat their supper on the hills overlooking the Valley of Gold.

Mary could only remember once in her life feeling the same excitement, the shortness of breath, the tingling skin, when every word spoken seemed to have two meanings or none at all and every laugh prolonged. How familiar it was all becoming! From the first early-morning mist and the silver dew and the tall black mountain peak that was so much like Caernarfonshire but warm in the sunshine and heavy with a perfume that was Africa's own.

Walrus had promised her they would outspan early so she might prepare something special for supper, and seeing the flush in her face he sent Jacob to help her and promised he would ride off in the afternoon to hunt for birds or perhaps a rabbit.

The oxen's pace was so casual now, Jollie Thomas had taken to walking by the side of the wagon holding onto the leather straps of the tent. But by mid-morning, once the sun had become too warm, she sat on the wagon box kneading Mary's dough in her lap and pulling seeds out of flowers Jacob brought her to press into the crust of the bread later. She would nod or shake her head in answer to Mary's questions and whenever she wanted to ask any herself she drew letters on the palm of her hand. Mary cut up one of her own dresses and during the midday outspan brought the sewing-machine out of its waxed wrappings and made Jollie a simple pretty frock from the roll of pale blue cotton.

They kept their slow but steady pace throughout the day with a breeze on their faces to freshen them. The oxen moved without the usual shoutings and whip cracks, helped by their breakfast of thick lush grass and their own knowing that the long and hard journey was almost finished and that soon they would rest in water meadows to grow strong again before turning around for the trek to the coast once more.

As he had promised, Walrus rode away in the afternoon and just before dusk came cantering back with pigeons, plovers and two plump and speckled guinea-fowl tied to his saddle. He looked especially pleased with himself. 'A good afternoon's shooting, Mrs Mary,' he said with his great grin. 'The small birds we'll roast tonight but the fowl we'll hang, just as the gentry do, so they'll be soft and juicy in two days' time for that special dinner you've promised me.'

Mary stopped feeding baby Tom. Huw looked up from his reading and William came running. Even Ianto paused from polishing his gun.

'And what special dinner is that, Walrus?' she asked, sticking out her jaw to him the way she did whenever she sensed she had a part to play in one of his jokes.

'Don't you remember?' he asked. 'Is it so long back you've forgotten the plan you had? Has the African sun addled your brain and sapped your memory? Two miles on is Graskop and on the other side of that is the end of your worries!

'And tomorrow is Christmas Eve! So be ready to roast my fowls for Christmas dinner, Mrs Mary, and I'll ask you to stuff them with herbs and a large onion just the way Mother Baines used to do!'

The men and boys cheered and Mary cheered with them and baby Tom did not seem put out as his mother's tears dampened his head.

That evening they outspanned for the last time. It was on the ridge overlooking the goldfields and they could see the diggers' camp below. Warm air lifted up their voices so that it sounded as busy as a high street; the tents might easily have been roof-tops and the flickering yellow fires, street lights.

They looked down in awe until Jacob rattled stones in an empty cooking-pot to call them to supper. Then they sat there quietly in a circle around the fire roasting the tiny birds over ashes on spits of mimosa twigs, with the juices dripping into the crust of Mary's seed bread, looking down at the twinkling in the dark they knew was Pilgrims Rest.

CHAPTER FOUR

In the greying years, Mary called back the memories and despite the distance and buffeting of time they came rushing to her, vivid and noisy, one recollection spurring another so that rather than diminishing, they grew in detail: forgotten places, forgotten names, a smell, a colour, a face, a fault, growing as her years grew; that morning they rode into Pilgrims Rest.

It was a sharp bright dawn. The sun was hidden behind the peaks but the sky was full orange and the still air promised a hot day. They were too excited for breakfast so Jacob boiled two billies of tea and they stood by the smouldering night fires drinking it as the boys harnessed up the oxen and made ready.

The diggers' camp below was covered in low cloud, the valley's cleavage hidden as mists swirled in and out of the creek, patches suddenly clearing to expose a tent or a man working and then, just as abruptly, bury them again.

They could see that the way down was steep. The track appeared to loop between the rock face and boulders, and its surface was black and shining, with stones as sharp as flint. Three hundred feet down it jumped a stream, passed beneath a waterfall and then disappeared into a grove of wild fig trees. The mountains and the rolling hills around looked so well made, as if God had been in no hurry shaping them all. Each was as round and smooth as a breast or a buttock, overlapping and folding into one another like a roll of dough, and spewing grey boulders, some as large as a wagon, others no bigger than a man's fist. It looked to Mary as if the world here had worn thin in places like a threadbare carpet, losing one pattern for another.

By the time they were ready to leave, the cloud had been scorched away and Mary was surprised to see a small cluster of houses. Walrus had spoken only of tents and the Africans' mud huts but she could see half a dozen single-storey buildings with windows and thatched roofs. One, in the centre, had a verandah and a porch. She held baby Tom tight to her as the wagon slid its way down, hitting the rockside as Walrus' boys, six to a wagon, hung on behind, a rope tied around their waists to slow it down. The oxen braced themselves against the gradient, skidding and stumbling, with Ianto and Huw each side of the back wheels wedging poles against the rims to brake. Walrus was on his horse at the front with his whip looped around the lead ox's neck to keep him straight and steady. Slowly they curled their way down, often turning back on themselves at bends, giving Mary a new perspective of her new home, which seemed in so many ways like the one she had left.

The night before by the fire, she had opened her Bible and for the very first time read out aloud the story in the newspaper cutting the young man from Cardiff had sent her. He had written:

'Hills upon hills upon hills sit on each other and make up a mountain taller and broader than Snowdon. In springtime it is thick with grass and fern and the slopes steeped with colour. The rocks run wet with springs that twist and jump off the black face and cascade in little purple waterfalls, coming together in the broad water below that the Boers have called the Blyde River – "The River of Joy".

'It is here that men spend their days digging and panning, chipping and chiselling on their lonely claims, breaking their backs and often their hearts searching for their fortune in gold.

For the hills of Africa, like the hills of Wales, are very jealous of their treasures.'

And now it was laid out beneath her and getting bigger with every yard the wagons dropped. The slope began to level off as they entered the green tunnel of fig trees, with the mountain peak now high above them, and Mary relaxed her grip on the wagon box and eased the ribbons that tied baby Tom to her. Then the avenue of trees ended unexpectedly and she was dazzled and stung by the hot sun again. She shut her eyes tight and when she opened them she could not believe what she saw.

Men were running towards them, so many men, so many shapes and sizes of them, shouting and whistling, men with picks in their hands and shovels held high over their heads, long men and short, old men and young, some half-hidden behind red or black or grey beards, some with hats, some stripped to their trousers, some with waistcoats and moleskins, all running from their diggings to come to see the valley's first white women. Those who had the energy ran alongside; those who had not, lined the track banging picks against shovels and shovels against boulders with each man lifting his hat as the wagons passed.

Walrus Baines turned in his saddle twenty yards ahead and shouted above the din: 'Get back inside, Mrs Mary, or we'll never end the commotion!' But it was too much like a carnival and Mary had no intention of missing it.

'Rubbish!' she shouted to him. 'We'll stay where we are. There's no harm in them looking and I think I'm quite enjoying it!' She saw Huw's frown. 'And don't you spoil it with those chapel looks of yours,' she said. 'Watch it and enjoy it because you'll never see anything like it again.'

Walrus slowed his pony until he was alongside her. 'I've never seen the like in all my years,' he said. Then with a grin, 'I may be presuming too much, Mrs Mary, but I think they're a might pleased to see you.'

She laughed. 'It's like going to a wedding!'

'Well, you've enough grooms to choose from,' he said, winking at Jollie.

'Thank you, Walrus Baines,' said Mary, 'but not one of them has washed in a year and if ever the introductions are made I'll ask you to add that preference too.' She bowed her head to men right and left as they raised their hats in salute.

'Not a wedding, Mrs Mary,' said Walrus. 'You're more like the Queen herself on coronation day!'

'That's all very well,' she replied, 'but they still need a good scrubbing-down!'

Now she could hear the names the diggers were shouting at her, each in turn. There was Yankee Dan and Bill Dawkins, Leger-Smith, Reefing Charlie, Blanket Bill, Spinning Holly, Moleskin, Hammerhead, and with every name a hat was raised. She did not count them, nor could she have done but it was said later by those who were watching that the diggers had turned out to a man. And there were one thousand and seventy working there that day.

Walrus led the wagons up the High Street like a general his army, sitting as stiff as a ramrod on his horse with his rifle over his shoulder. He halted them midway along the line of thatched-roof houses and then pushed back through the throng to Mary's wagon.

'Best sit along me, Mrs Mary, and leave baby Tom with Jollie until we find yourselves a place at the hotel.'

'Hotel?' she asked, surprised.

'Well, that's what they like to call it here, makes the place sound established. It's just a kitchen with a few rooms nailed to the side, and do you see the bar? That used to be a little Catholic church in Lourenço Marques before the boys brought it here all packed up in wagons. But it'll do till your boys find somewhere of your own.'

A man below them shouted, 'Introduce the lady, Walrus, and show us her man so's we know the odds!' There was a roar of approval around him and hats were thrown in the air. Then someone fired a gun.

Walrus sidestepped his horse closer to the wagon. Mary looked behind her as Ianto picked up his rifle.

'Put that down,' she said. 'You put it down now and don't you dare touch it again until I've said so or God help me, I'll break it across your back!'

Walrus stood in his stirrups towering above them and cracked his whip so that the men wondered if another shot had been fired.

'Thank you for seeing us in,' he shouted. 'I can't remember the last time you gave Walrus Baines such a welcome – for such is what I take it to be, and I'll be happy to take a drink with every one of you in turn.' There was a cheer. He reached for Mary's hand and she stood up on the wagon box.

'This lady,' he said, 'is Mrs Mary Llewellyn whose husband is buried in Wales, and a digger too. The girl is Jollie Thomas who lost her whole family to the Sekekune some months back and she's only just mending. The young lads are Ianto, and Huw and young William here, soon to be the greatest transport rider in the Transvaal. Then there's baby Tom. Come up, lads, and show yourselves!'

But the diggers had not come tumbling off the hills to see Mary's sons. After all, men came wandering into Pilgrims Rest every day unheralded, just as others left it. So a man with a monocle in his left eye led three cheers and then another digger with large gold earrings began singing, and they all joined in.

Huw helped Mary onto Walrus' saddle and the diggers parted, making a narrow corridor for them all the way to the steps of the Royal Hotel. It was as Walrus said, a kitchen, a bar and a cobbled yard with three tiny rooms on each side, connected by a verandah. The building was raised off the ground by stilts and steps led up to another verandah that ran along the front. The roof was thatched and tea-chest lids had been stitched over the worn and torn parts. Nailed over the front door, painted a foot high in red, was the landlord's name:

HONEST JACK MACINTYRE

And under it, in smaller untidy print, was:

ALSO P. J. HAMILTON SURGEON, BARBER AND TENTMAKER (AT THE REAR)

Honest Jack offered brandy but Walrus took gin and he sent one of the serving girls out to fetch tea and peaches for Mary. The owner of the Royal Hotel was as tall as Walrus but many stones heavier and thirty years younger. There was as much hair on his face as on his head, which made him come to an untidy end. Large black curly sideburns grew out onto his red shiny cheeks within an inch of his red shiny nose. He might once have been handsome but now he took no care of himself except to wax his moustache. The rest of him was sadly looked after. An enormous paunch toppled over the brass-buckled belt and rested on his knees like a money pouch when he sat down.

Stains from a month of dinners had mottled his shirt front and there was not a button left on his grubby waistcoat. He walked with a limp and Mary noticed his left knee was swollen inside the trouser leg as if it were bandaged. She wondered how long it had been since a woman had taken notice of all his problems and tried to put them right.

The girl returned with a teapot and a small basket of peaches and he handed Mary the largest, rubbing it first on his waistcoat. 'I'm afraid we live rough, ma'am,' he said. 'My wife and daughters live in Lydenburg, less than a day's ride from here into the lowveld. They weren't made for mining. Mind you, things are better here than they were, and getting better still it seems to me now you've arrived. My wife is good though, and she sends me a letter a day, though as we only have one post once a week, I have seven to read at once every Saturday. And the dear lady sends me a food parcel every month as regular as sunrise.'

Mary asked, 'Are the peaches hers?'

'Oh no, ma'am, not the peaches . . . she wouldn't send peaches, nor anything sweet. The peaches are from the creek though it's our biggest mystery how the trees ever got there.

Perhaps you didn't know but the place was called Peach Tree Rush till some years back. Shows we're not the first to come as someone must have dropped the stones here. No, she didn't send the peaches, but you'll have some of her surprises for dinner tonight. I think dinner would be a good time for you to taste her pickles. Her Christmas parcel arrived only yesterday, and an uncommonly generous one too, as you might expect for the season.'

Mary stopped eating her fruit. 'Christmas?' she said, surprised. 'Will you not see her for Christmas?'

'Oh no!' said Honest Jack and frowned. 'I couldn't leave the hotel now, this is my busiest time. The men drink well all the year round but they drink especially well at Christmas.'

'But can't she come here?' asked Mary.

Honest Jack wrinkled his forehead again. 'I wouldn't expect her to leave her friends at Christmas just to see me. And it wouldn't be fair to ask her.'

'I think it's such a shame,' Mary said, 'for a family to be so near at Christmas and not see each other.'

But Honest Jack did not answer. Instead he poured himself more brandy, topped up Walrus' glass and handed Mary a second perfect peach. She looked across to Walrus, who shook his head at her and put a finger to his lips and she was confused.

'You're a kind man, Honest Jack,' said Walrus, 'and a generous one too and I'm blessed if I don't feel obliged to honour your missus's cooking too by attending dinner myself this evening. Though I warn you, tomorrow is Mrs Mary's day and she'll need some space in your kitchen and a decent fire in your ovens for we've a brace of fowl hanging and I've been promised the finest Christmas dinner I ever expect to eat.'

The cabin Mary, Jollie and baby Tom were to share was only wide enough for two bunks with scarcely knee room in between. There were no windows, simply an open door covered by a curtain of woven grass to keep out the dust and flies during the day and the chill and mosquitoes at night. The rush mat that covered the mud floor was slowly being eaten away by an army of red ants nesting in the corner, but there was a candle holder at the head of each bunk, the mattresses were stuffed with fresh-smelling grass and the white calico coverings were newly washed and ironed.

'More than we expected,' said Mary and Jollie nodded. 'Though not as much as we deserve,' Mary added and the girl smiled. 'One thing I won't have, though, is ants eating my baby, so we'll find a way of lifting the cot off the floor.' There was a knock at the doorway and Honest Jack stood there, hunched so that he might see through it and holding a pot in his hands drooping with magnificent dark red flowers.

'Begonias we used to call them in England, ma'am. Brought the corms with me. Walrus told me to give them, said they'd look better with you than with me.'

She took it from him and held his hand. 'Walrus said nothing of the kind and you're a nice man to think of such a thing.' But already the blushing giant was backing away and crossing the yard before she could say another word.

She turned to Jollie, puzzled. 'Did you notice the gold ring?' Jollie shook her head.

'It was on his right hand, third finger,' said Mary, 'just like mine here. For widows and widowers. How odd! And his wife still alive only a day's ride away.'

Walrus Baines had already decided he would stay the fortnight and possibly longer before turning his wagons around for the return trek to Lourenço Marques to meet Captain Jeppe's grimy coaster again. His oxen were thin and some were bleeding after the sharp-stoned descent. He would give them a treat, a chance to fill out again on the lush grassy slopes, put on some weight and sort out their stomachs, and if any more had been bitten by the tsetse, they would show it. Anyway, he asked himself, wasn't tomorrow Christmas Day? And wouldn't it soon afterwards be 1875, another year gone, and he in his sixty-sixth year, or was it his sixty-eighth? So why not stay and help Mary settle herself in, she and her brave little family. Walrus Baines was fond of persuading himself that indecision and a change of plan was simply the ability to adapt.

It was decided that at least until the New Year the women and baby Tom would be Honest Jack's guests and Ianto, Huw and William would sleep in the wagon, and spend their first days staking out their claims. By slow and careful manoeuvring they brought their wagon along the narrow track to the rear of the hotel, Mary insisting that if she was to sleep well she must have her men and her belongings close by.

All through that hot day they worked, unloading and unpacking, sorting and checking their supplies and equipment. Every half-hour Honest Jack brought out jugs of cool spring water and bread and meat cuts – their 'tiffin' he called it – then stayed to watch, offering his advice on this and his warnings on that. He stood with his legs wide apart, thumbs tucked into his broad leather belt, telling them again and again how much trouble they might save themselves if only they would do it this way and not that, so that Walrus said to Mary, and Honest Jack's back, that 'saving trouble' seemed to be the purpose in life of every Englishman he had ever known and Honest Jack was no exception! The big man worked to a rule, said Walrus, that however a day's work was divided there must be a pair of hands spare, and by carefully distancing himself from the labour, he ensured that the pair of hands was always his!

The light was fading, the sun reddening and at last their first day's work was over. Ianto and Huw went down to the river where other men were bathing, and William followed Tongogara to a waterfall upstream. Honest Jack's girls brought pails of warm water and filled up the tin hip-bath that had been put between the bunks and Mary, feeling it already Christmas, broke open the pretty wrapping of the pink tin of scented soap she had bought for sixpence at Dartmouth.

The soft spring water drew the month's tiredness and the sweat and dust of the trek from their bodies and softened their hair. Jollie used her damp towel to brighten the colours of Mary's pinafore and within the hour they stood facing each other sparkling, their skin tingling, their hair brushed tightly back and shining. They pushed through the grass curtain and breathed in the warm scented evening air. It was dusk. The slopes opposite were already twinkling with camp fires and the wisps of smoke drifted down towards them with a smell like burning applewood. Mary thought she could hear a concertina, but then it was gone and she wondered whether she had simply wished it. There was a grand feeling of quiet movement all around them, a bustle, as if all the diggers were going about their evening chores whispering on tiptoe.

Quickly the moist air, caught up in the grey smoke, tinted the light purple, going dark at the edge of the forests and tingeing even darker on the humps of the hills. Below, Mary could just make out the silver gash of water in the creek. A dog barked and higher up a second one answered. She heard the clatter of pans, then shouting and laughter. Something darted above her, in and out of the yard. She thought it was a bat. Then there was a rustle of white which might have been an owl. More dogs greeted their masters back to their tents, up from the river and washed clean again. The smoke rose straight in thin, grey-blue columns, to the stars it seemed, and the thatch roof around them was suddenly white as the moon rose over the ridge. The moist air that had swept across the camp making it fresh and new again now slipped down the escarpment, giving life to the parched and wilting lowveld.

Mary turned to Jollie and took her hand. 'I wasn't dreaming! There is a concertina, I can hear it – listen!' They walked to the edge of the yard and looked out across the camp, standing together, hidden in the shadows. The music came louder down the hillside, as if the player, like a minstrel, was strolling from fire to fire towards his evening's entertainment at Honest Jack's. Men hummed his tune as he approached and then sang it louder as he passed, and men away from his path, sitting at their tents, joined him until the hillside was like an enormous choir.

'Just listen to them!' Mary whispered. 'It's Christmas Eve and they're away from their work, just like home. Oh! Jollie, Jollie my sweet, did you ever think it would be like this? Did you ever?' And Jollie shook her head and leant towards Mary and kissed her ear.

Above them, perched on the crest of the thatch, the white owl watched the scratchings of a mother mouse, hoping the two women would move indoors before his dinner went away.

'Pork?' asked Mary.

'No,' said Honest Jack. 'Not pork.'

'It's pickled, though.'

'Yes, it's pickled.'

'Pickled what?'

'Hippo.'

'Hippo?'

'Yes, ma'am, belly of hippopotamus pickled in its own juices.'

'Goodness gracious!' said Mary and put down her knife and fork. William, who had had three helpings, went pale.

Hippo or not, it was a meal they would not forget quickly. It was, after all, the first table they had sat at since Durban and the first tablecloth since Wales.

It began with Walrus asking them with the soup what was their opinion of their first day in the goldfields, and they were still loudly reliving it well into the cheese.

'And what of you, Ianto?' asked Honest Jack. 'You haven't said much.'

'Ianto thinks there are too many English here,' said William before Huw could kick his ankle.

'Too many English, is it?' replied Honest Jack, knowing nothing of Ianto except that he was too quiet for so large a man. 'Well, young 'un,' he said to William, 'there's precious few parts of this world where they ain't. Excepting a Boer's front parlour.'

'That is unless they've skinned him first and made him into a rug,' laughed Walrus.

'That's right,' said Honest Jack. 'You'll find out soon enough there's no love between us. Mind you, a Boer's love of money is always at war with his dislike of us and given the two, his money love will always win. If you've got gold or silver you'll never meet an unfriendly Boer.'

'But it wouldn't do for any of us to go suddenly disinherited among them,' said Walrus. 'I'd sooner drop among a pack of hyena.'

Honest Jack nodded his agreement.

'Why don't they like the English?' asked Mary.

'That's a matter of opinion, ma'am,' answered Honest Jack. 'Some say it's because we're greedy, that we've taken what's rightly theirs and taken more than we can cope with. Also that we should have stayed in the Cape, stopped at the Orange River, and there's a lot to that opinion. Cape Town was all we really needed, a good, deep port halfway to India. But we weren't content. We're always pushing on, exploring, it's as if we need to touch all four corners of what we own. Anyhow, we've pushed the Boers too far and there'll be trouble. It's coming, between us and them, next year, year after, I don't know. Once, you see, it was just land, but now it's diamonds and gold and damn me if we won't have to pay for it too. Damn English greed!'

Walrus interrupted before Mary could speak again. 'Honest Jack knows his Boers, Mrs Mary, knows them well. I'm afraid he's had a bad time with them too.'

'Yes, ma'am, I know as much as I ever want to know and more than I should and my advice is to stay clear and stick with your own. When God looked down and saw this empty country He put down three tribes, the kaffirs, the Boers and us. Now I reckon He knows it was a stupid thing to do, as none of us will mingle – now or never.'

'Not even here?' asked Huw.

'Especially not here, boy,' said Walrus. 'Especially not here. The Boers are farmers, not diggers. They love money but they won't leave their cornfields to find it. There's probably something in the Bible that tells them digging's ungodly.'

'No, I don't think so,' said Huw politely. 'There's nothing I remember that forbids it.'

'Well, something does, boy. They own all the land from the Vaal to the Limpopo but they've yet to leave their cows and corn to come up here.'

'And thank the Lord for it,' said Honest Jack. 'We've too many diggers already, can't see the gold for boots, the queerest assortment south of Dover. Just up the creek there's another camp called Mac Mac Falls. And d'you know why, young fellow?' he said, leaning forward and tweaking William's ear. 'It's filled with Scots! When the Boers' President Burgers came up here a few years back he was introduced to so many Macs this and Macs that, he called it Mac Mac Falls, and the name stuck. A year back, I remember, a couple of them wore kilts on Saint Andrew's Day and the gold commissioner – he was a stupid old fool called Houghton then – he fined them five pounds for indecent dress. Nearly caused a riot.'

Walrus thumped the table with his mug and refilled it with beer.

'And I remember him fining a man who tried to hang himself once,' he said. 'They cut him down in time but Houghton still had him in court before him and said: "As you have been found guilty of the attempt only, I will fine you five pounds. But be sure that had you succeeded I should have felt bound to impose a much severer penalty!"' And even Ianto laughed.

Mary was now feeling giddy with the heat of the room and the wine. Her face felt on fire and she found it difficult to shape her lips to form words, like the times that Owen had brought home a bottle of red ruby wine. 'Have there been many rich men here?' she heard herself asking.

'No, ma'am, not many, at least not many yet,' said Honest Jack, 'though there have been some lucky finds. First real gold was dug up along the Blyde two years ago and it had a mighty strong perfume because the smell of it reached all parts of the world and within a month over a hundred diggers came. They reckon a man named Osborne had the first find, a seven-pound-weight nugget. Then his partner Barrington had another like it soon after. But one of the best was old George Lilley's. He dug it out of the creek only about a hundred paces from here and it weighed seven and a half pounds! Maybe there's been a dozen men so far who've left rich, but there are plenty buried here and not all of them should have died so poor.'

'Like McLannigan,' said Walrus.

'Ay, and Tucker too,' said Honest Jack. 'They were the saddest pair of all, ma'am. Just over a year back, it was. They'd walked all the way from Maritzburg and they'd only enough money to buy one pick and a bag of mealie between them. They staked out on the far side of Big Rock on Slater's claim and in the first week Tucker kicked over a turf and there was a ten-ounce nugget looking at him. That's how it went on, day after day, sometimes good, sometimes not as good, but they always brought up something. Kept their nuggets in jam jars. Then they bought a second tent and filled it with Cape Smoke and whisky and those two dug and drank and drank and dug as if there was no next week. But then after three months their seam ran out just as suddenly as it started. Then the jam jars were emptied one by one. Shame was, they were only youngsters, no more than thirty years old, but they just couldn't face starting all over again. So when the last jar was emptied they dipped their hands in cyanide, each licked the other's palm so it's said, and went off to Hell together!'

Everyone was very still until Walrus gave a roar and jumped out of his chair. 'Honest Jack! Honest Jack!' he shouted, splashing beer from his mug across the table. 'This is not the talk for Christmas Eve! These good people haven't trekked six thousand miles and more to listen to your doom and darkness. Cheer us up, man, cheer us up!'

'Then you tell us a story,' said Mary, marvelling again at Walrus' timely interruptions. 'Tell us a Christmas story!'

'So it is, Mrs Mary, a story it is. Fill me up, Honest Jack, up to the top, for I've a thirsty tale ahead of me.' Then together the two men joined arms and sang:

> 'Oh surely the women are worse than the men
> For they dine with the Devil and come home again.'

Walrus sat down again with a bump, spilling beer into his lap. He began, 'Well, I ain't never known much of Christmas except to watch others at it but I did once know a man who could have been Santa Claus and that's where he came from, too, up in the north where the snow is. We called him Swedish Pete, though you'd need to take a pinch of snuff before you could say his last name the way he said it! He was half as big again as Honest Jack here, with a head of white hair and a great big fluffy white beard. He was a good kind man, though owing to his deafness he was growing mistrustful, at least deafness was his excuse for getting in and out of trouble so often. He knew of the diamonds at Kimberley and reckoned they'd be the easy way home to Sweden. He was a determined fellow and didn't shy at hard work, but he never did have the one thing men who make money always have – luck. Luck to Swedish Pete was as rare as a blue-eyed Hottentot. He never had the feel for it; reminded me of a badly trained gundog, always on the scent but never facing the right direction!

'Except that once, the one and only time. He came into Kimberley on a pony and cart – it was just about the time that old man Hardy got his diamonds back – remember that, Will? Well, Pete dug hard for a month, which is about as long as most men reckon it takes just to sharpen their shovels. But it was enough for him and he chucked it in. After only four Sundays he packed his things and pulled up his tent to move on. But then as the last peg came out of the ground a diamond the size of my thumb came out with it. They reckoned it would fetch ten thousand pounds, but whatever it was worth it was more than he expected and certainly more than he needed for a ship to Stockholm, where he was from. So he got into his cart and harnessed his pony for their trek back down to Cape Town.

'Now from Kimberley he had to cross the Karoo Desert which is the loneliest bit of sand outside the Kalahari. If the Devil made you travel it forever you wouldn't see a living soul more than once every hundred years, but on that day, it seemed, word of his luck had travelled ahead, the way good news and bad always does, and he came across a man and his kaffir boy sitting in the shade of a Kokerboom.

'"I'm a government inspector," said the man and so he might have been with his dark tunic and peaked hat, "and I've been commissioned by the government in Cape Town to trap an ant-eater."

'Well, Swedish Pete acted deaf, making the man repeat it, time enough for him to work out what an ant-eater was exactly. He'd never heard of one before, least of all seen one, not that many have, mind you, as they're shy creatures and they'll dig themselves into the ground quicker than you can say it.

'"Now," says the government inspector, "I've trapped one inside this cave and I'll pay you well to help me tie it up and carry it south." And Pete, kindly old fool and still not used to the idea of the diamond and its worth, thought it a good deal.

'So the kaffir tied a rope round him with more knots than the inspector had warts on his face and tied the other end round the ant-eater's leg. Then they lit an oil rag and smoked out the poor beast and he came running so fast, Pete was pulled off his feet and dragged hollering into the soft sand. That creature dug himself deep and didn't stop until he'd pinned Pete on his back, staring at the sky and with the noose as tight as a tow-chain around his middle. He hollered and he hollered but he would be hollering still because the rogue with the warts was already half a mile away with the pony and trap and his kaffir running alongside.'

Walrus stopped, leant back, drank his beer and eyed them across the rim of his mug.

'He lost the diamond?' asked Huw and William together.

Walrus took another long draught and wiped the froth from his moustache with the back of his hand.

'Walrus,' they all shouted, 'what happened to the diamond?'

'Now, boys,' said Walrus, 'be patient as it was patience that saved old Swedish Pete. You see, he'd kept the stone about his waist in a money-belt and being a patient man, as I say, he lay there burning in the sun waiting for the ant-eater to come up again for air. By evening he did, and after some persuading they went to Cape Town together, sold the stone, cut the rope and went their separate ways as happy as pigs in a puddle.'

William scowled and Honest Jack fell off his chair laughing.

'You're a wicked storyteller, Walrus Baines,' said Mary, 'and a bad example to my boys.'

But already Walrus and Honest Jack were into the second chorus of: 'Oh, surely a woman's much worse than a man . . .'

The revelry in the bar next door had now spilt into the street so that there seemed not only one but a hundred different parties going on. Then they heard a bugle and the sounds of gunfire and seconds later galloping horses, hurried along by cheering.

'They're racing their ponies to Browns Hill and back,' said Honest Jack. 'They're crazy to do it by moonlight. There'll be a few broken heads and legs by the morning.'

'And a few empty jam jars,' added Walrus. 'They bet here, Mrs Mary, faster than they can chase a tail of gold. It's a blessing and one I reckon God intended that Christmas only comes once a year.'

He was interrupted by the chiming of the tall, black-marble clock standing among the debris of food on the sideboard and they stopped their chatting as its gilt filigreed hands came together for midnight. And when the last of the twelve bells had chimed Honest Jack slowly and not very steadily stood up at the head of the table and held up his jug high in front of him.

'Mrs Mary,' he said in his sombre way, 'I welcome you and your family to my home and hope with all my heart that your days here will be as happy as this one and that your life will be long and full. A Merry Christmas to us all!'

Jugs collided above the table as Walrus Baines leant over and kissed Mary's hand, and she in turn did what she had been meaning to do all along the Delagoa Road and kissed him on the nose, which reddened the old man's face. Then William tugged at Mary's sleeve and nodded towards Huw whose Bible was open on the table in front of him. He looked up at her expectantly and she smiled and said loudly, 'Huw would like to say a prayer, just to round things off, the way we did in our parlour back home.' And Huw stood up and they stood with him and recited the Lord's Prayer.

They said 'Amen' and when they opened their eyes there was a man standing at Honest Jack's shoulder, as tall as he but some years younger. He had a head full of curls which were stained black with sweat where they touched his forehead. He had a young face, lined too easily for his years, but his grey eyes sparkled as they looked at Mary.

'Good evening, Mrs Llewellyn,' he said in a strange accent she had not heard before. 'And a Merry Christmas, too. Your name is everywhere and now I see why. I'm Carpenter, Major John to everyone here, and may I say, ma'am, you'll never be more welcome anywhere than you and your boys are here in Pilgrims Rest tonight.'

The moonlight horse-racing lasted well into the night and when it was over those who could climbed back into their saddles and prayed that their weary, sweating beasts would find their way back to the tents, beds and blankets. Those who could not find their horse or climb into their saddle walked, and those who could not walk or ride simply fell to the ground and slept.

It was gone one o'clock before the three men stood at the supper table to say their goodnights to Mary, and with a pleasantly affected ceremony each in turn bowed and kissed her hand. Honest Jack, Walrus Baines and Major John Carpenter, recently appointed magistrate and Gold Commissioner. Not at all put out by Ianto's scowl as he left with Huw and William and Jollie two hours before, she had been determined to stay and enjoy the three men's conversation and the extraordinary tales of Africa they exchanged. The more she listened, the more terrible the vast country seemed, terrible and exciting and yet more and more strangely familiar.

She left and crossed into the yard from the kitchen door and was astonished at the whiteness of the moon's light. With a little longing, she thought, it might almost be snow. At her doorway she waited, not anxious to go in, tired but not wanting to sleep because it would mean saying goodbye to all that was still happening. To sleep would be to wake and find the night and everything in it gone, boxed away into her drawerful of memories. Sleeping meant packing the day away, rubbing it out like a child's chalk sums on a slate.

But then she heard baby Tom moving in his cot and she breathed in the perfumed air once more before stepping through the curtain of woven tamboekie. As she did so there was a rustle above and the white owl spread its wings and for an instant hid the moon; a small ball of chewed-up bone and fur tumbled down the roof and hit the ground a yard from the hole where the family of baby mice were waiting, hungry and growing cold.

Mary smoothed the blanket over Jollie's shoulders, tucked the covers tight under Tom's chin and held her little finger for him to suck. His eyes were closed but he drew hard with his strong mouth. She leant down and kissed his forehead, smelling the sweetness of his skin.

'We've come home, my baby,' she whispered. 'You and I, Tom. We've come home!'

* * *

She woke and knew the sun was high, which vaguely irritated her. It was Christmas morning and she wanted to be up and be doing things. There were so many things to be done so she had to decide what was first and what must wait. Christmas came first but when that was over, Ianto and Huw must stake their claim and pay their fifty shillings' licence to Major John. Walrus said he would look for a good site to pitch their tents but Mary insisted they would not live in tents; they would build a house, so Walrus agreed that after the holiday he would send his own boys with Ianto and Huw to search for proper timber on the hills.

Already the heat was bouncing off the cobbles in the yard and the sun was scorching the thatch and Christmas so summer-like, she thought, was not Christmas at all. She would have to work hard to make it convincing.

'We shall need a tree,' she told William, 'and as near to a fir as you can find,' and he and Tongogara went off on their morning's search. She sent Jollie and Jacob to look for coloured berries, white and red and the fluffy white seed-balls like dandelion puffs she'd seen on their way down just below the grove of fig trees. Honest Jack sent his girls to the creek for tiny unripe peaches, bright and yellow that hung like baubles, and he gave her a dozen small hard shiny red apples and as many Cape oranges. Mary also persuaded him to empty the packets of tea in his kitchen into a single large chest so she might take the silver wrappings and cut them into stars and crescents. Then Jollie painted dried peach stones white so they looked like tiny crinkled snowballs.

By late morning the tree – what the diggers called an African Fern – stood seven feet high in the dining-room, proud and splendid and as heavy in colour and trinkets as any that stood in the drawing-rooms of wealthy England. And standing on top of it, not a fairy in pink taffeta nor an angel in shimmering tinsel, but Africa's own: a corn dolly woven and shaped by Jacob from dried yellow maize leaves.

At midday Major John called to take them to the chapel,

but Honest Jack first insisted they drank his rum punch and by the time they left, Mary felt much in the mood for singing.

The small church was built of rough-cut stone under thatch with a door at one end and a single window, thin and tall, over the eastern altar. Above the window was a thin, peevish cross cut from red wood. The climb from the High Street up through the cemetery was steep and the gravelled path went between a row of thirty or more headstones chipped from the local stone with the names of the dead clumsily chiselled on them. Mary asked Major John how they managed to carry the coffins so high and he replied that often they didn't, and the dead and their boxes frequently parted company! Mary clutched baby Tom closer and the major held her elbow.

Towering above the church was an old and tall fern tree, its lower branches sweeping down and spreading like a cedar, giving the building what looked like a second roof. It also kept the light from the window so it was dark inside. A single candle lit the altar table and a small simple crucifix lay at its centre. There were no pews and no hymnbooks and diggers shuffled and edged into lines leaving an aisle down the centre. Major John led Mary to the front and for some minutes they waited. Men coughed and whispered and spluttered behind them until, without warning, Major John stepped forward to the altar, bowed his head for a moment, and then turned and faced the small congregation.

'Gentlemen, it seems the man on the hill has forgotten what day it is, which is a pity for it's a very special one – Christ's birthday and the arrival among us of the Llewellyn family, including Master Tom here, the youngest pilgrim of us all! Last night I interrupted them at supper while eldest son Huw Llewellyn was saying prayers. So in the absence of our own preacher, I'm going to ask Huw to be ready with his book and read us some lines once we've done with our hymns.'

And so, after they had sung their way loudly through 'Jerusalem' Huw did as he was asked, quietly and hesitantly at first, so that men shouted from the back rows for him to speak up.

But already he felt his blood rise and his heart beat faster, the way it used to in the chapel at Bethesda as the Reverend Morgan Roberts fired him with brimstone and terrible threats of the doomed sinner's life hereafter.

Huw spoke the words from his Bible but not Morgan Roberts' way. This churchful of strangers were not Penrhyn's men, prisoners of the quarry, dying of slate. These were the freest men in God's world, bouncing across oceans and nations, men who did not fear living and thought of death only once in their lifetime. What would Preacher Roberts threaten them with here? Demons and pools of fire? Would he scream as he did in Bethesda until the spittle speckled his lips, threatening love as his fists bruised his open Bible, pushing love out of the chapel windows and up the devil's black slurry hills? But Roberts would not frighten these men. They were fresh to Africa and whether they knew it or not God was freshly with them, a little bit of Him tucked into their pockets.

So Huw read his Psalms and spoke his prayers, loudly and gently to his congregation, and when at the end they said Amen and Amen again, he felt strangely satisfied. No cold draught crossed his brow and no shaft of white light touched his shoulder as Preacher Roberts had promised. Yet something had happened. He had read from the pulpit before in Bethesda many times under the fierce unforgiving eyes of the chapel elders, but he had never felt like this afterwards. It was, he told himself, the hand of the Lord reaching down so that he might understand why he had come to Africa and what he was now expected to do in it.

He was about to begin a new career in a new land but digging gold, he now knew, was only the start of it.

They left the cool damp half-light and shielded their eyes from the sun. The boys went back to their wagon but Major John led Jollie and Mary with baby Tom in her arms into the shade of the church tree to wait until the untidy congregation had trundled back through the cemetery and spread out its separate ways.

'The boy's determined to be a preacher, ma'am?' he asked her.

'I think so. He's brought his chapel to Africa and I must say it sounds better here than it did at home.'

'Strange. What he said about the diggers, thinking of death only once.'

'Was he wrong?'

'Right and wrong! It's true they don't ever worry about dying; if they did they'd be dead long ago. But they do get anxious about being properly buried. Whatever else they do with their gold dust there's always a little put by for their funeral. Two ounces, no more, £7 for a piece of land, a coffin and a headstone. It's the same with the Boers. When they trek they always carry four planks of hardwood strapped under their wagons for their coffin too. Even in their farms you'll find the same four planks under their beds, waiting to be used!'

'I can understand,' she said. 'I'd hate to be put down without a proper cover on me!'

He laughed and swept his arm across the graves. 'Well, you'll not find a man who's not decently attired here, ma'am.'

Mary handed baby Tom to Jollie's care and then stepped between the rows of headstones and he followed her. One read 'TATTERSALL OCTOBER 74', and he had been buried so recently the headstone had been pushed askew by the moving earth as if Tattersall had not been comfortable.

Across from him lay 'BOS'UN MOCKETT DIED OF WHISKY 73' and by Mockett's side was 'SCORCHER HARE' but his stone told no more. The life and death of 'GERMAN GEORGE' across from him was just as secretive.

'It seems such a shame,' said Mary, scratching the lichen from a name with a pebble, 'that a man should come so far and live so long and only have this to be remembered by.'

'That's how they would prefer it, ma'am,' he said. 'They're loners, every one of them. The only thing they have in common is their optimism. They seldom tell me or anyone who they are or where they're from. They arrive with a pick and a pair of new boots and in six months they've gone away with a pocketful of gold dust or they're dead with fever, or like Mockett here, pickled in malt. If that was his real name. You see, they assume a name the moment they hit camp. A man may have left England as John Smith or Jack Jones but when he comes here, by the colour of his trousers or the shape of his hat, the way he walks or his accent, he'll take on a new label. You won't believe it but we've got a Dungaree Jack, French Bob, Yankee Dan, Old Pipes, Charlie the Reefer and One-Eyed Spinner. And you'll have heard about Wheelbarrow Patterson. I sometimes reckon half the world's square pegs find their way to this little valley. Back in my home we would call them "no-gooders" though they've little enough to take exception to. So far we've had a French count and an English duke, deserters from the British army and navy, veterans who've known the Yukon and even Australia. One of the strangest was a sailor from Liverpool who brought his cat-o'-nine-tails with him, the real thing with eighty-one knots on it. Curious thing for a man to grow attached to. But he never had reason to use it here and we buried it with him just the other side of young Tattersall there. He died of fever, same as a lot of them. Some have caught the liver-worm, others have been crushed in rock-falls. It's a dangerous sport they're at. But they're still loners, alive and dead. They don't have many rules but there's one they do obey. "All things may be dug up here except a man's past."'

'Like the man on the hill?'

'Oh no,' he said with a smile. 'The man on the hill has a past and there's not a digger here who doesn't know it. He's got a name too, though while he's up there hiding I don't suppose he'll remember it.'

'Hiding? Who? And why did you expect him here in church this morning?'

'Because that's where he belongs.' He walked a few yards from her, leant over a headstone and picked a single flower. 'They call it morea,' he said. 'The sun burns it up.

Only lives a day, like the mayfly. I reckon it's safer with you.'

She took it from him but said nothing. He sat down by her feet. 'The man on the hill is the Reverend Bernard Makepeace, once of England.'

'A vicar? Hiding on a hill?'

'In a cave on a hill, to be precise.'

'But what's he done?'

'What he's been doing every three months as regular as sunrise ever since he came here. Blind drunk night and day until the money runs out, then they carry him to his hideaway with a blanket and a billy of water till he recovers. Honest Jack sends his girls up there with soup and slops every evening and they report to me on how he's doing. I was hoping he'd make it back today, but perhaps he'll manage it in time for this Christmas dinner Walrus has been telling me about.'

Mary sat down on the grass by him, between the gravestones and the speckled light of shade and sun. She looked across to Jollie, who was on her knees, rolling baby Tom gently up and down the short and shallow grassy slope of a mound of moss covering the remains of a digger known only on his headstone as 'THE IRON PIRATE'.

'Tell me more about the vicar,' she asked. 'You see, at home in my village the churchmen were very important. They almost ran our lives for us. They were very proper and never ever drunk in public.'

He nodded. 'The vicar's the son of a dean from a place called Wells in the county of Somerset. Seems he went to Cambridge University and he told me he once had ambitions to become a professor, but he never did, because he came to Africa; first Cape Town, then Durban, then travelling Natal, until ending up here. I believe he came to the valley to get away, though only he and God know why and neither of them are saying. Every quarter, our vicar is sent a payment, a remittance; he tells me it's fifty pounds and I've a feeling it's sent by his father the dean to keep him as far away from Wells and England as possible. Just as soon as that money arrives from Lydenburg he hands over twenty pounds to Honest Jack for food rations, ten pounds goes into a chest he keeps in his tent, and what's left over he spends in the bar. Sometimes he's stinko for a week, sometimes two, but when the money's gone they tie him to a horse and up to Black Rock Hill he goes till he's able to walk back down again on his own. Sometimes on a still night you can hear him singing in the cave, in the strangest way, like never-ending hymns in Latin. Once he had me send him a book from his tent, kept it in his chest, that's how I know the money's there. And I saw what else. All the treasures and trappings of a high churchman: gold and crimson vestments, strings of beads, tiny brass caskets and a painting of the Virgin Mary in a gold frame.'

'And the book?'

'It was foreign. Not Latin, I'd have recognized that. Later he told me it was the Greek Testament. Can you see him sitting up there stinko, reading Greek?'

Mary sighed and looked across the graves towards the hills. 'Why are men so sad?' she asked but he did not answer. Then she asked, 'Can't you stop him? Can't you take the money away?'

'Sure, but you'd have to fight him and he's a powerfully strong man. I've seen him lift Honest Jack over his own bar and he's taken his coat off more than once in his own church to the blasphemers.'

'Is he alone here?'

'D'you mean does he have a black woman? No! Though he has a daughter in England. I think that's why he puts money away.'

'And when he's sober is he a proper vicar?'

'Oh, he does his duty though I've a feeling God turned His back on him a long time ago.'

Jollie Thomas now lay on her back holding baby Tom above her at arm's length with him kicking and gurgling his pleasure. White clouds came scudding off the mountain peak, their shadows slipping like giant stains down the slopes towards them. The ground air was still and there was a distant drone like a swarm of bees, something Mary had heard many times on the trek on such still warm days. The camp was quiet. Men were sleeping off the week's work and the hard night's drinking and far off, in the broadest sweep of river, men swam naked in the clear fast water. The valley seemed enormously contented and at peace; as if it had never known aggravation. And Christmas seemed at the other end of the year.

Mary turned to Major John. 'Why does he do it?'

'Don't know,' he said. 'There could be many reasons or none at all, though once he told me he was trying to drink himself to death. Maybe he's unhappy in love.'

'Oh no! That's nonsense,' she said. 'Nobody dies of a broken heart, the body's too sensible for that.'

He looked away. 'Perhaps. But he was quite sober when he said it!'

Baby Tom was no longer content. The ache for food had outgrown the fun of Jollie's attention and she brought him crying to Mary. Major John stood up and walked some yards away as Mary organized her breast. She watched him as the baby nestled into her, suckling. Against the sky his hair seemed almost white.

'And what of you?' she asked. 'Will you tell me all about you?'

'Are you comfortable, ma'am?'

'I am, yes, very content.'

'Thirsty?'

'No.'

'Hungry?'

'Not at all.'

'Then if we've an hour to spare I will, though on one condition only.'

'Which is?'

'That you will now or at some time tell me all about the

remarkable Mary Llewellyn who's come all the way to Africa from England.'

'Wales,' she said, 'Wales. It's wise to know that particular geography when you're with me and my family.'

He sat down again, and lay on his back with his hands folded under his head. He stretched his legs and looked at the clouds.

'I'm thirty-two years old and fit of mind and limb and was born in New Hampshire. That's New England.'

'And where is that?'

'Ma'am?'

'Where is New England?'

'In America.'

'Then you're the first American I've ever met! Go on.'

'My ambition was to be a builder, or rather, an architect. I always wanted to build – houses, schools, museums – entire streets full of my buildings. I even dreamt of having a town named after me, Carpentersville, though it never did sound right. The old family name is Carpentier. My grandfather was French; the English chased him south across the Canadian border. The English are always chasing someone, somewhere! In time he drifted down through Indian country and settled by a lake called Winnepassakee. Doesn't that sound nice? It's Indian. Well, I never did become a builder, because father put me into a law company, his company, so you might say I had a sympathetic apprenticeship!'

'That was nice,' said Mary.

'No, it wasn't. It was awful. Hateful. Promise me you'll never put young Tom here into law.' He paused, then sang:

> 'He saw a lawyer killing a viper
> On the dunghill by his own stable
> And the Devil smiled, for it put him in mind
> Of Cain and his brother Abel.'

He laughed and she could see her reflection in his eyes. 'I did my best by my father,' he went on. 'Had he been old and ill I would have stayed and sold the business when he'd gone.

But a stronger, healthier, more upright man never lived, which was a shame. D'you know, I used to feel positively unwell just being by him! That's possibly why mother decided to go first, which made me sad because I think I loved her a little though it was hard to tell with her. Anyway, at her funeral I decided it was the end of Carpenter and Carpenter. Funerals, I've since discovered, have an odd way of sharpening things up all of a sudden. Anyway, as mother went into the ground I hopped off, trusting that father wouldn't send the law enforcement men after me. And he didn't. But the war caught me up. I joined the Union Army and fought at Bull Run as a trooper, finally crossing half the country with General Sherman, and ending up a major.'

He turned on his side, picked a blade of grass and chewed it. 'A lot of things have happened in between that day and this. I signed on as sail-hand aboard a clipper and a year later, having circumnavigated the world or so it seemed, I jumped ship at the Cape. As it happened and not for the first time, I got my timings wrong, because it was winter and the sky stayed black for three months. Then the rain turned to hail and the hail to snow and it was cold as any winter I'd ever known back home and the coldest they'd ever known in the Cape, too! I spent the first month of the three at kip shops without enough money for a blanket and queueing at the kitchen doors of boarding-houses to dab for food with a fork in a bucket for a penny. I mean never to be hungry or cold like it again. That's how quickly this country is changing. Five years ago I was starving but nowadays a man might travel from the Cape to the Limpopo without a shilling in his pocket and be entertained all the way. But then it was bad times.

'I teamed up with another fellow, said he was German though I think he was a Boer running from home like me. We decided we'd try for diamonds and stowed aboard a train bound for Kimberley through the Karoo Desert. But I think it must have been one of the first trains in that direction because I thought we'd starve before we ever got there. It was so slow, we passed some cows and three days later we saw some more. "They ain't more cows," my German friend said. "They're the same cows who've caught us up!"

'We knew nothing of the Karoo so we hopped off to walk it. But deserts are strange things, Mrs Mary, they're always your enemy. The Devil made the desert. In the day it burns you till you're screaming for shade and at night the air cuts you in two and your toes and knuckles freeze solid. On one of those nights I got frostbite and we waited for dawn and the sun to thaw me out. But the Devil decided we wouldn't have sun that day and the winds blew and the sand cut us to ribbons and my feet began to swell and turn blue. So then my friend went off and I thought that was goodbye but five hours later he came back with a springbok. He cut open its belly and shoved my feet into it, and that's what saved me, he and that warm dead thing together.

'I think we might well have made it to Kimberley. We might have become rich men and he could have bought his grape farm in the Paarl and I could have sailed first class back to Boston and lived a life of Old Riley. But the desert hadn't done with us. We'd beaten it once but it wasn't going to let it happen again. We were just about to come off it with only a couple of days still to go when he stepped on a boomslang – that's a snake you'll never want to see – and it bit his instep. He shook for five days and nights like he was a puppet. He couldn't shut his eyelids, so I had to close them when he wanted to sleep and open them again as soon as he stirred. It's the worst way of dying I can ever imagine but I had to stay with him till he'd gone. Then I buried him in the sand, so the desert got its way in the end. A week later I made Kimberley but I never dug for diamonds, couldn't have done, anyhow. Six months before I was a fit young fellow who might have shifted half of Africa given a month and a shovel but those six months almost finished me so I became a lawyer again and worked in the company offices, which is how, eventually, I got here. End of story, Mrs Mary. And you might think it serves me right for leaving my old Papa!'

He laughed and sat up. For a while he looked at Mary and she at him. 'D'you know, ma'am, and begging your pardon, but I reckon you have some Indian blood in you somewhere!'

Mary was surprised and showed it.

'I'm sorry,' he went on, 'but it's all this talk of home. The Indians used to come over the Notre Dame mountains selling furs and skins and some of their ladies had much the same colouring as you.'

Mary turned away, handing baby Tom back to Jollie. She hadn't blushed for so many years, she had quite forgotten how to cope with it. Major John did not see it though, or he would not have persisted.

'I reckon you must have some Indian stock in you,' he said again.

'Welsh,' she said, 'through and through.'

'Are you certain your grandma wasn't ever in Canada?'

Her eyes were sparkling now. 'My grandmother,' she said, 'only left her parlour twice in her lifetime. Once to be married and once to be buried. Now we'll talk of other things.'

But he would not be put off. 'It's a silly thing to say but it's as if you've always been in Africa.'

'What?'

'Your skin, I mean. It's the colour of honey.'

Mary rose quickly and almost ran to the path. 'Come, Jollie,' she called, 'we've some cooking to do if those guinea-fowl are to be tender in time for dinner.'

He watched them as they stepped their way carefully down between the aisle of headstones until they reached the gate above the High Street. And he was curious.

The Reverend Bernard Makepeace came late out of his cave behind the towering ironwood tree on Black Rock Hill. Not because he was smelling of whisky or still suffering from its poisons; nor was he so casual about his duties that he had not cared whether he missed his Christmas morning service or not. He had intended returning a day earlier, to stumble his way down to the River of Joy, strip and wash away the sweat and dirt of nearly a fortnight's hibernation. He had even unpacked the clean set of clothes Honest Jack's girl had brought him and had dug a hole ready to bury the soiled and shameful tatters he was wearing.

But yesterday morning's commotion had woken him and brought him stepping out from the high ledge of the cave onto the boughs of the tree for a better view and he had watched Walrus Baines on his horse and then the women in their wagon behind him. He saw the baby in their arms and it was then that he wondered if he was ready to greet them, whether he ought not to wait until the smell had left his breath and his hands had stopped shaking. So he decided to sleep out another night and another day, and come dusk this Christmas evening he went down to the river to begin the ritual of return. He let the water cover his hips, he scooped up handfuls of soft mud and scoured every wrinkle and cranny of his body, rubbing it hard into his hair and into his gums and teeth. Then he stood and plunged into the river's cold deep centre and swam and kicked and blew fountains high into the air and roared his delight like an old buffalo coming to water after too long in the lowveld's heat and dust. It was at times like this that he made his resolution never to drink again. The resolve was as regular as its cause and he made it so frequently he had even stopped appealing directly to God for help.

But now a family had arrived and with a baby, the first white women in the valley and wouldn't they need his help, and the comfort of his church? Wouldn't there perhaps be a baptism and even a marriage one day? Wouldn't they be proper parishioners, not the blaspheming rogues that littered his little church every Sunday simply for somewhere different to be? Wouldn't it change now a family had come? Wasn't there a purpose?

He swam back to the shallows and knelt and closed his eyes

and buried his head in his large hands, an enormous white and naked man alone in the darkness trying to speak to God and knowing only the nightbirds were listening.

He was not tall but he was very broad and men joked that had he been a few inches wider he would have been quite square. Not that men joked often in his company because the Reverend Makepeace had a quick and violent temper and his punishments were severe whether he had misheard or misjudged a man or not. His large brass-buckled belt had been used on many who had been slow to respect the cloth or had ridiculed the message he sometimes preached.

Whether he liked it or not he was indeed very square-looking. His jaw was square and his head appeared to have corners. His body was rectangular and his hands looked from a distance like large pink books. He was bald though coal-black curly hair grew fast on his sideburns and spread across his cheeks. He had a broad flat nose and it had once upset him to hear a digger say that because of the shape of it and his wide nostrils and the wiriness, curl and colour of his side hair, 'somewhere and sometime his people have been meddling with the kaffirs'. The digger was carried, broken, to the Boers in Lydenburg for treatment as men in Honest Jack's bar heard the Reverend list his ancestors, none of whom, he vouched, had ever been to Africa or even out of the British Isles!

Despite, or possibly because of his pedigree, he had always been a misfit, through school, through university, even in his last refuge, the Church. He was a fugitive from fate and believing his Maker had deliberately set him apart from others for a purpose, the child Makepeace decided to distance himself further. At school he trained himself to leave his bed empty and sleep on the hard floor; he washed in cold water in winter and chose thin shirts and left off his topcoat so that the chill wind bit and the rain stung. He courted punishment and committed petty crimes to test his resolve at the end of the cane. He was the outsider, who looked through other people's windows with awe at the warmth and the love inside, cursing his God for making him in such a way and not telling him why.

When he was sober he lived in his little church, and slept on a thin grass mat beneath the altar table. Every morning he swept the church himself whether there was dust or not, visitors or not, and early every Sunday, excepting those when he was away on the hill, he scrubbed the stone-flagged floor and picked wild flowers and coloured grasses for the vase by the cross. In the winter months, while it was dry, he repaired the thatched roof with reeds he reaped himself and repointed the stonework with his own mortar made from lime and mud. Often, sitting so many hours alone looking at the door that so few opened, he thought of the chest in the tent and the holy trinkets he kept there. It was his great and terrible secret. As an advanced ritualist he would dearly have loved to adorn his church with all those scents, symbols and dolls that horrified the good Protestants, of whom he was not one. That was also his secret. He served a common God but in a Church and of an Order not of his choosing. That was why his father, dean in the Anglican High Church, had been so horrified at the discovery of his son's treachery and had sent him from England and paid him to stay in Africa. That was why he kept his little stone church so bare, as if to impress upon his Holy Witness there was no deceit, that no sides had been taken. But there was no deceiving. God, he knew, would never forgive him his unholy hypocrisy.

Which was why he lost himself in drink and the Greek Testament each quarter year when the Judas money came.

There were those who had still to travel the dangerous dirty way to the valley from Lourenço Marques in Walrus Baines' wagons, and who had still to listen to him by his large fire, full of his chicken stew and watch the pipe smoke curl above his head, who would wonder if that dinner he spoke of so often had really been so grand. Could it have been so special that

Christmas night? Had there really been roast guinea-fowl stuffed with onions and herbs? And braised redwing in hot peach sauce, pickled fish and partridge, rabbit, sweet potatoes, tomato chutneys, and stewed oranges swimming in burnt treacle? Had there really been wines from Stellenbosch in the Cape and brandy from France and a Christmas tree cloaked in as many colours as you can count in a day, heavy with mystery parcels and topped by an African angel made from maize? And was there really a cripple who played carols and all kinds of magic on a concertina who had danced with a girl with a torn face called Jollie? Could all this have happened in such a faraway place as the end of the Delagoa Road?

The Reverend Makepeace stood on the verandah peering in through the open window, wary of his own excitement. His church was less than a hundred yards away and he thought of the mat beneath the altar and the solitary night's penance due. But he was watching what he considered a minor miracle and an act of faith. Teddy the music-man whose crippled young legs would not carry him in a straight line for more than a song, was dancing with a girl who seemed perfect in every way except her face, which God seemed to have cruelly and hurriedly stitched together. Honest Jack's hotel was shaking on its wooden piles as the diggers stamped their great boots in time, and at the far end, beneath a magnificent tree, was Major John, dancing with the fine woman he had seen yesterday holding a baby to her breast as the wagons came down. And there was Honest Jack, nowhere near as drunk as he ought to have been on such an occasion, oblivious of his bad leg, jumping up and down on the same spot like a man treading hot coals. And Walrus Baines at his favourite sport, eating, and as ever with his hat on. The noise, the colour, the singing and dancing, the smell and heat of life billowed out of the window. It was like every party the Reverend had ever dreamed of going to, like every Christmas he had ever been denied. He breathed in the flow of warm air and made his decision. He would wait until the music stopped and with a cough and just a little drama, enter.

But then the voice said no, the voice that plagued him inside, the voice that made him two men, hateful of each other, that sent him drunk into the hills and then condemned him on his return. The voice sneered at him, reminding him of his guilt and the need to repent to a deaf God, and the Reverend turned away from the window and walked back along the verandah. But as he came to the steps he stumbled and had he not been sober, his weight would have broken Tongogara's neck.

'What in heaven's name are you doing, boy, hiding in the dark?'

'Watching, baas, only watching,' said the little boy, frightened and shaking under the Reverend's tight grip. His eyes were wide and he wondered what this man, the one they called 'Sagafi', 'the Severe One', would do to him.

The Reverend Makepeace let go of his shoulder, paused and then sat down, his short thick legs dangling over the edge of the steps.

'Watching was what I was doing too, little lad,' he said quietly, 'just like you. Watching and wanting to go in.'

Tongo shuffled uncomfortably on the planks by his side. 'But you can go in, Sagafi,' he said.

'I can. But I mustn't.'

'Mustn't?' asked the child, hearing the word for the first time.

'Yes! Mustn't. Sometimes, Tongo, it's wrong to enjoy things.'

The boy was puzzled. His mother had always taught him that it was wrong not to enjoy things. And yet Sagafi, the white man's witch doctor, now said otherwise and white men were always right, his mother had taught him that too. So he said nothing but looked up at the big square face and followed Sagafi's gaze to the moon, hoping, as he always did when he sat with white men, that Sagafi would speak again, so that he might listen to the wonderful strange words. But when the

Reverend spoke it was with a new voice, soft and faraway. 'Do you know, little lad, why they're singing and dancing in Honest Jack's tonight?'

'No, Sagafi.'

'Do you know what day it is? A special day?'

'No, but Baas Walrus has eaten a big dinner. Better than Jacob's.'

The Reverend Makepeace held his hand up to the moon and saw its silhouette was steady and he was pleased.

'Today, Tongo,' he said, 'is the birthday of the greatest white King. His name is Jesus. Can you say that?'

'Jesus,' said Tongo and said it again because he liked its sound. Then he asked, 'Is Jesus greater than Chief Sekekune of the Bapedi?'

'Oh yes,' said the Reverend. 'Greater even than Shaka Zulu.'

'Not Shaka Sagafi?'

'Oh yes! Shaka died, Tongo, but my King will never die!'

'Is he old man?'

'Old and young. Young and old.'

Tongo did not answer. Sagafi, he thought, speaks in riddles the way his own father and grandfather did, saying silly things very solemnly so they sounded wise. And yet Sagafi was the wisest of all the white people, so surely what he said must have meaning.

'Not old and young same time, Sagafi? Young men grow old and old men always die.'

'No, Tongo. Not all men. That is my King's secret. And if you serve Him well, even better than you do Baas Walrus, then maybe one day He will call you and tell you His secret. Then you too will live forever.'

'Oh no, Sagafi! Your King will not talk to kaffir boy. White chiefs not talk to kaffirs . . .'

'Dear God,' said the Reverend in a whisper to the moon, 'why do you make us so blind and deaf if you wish us to see and hear!' Then he said, 'I think He will, Tongo. He once told all little children to come to Him.'

Tongo sat still, thinking. Then he said, 'You will show me how, Sagafi?'

'I will.'

'And you live all time too?'

'No, Tongo, I may not. I have made my King Jesus angry and He may never talk to me again.' Then he pulled himself up onto his knees and looking beyond the moon he prayed aloud:

> 'And He said give me your lamp
> And your arm, so I may see in the dark.
> And the man answered, take the arm of the Lord
> And use His eyes that you may have
> Light from this place to eternity.'

He did not know how long he knelt there but when he turned he saw Tongogara in his dirty ragged shirt kneeling by his side, his eyes tightly shut and his hands clasped under his nose. The Reverend leant down and slowly drew the sign of the cross on the little boy's forehead. He waited. Then he said, 'Come, fellow Christian. We've made our peace. Now we've other business to do.'

He picked him up and sat him on his shoulders and marched back along the verandah, and not waiting for the music to stop, stood in the doorway with his little load above him and shouted in the voice he normally reserved for transmitting messages across the valley:

'Gentlemen, ladies, a Merry Christmas to you all. Make way for Bernard Makepeace and his friend Tongogara who've come to join in the last hours of this special day with you and who have every intention of making what so far seems a very sombre affair into something of a proper celebration. But to begin, lift your jugs and toast the health of Victoria, about to begin the thirty-ninth year of her reign.'

And with that, Teddy the music-man sat down with a thud and, red-faced and puffing at the foot of the tree, pulled apart the bellows of his concertina and began the rousing first verse of 'God Save the Queen'.

And those few who were alone in their tents that Christmas night stirred in their sleep as the tune drifted with the camp-smoke across the valley of Pilgrims Rest.

CHAPTER FIVE

They were eight days into the New Year when Huw and Ianto found fool's gold. It was the day Walrus left the valley, the day Major John rode to Lydenburg to help bury four Englishmen and twelve Boers slaughtered by the Sekekune.

Ianto and Huw had staked their claim on the near bank of the Blyde River, along from what the diggers called Darkes Gulley. It was a piece of land shaped like a horseshoe with the river all but encircling it. Their claim had been worked before but other men had not dug deep enough and Major John showed Ianto and Huw where to place their pegs and how to work the topsoil for at least another twenty feet. Only then, he said, could they expect to touch bedrock and find the treasure dust.

Tents lined the river on both banks. The diggers ate and slept close to their claims and although a few of them erected simple shacks, most were afraid to in case they were building on gold. The river bank looked like a giant sprawling pincushion with more pegs, it seemed, than blades of grass, each peg driven four feet into the ground with a card pinned to it and the owner's name on that. The claims were a size regulated by the Transvaal government and a licence fee was paid for each. The claims were one hundred and fifty feet square and if the name-cards and pegs stayed in place no one dared stray onto them.

In the beginning there was a rule that if a man did not work his claim for three days running, anyone could jump him and take it for his own. But the rule did not last long. Too many diggers went down with the fever and too many claim-jumpers died with a bullet in their chest, fired by a sweating, shaking hand raised from a sick man's bed.

A digger's day began at sunrise as he crawled from his damp blankets still in his moleskin trousers and flannel shirt. He pulled the balls of rolled-up grass from his hobnailed boots, put there overnight to keep out the snakes and scorpions, and breakfasted on a billycan of boiled tea and a cut of meat in his bread. Ahead of him was twelve hours' work. He was his own taskmaster, he and the claim, with the fortune in gold he knew for sure lay beneath it. No man ever slackened and the only absentees were those who lay wet between their blankets on fire with the fever, or those dying from the worm that had pierced their liver and turned their blood black.

Work stopped at six to give a man enough light to wash and kindle his fire to heat his meat and tea for dinner. That was a rule that all men obeyed. It gave them rest, because those who had struck gold would work all night, and no man would sleep. Nor in the dark would any of the rich claims be safe and the owners would be forced to stay awake and keep guard. Some men in the past had tried jumping claims at night, thinking there was somewhere to run to and somewhere to hide. But there was not. They were lynched, those caught a second time. The first timers were whipped and had their heads shaved and half their beards cut away and led a hermit's life, speechless and unspoken to.

The lower diggings were alluvial, the nuggets and dust washed down from their seams in the mountains, sinking through the topsoil to the bedrock twenty feet or more deep. Each digger had to build his own race, a narrow channel to take the water from the river to his sluicebox. This was like an open coffin, two feet wide and sometimes as long as fifteen feet with thin slats of wood nailed across the bottom which the diggers called ripples. The first job each morning was to fill the sluicebox with earth and when the water had a good head, let it race through to wash away the soil. The gold dust, being heavier, sank and was trapped by the wooden ripples. Sometimes the dust was so fine, a man would nail a sheepskin or an oxhide to the floor of his sluicebox so that the particles were caught up in the hairs.

One digger was so poor when he came to the valley, he did not have a race or a sluice or even a shovel. He simply scooped up the soil with his hands into his blanket and then let the river wash away the debris. Sticking to the blanket's weave was his daily income. They called him Golden Fleece Johnson.

The greatest moment in the digger's day came when he cleaned up his box, scraping out the mud and panning it with water in a shallow basin, tipping it left and right, slowly sifting it, flushing away the mud and stones until all he had left was a tail of fine gold. If he had gold at the end of his day a digger considered himself 'flush'. If there was only caked mud he was said to be 'hard up'. Too many months of being hard up made some men end their lives with a bottle, and others with a gun.

It was not the hard work that broke a man. It was not the smell and taste of his sweat that hurt, or the back that would not straighten, or hands so blistered and heavy with corns he could not sleep with the pain. It was not fatigue that took a man's heart away. It was the unfairness: that good fortune should smile on some as the Devil sneered on others. A man could spend months shovelling and not find gold to cover a sixpence, while his neighbour, a stone's throw off, made £20 a day. But such was the gamble and it kept men digging until they died wealthy or exhausted.

Huw quickly became popular with the diggers. Remembering his first Sunday sermon they called him Preacher which seemed to please him. They found him whimsical and although some laughed at his quaint ways, they all listened when he spoke and helped him when he asked. They taught him how to turn the earth and move water and sift the mud. He studiously copied the ways they worked, kept their hours and they were pleased with his apprenticeship.

On the morning of the eighth of January, his shovel clanged

against bedrock for the first time and he yelped when he saw the shining seam at the end of his steel blade. The diggers came running but turned around just as quickly, all except a tiny man with the strangest accent and a knitted woollen scarf, much longer than himself, wound around his neck, who took Huw's shovel from him and pulled more of the earth away.

'That's fool's gold, dear boy,' he said in a foreign voice so deep it seemed to come from his boots. 'Cheap metal you'd not make a hairpin from. Real gold, my dear, does not show itself that easily. Real gold is shy! Remember the rule,' he said, wagging a long finger. 'Nothing's gold that glitters!'

The diggers did not speak to Ianto because he did not seem to need them. He would not take help from them, nor ask for it, so they left him alone. That was another rule. You did not try to prise open a man who wanted to stay closed. So Huw spoke for both of them and men would speak in Ianto's company as if he was not there at all. Soon it was being said in the tents and bars that the big black Welshman would not be staying in the valley. They all agreed. They had seen others like him and none had stayed long.

Walrus had already sent his empty wagons ahead early that morning. The descent from the peaks had taken only a few hours but the return climb would take most of the day. So it was mid-afternoon when he led his horse out of the stables and prepared to follow, expecting to catch up with them by early evening.

Tongogara and Jacob had said their sad farewells. Jacob had made a corn dolly for Mary to hang from Tom's cot and a larger one with a pretty dress and cap made of coloured grass for Jollie. Tongogara had searched since dawn for William but he had hidden away, refusing to say goodbye, even though Walrus promised they would all return to the valley come what may before the middle of winter. William had hidden high up in the boughs of the church tree. He watched the wagons roll along the High Street and saw Tongo sitting up on the driver's box waving to him, knowing he was hidden there and knowing why.

Mary had cooked Walrus half a dozen special loaves stuffed with chicken meat, herbs and onions, which she said would last him a week if he rationed himself sensibly and the old man smiled as he tucked them into his saddlebag. For a week she had pleaded with him to stay, to settle with them in the valley and make his living plying his wagons to Lydenburg and around. She argued that there was already enough trade in timber and supplies and as the camp and village grew so would his share in the trade it brought. But the old man said nothing and Jacob and Tongo shook their heads as they listened. How many times in the past years had Walrus told them it was time he settled down! How often had he said he would sell his wagons and spans of oxen and set up a trading store along one of the trekking roads? But they were a little encouraged. This time their master had stayed longer, delaying his turnabout for the coast, and there had been moments when they thought they might finally have seen the last of the Delagoa Road.

Walrus had almost changed his mind. The country was opening up now, he had always known it would, and the trekroads were getting busier all the time. No doubt he would make a living. But only if he survived! And that was the rub! The kaffir chiefs were sending more and more of their warriors out to wash their spears in white men's blood, determined to stop the white farmers and their cattle spreading any deeper into their tribal lands. Chief Sekekune was doing it now, tomorrow it might be Sechele, or Gatsisiwe, Montisiwe or Mankoroane. Perhaps even the Zulus. And that's what kept him on the move, because if he put down four wooden walls out in the veld and lived within them, maybe he would end his days the way old man Hart did, with a bullet in his neck and a spear through his chest.

But now he had another choice. To settle here with people

he knew, with a family he was more and more fond of every day. And here he would be safe. He would think hard about it on this trip. Maybe this one would be his last.

He kicked a stone and sent it hurtling into the side of the Royal Hotel. It rebounded into one of Honest Jack's many dogs and sent it howling away. Mary was waiting for him by the halter rail.

'Mrs Mary,' he said, 'I would have stayed longer. That was my intention. But Major John tells me he's heard some more of Sekekune's mischief and it wouldn't be wise to wait longer. It's best I push along the road before he moves too many of his black devils east.'

'William won't forgive you for taking Tongo,' she said.

'I know, I know, but it wasn't my doing. You tell young Will that from me. Tongo could have stayed, I said he could, but you see, he reckons I saved his life and now he owes me one. That's what they believe and Tongo wouldn't dare upset his spirits by leaving me until he's paid me back. But we'll soon be here again, Mrs Mary, you tell Will that. And tell him next time maybe we'll stay for good and do some trading with the Boers and make a decent penny or two out of them!'

She waited as he tightened the girth and slotted his rifle into the leather saddle-holster. The sun was already midway down the sky and in three hours it would be dark. He slapped the horse's flanks and he jumped. He was heavy with so much of the valley's lush grass and stamped the ground with his forelegs. He knew the climb up the ridge well enough and was anxious to have it done before the long shadows tricked his eyes and slowed him down.

Mary stepped closer to Walrus and held his arm. 'Before you go,' she said, 'will you tell me about Honest Jack's wife?'

He cocked his head. 'You been saving this up?'

'Yes. I'd been hoping he would tell me on his own but I don't think he will.'

'No, Mrs Mary, I somehow think you're right, not that it matters. You'd have heard it soon enough. It's no secret.'

'Is she dead?'

'Not exactly! Why should she be dead?'

'Because he's wearing his wedding ring on the wrong hand.'

'And what's the wrong hand?'

'This one.' She held out her right hand and showed him her own band of gold. 'It means you're a widow or widower.'

'Well, that's not what it means at all, at least, not with Honest Jack. Truth is, she's alive but she's as good as dead to him. I mean, although she's living he don't ever expect to see her again.'

'Has she run away?'

'Oh no! She wouldn't've done that.'

Mary waited as he turned his mare and together they walked to a pile of logs neatly stacked at the end of the halter rail beyond the hotel verandah. Walrus lapped the reins around it and they sat down. She held his big hands in her lap. 'What did she do, then?'

He looked over her shoulder towards the lowveld. 'Honest Jack's wife,' he said, 'is a prisoner, and by her own flesh and blood, locked away down there in Lydenburg. Sad, all of it, from start to finish. We knew it would end the way it did, all of us except him. It's two years now but it'll kill him in the end. They almost killed him themselves the time he went to get her. I know I've said it before but God didn't mean us to mix.'

Mary stopped him. 'Tell me from the beginning, Walrus.'

He nodded. He took his hands away and lit his pipe. The sun played on the lone red hairs in his grey beard like the gold seams themselves. She had a sudden feeling of panic as she watched him, something telling her to concentrate on the face, to make all of it indelible; the long nose and the long drooping moustache that curled in and out of the beard as if it had been stitched in place by a careful weaver, the sag of his lower lip with the weight of his pipe, his bright grey eyes. Suddenly she wanted to say, 'Let's not talk of Honest Jack's wife. Let's talk of your journey and how soon you'll be back,' but he began.

'Two years this winter it'll be. He was coming up here the long way from Durban through Natal edging on Zululand. Didn't trust himself with me along the Delagoa. He'd heard about the Sekekune and the Swazis were bickering and fussing then, too.

'But along by the Buffalo River he went down with the fever, or a snakebite, nobody knew what, but he was close to dying. Some Boers found him and carried him in their wagon and looked after him, at least the youngest daughter did. And it was because of her that he lived, because once he started shouting out in his dreams in English they might just as easily have dumped him over the side again.

'Anyhow, she wouldn't let them and she nursed him back again and all the time he told her his stories, about what he'd done, about the Cape and Kimberley and about the goldfield he was going to. He was a handsome man then, Mrs Mary. You can't believe how quickly a man can go down. You'd never have recognized him two years back. He was a lively boy and it wasn't unknown for the ladies to love him for it. Anyhow, with the fortnight out, that's the time it took them to reach Lydenburg, she loved him too, which ain't surprising because the Boers aren't the liveliest folks and I don't suppose there's one among them could have talked the way Jack did then. Believe me, if you overheard a couple of young Boers courting, for certain they'd be holding hands and swapping the prices of kettles and fowls!

'Well, we thought he was holding her on a piece of string so you could have swept us down with a feather when Jack said he was going to marry her. I never did see her, but those who did said she was pretty. Very Dutch, mind you, but pretty.

'Not that Jack ever got near enough to her folks to ask permission. They'd have taken his head off with both barrels, had he tried. So one night he waited just outside the town and they ran off together. But the poor things scarpered the wrong way, going south deeper and deeper into the Transvaal, right into the heart of Boerland when they should have headed south-east for the English in Natal. They were married by an unsuspecting trekpriest and maybe for a few days they were happy. But then the girl's brothers, cousins and uncles caught up with them and boxed them in near Heidelberg and they didn't delay. They tied Jack to a tree, stripped his pretty little wife naked and whipped her in front of him. Not to punish her, mind you, but him. That's how the Boers are. That was his punishment for meddling with them and taking what wasn't his to take. They're hard people, Mrs Mary, very hard. If they think you've done them a wrong there's nothing they won't do back. And if they think God's not with them they'll turn their back on Him until it's all over and then open their Bibles again as if nothing had ever happened.

'That's probably what those folks did. Whipped their youngest girl till she bled, left Jack to the hyenas and then went home and prayed for charity and a good harvest!

'Anyway, they took her back to Lydenburg and Jack came up here, wondering what next he could do, trying to work out how he could get her away. He waited till well past winter. Then he heard she'd had his babies, twins they were, daughters, and he couldn't wait no more. He took two horses and two guns and reckoned he could take all of Lydenburg too, which damn me, he very nearly did! He had them firing at him for half a day until his guns were empty and then they took him. He hoped they would hang him 'cos that's what he wanted. But the Boers are cleverer than that. They took him to see his wife and his little baby girls, just to make the pain worse. Then they shot him through the knee so's he wouldn't never stand up against them again. I suppose they reckoned that to kill him would have been to sin, but by doing what they did, they'd stay on the right side of God!

'Two years now and Honest Jack's not seen them since. Something must have changed down there though, because just last time I was here, they'd let her send letters and parcels. I thought that would have made him better but it hasn't. He's much worse now, dirtier, drunker, which makes me wonder if it wasn't the Boers' own way of stretching him further on the rack: letters from a wife you can't see telling of two little girls you'll never hold. He gets seven on the Saturday post and you won't see him all Sunday. And on Monday he looks as if he has no inside.'

Walrus paused and wiped his lips with the back of his hand. Then he said, 'It's a strange thing too, the Boers calling the place Lydenburg. In their language, it means "the Hill of Pain".'

Mary did not speak. Tears filled her eyes and Walrus gently patted her shoulder and stood for a while in silence.

Then he leant down and kissed the top of her head and whispered, 'Now don't you worry, Mrs Mary. You be a good girl and I'll be back soon enough. Then we'll have some more of those special times, you and me and the boys. You'll see!'

He mounted his horse and trotted slowly off towards the lower pastures and when she looked up he was already cantering and lost in the avenue of wild figs.

There was no bank. A digger's vault was his jam jar and a pennyweight of gold dust was enough to provide him with rations for a week, though prices were rising and men grumbled at paying half a crown for a saucerful of shelled peas or five shillings for a pound of beef dripping. Even a kitten, bought at one of the lowveld farms, might now cost a man ten shillings.

The owner of the store was a Mr Phelan. No one knew his Christian name though many had asked, and it was his store that served as the bank. Men weighed their gold on the counter and Phelan gave them his 'goodfurs' in exchange, credit notes to the value of the gold dust on his scales. First Mr Phelan would blow the gold; it was his right, to take off any dirt that might make up the weight unfairly. There were many diggers though who reckoned he blew too vigorously and that one day he would put his mud floor through a sluicebox to recover the gold he had deliberately blown there for his retirement!

Phelan's store was tiny. It measured fifteen feet by eight with the walls made of mud and stone and a roof of packing-case lids. The door was made from the lids of two boxes nailed together, hinged with sisal. Phelan hung a square of sacking across the window to keep out the prying faces and the complaining obscenities of diggers kept too long queueing in the sun or rain. Four poles rammed into the mud floor with more packing-case lids nailed to them was Mr Phelan's counter and a row of upturned boxes served as his shelves. A large hogshead of Cape brandy took up much of the room, and sacks of potatoes and oranges occupied the rest of the floor space. Second-hand saddles hung from the roof timbers and shovels, picks and tin basins were pegged to the walls.

Behind him, on Mr Phelan's side of the counter and out of bounds to everyone else, he had pinned up pictures from *Punch*, the *Graphic* and the *Illustrated London News*. There was Florence Nightingale and a lithograph of the Queen and Prince Albert. Below them he paraded what he called his shelf of 'specials'. At the start of business every morning, and with the care of a Bond Street milliner, he arranged a brass egg-timer, a box of coloured candles, a bottle of Worcester sauce, a tin of condensed milk, a pound pot of Dundee marmalade, two small tins of Colman's mustard, a jar of Macassar and a box of Keating's Best Persian Insect Powder. Together they represented his 'valued stock' and he was so fond of them it seemed he did his best not to sell them.

Mr Phelan's most prized possession was his scales. They were brass and so delicately made with their filigree balances and fine chains that gold dust, enough hardly to cover the top of a pin, would send them cavorting about in his hand. He polished them so often, the gold lying in their pan looked quite shabby.

Mr Phelan did not speak much in business or much about it. He was a very quiet man who looked after his words the way he did his shelf of specials, as if he valued every one before he spoke it, like a pennyweight of gold dust, not to be squandered. But the habit did not make him unpopular. He spoke when he had to and never refused a reply.

Behind his store was a thatched lean-to and there lived Mr Phelan's wife. She was a Hottentot from the Cape of Good Hope, tall and heavy-limbed but with fine sturdy breasts and a small round firm bottom, which was unusual among the African women. Although Mr Phelan slept on a camp bed under his counter, he ate his meals with his wife by her stove and it was generally assumed that in return for cooking and washing she was sometimes allowed to join him under the counter.

He did not go to church but he was very strict to observe British public holidays, including Saint Patrick's Day. On these occasions he would close the store at twelve o'clock, loosen his tie, undo the buttons of his waistcoat and walk the hundred yards to the bar of the Royal Hotel, followed by his wife. She was not allowed in; Honest Jack was very rigid about such things. But every time Mr Phelan bought himself a brandy he bought a beer for his wife too and took it out to her on the steps. Drink for drink they went at it and come dusk, Mr Phelan would nod his goodnight to Honest Jack and walk unhindered and a little unsteadily back to his bed under the counter, with his wife doing her best to follow some distance behind.

At the back of Phelan's store and within sniffing distance of his kitchen was the jail, the only one between the Portuguese border and Lydenburg. It was flimsily made of wattle and daub and the walls so thin a child might easily push a finger through. Because of this and a disinclination to spend time or money building a stronger one, Major John, who was magistrate every Monday and Thursday morning, continued a practice first introduced by his predecessor, Major Macdonald. He had been so afraid that prisoners might break out and thereby commit a further offence, he ruled that white prisoners should be released between the hours of sunrise and sunset to work their claims just as long as they returned to sleep in the prison at night. It was a popular penal innovation and never disobeyed.

'And what of the black prisoners?' asked Mary as Major John opened the wickerwork door of the jailhouse, explaining the rule to her. 'Are they allowed out during the day too?'

'No,' he said, 'that's a little different. With the kaffirs it has to be.' He took her by the arm. 'Come, I'll show you.'

He led her along a path which wound uphill for about a hundred yards until they came to a clearing where the grass and bush had been burnt away in a circle. The ground was thick with charcoal and clouds of black dust rose as they crossed it.

In the centre were two sets of wooden stocks and in them sat two blacks, one young, one older, with their wrists and ankles held in the wooden clamps. Behind them was a tall mufuti tree, its trunk shaved bare and a thick plaited sisal rope hanging from it. The blacks did not look up but together chanted: '*Mohamba t'chenga – nkose – Mohamba t'chenga.*'

'What are they saying?' Mary asked.

'They have their own name for me. It means "He Who Laughs As He Walks".'

'And what have they done for this?' she asked.

'Very little, or they wouldn't be here.'

'Very little?'

'Yes, Mary. Samson, the older one, stole a dozen chickens and he'll sit here a day for every bird. Nyoka is more of a problem. He's a wild boy – tried to set his mother's hut on fire. I had him thrashed last week and he'll sit here for at least another to reflect on it. He's a bad one. His name means snake. They named the baby well!'

'What's the rope for?' she asked.

'We don't put women in the stocks.'

'I think it's uncivilized,' she said angrily.

'They're uncivilized people.'

'You won't improve them this way.'

'Would you rather I gave them back to their own people? Do you know what they'd do to them if I did?'

Mary did not answer but Major John would not let her be angry about Africa so soon.

'Samson,' he said, 'would lose his fingers once they had decided which hand led the other in the theft. They'd simply chop them off. He might bleed to death, he might not. He might catch a poison in his hand and end up losing his arm too. And Nyoka's punishment? I'll not describe it, but the kaffirs, like us, are not pleased with a son who tries to kill his mother, and they'd make damned sure he never had sons of his own. Mary, this is Africa! Do you understand? Don't weep for these fellows. They're pretty thankful to be punished by the white man's laws and not their own, believe me!'

She came back to him and held his hand lightly. Then she said: 'Can I bring a piece of sacking for them to sit on?'

'No!' he said.

'Was that part of your punishment too? No sacking?'

'No.'

She squeezed his hand, then let it go. 'Well, unless the good magistrate has fierce objections, I'll put some sacking under their bottoms this afternoon.'

She turned and he hurried after her. The young Nyoka spat between his knees and watched the phlegm sink into the charcoal dust. But the older man, Samson, nodded his greying head and began humming.

'Kaffir hens are not made to God's design. They are creatures of Satan, made purposely to torture us. Their presence on earth cannot be explained any other way.'

The Reverend Makepeace was fond of using the dinner-table as a pulpit and the chicken leg in his hand had suddenly prompted a dissertation about the African and his problems, including his chickens.

'I've seen kaffirs hang chickens by their legs from a stick

over their shoulders with their necks screwed round so their beaks pecked their tails and carried that way for days on end without water. But their energy is terrifying. Within an hour of being freed they're screeching and kicking and pecking, turning over the same sod of earth with the same silly kick a hundred times, convinced there is a single seed hidden inside. I've always found it extraordinary that anything God created could be so furiously and uselessly busy.'

It always seemed to the Reverend that the dinner-table was a far more natural place to sermonize than a dark and lonely church where gossip was forbidden and pleasant nonsense denied. Churches, he thought, were like giant grey courtrooms, where confessions were enticed from sinners and punishments hinted at. If only God could be brought to dinner, how much easier His job would be!

But tonight the talk was not of the church but of the unbelievers, the kaffirs, and all because the Reverend had heard of Mary's act of charity for the two in the stocks. 'Sackcloth and ashes,' he joked and then laughed so much, he spilt chicken gravy all down his shirt front.

Mary and the Reverend sat together facing Major John in his tiny room on the uphill side of the Royal Hotel, eating the supper sent from Honest Jack's kitchen. For the occasion he had opened a bottle of Cape sherry. The room was warm and the candles and the sherry made the Reverend's eyes sparkle.

'You mustn't die of remorse, Mary, for two kaffirs kept safe in our great wooden locks. As Major John must have told you, they're lucky to be in one piece, let alone alive. If it had been me sentencing them I'd have given them solitary and a spare diet, the two things a kaffir dreads most: lack of conversation and any interference with his belly.

'Mind you, and if you'll let me be solemn for an instant, the thing to remember about the kaffirs, Mary, is not to believe the white man's account of them. I've met plenty of these so-called savages who are as well educated as their Boer masters and sometimes considerably more cultured and quite as much entitled to our respect. There's some appalling rubbish spoken of them, about their laziness and their inability to recognize the nobility of toil.

'The poor African, my dear, is denounced in every white man's bar from Cairo to Cape Town and his faults are prayed over at every church, chapel and synagogue in between. Legislation is passed to protect him and taxes devised to prove to him the necessity of making money.

'But it's all wasted, every breath and penny of it. An African will remain thus, long after we've left his country, and whatever we give him now, whatever we leave behind, he'll discard and give it all back to the bush. Africa will remain Africa and its peoples will not be so easily changed by a short visit from us. The poor savage may be black and crude and evil-smelling but nonetheless he is painfully human and because he is a creature with dignity he will not be moulded like clay in our image.' Then he nodded and said briskly, 'End of sermon. Pass me some biscuits, please.'

'I've been watching them,' said Mary. 'I went with Jollie to their village. Their wives are tidy and well kept and their babies are plump and cuddly. I saw them hug their children just as I do mine and they're respectful to their elders, which is not always the same with our young, is it? I can't see it's their fault God chose us first.'

'If such a thing He did,' laughed the Reverend. 'And anyway, it's not too late for Him to change His mind.' He sipped his sherry and winked at Mary over the rim.

Major John spoke. 'What else did you see there, Mary?'

'Oh, very little else,' she said. 'It was peaceful. They hardly seemed to notice us. What might I have seen?'

The Reverend interrupted. 'John's worried. There's a mood about, and a troublesome one. Chief Sekekune's behind it, of course, though there's talk the Zulus have put him up to it, to test the water as it were.'

'Test the water?' asked Mary.

The Reverend nodded. 'Yes, they're prodding us, like a stick in the ribs, to see how soft we are, to see how far they can push us before we kick back. The English and the Boers are taking too much of their land, you see, barging through without even the niceties of negotiation or payment, a very un-English thing to do. But there are some very hungry people around, Mary, very hungry indeed, and in too much of a hurry to bother to do things properly. The kaffir chiefs won't have it, especially the Zulus. And we must be careful, very careful indeed not to upset the Zulus.'

He looked across at the major. 'It worries me, what is going on, John, between the Zulus and the Boers and the Boers and us.'

'I'm sure that the Prime Minister, Disraeli, will do the right thing,' the major replied.

'Rubbish! British prime ministers are seldom fond of doing the right thing at the right time, especially if it passes the notice of Parliament.'

'Surely there are enough good men out here in the Colonial Service to keep their masters back home well enough informed.'

'John, you are a dangerous optimist. The politicians in London know desperately little of the vast foreign lands they govern. And the upper classes who pay them, while intensely proud of the Empire and well aware of its commercial advantages to them, are nevertheless scornful of the lower classes who found, fought and hold it for them. Sooner or later there's going to be a war, in or out of the Transvaal, and God help any man who finds himself in it.' He took Mary's hand. 'Promise me, Mary,' he said, 'promise me you'll not let your sons join the army.'

But Major John thumped the table. 'The Reverend's a prophet of doom,' he said, 'and I'll not have you preaching this way.' Then he leant back in his chair, his face in shadow. 'But next time you want to gawk at the kaffir families, Mary, let me know and I'll send someone with you. The Reverend is right in one thing. There is a lot of mischief around and you mustn't be reckless.'

'You think the Sekekune are in the village?'

'No, but their *inyanga* might be.'

'*Inyanga?*'

'War doctors, witch doctors, call them what you like! If Chief Sekekune is hoping to make trouble he'll be moving his *inyangas* across the country, village to village, whether they're his people or not, terrifying them, dancing on fire in their leopard skins and masks, urging the terrified fools to kill.'

The Reverend poured out more of the major's sherry. 'It's quite extraordinary, Mary,' he said, 'how they force their will on the poor savages simply by fear. You see, they believe in the Supreme Being just as we do, but unlike us they have absolutely no confidence in Him. They simply don't believe He can protect them from all the evil things around them. Evil to them is the most powerful force in this world and the next. From babyhood they have listened to stories that frighten them. When I was a child, Mary, my mother read me the tale of Shockheaded Peter and the Long-Legged Scissor Man who cut off little boys' thumbs when they were naughty. Very clearly horror indeed, but the Africans do the same with their children too. There is a custom common among many tribes here called *ingqithi* or the short finger. If a child, boy or girl, continues to wet its bed after it's six or seven, the mother threatens it with the same scissor man, the *ingqithi*, except that here if the terror fails, they do cut off the little child's finger. From the moment the child can listen, he has heard of ghosts and the will-o'-the-wisps that haunt the woods and the half-man half-serpent *Thikoleshe* that lives in the rivers and they know of the wizards that come howling out of the night riding on baboons bringing disease and death. And the kaffirs believe all these evil things can only be defeated, not by Good, as you or I believe, but by even greater evil. And its agent on earth is the witch doctor, the *inyanga*, who, with his medicine, his *umtagati*, is the only one who can save them.

'People laugh at their powers but I've known white people go to the witch doctor to help them have children or stop their having so many. Diggers pay them to tell where the greatest amount of gold is hidden and even the Boer farmers pay for advice on when it's going to rain. I remember one farmer who had horses and cattle stolen some while back and paid good money to the witch doctor to have a smelling-out feast. The frightful creature squatted in the middle of a circle of village men and rattled the bones from a newborn goat in a calabash and threw them across the ground like dice. Then he jumped and screamed, waiting to point the finger at the culprit. But these *inyangas* are clever fellows and they do a little bit of smelling-out beforehand, and this one found out who was the most unpopular man in the village. Then he pointed the finger at him and they beat him to death. Of course he was not the one who stole the animals but the fellow who did was so terrified, they were back in their pens long before the farmer returned home.'

He sipped more of his sherry. Then he said, 'Don't worry, Mary. John's being a little over-anxious about you. You're safe enough during the day. The *inyangas* are like the scorpion and the bat, they don't like daylight. But if you ever see a big fire there at night you stay here, because that's a sure enough sign the *inyanga*'s arrived and is up to his evil mischief.'

'Fire or no fire, I reckon she's . . .' But Major John did not finish his sentence. Honest Jack came into the room breathless, sat down heavily by him and handed him a piece of paper.

'A rider's just come up from Lydenburg,' he said between gasps. 'There's been shooting on the Middleburg road . . . Sekekune stopped the stage . . . killed four passengers . . . then went on to a farm . . . set fire to it . . . ten or more in the same family . . . all Boers . . . all dead. Runner said there were some papers on the stage for you . . .'

But the major had already finished reading the neatly hand-written letter from a Boer who had not signed his name, telling him the four dead were English government officers from Durban. Major John had been expecting them. They were carrying government papers dealing with British security and

British intentions in the event of hostilities with the Sekekune, the Zulus or the Boers themselves.

Major John left for Lydenburg an hour later. He did not return until the end of January.

Mary kept her promise to the major and did not venture to the village again though she did climb Broken Hill to watch it from a distance and follow the movement of people in and out of the high stock fence that surrounded the ring of mud huts. Whatever Major John and the Reverend had said, she could not believe they could ever be a threat. When the wind was right she could hear them talking to each other and the delightful yelps and laughter of their children. She watched the women work, digging and planting their corn in the soft earth beneath the rockface, with their sleeping babies tied in a bundle on their backs. She watched others walk from the springs carrying tall pitchers of water on their heads, gliding gracefully through the tall grass, as straight as ramrods; and the younger women further downhill in the bigger pools slapping their wet laundry against the boulders with such a rhythm, it was like listening to the small steam engines in Penrhyn's quarry. Mary watched and wondered how they could ever be sinister. How could she ever be frightened of them, whether they burned their fires brightly at night or not?

That evening as she returned to the valley she saw her first baboons, a family of them jumping and screeching in the wide spread of an acacia tree. Two sat perfectly still on the very top branches, ignoring the pandemonium below, copper statues facing the sunset.

Mary began to build her house. She had arranged the routine. Ianto and Huw spent their mornings working their claim, and after a lunch of tea and bread and dripping they came up from the river to work the afternoons, lifting and cutting timbers for the house frame. It was coming into shape on the strip of land Mary had bought off Honest Jack for thirty-five shillings, a little over two acres, standing in its own valley, walled in by the grassy slopes of the ridge. Spring water ran out of a crack of black rock at the eastern end, turned into a stream, which just below the site of the house formed a pool and ran on down the creek into the river.

Mary placed the cornerstones of the house so that her front porch would look down her valley and she would see, on hot summer afternoons, the river splashing below and the green, stretching to the horizon like a limitless lawn. She was fascinated with the trees around her and scattered across the slopes in such a perfect way they looked as if they were part of a rich man's estate. And they had the most delightful names which perfectly fitted their shape and colour.

There was the cabbage tree, and the livelong, the rubber tree and wisteria, the monkey bread and the giant candelabra tree, its green and flaking spirals rising thirty feet high. Below were clusters of wild figs and marula plums, and one nicknamed the hissing tree though nobody knew why.

While the men hammered away at the timbers, William, Jollie and Mary with baby Tom tied to her back, the African way, gathered long grass for thatch. In their wanderings they found brilliantly coloured white arum, yellow iris, red montbretia, wild peach and shot apples. They dug them up carefully with plenty of earth about their roots and kept them in the shade well watered until the house was ready for Mary to plan her garden.

It was to be a very special garden. She dreamt of having flowers from all parts of the Transvaal and from Natal and the Cape. Walrus had promised to bring her seeds and cuttings from the jacaranda and tulip trees of Durban and Major John said he would sneak some shoots off a climbing bougainvillaea he had seen on a Boer's house in Lydenburg. He promised her loquarts, and the giant white and yellow African daisies, primulas, flowering quince, and the little blobs of purple that he called bachelor's button, and poppies of red, yellow, mauve, some of all colours.

Special too because it would be her first garden. In Bethesda there were only back yards and if the earth had ever been fertile the slate dust had long killed it. The only flowers she could remember there were made of wax and stood sterile and soulless in a black marble vase by the chapel door. How she had yearned for colour in that black Welsh valley; for forests to spring up in the quarry yards, for the slag heaps to sprout grass, for daffodils to grow and cover the slurry; for nature to take Bethesda back and make it clean and green again!

In his searchings William found a row of slender, two-feet-high saplings with thin, heavily ribbed leaves like a willow and one of the diggers said they were bluegum trees and the seeds had been scattered by an Australian two years back. He had called them eucalyptus. Again Mary carefully dug them up and on Honest Jack's warning of the winter's winds, she planted them in a line for shelter, interspersed with a dozen more young saplings nobody could identify but which had leaves like a sycamore.

The four walls were up in the first week and by the end of the second there were four rooms inside, though there were no doors, simply sacking curtains hung from hooks in the lintel. The rooms were bare, the floors rough and full of splinters, the wood oozed sap and insects spilled out of holes and scurried to dark corners. There were window openings but no panes, so Jollie patiently unwound a cotton apron and then rewove it loosely into squares to hang across the openings to let the air and light in and keep the unwanted night insects out. The doors front and back were in line with each other, as too were the window openings on either side to provide the draught on hot days. Honest Jack lent them candle-holders and Mr Phelan, to everyone's surprise, walked from his store with a gift of the pack of coloured candles off his specials shelf. Even Mr Hamilton, the seldom seen surgeon, barber and tentmaker who lived behind the hotel and whom few ever saw out in daylight, sent the cured and beaten hide of a cow as a rug for the floor. By the end of the third week there was a porch and the beginnings of a verandah.

Every evening now Huw made furniture. It was plain, heavy and simply joined and yet his high-back chairs, the tallboy and cupboard filled the house and made it look almost elegant. Soon, he promised, he would design his own bow-lathe and turn spindles and Mary, he promised, would have her own rocking-chair before her next birthday.

She saw him enormously contented, happy to partition his day on the claim, the house, his furniture and his Bible, dividing his time and energy to them all equally and with the same devotion. He never spoke of Wales or of Owen, except to chide Mary for forgetting to wind up the silver watch that hung on its chain by the chimney breast. More and more now he spoke of the church, and of the work he had to do among the Africans.

William had retreated into a shell the day Tongogara left but the mood did not last long. Soon he came bouncing out again and on the second Saturday afternoon and without Mary's permission, he borrowed Honest Jack's brown and white mare Biffel and entered the races.

Under Walrus' firm hand he had very soon become a clever rider and he ran Biffel so hard in the first two races that he became the betting man's favourite for the rest of the day, some staking an ounce of gold that he would be first to the top of Browns Hill and another ounce he would be the first back to the Royal Hotel. He might well have made Biffel's owner a little wealthier that day but Honest Jack took the halter and led Biffel, sweating and in a white lather, safely away to the stables for the night.

Saturday was a day of many men's mixtures and moods. Some continued to work their claims until dark, men who would not, nor could not, put down their picks and shovels on any day except Sunday, and who considered others to be quite mad to race horses or play football when they could be at their sluiceboxes.

The English and the Welsh were the footballers. They used an indiarubber tennis ball covered in tightly sewn chamois leather. Sometimes there were only five a side but more often twenty-five.

No one cared to be referee since the last man who ventured it, a small Italian, was marched backwards off the field, stripped and thrown into the river following two unpopular decisions. So games were played without stoppages, whatever the fouls, whatever the injuries. Nor did the pitch have boundary lines and often the ball was chased halfway up the Ridge and the teams would send to Honest Jack's for beer while they waited for the ball to be dribbled back down again.

There were thirteen Welsh diggers in the valley plus a man called Jones who had lived in Gloucestershire and who, because of his name and the nearness of his home to the border, considered himself more Welsh than English, and played on their side in football and was a powerful tenor whenever they sang 'The Ash Grove'.

The Welsh kept much to themselves. They got drunk together and sang their songs together though not all of them in Welsh. One by one, and never together, they came to see Mary and talk about the old times, about other valleys and the families they had left behind. All spoke with what the Welsh call *hiraeth*, a longing, yet none said they ever intended to return. They would continue to dig here, they said, and if the gold didn't show itself they would move on and begin again somewhere else, but in Africa, always in Africa. They had brought some part of Wales with them, they knew that, and had left something of themselves behind. But there was never any going home again to join the two together. Mary nodded because that was how she felt too. She spoke in Welsh to the men from the North and in English to those from the South. But she said the same thing in both languages. This was home now and that was the end of it!

Every Saturday evening before the men went indoors to the bars, not to emerge again until Sunday was already a few hours old, some had their fun with the African women who came down from the village to cook corn cobs over bowls of hot ashes to sell two for a penny. At the lower end of the hotel's verandah was a large hooped waterbutt never less than half full, and once the women had sold their last corn the diggers threw pennies into it. The women scrambled for them, struggling to reach the bottom, exposing their large bare rumps which were then soundly whacked. They squealed but would not shift until they finally came up grinning with the pennies between their shining white teeth, well pleased with the evening's takings.

Then the men dangled their legs over the verandah's edge, their mouths full of corn and beer, waiting for the final Saturday ceremony, the arrival of the postboys. Two young Africans ran the thirty miles from Lydenburg together with the post bags strapped to their backs, one carrying a rifle, the other a long African spear. They left the Square in Lydenburg punctually at midday and six hours later they could be seen kicking the last of the lowveld dust on the slopes of the escarpment to begin their final jog up Pilgrims Hill. Once they were sighted, Honest Jack blew his bugle and men ambled up to the High Street from their work or tents to bet on which of the two boys would race past the hotel first, rifle or spear, spear or rifle. There was nothing the diggers would not bet on: how far a man could spit, or urinate; whether, as they watched a hawk in flight, it would swoop left or right, or whether a spun coin would show the face of the Queen three times in a row. Sometimes when the betting on the postboys was fierce there was a suspicion that one or both had been nobbled. It was more of a suspicion and nothing was ever proved, but with so much digger's gold at stake, sometimes 'Rifle' and sometimes 'Spear', after thirty miles of effortless running, would develop a strained ankle or a stomach pain a mile from Honest Jack's porch!

* * *

Major John came back at the end of January very excited and with a two-wheeled trap in tow containing two presents for Mary. One was a diary, the other was in many parts and very large, and carried with much huffing and puffing by Honest Jack's servants up to Mary's house. There, with great ceremony and a speech of explanation he tore open the brown tar wrapping-paper, and exposed sheets of wavy sheet metal six feet long by three wide. This, he said, was called corrugated iron and it was roofing every Englishman's house from the Cape to Natal. It was strong enough to carry a man's weight, never rusted and would be the crown on Mary's new home.

Immediately Huw and William, helped by Honest Jack's boys, tore off the beginnings of the thatched roof and by sunset all but a few sheets had been firmly hammered into place. That night, for the first time since they had begun to sleep within the walls of the house, they went to bed and shut out the stars.

But the major's excitement had little to do with roofs. It was about gold and the wealth that lay just beneath the ground in Pilgrims Rest. The day after he had buried the four Englishmen in Lydenburg and had recovered the dispatch case with the monogrammed crest of the British Natal Administration embossed on it, a horseman came to him with a summons from Middleburg. He was to attend an important meeting. It did not say with whom or for what, but the letter was sealed with the stamp of the Volksraad, the Boers' Parliament. Two days later he was escorted into the middlerooms and waiting for him was Johannes Burgers, the newly elected President of the young South African Republic. With him was a small bespectacled man dressed entirely in black, and grey canvas spats, who was introduced as Perris, from Berne in Switzerland.

President Burgers had come to discuss gold and the diggings in Pilgrims Rest. His young republic, he explained, was close to bankruptcy. It owed the British Cape Commercial Bank upwards of sixty thousand pounds and could not repay the loan; he could not even find the money to service the interest.

The British could foreclose on the loan at any time and humiliate every Boer in the Transvaal, and that was something he would not contemplate. Now that gold was being profitably mined in the Drakensbergs, it was an unexpected source of revenue his government meant to tap. He was advised that within a year, if it were properly managed, he could repay the entire Cape Commercial loan and a year later begin investment in railways and schools.

However, the diggers were a problem, because no one knew how much gold they were mining and despite the law they still refused to declare how much they were taking out of the Transvaal and selling to the English bankers in Natal and the Cape.

Therefore he had invited Herr Perris, who worked for the Swiss State Mint, to South Africa. Perris had convinced him the republic should have its own mint so that the government might profit directly from the buying of gold and the sale of coin.

The President was so confident of Herr Perris and so impressed by Switzerland's impeccable financial traditions, that he had written, without waiting for his Parliament's approval, to the South African Consul General in London instructing him to negotiate a contract for the design of the republic's first gold coin. It would be equal in value to the British sovereign and it would have the President's face on it. Major John's task was to persuade the diggers at Pilgrims Rest to co-operate.

'And if they will not?' he asked.

If they did not, replied the President, he would be obliged to abandon the system of licences and take the goldfields for himself. 'The land,' he said, 'belongs to us, the Boers, and so it follows that what's beneath it is ours too. We will not have the British bankers in the Cape bringing our young republic to its knees. If the diggers will not agree, a law will be passed. It is as simple as that.'

He put on his black top hat and did up the buttons on his waistcoat, ready to leave.

'And I warn you, Major Carpenter,' he said, 'it will be one

of many new laws to make this gold work for us and not the immigrants. We are determined that where gold is not found in sufficient quantities to pay diggers to work it – or if men simply do not wish to make a claim on any parcel of land – we shall offer those concessions to companies. There is a lot of interest in London. A syndicate of Jews there has already made an offer.'

Major John shook his head. 'The diggers will not take easily to your demands, Mr President. They could get angry. Yes, sir, they could get quite violent.'

'Is that so?' said the President, tapping the top of his hat as the doors opened for him. 'Then let them, Major. Let them!' With that he turned and walked away, Herr Perris running at his heels.

As he returned to the camp Major John had looked at the scattering of tents and the claim pegs dotted across the slopes like a thousand crosses in a battlefield, and realized he had witnessed not only a new page of history being written, but the beginning of a new chapter. All of a sudden land had become precious. Not just for a few hundred fortune hunters and mavericks but for a young aspiring government of an infant nation. The Boers were coming to terms with what it was they owned, fields of gold, God given. And it had taken a bespectacled little Swiss money man with canvas spats to show them how to use it.

Ianto did not take well to the major's gifts, nor the way Mary received them. He resented other men's attention to her, and had done since childhood. Then his face was often red and stinging with her slaps after he had scowled at any one of Owen's friends who had stopped her in those dark and dank Bethesda streets for a chat on their way home from work.

Now, since Owen's death he had become even more jealous

and possessive and it ate into his love for her. Whenever she spoke to men, like the Welsh diggers who sought her out simply to talk of home, he saw her openness and friendliness as flirtation. So that afternoon, as he had watched her excitement at Major John's return, he felt physically sick and sat in the shadow of the trees. And when Huw and William began hauling the corrugated-iron sheets to the roof he crept deeper into the forest to shoot the singing birds.

He came back long after it was dusk. Mary had left no supper for him and she did not look up as he sat down at the empty table.

'If you want supper, Ianto, boil up the beautiful little birds you shoot for nothing.'

He hit his fist hard down on the table-top. 'You've soon forgotten who you are and where you're from. My God, I've never known a woman who was so quick out of mourning!'

Still she refused to look at him but sat there embroidering the pair of braces she meant for William. Then she said quietly, 'And how many women have you known, Ianto Llewellyn? Two I know of. One you will not talk to and one who can never answer. And if you stay the way you've been these past months you'll never know any others, not women with love and pity in them, anyway.'

'Damn your pity!' he shouted. 'From you and from her. I don't want it.'

She turned on him angrily. 'Then what is it you want, boy? Tell me. Do you want me in black till I die too? Have you stopped loving me because I left him dead and alone? Is it because I will not sit still and weep like the women did in the quarry, because their men had gone and they were nothing any more? Is that it? Say, Ianto, is it? Well, lad, you just learn a little of love, learn how to, and then you'll know that I loved my Owen well and mourned him with all my heart every day and all my nights from the moment they hid his face from me with Welsh dirt. But get this into that head of yours: he is buried in Wales and I will not mourn him forever in Africa.'

Ianto slumped in his chair. 'It's not decent,' he growled, 'this way you are. He hasn't been dead a year and already you're looking for another.'

She stood and let the braces drop to the floor. Then quickly she went to him and hit him so hard across the face it turned him in his chair. Memories of a stinging face and swelling eyes confused him but he heard her say, 'You have a black heart and may God forgive me for helping to make it so. Hate us if you will, go and find another place if you want, go back to Wales if that's where your peace is. Go and empty your hate anywhere you like, but not here, Ianto, not here because we are too happy to have you spoil it. You will not, Ianto. I won't let you. We have come too far. We've left it all behind us, all the fears and bitterness. It's buried in Wales. We are Africans now, Ianto, until we die.'

He turned to her. She saw his dark eyes glistening and the red weal of her fingers on his cheeks and then she too remembered the little boy who kicked men's shins on the drizzling pavements, the little boy with the black flannel shorts made out of his father's tired and tattered trousers. The father who was not his own.

She stepped close to him and held his bruised face against her breast. 'Oh Ianto, Ianto,' she whispered. 'You silly sad boy, always so fierce about me. I think you were even jealous of my Owen.' And then she heard herself say, 'It's not your fault, my darling, you're only half what you think you are.'

She felt him stiffen and she stroked his small black curls but they would not stay put. Quickly she said, 'You mustn't worry about your silly old mother. I've too many years in my apron pockets to think of starting all over again with a new man. And anyway, who would I find to match my Owen? Whatever you think, Ianto, I did love him in my way and I do believe that if the world was peopled by men like him we would be in paradise now. That's my opinion, anyrate!'

He kept his head against her for a while longer, feeling her warmth and softness, listening to the throb of her heart, until his sadness chased his anger away. He looked at her and she saw the question in his eyes, but she would not let him ask it. 'Now off you go to bed,' she said, 'and we'll have no more talk like this. We mustn't spread misery like muck in a farmyard.'

He smiled, the first she had seen on his round, tanned face for a year or more. He stood, kissed her forehead and walked to his room and she watched until his curtain fell. How near she had come to telling him, closer than ever before. But she had not. Perhaps it was not the time. But then there never had been a proper time and she knew there never would be.

Every night now, after she had brushed her hair and wound up the silver watch, she prayed for Ianto. It became her ritual before going to bed, urging God to do more to help him. But day on day she saw him drifting further away until she was convinced God had left them as well. It did not surprise her. She had committed sin, however long ago it was, and there had to be punishment. If it was long in coming, then that was the holy strategy.

One evening in mid-March she said to Jollie, 'We have been happy too long,' and the girl gave such a look and with such fear in her eyes that Mary stayed awake all night thinking of nothing else. The following night Jollie had the first of her silent nightmares. Mary sat up and in the dim flickering of the small nightlight candle saw her sitting upright, staring at the wall and wringing her hands as if she was washing them clean. It happened again the three nights following and on the fourth she began sleep-walking and Mary led her back to bed and held her arms to her side until she relaxed and fell into deep sleep.

Then Jollie no longer helped Mary with the house or with baking the bread, or with sewing. She would not take Ianto's and Huw's tea and dripping to them at midday, and more and more now baby Tom was crawling around Mary's legs, wet and dirty.

It happened on a Friday. At midday as Huw and Ianto came walking slowly up the hill towards the house at the finish of their work Mary saw Jollie beyond the stack of timber, asleep in its shade. Baby Tom was crawling towards her, when suddenly Mary felt alarm, something inside telling her to run and take her baby quickly. But she was confused and hesitated and then it was too late. Baby Tom fell onto Jollie's back and as she turned, Tom's face was inches from hers. She opened her mouth wide like a woman screaming in terror and pulled at the grass, desperate to get away from the child. Mary ran and picked him up and Huw then took him from her. Jollie was still now, staring at the spot where Tom had been, with her wild nightmare eyes. Mary knelt and took her hands, but Jollie would not look up.

'What is it?' Mary whispered. 'Tell me, child. Do I know already? Jollie, do I know?' Still the girl would not look and Mary leant lower to see her face. 'Jollie, do you know? Are you afraid of baby Tom because you know?' The girl closed her eyes, squeezing them tight to keep out the light, and put her hands over her ears to shut out Mary's questions.

'Tell me, Jollie. Don't be afraid. Are you big? Is it a baby?'

The girl suddenly swung herself around with such force she threw Mary over and by the time she sat up Jollie was already into the forest, her long light hair and the tassels on her blue dress streaming behind her until she was lost in the trees. They searched all afternoon but the forest hid nothing human. Major John and the Reverend organized search parties, one following the river upstream, the other to the line of trees that spread out across the slopes towards the Ridge. But at dusk they all came back shaking their heads, saying it was the hardest thing to find someone who didn't want to be found. The Reverend scolded one digger who said that by now the girl's body might already have been taken by the river.

Mary kept her secret despite the questions and Ianto's dark

accusing stares, but as soon as the diggers had gone to their tents there seemed no point in keeping it to herself and she told Major John and the Reverend in front of Ianto and Huw.

'She's carried it from Lourenço Marques,' she said, 'all this way.'

'Like something rotten inside her,' Ianto spat out the words. 'Part of him, burning her up.'

'But it's only a baby,' said Huw gently. 'And it'll be clean and fresh when it comes. And hers.'

'If she has it!' said Ianto.

'What do you mean?' asked Mary.

'I mean she's gone and she might rather kill herself than have the Portuguese bastard.'

Mary gripped the back of the chair so tight her knuckles were white. Colour dropped from her face and almost in a whisper she said to him, 'Go away, Ianto. Don't talk, don't speak, just leave me.'

The Reverend came closer and held her arm. 'Come, Mary, come with me, we'll go to the church. Someone may help us look for her. Let's go and ask.'

The single candle was alight on the centre of the altar and they knelt under its halo, side by side, in their silent prayers. For half an hour or more they stayed there, when suddenly he held her wrist, and whispered, 'Mary, look at the window. It's alight!'

She looked up and saw the narrow slit of glass glaring yellow as if somebody was waving a large candle behind it.

'There's a fire in the kaffir village,' he said. 'Listen, you can hear them!'

They stood up. He took her hand and they ran to the door, out along the outside wall to the altar window facing east towards the village. They could see the fire quite clearly, its flames rising above the tall stock fence that enclosed the mud huts, and they could hear the chanting, low and slow, like a hundred drums rolling, and in between, the screaming and trilling of the women.

'The Lord help us . . . it's the *inyanga*, Mary. The witch doctor has come!' He turned to her, the distant flames catching his eyes. 'Give us strength, Mary . . . she's there. God help her . . . she's there!'

But Mary was listening to another voice, Huw's, from the far end of the church. 'Mother,' he shouted, 'Ianto's gone. He's run off and he's taken his gun.' And she already knew he was out there towards the fire, searching for her.

He moved quickly for a man so large, so that the two African sentries did not hear even a twig snap or a leaf rustle as he passed between them. He remembered his terror the night under the wagon when the Sekekune had attacked, but now he was astonished how easy it was and how calm he felt. It was because of the gun, his gun, the gun he could use better than anyone now.

The flames lit up the sky like an orange dome. Sparks spun into the air like butterflies on fire racing out of the kraal to settle and smoulder in the bush outside. He circled to the right so that the flat shining face of black rock protected his back, and he crawled towards the fence. Carefully he eased the woven grass apart and looked in.

Squatting around the fire were a hundred or more naked men and prowling in and out of them was a hideous old man, half-crouching, sometimes pouncing, his arms shooting out like a snake's tongue, screaming at them. On his head was a baboon's skull, its eyes still in their sockets, its teeth grinning, and strung around his neck and chest were strings of cowries, tortoise shells, the teeth and claws of animals and the shrunken heads of wild cats, eyeless but with their teeth bared in the pain of death. In one hand he carried a warm stomach torn from a baby goat and in his other and wedging its neck between his middle and forefingers was a green boomslang flicking its lethal tongue and coiling its body around his shining sinewy arm. The beads and shells and skulls rattled as he screamed his curses and held the snake's head to each man in turn, its death tongue an inch from their terrified eyes. Around and around he danced, a dozen shadows leaping from the fire, writhing like someone in his death throes, hissing like a cat, howling like a dog, as red betelnut juice ran down his chin and onto his chest like blood from a broken artery. Suddenly he stopped and faced a man. The chanting stopped too and the women were silent. Only the fire crackled. Then with one last scream he threw the snake at his victim and the man fell forward onto his face, dead with fright before the venom had even entered his flesh. The others fell on him with their spears and ripped him apart.

Ianto let the grass close again and shut his eyes. Sweat ran down his temples, his hands shook, and he could feel his heart beating at his fingertips. Was that how they would kill her? With the baboon head grinning, the snake at her eyes and a hundred spears splitting open her body? She had something rotten inside her but he would not let them tear it out like a goat's belly. He would not let her go their way. She had suffered too much already and he had suffered with her all the way from the sea.

He crawled to the rock face and in the flickering light looked for a ledge high enough to see over the fence, high enough to look down onto the circle of fear. He strapped the rifle to his back and began climbing, searching with his fingers for a hole or a ridge to cling to. Inch by inch he went, hugging the rock, whispering to it, urging it to help him up, until thirty feet high he found a narrow gulley and fitted himself into it. Slowly he turned in shadow, the fire's light barely reaching the rock, and pulled the rifle over his shoulder and eased himself back into the cleft. He could see her now, tied to a single stake like a dog on a chain, lying with her head to the fire, her fair hair spread out. But then his eye caught lanterns bobbing in the darkness from the camp. Major John was coming and bringing an army of diggers.

He lifted his rifle and saw her again, between the wedge of

the ivory sight, blue and white in his aiming eye. His forefinger curled round the trigger and again he felt his heart beat against the cold metal as he pressed against it. A trickle of sweat stung his eye. He blinked and aimed again but now the *inyanga* was over her, shaking his terrible body, holding the green writhing snake high above his baboon mask.

Ianto pulled the rifle butt hard into his shoulder. He must not miss, or worse, must not wound her, for that way she would die twice over. He felt his panic rising, like that first time near the Komati River. Major John's lanterns were rounding a hill and in a minute or less they would top the brow and be seen.

The blue dress was in his sight again, brilliant in the firelight as the shadow danced about her. 'God take her quickly,' he whispered. 'The Devil fought hard for her and put something of himself inside her but God must take her back now,' and he squeezed the trigger. Even in the explosion and the flash of light at the barrel's end, even as the butt pushed deep into his shoulder, he knew he had killed the shadow instead and when he looked, the *inyanga* was standing over her, his spear raised high, the yellow light dancing on his black glistening dying body, and in that instant, as life turned to death, he was perfectly still, the beads and cowries, the tortoise shells and skulls hanging noiselessly. The only moving thing was the boomslang, a flash of green that wormed its way out of the dead hand as he fell forward onto her, his unseeing eyes towards hers, his blood turning her blue dress crimson.

Ianto reloaded as he heard the sentries cry out and saw the pandemonium around the fire with men running and women screaming and he sighted and fired again. But there was so little of her to see, so much was covered in the *inyanga*'s mess of death. Only her face showed but it was a white blur among a scattering of red and black and confusion. For the third time he reloaded and fired again but he knew it was too late. They were up and moving, the men and women screaming, as Major John and the diggers came in firing their guns into the night so that bullets bounced off the rock.

He heard the major shout: 'Come down, Ianto. Come down. She's safe!' But the diggers looked towards the black rock and saw nothing because Ianto would not be seen. Instead he watched them push the Africans into a corner, the men cowering, the women wailing and beating their breasts; he watched Major John pull the *inyanga*'s body off the girl and rip away the baboon's mask and the beads and skulls and the paraphernalia of terror and hurl them into the fire; he saw him order the villagers to look at the old man's body, to see its nakedness and the gaping wound where the bullet had torn the neck away. Then he lifted Jollie in his arms and as he walked out of the kraal the villagers groaned and the women fell to the ground and beat it with their fists as the diggers lifted the *inyanga*'s body high above them and threw it like a sack of soiled straw into the middle of the flames.

Ianto waited for the last digger to go, until the last lantern had disappeared over the hump, then dropped into the bush below. He would not follow them. He would not see the valley again. Instead he moved off through the long grass, following the natural fall of the ground. It would take him to the river and beyond that to the escarpment that dropped away to the lowveld. He would take the road to Lydenburg and there he would meet the Boers and he would talk to them about the English and he would show them his rifle.

At midnight and with the moon as bright as day he waded hip-high across the Blyde River with his boots about his neck and stood on the far bank wringing out his trousers. He breathed in the thick soft air of the Transvaal and looked back at the twinkling of the diggers' fires, just as he had seen them that first night he had looked down from the ridge. He could just make out the string of lamps along Honest Jack's verandah and behind it, in her tiny valley, his mother's house and the lantern hanging on her porch. For no reason he knew of memories came flooding back: of the games he played with

Huw and the other boys in Bethesda among the heaps of slate waste that stretched to the sky from his back door, games of hiding and seeking, or tumbling and screaming, of fighting with cannons and swords, and horses that winged from tip to tip, carrying frightened little sisters from their quarried dungeons. He remembered, but he could not think why, the army of a dozen boys who slid and rolled to their rescue, blacking themselves in dirt, and how he fought like a winner because he had always fought alone, always on his own against the others' camp.

That was how the valley looked now, the other camp where he did not belong. His mother's and his brothers' but not his. For some strange purpose he had left it and he knew it was because he was not of them. What had she said? 'You're only half what you think you are!'

He looked once more across the River of Joy and shouted his goodbye and felt almost light-hearted as he heard the breeze carry his words across. Then he turned west for the lowveld. There was no other way now.

The baby was stillborn and although Mary cried when she carried the tiny thing in its box to the graveyard, Jollie did not. Nor would she go with the Reverend into the church to see the boy child to heaven, and when Mary suggested they plant wild violets over the little mound of soft earth, Jollie shook her head and tore a handful of weeds from the ground and held them out instead.

The diggers talked of Ianto and went on talking. Why he had left without even saying goodbye to his mother and why he had been seen in Lydenburg and even further south with the Boers. Why, on that strange last night, he had fired three bullets at the *inyanga* when only one had hit him and he the expert shot that never missed. There was much talk but it was kept to the diggers' tents after the day Reverend Makepeace whipped a man with his belt until his back bled for the strange and unlikely story he told. But not even the Reverend's belt could stop the story from becoming a whispered legend.

The big silent black-haired Welshman had not stayed long; they had not expected him to. He would not be missed, but neither would he be quickly forgotten in Pilgrims Rest.

CHAPTER SIX

Throughout the following months of autumn, Mary lived with the certainty that Ianto would not come back. On bright blue crispy cold mornings she stood on her verandah and looked out towards the lowveld, searching the dark line of the Lydenburg road for a lone horseman or the spiralling dust clouds that followed a wagon. And when the sun went down early on its winter round, yellow in the pale evening sky, she stood there in the chill air, looking for the same tell-tale signs. But as the days turned to weeks and the weeks into July, her start- and end-of-day vigils became shorter. Then, at the beginning of August, a Welsh digger up from Kimberley told her of a young dark-haired giant who had spoken Welsh to him as far south as the Vaal River. She waited no more, and pushed his memory away from her, like Owen's, among the loved and gone.

Jollie blamed herself for everything that had happened, her running away and capture, Ianto trying to kill her to save her; even the baby's death in her womb. So she resurrected the memories in her mind and walked every morning and evening to tend the baby's grave and each night endured the endless silent pain as each experience was relived. She saw it as her penance.

Mary knew it was happening. So did the others. They watched but they could do nothing to help. Jollie spoke only to herself, and was deaf to their comfort and coaxings. It was ageing her. Her twisted face was filling out and her body becoming plumper and her fair hair was prematurely streaked with grey. During the day her young head outshone it but at night the glare of the oil lamps played unkind tricks, as if she was growing older so much quicker in the hours without sun. But little by little her horrors grew less familiar, and the torments died like a storm losing its rage at sea; and like the sailor who survives it, certain that nothing could ever be so terrible again.

Once she was better there was no limit to her devotion to Mary and the growing blustering Tom. She was a constant reassuring companion and a tireless nanny, and when she saw that Mary no longer opened the front door early and closed it late in her watch for Ianto, Jollie took her place, and stood those few extra moments every day, a dutiful caring sentinel, waiting for a man she knew could not come home again. Sometimes, and always in the afternoon when Tom was asleep, Mary saw her standing beyond the hotel, on a high mound of rock between it and the church, looking towards the kraal and the thin wisps of blue smoke from the cooking fires inside the stock fence that had been her prison and almost her grave. Sometimes she stood for an hour or more, ignoring Honest Jack's girl-servants who brought her water or an orange, turning back only when she heard Mary's call that Tom was awake.

Maybe the elders in the kraal had watched her too from their own lookouts, because one morning three of them came to Mary's front door pulling a pretty brown-and-white calf behind them. The old men brought Honest Jack with them to explain that the calf was a gift to Jollie from the villagers. She watched them release it but she didn't move from the porch. Instead it ran to her and she knelt and let it nuzzle its soft wet nose into her neck, and the old men went back to the village happy, carrying jars of Mary's jam.

It was a hard winter. Snow settled on the Drakensbergs and no one could ever remember it happening before. The old saw it as a bad omen. It was a light fall, deeper on the peaks above the ridge but stopping abruptly at the edge of the escarpment, where the olive green and tans of the lowveld stretched away untouched and unchanged as if there were no seasons at all. The night winds from the Lebombo Mountains in the east spun the powdered snow in icy spirals and the ground was set so hard men could not drive their picks into it and the Welsh and Scots woke in their tents and wondered whether God had turned the hemispheres around.

On the second frosty morning William was called by a digger named Big Macpherson to Folland's Corner a half mile up the creek where the enormous man worked his claim and kept something of a farm to feed his giant appetite. He had chickens and geese and wild duck with clipped wings and a cow that showed her ribs and haunches but gave him over a gallon of milk a day. Until that morning, he had a black Mashona goat suckling two newborn, but the night's frost had killed the mother and one of her babies. Big Mac was about to kill the one who survived when he remembered William.

'One was called Peter and the other Paul, but I can't remember who's dead and who's not,' Macpherson said as he lifted it to William and told him how to wean it on warm milk and sugar and how to use his little finger as a teat to dip and feed.

William tucked the tiny crying thing under his coat and turned to hurry home. But instead of following the river, anxious to keep the tiny thing warm, he took the short cut through the woods. He got as far as the hump in a clearing called Knobby Hill when he saw a family of Africans squatting on top of it by a gnarled and bare thorn tree. He called out but they didn't answer, nor did they turn, which puzzled him. The wind was bitterly cold and gusting, yet nothing moved about them. Holding the goat tight against him, he ran to them, calling.

Their blankets were pulled tight and their pots and pans were placed neatly around them in a circle. He called again but still they would not turn. Breathlessly he reached them and laid a hand on the man's shoulder, then he pulled it back as if he had touched a nettle. They were frozen to death, sitting together, father, mother and their two children, their eyes closed, their skin strangely grey, their black hair white with frost. The little ones' hands rested, one on top of the other on their father's knee as if it had been the final source of warmth. William touched them gently one by one on their stiff grey cheeks and then ran off as fast as he could, holding the baby goat hard against him, the tears streaming down his face, to tell Mary.

For an hour or more she comforted him. She wrapped the baby goat in a towel and said that now they had it as well as a calf, William should help Huw build pens to keep out the cold and the hyenas. And, she said, as they now had the beginnings of a farm they must give it a name because all farms had names. Then as William sat by the fire dipping his little finger in sweet milk, Mary went off with Major John to cover the dead family in the hay they kept for the calf, and wait for the thaw so they could bury them.

There had been no message from Walrus, autumn or winter. Major John thought the Sekekune raids on the farms and trek-roads both sides of the Drakensbergs had kept him in Lourenço Marques, and would keep him there until the Delagoa Road was safe to travel again. Then, towards the middle of the month, some Australian diggers arrived, coming the longer, safer way from Durban, and they brought with them a letter. It was neatly handwritten, not by Walrus, but they were his words:

> Mrs Mary:
> Some fool Englishman is causing trouble in Lourenço Marques and the Portuguese have put a stop to our ships dropping there. So I came down to Durban to pick up some seeds for your garden and more pilgrims too. I reckon I shall be on my way shortly, so oblige me and find a patch of grass and I will stay put this time, then we shall have those special times.
>
> Your old friend,
> Walrus

Late that afternoon the Reverend Makepeace came to the house so excited Mary thought he was drunk again. He was not. He too had received a letter and he waved it at her, pacing up and down the room, puffing and stammering as if he was about to begin his most explosive sermon ever.

Mary sat still, and watched and waited for him to stop and speak. It was a minute or more before he did.

'She's coming, Mary! Can you believe it? She's coming. All this way and not a word, not a line till now. Simply caught the boat and all on her own. Extraordinary! Quite extraordinary!'

He began his pacing again but as he passed her chair the second time she caught him and held him.

'Reverend,' she said, laughing. 'What? Where? Who's coming?' And she pulled him down beside her.

He looked at her solemnly and took a deep breath. 'My daughter Polly. She's in Durban, and sent a letter with the diggers just in. She says they've landed in Durban because the Portuguese have banned British ships anchoring in Delagoa Bay. She's with another family bound for here. She says Walrus is waiting for a second ship to arrive and then they'll come up through Natal.'

Mary let go his arm. 'Is that safe?'

'Nowhere is nowadays, but she's safely crossed two oceans so I won't worry about a few hundred miles across land with Walrus.'

'She's a brave little girl.'

'She was always brave but I wonder just how little she is now.'

'How long is it?'

'Five and a half years. And that's exactly right! Five years and six months next Friday. I've pencilled in every day on five and a half calendars.'

'You had to leave her?'

He nodded and sighed. 'Oh! Yes, I had to and in such a fashion, I couldn't take her with me. It was part of a contract I made then with my father. Polly was at school: her mother was already dead, you see, and she was only eight and I was in no right mind or health to look after her. It was the best way things could be sorted out.'

Then he brightened and waved Polly's letter at Mary again. 'But this, Mary, is God's work! He did it. For me!' He stood up and stamped his feet the way Mary had seen him do at the party on that first Christmas night. 'You see what it means, don't you?' he shouted. 'I'm forgiven. He wouldn't have done it otherwise. God's wiped the slate clean, Mary, and sent her as a blessing.'

She watched him, a great roly-poly man shaking with laughter and gratitude like someone reading his own reprieve, crossing and uncrossing his arms as he paced to the fire and back, stopping every few yards to recite a prayer in a language Mary had never heard before.

Just as suddenly he stopped and stood perfectly still with his back to her and his head bowed and she knew he was weeping. After a while he said quietly, 'I apologize, Mary, for my silly behaviour. And me perfectly sober! But you see, I have grown unused to good news over the years and this was one little bit I'd given up all hope of ever receiving.'

Without turning his face to her he went to the door. 'May I come to supper, Mary? I couldn't bear to eat alone tonight.'

'And you'll tell me all about Polly?'

'Oh, yes! Most certainly I will.'

He closed the door carefully behind him. She waited for him to drop the latch, then moved to the window and watched him walk down the sloping garden towards the High Street, quickening his pace until he was running as he passed the hotel.

Above her window the icicles hanging from the roof were dripping and the trees beyond the grass were perfectly still. The cold mountain winds had gone at last and it was beginning to thaw.

* * *

Come September, the last chill had left the mountain air and the sun stayed longer and higher in the sky. The sap was rising and the trees were tipped green and the plants carried the morning dew easily on their sturdy new shoots. Jollie's calf had filled out into a heifer, and kicked and sprinted up and down the slopes, and the fur on the head of William's baby goat had split to show the first stubs of horns and he pounded the ground, stretching his rope taut to reach the new grass. It was the end of the highveld winter and the beginning of an African spring. And Mary had called her little farm 'Tambootie', after the trees that sloped down from the mountains.

Baby Tom celebrated the new season with jaundice. It threatened Jollie's health too because when she saw him puffed and yellow in his cot, she worried everyone and ran in circles searching for medicines, pleading with her eyes for help. There were a dozen people gathered around baby Tom; all agreed on the problem but none was sure of a way to cure it. None that is, except Mr Phelan. Shortly, he came to the house carrying a small pot containing an old Hottentot medicine, his wife's remedy. Mary looked alarmed but he soothed her in his brisk Irish way, saying that his good wife's potions were sometimes a little irregular but he had never known them fail to cure.

Mary hesitated but Jollie fussed so much (with Mr Phelan saying under his breath that he'd never known anyone so dumb make so much noise!) that eventually she agreed to take his jar and give the yellow Tom a spoonful of the milky mixture once an hour for every hour of daylight: that was the Hottentot's instructions, said Mr Phelan.

They did it punctually throughout the day, Jollie cradling and Mary spooning and Owen's silver watch witness by the fireplace. Gradually Tom became noticeably less puffed and less yellow and by early evening it was obvious his fever had gone. Jollie rushed to Phelan's store with the news and minutes later the man himself appeared. Baby Tom giggled and kicked, which amused the Irishman who took a brass egg-timer from his pocket and tipped the sand one way and then the other, interrupting time to amuse the child.

'Mr Phelan,' said Mary, 'would you ask your wife what her medicine was made of?'

'I already have, ma'am,' he replied.

She waited. 'And?' she asked.

'It's something of a secret,' he said. 'You must understand that the Africans are very sensitive about their secrets, very sensitive indeed. Sometimes that's all they own and to give it away would leave them with absolutely nothing.' He looked at baby Tom, poked out his tongue, and then put the egg-timer back in his pocket.

'Thank you,' said Mary. 'I understand, Mr Phelan, and I'm grateful all the same. Please tell your wife that.'

He hesitated. 'Well, I can tell you what she calls the main ingredients, as it were. It's *n'taa* crushed in warm goat's milk. That's as much as I know and you mustn't say I told you. Goodnight, ma'am.'

'Goodnight, Mr Phelan. And I'll remember. Not a word!'

That evening as Mary sat with the Reverend at supper she asked him, 'What's *n'taa*?'

He laughed and then grimaced. 'Something you'll not want plenty of,' he said.

'Why? What is it?'

'Lice, Mary, it's kaffir for lice, a little juicier and better-fed than the ones we're used to back home, but lice all the same.'

Mary was sick on the floor and the Reverend fed her with tots of unwatered brandy until he saw the colour come to her cheeks again.

It was the middle of spring when the Boer wives came to visit.

They lived on the lowveld farms and they had known about Mary from the day she had arrived and were naturally curious, this one white woman among so many men. They became doubly curious when they heard she had a baby and that she was not English at all but Welsh. They knew nothing of Wales and no one in or around Lydenburg could be sure where it was except that it was in Britain and obeyed Westminster. But still they made no arrangements to visit her. No Boer woman who prized her dignity – and they all did – could visit a stranger who did not have a home, or at least live in somebody else's. So it was not until it was confirmed by travellers passing south that Mary had a timber-framed house with the new iron roof that they boarded their traps and whipped their ponies up the long stony staircase of Pilgrims Hill.

They agreed they would not stay long, simply view this Welshwoman and her child, drink her tea and eat her cake and hear how she accounted for herself among the evil-smelling diggers who had come to dig Boer gold.

But they were not prepared for Mary's sewing-machine! They had of course heard of them. Cousins of cousins had seen them in Cape Town and an Indian tailor was known to have two in Durban. But they had never expected to find one perched on the top of the Drakensbergs.

They came unannounced one Saturday afternoon, as the men were racing up and down Browns Hill and the Welsh were rehearsing their various anthems on the football field, eight stern women, young and old, dressed in navy blue dresses, blue bonnets, aprons and heavy crochet shawls around their shoulders and escorted by four young Boer horsemen, each with a rifle but not a smile between them.

There had never been such a visit to the valley before and many of the diggers stopped their work and ambled up the hill to the Royal Hotel to gawk and joke with the brooding young Boers who would not or could not speak English back. Honest Jack watched them too, sitting in a chair on his verandah, rubbing his knee with part of a Boer's bullet still in it, drinking gin and spitting out balls of chewed tobacco in their direction.

The women were dressed so soberly they could have been widows, but they were quick to tell Mary of their husbands and the hard work they did, the acreage they farmed, the number of cattle they owned and the number of Africans they employed. In turn Mary was asked to describe Owen, what he had done and why he had died. She did it as best she dared in front of strangers but she felt suddenly vulnerable and foreign. They mouthed their sympathy yet there was none in their eyes. They spoke English in a clipped quaint way, but Mary thought that was all she and they had in common. They tried, at the turn of every new conversation, to ally themselves with her, emphasizing her Welshness and assuming a shared dislike of the English.

But even in front of her, the stranger, they pecked at each other, changing so quickly with an unkind word or a sullen silence that they seemed to be taking all sides at once and none for long.

Mary had long forgotten the women's chapel meetings in Bethesda and she did not thank these dour Boers for reliving them again here in her own parlour.

The one thing the women had agreed among themselves before they arrived was that they would not stay long. But when they saw the sewing-machine, they made Mary show them how to turn the seam of a linen sheet in seconds when it would take them an hour, and stitch a patch on a pair of trousers almost as quickly, and they remembered their own pricked fingers red and sore in an evening's work and the thimble lost. And when they saw the fine needlework on the dress of the silent and disfigured girl called Jollie they quite forgot themselves and their waiting horsemen outside. They pedalled and practised, and competed with each other for Mary's time, offering Dutch and Cape recipes, jars of preserved fruit, vegetables and game meat if only, they said in a chorus, they might come the following Saturday with their patterns and cloth.

Mary gave them pickle and cheese, then hot bread and jam with tea and more tea but it was not until late afternoon, when she finally agreed to make dresses for them, that they let her open her front door. Then they boarded their traps in the High

Street and clip-clopped off towards the ford for the long, braking descent to their farms below. And behind them rode their silent mounted escorts and following them, the drunken whistles and jeers of the diggers on the hotel steps.

The last and youngest escort turned in his saddle to look back but quickly turned again, kicking his horse to a canter to catch up with the rest, taking home with him a picture of the village he would never forget: a mass of sprawling drunks cheering a dozen steaming horses and a row of large black bottoms spread across the edge of a water butt being loudly and soundly slapped!

That evening, in Honest Jack's private room, Mary sipped gin for the first and last time in her life. With the women gone she had rushed to the Reverend for comfort. He suggested a bowl of Honest Jack's chicken stew and Honest Jack in turn suggested a glass of gin and water to calm her first.

'I think they're the oddest people I've ever met,' she said. 'Questions, questions, but they never answered mine. And they were so rude, sitting in my own parlour eating me out of larder, and jabbering among themselves in their language as if I wasn't there at all. And then when they decided to speak English to each other it was as if I mustn't hear, all secret, like wrongs hushed up.

'There was a great deal of chaff among them, but not a lot of wit that I noticed. And if there was, it was lost in the strange English they wrapped it in. I think one or two might have been friendly but the older women watched them like teachers and spoke to them like a classroom of children. Married women as well! It was the same with the cake and the cheese and the cups of tea. The older ones ever so careful they didn't get less than the others. And they kept quoting from the Bible, worse than my own preacher ever did. Everything they told me they'd done and all the things they were going to do was right because the Bible said so, as if the Book was written just for them!'

The Reverend laughed and slapped the table with his hands. 'They love it, Mary, hard and cunning as they are. They wouldn't move outside their homes a hundred yards without the Scriptures in their pocket. They love the Old Testament especially. It means more to them in their daily lives than anything else. They reckon it mirrors their own image, you see – Abraham going out into the wilderness not knowing where; remember? Into a place where he would receive an inheritance, and didn't he stay in the land of promise in a strange country, living in tents? Isn't that what they've done? Isn't that what the Great Trek was all about?'

Mary sighed and looked up at the Reverend and then at Honest Jack, not caring.

'Oh, Jack,' she sighed, 'give me some more gin. They're coming back next Saturday with their dress patterns and prattle and I don't think I'm up to it. Really I don't!'

'The Boer will always smell out a good bargain, Mary,' said Honest Jack. 'Nothing delights them more than getting something for nothing.'

'Bit like the Welsh then, I suppose,' she replied wearily. 'Never open-handed till the shops are shut!'

Exhausted by her day and sleepy with gin she dozed where she sat. So they wrapped her shawl around her shoulders and turned down the lantern and tiptoed to the door.

'Mrs Mary's seen her first Boers, Jack,' whispered the Reverend, 'and I fancy she's not taken by them.'

Honest Jack nodded and said, 'I'll tell you one thing, Reverend. I'm only happy with a Boer when he's lying in a coffin. And even then I tell the undertaker to bury him face down so if he's not dead he'll dig the wrong way!'

'Then God forgive you, Jack, for saying so.' But the Reverend was smiling as they went out, closing the door quietly behind them to finish their soup in the kitchen.

* * *

Because of Huw's hard work Mary now had forty ounces of gold dust in her secret hideaway in the larder, worth by Mr Phelan's reckoning one hundred and seventy-five pounds on the slowly rising market. On Major John's advice Huw took out three more claims on a strip between Mary's two acres and the creek. He took on an African to help him, the man Samson who had been locked in the stocks for stealing chickens. Having an African on the diggings upset some. The diggers had always worked their own claims so that what they found remained their secret and their profit was shared with no one. Occasionally, if the work was hard, or if a man was only half-fit from the fever, or injured, he might take on someone, but it was always a white man. Blacks were not welcome where white men worked.

But gradually Huw won them over and when they reckoned an African need only be paid a fraction of a white's pay, some even thought of employing one themselves. So Samson became a familiar face, and they accepted he was easier to work alongside than the scowling Ianto.

Samson had learnt his English odd-jobbing his way south from the home across the Limpopo River he called Mashonaland. He said he was from the Karanga tribe and his kraal was close to where there had once been gold too in what his ancestors had called the Kingdom of Manomatapa. He described how great kings had lived in castles and fortresses with walls of square-cut stone built higher than the tallest tree, and how the kings had traded in gold with the Arabs who brought different wealth in exchange. But when the gold ran out the kings had been killed and their treasures plundered. Now the walls were crumbling and the fortress of Great Zimbabwe had been taken back by the bush, buried and forgotten in the forests that lay between the Lundi and Sabi rivers.

Samson was older than Huw though it was difficult to guess his age. His body was firm and strong and supple but the hair that touched his forehead was fringed grey and the first flecks of red were beginning to show in the whites of his eyes. He often spoke of his tribe and his village and the wives and children he had left behind on the northern banks of the Great Limpopo. He would sit cross-legged on the rocks with Huw, cooling his feet in the stream as he explained his tribal customs and his own manner of living. He held out his hands to Huw, palms cupped, to explain that when an African accepts a gift, he takes it with both hands to show that however small, he considers it of great value. 'Yet,' said Samson, 'the white man thinks we are greedy.' Then he dropped on his haunches. 'It also angers the white man that the kaffir does not stand up for him. Yet our mothers tell us we must never be taller than our chiefs. And we must never look our chiefs in the eyes because that means we have no respect. But Master Huw, when we drop our eyes to a white man, he thinks we have two faces and cannot be trusted.'

Samson explained that the African did not have the same sense of time and distance which also angered the white bosses. If he stopped an elder and asked the distance to the next village he would be told it was a day's walk away. But if he asked his stronger, faster son, he would be told it was only half a day. Samson told how his children were taught obedience and the etiquette and complicated ties of village life. He told how friendship and family loyalty were valued above all things and how this love and loyalty went beyond the grave, which was why the spirits of the dead were so revered.

So little by little, through Samson's eyes, Huw learned more of Africa's ways. But he also wondered how he could reconcile the order and gentleness as Samson described it with what he had seen that terrible night when they had gone to rescue Jollie.

It was then Huw's turn to remember and, like Samson, describe the life he had left behind. He painted his picture of Bethesda and the quarries and did it without bitterness or blame. He spoke of the strike and the fight with Lord Penrhyn, and the hungry winter, the lean spring and then his father's death. He told Samson that a man might work his whole life digging for slate and die before he should, with the dust clogging his lungs and still not earn in that lifetime what a digger in Pilgrims Rest might take from the earth in a week. He told how few men in the quarries ever lived long enough to see their sons full grown. And yet beyond their own yards, on the other side of the dust and slurry mountains, were the green pasturelands of England where their masters grew plump with profit and died of old age asleep in their beds. Samson listened and was astonished that whites treated whites in Wales the way they treated blacks in Africa.

'But you were a free man,' he said. And Huw nodded with a smile.

'Oh, yes,' he replied. 'Free to work in another quarry for another master for the same wages; free to go underground and be buried in a coal grave; or free not to work at all. All men have that freedom, Samson – the freedom to starve and their children too. We worked hard and to another man's whistle, a whistle to start and a whistle to stop. To hear a whistle blow and know it wasn't for you – that's all I ever imagined freedom to be.'

'It was all bad, Master Huw?'

'No, Samson. Not all bad. There was love in between. We had our family and our chapel and our singing. The Welsh are always singing, wherever they are, always singing about home!'

'The African only sings when he wants to be strong,' said Samson. 'Or when he wants to kill. And when he buries his dead.'

Huw shook his head. 'And yet when I was a boy and a half,' he said, 'my mother told me singing was simply people being beautiful.'

They worked the claims from dawn until midday and then after their lunch of tea and meat cuts they walked up to Tambootie. There was always building to be done, a window, a fence, pens for the animals or traps for the skulking hyena and raiding baboons. Huw, guided by Mr Phelan, who had read about a new invention, constructed a cooler. It was a simple design, a box with many slats, like a cage, and within it another one. And in the gap between the two he packed crushed charcoal and channelled water from the tank above to seep through. Huw put it in the shade between the foundations of the house and the evaporation was so effective, Mary's meat and cheese and butter were always kept there.

While Huw worked his carpentry, Samson planted and hedged and carried stone for Mary's garden paths and rockeries. She arranged it all from the rocking-chair on her front porch because she said it was from that chair the finished mature garden would best be enjoyed in her old age and so it should be planned from there.

As the months passed into winter and on into the spring there was less and less for Huw to do at Tambootie. The garden was growing quickly on its own so he took out his Bible earlier in the day and Samson sat by him and listened to stories about Daniel and the lion, about a man turning his wife into a pillar of salt, about the man called Moses who split the sea and another who made cripples walk and the blind see and fed thousands on a handful of fish and loaves. Now every Sunday evening, after an early supper, Huw held a prayer meeting at the house, which Major John, the Reverend Makepeace, William and Jollie attended as well as Samson and Honest Jack's girl-servants. At first the girls were overawed, sitting on Mary's chairs, eating her fruit cake, as still as a rock, and listening wide-eyed to Huw standing by the fireplace, speaking of God. But on the second Sunday, with Samson's encouragement and translations and more of Mary's cake, they unfroze and by the fourth meeting were able to recite the Lord's Prayer and, with their own improvised and delightful harmonies, sing the chorus of 'Jerusalem'.

Then one Sunday five weeks on, Samson unexpectedly brought two men from a village twenty miles, or a day's walk, away. He had sent them a message and they had walked that afternoon to be there for the evening service and intended to walk all the way home again that night. Huw was overwhelmed by it but certain they had only come for the novelty and he did not expect to see them again. He was wrong. The following Sunday they came striding up the garden path with wives and friends, fourteen in all, and the evening prayers overflowed into Mary's kitchen and Honest Jack's girls were quickly sent off to fetch more tea.

The theme of Huw's sermons was always simple. 'You are black,' he would say, 'and I am white. But this whiteness is only a colour on the outside, for we all have a soul hidden by our skin, a soul which Christ suffered for and gave His blood.

'If a black man has his soul washed white, he will go to Heaven. But it may be that some black men have such black souls they will go to Hell.'

The newcomers learnt the music and recitation quickly and the evening ended with a final mighty rendering of 'Christian Soldiers' and was so amplified across the valley that diggers, dozing in their tents, pulled their blankets tighter over their heads.

That week Huw was as excited as Mary had ever seen him. He would not tell her why, nor could she find out from Samson. It was William who eventually broke the secret to her. Huw had decided it was too far for the Africans to walk every week. He said it was rough lion country, that the women had babies on their backs and the men only had sticks for protection. They should not come to him to be Christians. In the tradition of things he should go to them. He should carry the Lord's word to the villages as all teachers had done since the first had walked the shores of Galilee. And anyway, the house was now too small to cope!

But the problem, and Huw did not need Mary to tell him, was transport. He could not walk twenty miles so easily. Nor could he ride it because a horse was no more familiar to him than the antelopes and bushbuck grazing on the mountain slopes. So for a while he fretted and Mary was frantic for a solution. Again it was William who provided it, as William more and more had the habit of doing.

On the Friday, he disappeared. The diggers said they had seen him on Honest Jack's horse sliding down the track beyond the ford to the lowveld. That evening, in the moments before dusk and with exceptional timing, William reappeared, on horseback, pulling behind him up the garden path – a mule.

'It's what Jesus had,' he shouted at the amazed Huw standing on the verandah beside a speechless Mary. 'He's perfect for you and he's called Blom.'

'William,' said Mary, 'who called it Blom? Where did you get it from?'

'Not *it*, mother. Blom is *he*!'

'Where, William?'

'From one of the farms, mother. From Mrs de Wet. She's one of the women who comes up here for your sewing-machine – the nice old lady who smells of aniseed.'

'She gave you this . . . *him*?'

'No. Not really.'

'You couldn't buy him!'

'No, I couldn't.'

'William!' she shouted.

'Mother,' said William back quickly, 'I made an arrangement! We have Blom, you make Mrs de Wet a cotton dress and Huw rides to his prayer meetings just the way Christ did.'

And that's how it happened. Huw sat astride old broad Blom and went off to preach with Samson as his guide. And Mary spent the following Sunday evenings at her machine sewing Mrs de Wet's massive cotton dress.

Little by little it filtered through. A story from a digger up from Kimberley, a traveller from the Cape, a sniggering remark, regretted as it was spoken, by one of the Boer women, the thin columns of black smoke of distant fires. And then Major John's sudden departure.

He was gone for a fortnight and when he returned he was

dirty and grey-faced and stayed in his rooms for two days writing his reports. On the evening of the second, the Reverend persuaded him to eat supper at Honest Jack's with him and Mary and when he arrived they saw he had washed but had quite forgotten to shave. For a while he sat there silently eating and drinking the bottle of Cape Red the Reverend had taken from Honest Jack's cellar. They waited for him to speak and when finally he did, spurred perhaps by the wine, he spoke in an angry voice Mary had not heard before.

'"*Eendrag Maak Mag!*" That's what they're shouting down there! "Unity Makes Strength" and yet the butchers have none!' And he hit the table so hard with his fists the glass jumped and broke its stem and the dregs of wine spread across the table, turning the breadcrumbs red. 'The Boers are going backwards so fast, they'll be in the Dark Ages before the year's out! Their republic's breaking up all around them. Farmers are refusing to pay taxes, they can't pay the government officers, Parliament is openly defying the President. They reckon there's twelve and six in the Treasury and they're releasing convicts from the prisons because there's no food for them. Now President Burgers has gone off to Europe and they're saying that by the time he's back there'll be someone else sitting in his place.'

'I've heard the name Kruger,' the Reverend said.

'That's right. He's a commando leader and as stubborn and spiteful as the rest of them.'

'Why has President Burgers gone abroad?' asked Honest Jack.

'To raise money. And can you guess why? To drive a railway from the Transvaal to Delagoa Bay just so the Boers can have their own route to the sea. As if they have anything to send there!'

'The British won't like that,' said Honest Jack. 'Taking trade away from Durban and Table Bay.'

'They needn't worry,' the Reverend said. 'There'll be no money from Europe, not for a pack of half-washed Boers.

Even if there were, there are more urgent things to spend it on than a railway.'

'Like gold coins with his face on,' said Major John, 'and other worthless rubbish. They say he's like a man wanting to build with marble when all he's got is clay, like a balloon, soaring in the clouds unable to be steered.'

'And dreaming of a blessed republic that none of his Boers want.'

'No, Jack,' said the Reverend. 'They want it but they won't pay for it.'

'Nor will they,' Honest Jack replied. 'There's not a dozen men in the whole Transvaal who've paid their taxes this year, and I'll wager none will next. They say even the Postmaster General is taking his pay in stamps.'

'And I believe it,' said Major John.

'But that's not what's depressed you, is it?' Mary spoke for the first time since supper began. She had listened to his anger but she knew it was not the reason for his despair.

He looked across to her and nodded. 'No, Mary, it isn't, though the Devil only knows how you can tell.'

'Was it why you were away for so long?'

'Yes!'

'Tell us!'

He pushed the plate of half-eaten food from him and they waited as he rubbed his eyes. They were red when he took his hands away. When at last he spoke his voice seemed faraway and sad, like someone grieving.

'We're on a little island here, you know, on the top of Pilgrims Hill, like a fortress perched above the world's troubles. As you know, I went to Lydenburg to meet the stage, I wanted my letters before the Boers touched them. They're such clumsy people, a child could have opened and resealed my last post more cleverly than they had. Anyway, it's well I did because there were instructions from Natal for me to travel further north, beyond the Zoutspanberg Mountains as far up as the Limpopo. They asked me to make a report on what I found there; no other guidance, no clues, simply to go and report back what I saw. So I went straight to some old chiefs I knew, Mapoch and Shatane, but still not knowing what to ask them. But I was not confused for long. As I went I passed villages in ruins and villages picked clean.' He paused. 'Tracks led me to caves a mile further up and there I found the ones who'd escaped. They'd hidden inside but fires had been lit at the entrances and they'd all been smoked to death. The roofs of the caves were thick with soot and the floors strewn with a hundred or more bodies, mostly women, some with children still in their arms.'

Only the tick-tock of the sideboard clock and the faint whistle of a draught under the door broke the silence of the room.

The Reverend spoke first. 'A hundred, John?'

'At least. If I'd had the stomach I would have stayed and counted more.'

'Was it the Sekekune?' asked Honest Jack, 'or the Swazis?'

'No! It wasn't any of the kaffirs. It was the Boers.'

'My God!' whispered Mary.

'Yes, Mary. And their God, too! The One they're always speaking of, the One whose Book they carry in their pockets and whose cross hangs over their mantelpieces. The Boers did it, killed the men so they could take the women and children and when they realized they had already fled up the hill they killed them too. I heard it all from Shatane. They went for him too but he was warned and ready and killed a few. At first I simply couldn't believe it. So they dug open the graves and pulled out the bodies. Five Boers. One I think I recognized from Lydenburg.'

'John,' said the Reverend, 'that proves nothing. Who knows how or why they were killed? It doesn't mean there was a raiding party.'

'Reverend! Shatane took me to a pit where they'd herded some children. Covered them in dry grass and set it alight!'

'No, John. No!' said the Reverend, now white-faced. 'They are hard people, we all know it, but they're not capable of that. It's a trick. John, you know the kaffirs well enough, they're always fighting among themselves, always have been, always will. It smells of them, and they're blaming the Boers.'

Major John stood up and with his hands deep into his coat pockets leant against the wall. 'Reverend, the words of chiefs like Shatane and Mapoch are as good as a magistrate's. But if you doubt him I'll give you the names of the two who led the massacres. Von Schliekmann and Abel Erasmus, both from Lydenburg. And furthermore I've brought back a written testimonial from a Scottish missionary who was on his way to Chief Sechele. He witnessed another attack and saw the Boers carry off two hundred women and children in their wagons.'

'A missionary?'

'His name is David Livingstone, a doctor from Edinburgh. I have his letter with me and he is sending others to the Cape and London.'

Mary spoke. 'John, why are they doing it? Why should they?'

'Land and slaves, Mary. They're filled with land hunger. They want it to be Dutch from the Orange River all the way north to the Zambesi, all of it theirs. To get it they must destroy the people who now own it, but as they get it they need more people to work it and so they're gathering the women and children. The Boers are calling them "Black Ivory" and they're buying and selling them at fifteen English pounds apiece and exchanging the smaller children for a heifer if it's a boy, a goat if it's a girl. It's wholesale slavery.'

He opened his jacket pocket and took out a letter. 'This is from a Boer who works a farm near Smitsdorp, sent to another who's probably off murdering, God only knows where! It's in Dutch but it reads:

> "Dear friend, If you come across some small kaffirs be good enough to send them by your first opportunity . . ."'

He threw it onto the table. 'There, Reverend, now do you believe me? And you, Honest Jack?'

Honest Jack took the letter and read it. 'Major,' he said. 'I don't doubt it. You know my circumstances. They are capable of all the things you describe and, in my own experience, much worse. The kaffirs are sent on earth for the Boer's use, that's what they believe and they say it's in the Bible.'

'Will no one stop them?' asked Mary. 'Will you, John?'

'No, Mary. Not me, nor the English. They'll not risk a war with the Boers over a few thousand kaffirs, at least not unless someone in London kicks.'

'Maybe this is what started the Sekekune fighting,' said Honest Jack.

'Maybe. The Boers have taken a lot of their cattle, and they're fighting the chiefs all along the western border. Now I hear the Volksraad is threatening to raise the price of a pass.'

'Pass?' asked Mary.

Major John nodded. 'Any kaffirs who travel through the Transvaal need a pass from the magistrate's office. It used to cost one pound – now it's going up to five and if they're caught without one they pay double and get twenty-five lashes, too. The Boers can find justification for that in the Bible too, you see if they can't.'

The Reverend Makepeace exploded, red-faced and angry. 'Nonsense, John! And blasphemous too. God won't stand for it, and nor will the British. They can't, not once this gets out. Victoria won't have a handful of murderous Dutch causing mayhem here. There's too much to be lost, too many British interests at risk. We gave them Transvaal at Sand River a good twenty years ago and it was in the treaty – no slavery. The kaffirs were to be respected, that was a condition. Dammit, we gave the Boers their liberty, liberty to possess what was theirs, not to take what was others'!'

'Maybe we should let them alone,' said Honest Jack. 'Let the kaffirs and Boers fight each other and kill each other. There'll be a dreadful number of dead on both sides but they'd not be ours.'

'No, Jack,' said the Reverend. 'Let the Queen send an army

out here to put an end to it. And she will before the year's out. She'll have to. Before the year's out. You mark my words.'

The Reverend Makepeace was wrong in his timing. The Queen did not send her army; her Prime Minister Disraeli did not think it necessary at the time and he was right. There were, after all, too many people in and out of the Transvaal, Boer and English, farmer and burgher, the greedy and the wise, who took alarm at the pace of events and the anarchy and bloodletting around them. So little by little, the Transvaalers prepared for the ending of their independence and to accept the introduction of the rule of law, the payment of taxes, the just treatment of the African and all the other limitations of British rule they found so abominable.

It was not until some few months later than the Reverend had predicted that the Englishman Sir Theophilus Shepstone, newly arrived from London, though not new to Africa, rode into Pretoria with an escort of Natal police and began the annexation of the Transvaal to bring it under the British rule. For a while at least the Boers forgot their hunger and put aside their ambitions. They were, whatever else was said or done, in occupation and they could wait. The British would one day have to go away.

In the meantime they kept their rifles well oiled and began to stockpile cartridges and explosives in their attics and cellars in readiness for another day and another man's call. And they recited to themselves in their parlours and churches:

> 'The good old rule
> The simple plan
> Of let him take who has the power
> And let him keep who can.'

Still there was no news of Walrus and his wagons bringing Polly Makepeace and the other pilgrims. The Reverend became less and less exuberant and there were times when Mary worried he would slip into Honest Jack's bar and stay there. Major John told them he was receiving almost daily reports of increasing activity by the Zulus all along the Natal border and that King Cetshwayo's impis had been in skirmishes with British troops as close as Ladysmith. He said it was perfectly understandable for Walrus to stay put until the British had made the road safe again. And so for a while Mary was content to believe that no news was for the best.

It was Major John's birthday and with much plotting Mary and Jollie prepared a surprise tea party for him. Mary baked a cake stuffed with ginger, dried plums and nuts and covered it in raw sugar crystals topped by one of Mr Phelan's coloured candles. It was a hot day so the table was carried from the house and laid out in the shade of a full-leafed syringa tree, and Jollie cut sprays of oleander and intertwined them to make a cloth of flowers. Diggers came too, so Honest Jack sent his girls running back to the hotel for jugs of what he called Cape Smoke, cheap brandy mixed with cayenne pepper; he said it kept the diggers happy and with enough cayenne stopped them being greedy!

Mary gave Major John a present of braces which she had embroidered herself. The Reverend gave him a blue silk tie taken from his chest in the tent and Huw, on behalf of William and Jollie too, gave him a three-legged stool made from stinkwood with the major's initials burnt on the underside.

It was a happy party. The candle was lit, and ceremonially and with great applause blown out again. Then everyone sang a song in turn between mouthfuls of cake, all, that is, except the Reverend, who with sugar and crumbs sprinkled across his face and pointing a finger at William, recited instead:

'I'm told swans sing before
They die.
'Tis no bad thing.
Though I wish that certain souls
would die
Before they sing.'

Then two brothers named Treloran, who had once worked tin in Cornwall, danced the strangest dance, making out they were a horse, one the head, the other the rump and singing a song no Englishman would understand. The horse weaved and twirled between the table and tree, in and out of the watchers, and one by one they joined in, hands on each other's hips, one long prancing horse, twisting and turning, the men whooping and hollering.

It was William who saw it first, though he was not certain because the sun was beginning to sink, turning everything on the ridge flat and yellow. But when it moved again there was no mistaking and he pulled himself out of the line and shouted as loud as he could above the singing.

'It's Flansman! Look, everybody! Flansman, up there beyond the staircase, above the figs.'

They stopped and turned and shielded their eyes from the glare, and saw, in the shadow of their hands, Walrus' brown and white horse. In the saddle, hanging on to his mane, was Tongogara.

The blood was hard and caked and his wounds were already beginning to scab. They washed and bandaged him and fed him with hot soup and stood by his bed waiting for him to speak more than the one word he kept repeating again and again: 'Zulu. Zulu.'

They took it in turns through the night to sit by him, though the Reverend left them a little past midnight to begin his own lonely vigil on the prayer mat by the altar table. Major John was already making the rounds of the diggers' tents asking all those with horses to volunteer, and at first light there were twenty mounts tied to Honest Jack's halter rail and twenty men eating breakfast inside, as their saddlebags were packed with food and their water-bottles filled.

But still Tongo only whispered, 'Zulu, Zulu,' and they had to wait another two hours before he opened his eyes. He saw Mary and began sobbing and she hugged him tight and pressed his head hard against her and sent Jollie off to fetch the major.

'Hush, hush, little boy,' she whispered, 'you are safe now, it's all over.' And she held him until the tears stopped and he was still again. Then gently, he pushed her from him and wiped his eyes with the back of his hand as Major John came in and went down on one knee by him.

'Tell me, Tongo, where are they? Where's Walrus? What happened?'

The boy nodded. 'Zulu waiting at Rolfontein and chase us to Elansberg. Master Walrus –' and the tears began again, 'he fight them with men in wagons, wagons on fire and Zulu go away at night.'

'Tongo,' said Mary quietly, 'is Master Walrus . . .?'

'Not dead, missus, but he . . .' and he hesitated, not knowing his English well enough to describe what he had left there. So he began to speak in his own tongue. A voice from the door translated.

'He says Walrus is wounded. He says he cannot move and is very ill. That was four days ago and God knows what's happened since.' It was the Reverend. 'Tongo says there's only one wagon left and they can't move it. The Zulus have burnt the rest and killed the oxen and there's a lot of fire and people dead.'

He walked slowly from the door and stood at the end of Tongo's bed and looked down at him. Then in a whisper, and almost beseeching, he asked, 'Polly Makepeace, Tongo? Polly Makepeace?'

The boy looked up at him but there was no answer in his eyes.

* * *

By midday they had cleared the peaks and that evening lit their fires on the southern slope of Pretorius Kop, the twenty diggers, Major John and William. Tongo had placed the attack near to Amersfoot on the Post Road from Durban which was well inside the Transvaal border. By the major's reckoning, that was a hundred miles and more from King Cetshwayo's kraal in Zululand and he had never known his impis come so far into the hinterland of British or Boer territory. The attack had been much closer to the border of Swaziland but Tongo was adamant: it was the Zulu.

Amersfoot was on the far side of the Komati River and if they rode hard they could reach it by dusk the following day. But the Zulus might still be there sifting among the corpses, waiting in ambush for another chance to wash their spears in the white man's blood.

Whatever their fears as they sat around their fires that night eating their stew and listening to the barks of wild dog and the sobbing of hyena below, no man spoke them. Nor did they hesitate or delay the following morning when the call came to saddle up, and they were away long before the sun turned the dawn sky pink. By the time it was high they had covered over forty miles and ahead was the thin, dark, meandering line of the Komati River.

The afternoon's dust and heat slowed them. Most of the diggers had not ridden such a distance since they had settled in Pilgrims Rest, nor had their horses done more than charge up Browns Hill and down again on the Saturday races. So Major John, riding at the head of the column with William alongside him, kept the pace down, stopping every hour to let men dismount and stretch themselves and loosen the girth straps under their horses' sweating, swollen stomachs. Whenever they stopped William saw tiny specks of black appear from nowhere in the sky, vultures, the sky hunters, spiralling and watching, heralds of the dead and dying, just as he remembered them on his trek with Walrus along the Delagoa Road. And somewhere ahead he knew other vultures as big and as black had already congregated in the same silent spiral, waiting their turn.

The heat left the sun at about five o'clock and the men, sore and with their backs breaking, thanked God out loud for it. There was not far to go now. They could see in the grey-purple haze the gradual curves of the Randbergs towards the Boer town of Wakkerstrom and the major warned them again that it would be dark by the time they reached there. He said it to them twice over: 'We have come too far now to do anything but go on. If the Zulus are in the canyon we are already being watched and waited for and can therefore consider ourselves already dead.' The men kicked their mounts and quickened their pace.

The sun dropped but the moon did not wait and day became night without shadows leaving the ground. The outline of Elansberg was clearly silhouetted in the moonlight and as they approached the opening of the canyon, Major John told them to spread out wide, line abreast, with the outer horsemen as close as they could be to the walls of rock each side. They pushed out and laid their rifles across their laps and opened their cartridge pouches.

The clip-clop of the twenty-two horses was muffled in the soft sand; even the nightjars and hyena that usually kept the night awake held their peace. William's throat was tight and he wanted to cough, but dared not. His hands were wet around the reins and rifle.

'If the Zulus are here,' the major had said, 'we are already dead.' But nothing moved except them, no sound but the dull plod of the hooves and the creak of saddles. No cloud touched the moon, no star twinkled, even the air was still and William wondered how such a giant of a land could be so quiet, as if it was already dead and petrified.

Then, before he realized why, his heart stopped thudding and sweat dried in his palms; a bat swooped low and an owl screeched. Directly ahead he saw the light of a camp fire, tiny and flickering. It was as if a vast black curtain had been drawn and they knew their search was over and they would live at least the night out.

There were some that night who, in the later retelling of their stories, would stop and wonder if the years had played tricks. There were others whose memories were so vivid they could not bear to tell them at all.

Five wagons had left Durban a month previous but only one had survived and that because Walrus had been by its side. The Zulus had attacked on the run from the hills on both sides and Walrus had pulled the lead oxen into the shelter of an overhang of rock which protected it from the spears above. Then, as he cut the dusselboom free, it rolled into a dip protecting them on both sides, and there Walrus, a doctor called Finaughty and a man named Jenkins who had never fired a gun before, fought for their lives, the guns loaded by Jenkins' wife and daughter and a pretty girl of seventeen with black hair and blue eyes and a firm square chin whose name was Polly Makepeace.

All day they defended themselves, firing the rifles until they were too hot to hold so the women ripped up blankets and dipped the strips in water and wrapped them round the barrels, afraid to look at what was happening in the open bush beyond. The Zulus pulled the wagons apart and set them on fire and the men, women and children ran in flames and when they were caught they were staked to the ground by spears. Before their bodies had cooled, the Zulus ripped open their stomachs, spilling the pink entrails onto the sand so the white man's spirits were released and would not haunt them for what they had done that day. They were gone before the sun set, and the blackened bodies, stretched, twisted and grotesque, were left to the lion and hyena – eighteen Pilgrims who had been only four days' journey away from their Rest.

The women had made a bed for Walrus by the fire only a few yards from the wagon and he lay there quietly with his slouch hat still on and his pipe clenched between his teeth. His right leg was hidden in a thick layer of dressings made from torn calico, eighteen turns of bandages but the last was already seeping red. They had covered it in a blanket to hide the smell. Mr Jenkins had collapsed in shock and fatigue and they could not wake him. Dr Finaughty was in the wagon alone and the three women sat by the fire with rugs around them, their faces covered in flecks of blood and soot, staring at the embers, seeing and hearing nothing. Only Polly looked up as the horsemen came towards them, but she did not move or speak or even cry, and there was nothing else to do.

The diggers unpacked their saddlebags and coaxed the women to eat cheese and bread and sip from their brandy flasks and they tipped water onto their neckerchiefs to wipe the filth from their frightened faces. The major arranged beds for the women beneath the wagon and he stayed with them until they were asleep.

William knelt by Walrus and held his hand. The old man's face was as grey as his beard and his eyes as yellow as the flames. One of the diggers warmed soup over the fire and mixed a little brandy with it and as Walrus slowly sipped it his eyes began to glisten again.

'Closer, Will boy,' he whispered. 'I've not a lot of steam left. Draw me up, lad, and put my head on your knee. I was never made to look at the sky. It's the bush I want to see.'

Carefully William raised him and saw the pain spread but he made no sound. Once Walrus had settled himself he smiled and said, 'You're meaner than most with the brandy, Will. Has that Bible-thumping brother been nagging you? Hand me a noggin, lad, and put it on the slate.' William raised his flask but the lips were cracked and bleeding and the brandy dribbled down Walrus' beard. Major John came back from the wagon and sat by his side and Walrus lifted his hand in a wave, then let it fall gently against William's face.

'I knew they were there,' he said. 'Didn't know how many but I'd seen their scouts about three days back, north of

Ladysmith. But my God! I never knew they meant to do this!'

'Why, Walrus?' asked Major John.

'Could be war, John, or the first pokings at one. They were saying in Durban the Boers had gone into Zululand and brought back a lot of cattle, two thousand or more. That's a lot of beasts, John, and you know the Zulu loves his cattle more than his wives. The Boers know it too but they did it all the same. There's a chance of a war there, I reckon!'

'But why go for the trekkers? Why the wagon trains?'

'White is white. Boer or English. We're in the Transvaal, John, and that's Boer country.'

'But they followed you from Natal and that's English.'

'That's as maybe,' said Walrus. 'Cetshwayo was the English's friend last year but maybe he's not this. He's been sending some nasty messages to Durban and I also heard Cetshwayo's mother's dead and his *inyangas* have told him to smell out the whites. They're always full of mischief and even the King does what he's told by them.' Walrus paused and sipped more brandy. He looked up at William. 'You won't know what they are, Will boy, the *inyangas* and their smelling-out feasts, eh?' But William said nothing.

Major John said, 'We must move you tomorrow. The wagon is damaged but we can work on it and leave before it gets too hot.'

'No,' said Walrus wearily. 'You'll not move me from here – leastways not alive. This leg of mine is split apart, right through the knee. Can't be much keeping the two bits together. No, John. We're four days and more away and I'll not last it out. I may be losing my mind but I ain't lost my sense of smell. The women tried to hide it under a blanket but I know the taste of gangrene and not even brandy can take it off my tongue. My leg's rotting and unless it's taken off quickly the poison will get all of me.'

'Walrus, I can't saw your leg off!'

'No. That's right, John, you can't. If you do, I die and I think I'd rather die with it on. But if you can make him sober in time there's a doctor in the back of the wagon, dead drunk. He helped us fire a few shots but when he saw what they were doing to them out there I never saw him again. Must have found the cask of whisky I was taking to Honest Jack's. He's a Scot, calls himself Finaughty, and seems he's a secret tippler though he's not to be blamed. He was caught by the Zulus five months back in the Hlobane Mountains in one of the smelling-outs. They took all his kaffirs and cut them to pieces in front of him, tore the women apart by their legs and then stayed all night with him, drinking his whisky, and all the time he thought they would take him next.'

In the back of the wagon, hidden in blankets, was the doctor, his eyes half open, his mouth twisted as he lay awkwardly against the backboards, his right cheek resting in a pool of vomit. William pulled his red hair and shook him hard; the man grunted, then retched again and William stood back as bile dribbled from his lips through the gap where the tailgate joined the floor. The major shouted, 'Drag him out, Will, pull him into the air, rip off his shirt.'

William unlatched the tailgate and the man dropped to the ground. He groaned again but did not move. Then a digger came and helped strip off his coat, shirt and boots and they left him there for the cold night air to bite.

William sat by Walrus again, and the old man held out his hand. 'I reckon I've done the last Tsetse Run, eh boy? But I'm not complaining. I reckon I've been lucky to come this far. Mind you, I'll miss it. It's a grand country, not that I've known any other. Old Mother Baines used to say that when nature stirred up the rich plum pudding of earth she did it here with a generous hand. Mind you, I've always reckoned she's a sly old cook burying all that gold of yours so deep. Stoke up the fire, boy, we've had some hyena these past few nights, gorging themselves out there.' He shook his head and heaved a deep sigh. 'God help me, Will, but I never thought it would ever come like this, never like this.'

'You saved five of them, Walrus. God will thank you for that. And Reverend Makepeace.'

'Makepeace?' The old man looked up. 'The girl's his?'

'Yes.'

The old man nodded and smiled. 'Thought she might be. Square jaw like his and a lot of guts, too. Look after her, Will.' He let go of William's hand and let his own drop to his chest. 'Is he still on the bottle?' he asked.

'No. But he may be by now.'

'I wouldn't worry,' said Walrus. 'He'll stay sober once she's there. I reckon that's all he's been waiting and worrying for.' He coughed and William saw specks of red edge out from the corners of his mouth. 'Come on, boy, give me some more brandy and get some diggers to shove the doctor's head in a bucket of water or I ain't going to see the morning!'

William dribbled the brandy through his lips. 'At least you'll have to give up trekking now, Walrus,' he said softly.

'That's right, Will. I reckon I've only got one more journey to do.' Then, suddenly anxious, he pulled William closer. 'Listen, boy,' he said fiercely. 'Promise me, promise you won't take me up to the Drakensbergs, don't put me into the mountains, not even in the Reverend's cemetery. I don't belong up there, I wouldn't be happy there. I'd be turning so often, the earth would never settle. I belong down here, on the roads. I know a place not far on, called Vaal Water, a little river that flows into the Komati just up from Steyn's farm. It never dries and there's a thorn tree a lot older than me alongside it. Will you put me there?'

William nodded and pushed him gently back onto his pillow and turned so the old man would not see his tears.

The poison was rising. Throughout the night Walrus sweated with fever one minute and shivered with cold the next, sleeping only to wake suddenly and then begin talking easily and fluently as if there was no pain and no creeping death in his veins.

'*Managa*, they call it, boy,' he said, 'the wilderness,' and he waved his arm in a half-circle across the night. 'A lot of men dead in it and a lot of men lost in it. I remember once a parson coming up from Pretoria to hunt for beetles, that was his passion, Will, used to collect them for a museum. But he wouldn't listen to advice, which there's always plenty of, and he got lost. We found him a week later with his prize specimens feeding on his eyes. But the strangest thing was when I was young, younger than you, lad, trekking the Orange River, going east towards the Kalahari on a night just like this, all bright and empty. We were camping by some fever trees, all pale and ghostly they were, draped in yellow lichen, and us half asleep and half awake. Suddenly we heard it, a kind of "hullo" but we knew it couldn't be as there wasn't another human for a hundred and more miles around. But as we listened it got nearer, and there was no mistaking. "Hullo" it said. "Hullo," every few seconds, like a question, closer and closer. We stoked the fire and shouted and waved firebrands, but still it came on, so we let our guns off, all three of us. But whatever it was out there took no notice, just passed us by, not more than a hundred paces away and so clear you felt you could touch it. Then it went on with its "Hullo . . . Hullo", the cry getting fainter and fainter like a lost and lonely trekker wandering the veld looking for a path or someone lost. Then it was all quiet again. We took it in turns to keep watch that night, Will, though none of us slept. But we never heard it again.'

He tried hard to sleep but the fever took him and turned him from side to side and he jabbered pieces and parcels of his life. William wiped the sweat away and stoked the fire. The flickering light made his face yellow too and as the sweat dried it tightened like a drumskin ready to split open and show the bone beneath. His face seemed to be shrinking, as if there was nothing inside and the cheeks, once full and brown and criss-crossed with tiny blue and red veins pumping life, were now empty and falling inwards like the stomach of a starving dog.

An hour later Walrus woke again and with the same fierceness shouted, 'Go across the Limpopo, Will, don't get tangled up with all the mess that's coming. Get my wagon, get it, boy, and quick, whip it up! Whip it up! The water's low into Mashonaland, King Solomon's Mine, Will, there's gold still there in the trees, in the trees I said, and look high, boy, look for the bird, that's where your fortune is . . . look for the bird . . . no Boers, no English, no mess . . . look for the bird in the Graves of the Chiefs.' And then, fading, he whispered, 'Do as I say, boy, trust old Walrus Baines. Go as soon as the floods are over, as soon as the river's down. And say goodbye to Huw, boy, kiss your brother goodbye.' And then in a voice, clear yet distant like an echo, he said, 'It's odd, Will, it's odd. But now I'm dying I've never felt so close to life.' Then he fell back and slept until dawn and William sat the hours with him, listening to his short sharp puffs of breath, and with his strange words echoing until he saw the first speckle of sunlight touch the old man's beard.

Two big diggers held the doctor against the rock face as Major John pushed the barrel of his revolver into the drunkard's mouth. But still he would not budge.

'No drink from you bastards,' he shouted, 'so no chop chop from me. Whisky, and I cut off the leg. Savvy?' Major John turned and hit him full in the face and the diggers let him fall. Blood spurted from his nose and upper lip but no one moved to help.

The major called William. 'Polly's awake. She says there's a cinnamon under the buckboard to hide the smell. Do it now, Will, before he wakes. It's not right a man should smell his death before it comes.'

Polly Makepeace sat under her blanket between the wagon wheels with the scene etching itself on her mind as certainly as acid cuts wax: the young man sprinkling spices over a dying stinking man; out in the open, the horror of hyenas and wild dogs skulking between the black shapes, the vultures swooping and screeching at their backs; and the curses and cries and the smack of flesh as they hit the drunken coward who would let a man die for want of whisky.

Walrus was now very weak, but he did not seem in pain any more. His pipe fell from his mouth and William picked it up, wiped off the sand and the old man clenched it tight again. 'No use with the doctor, then?' he asked.

'There's time, Walrus,' said William. 'There's still time.'

'No, boy,' said the old man feebly. 'He's too shot up. He won't cut it off without whisky and he won't be able to with it. So leave him be, leave him be. I'd rather not have him send me off in pieces.'

'Don't say that,' said William angrily. 'You're not going anywhere. Not without us. Nowhere!'

'Now don't you start fretting, boy,' said Walrus gently. 'It's only a matter of timing. We all end up in the same place sooner or later. Most of us, anyway.' He turned his face so that he could see William better. 'But I would like to have had a party. Yes, I would have liked to have had just one more like that Christmas Day. Always being on the road, you never have time to prepare things properly, when it comes to the end. Mind you, the Boers are always careful about it, as you might expect, always carry four planks of hardwood wherever they go so they're sure of being properly put down. I knew an old Irishman once and when he went they found four planks under his bed and a pouchful of coins for a party, too. It went on for three days and nights and they used his coffin as a table and there was so much frolicking, they had to tie it down to stop him jumping out and joining in!'

He laughed and then coughed. He lifted his long hand and beckoned William closer. 'Will, good lad. Thank your mother for that Christmas dinner and those special times we all of us had. Tell her my only regret is that you didn't all come to

Africa sooner. Tell her there's some seeds in my saddlebag for her garden, Will, some flame lilies from Durban. And tell her . . .' But his last message would have to wait. The pipe fell from his lips and his eyes saw no more.

They buried what was left of the charred remains of the eighteen dead in a single grave and piled stones above it and the diggers made a cross from pieces of charred timber from the burnt-out wagons. Major John read the service and they said the Lord's Prayer and those who did not know the words bowed their heads and closed their eyes and said 'Amen' anyway.

William told the major of Walrus' wish, so they wrapped his body in a clean blanket and Polly sewed the ends together with a sacking needle to make him neat.

At midday they prepared to leave.

'Where do I ride?' shouted the drunk and bloody Dr Finaughty.

'You don't ride with us,' Major John answered. 'There are no horses spare and I'll not have you in the wagon with the women. You walk behind and when you drop we'll tie you like a sack of corn to the back. You deserve no less.'

There was not a digger there who would not have shot the wild-eyed, red-haired man in the face where he stood, but despite his ranting and his curses they let him follow. After a mile he held on to the wagon rail but a digger cantered back and whipped him away so he kept his distance, sometimes screaming, sometimes singing, sometimes talking to himself. Then he became silent and without anyone noticing he increased his pace until he was level and alongside the last rider. Suddenly he snatched the digger's rifle off his saddle and fired it over his head and they stopped.

'You bastard crew,' he screamed, 'kill me but I'll have one of you first. Now, give me a horse and water and give it quick before I clear a saddle with this.' He fired again, only yards from the rear oxen, and the sand erupted in front of the women. One of the diggers went to dismount.

'Stay put there,' shouted Major John. 'No man gives up his horse for that. Stay where you are!' His hand dropped to his saddle holster inside his right knee. The doctor saw it and raised his gun to fire again, but William, only five yards from him, had already made up his mind and with a quick movement turned and fired Walrus' rifle. The force of the bullet spun the doctor round and split his chest wide open.

The diggers would not let him be buried and Major John was in no mood to argue. So they rode off, and William looked back to see the hyena already creeping in, and around them the shadows of the spiralling black birds.

That evening they buried Walrus in a deep grave on the banks of the little slow-flowing river under the shade of the thorn tree. They rested his head between two roots like a cradle and put in his hat and pipe before they covered him. The diggers brought boulders from the river bed and set them in a rectangle and the women stood in the shallow water and filled their aprons with pebbles and then spread them between the boulders so that when men passed they would see the stark silhouette of the thorn tree and the Christian grave beneath it and lift their hats and say 'Good day' to Walrus Baines.

It took four days to reach the valley. A wheel buckled and an axle split and the oxen were weak and covered in sores for lack of grass, so the outspans were long and frequent. The Jenkins mother and daughter were only now beginning to realize what they had done and what they had seen and they became sick and would not eat and suffered bouts of weeping that no one could stop.

On the Wednesday the wagon and the twenty-two riders came quietly into the valley like a funeral procession, and Mary and Huw, standing on the porch, saw Walrus was not at its head. The Reverend ran towards it and a girl with black hair leapt into his arms. Then Mary saw the pale frightened faces of the Jenkins women peering through the canvas flaps and she too ran down the High Street.

That night, long after the valley was asleep, Mary sat on the verandah in her rocking-chair staring out at the blackness. A breeze moved the trees and the crickets buzzed and a fruit bat dipped in and out of the lamplight where moths scorched themselves on the glass and fluttered dying at her feet. She heard a single nightjar and the faraway call of a fox and the jabber of an irritated baboon half asleep. The air was thick like velvet and warm and heavy and smelling of jasmine. She closed her eyes and breathed it in deep. Later she stood and took the lantern and very slowly walked down the steps to the garden and knelt by the rockery and one by one pressed the flame lily seeds into the soft earth. Then she lay down on the grass and wept and stayed there crumpled until the new crescent moon rose over the peaks and spread its thin white light over Pilgrims Rest.

CHAPTER SEVEN

Not a month passed when Major John did not promise Mary that come the next, he would take her to the grave. Huw made a cross with a tiny slouch hat and pipe carved on it. They tried to agree on a verse or line of prayer but nothing seemed to suit his memory. So Huw simply put

WALRUS BAINES LIES HERE
20th JANUARY
1878
BLESS HIS SOUL

But the cross remained in Huw's workshop, covered in tarpaulin to save it from the dust and flies and the worms that ate everything, and it would be some time and many, many African seasons later before Mary finally got her way and placed it at the head of the pebbled grave on the banks of the Vaalwater River.

There were no travellers now from the Indian Ocean along the Delagoa Road nor the English way from Durban and Mary felt the village was more of an island than ever before. Major John told her of reports coming to him daily of the commotion along the Transvaal's south-eastern border: the Zulus and their hated enemy the Boers clawing at each other, attacking each other's farms, stealing each other's cattle, claiming each other's land and killing for it.

The Engish administrators in Pietermaritzburg and Durban

dispassionately called it the 'disputed territories', a giant tract of land that swept down from the Drakensbergs on their eastern side to the Buffalo and Tugela rivers. A vast land but lacking the well-watered grassy pastures on which both the Boer and Zulu cattle-farmers depended for their survival. But nature, in her even-handed vindictiveness, had infected the grass with lung fever and red-water fever, and the scarce irrigation ran through rocky hills and steep ravines that the cattle could not reach.

Throughout the previous year's drought Boer and Zulu had fought for the surviving grasslands and for control of the rivers that watered them.

In Natal the Lieutenant-Governor, Sir Henry Bulwer, counselled arbitration though there were many close by him who whispered in his ear that the Boers and the Zulus should be left to fight it out alone until, exhausted and tamed, they fell like ripe pears into Britain's Colonial lap. But Sir Henry ignored the war-mongering and chose instead to act as honest broker, hoping there was a just and even settlement of the territories which both Boer and the Zulu King Cetshwayo claimed as their own.

Cetshwayo, since his father M'Pande's death, had kept his peace with the British in Natal at their shared border along the Tugela. Not because he feared them. Among the Zulus fear was unknown. For half a century since Shaka, the creator of the Zulu nation, they had been the greatest and most feared in Africa and it was inconceivable that any other army, even the British, could defeat them. But Cetshwayo had always known that any extended war with the Redcoats and their field guns would leave his own regiments severely mauled, so he was happy that they were not his greatest threat. He sat with his *indunas*, his chiefs and his counsellors, under the great thatched dome of the Great Royal Kraal in Ulundi and told them that their first enemy was the *Amabunu*, the Boers. But he said, now that the British had taken the Transvaal and had humbled the Boers, and as long as the British patrolled their new possession and ensured their Great White Queen's laws were obeyed, the Boers would keep the peace and not cross into Zululand. But the King was wrong. The British did nothing when their laws were broken and the Boer commandos continued their raids and left a trail of bloody insistence that the land was theirs. It was then that Cetshwayo remembered, for the first time since he was a child, the words of the dying Shaka. 'When I die, stars will break forth and our land will be crossed again and again by swallows in every direction.' Now he understood the prophecy. The swallows were white men riding their horses and driving their cattle across half of Zululand, half of his entire kingdom; Shaka's swallows were the Boers.

But then, and to his surprise, Cetshwayo began to receive letters from the British whenever his warriors sought revenge, letters that warned him, cautioned, reprimanded, as if he were their enemy, as if he were the aggressor. So late that African spring he gathered his regimental commanders and counsellors around him under the great dome and warned them that the sky was growing dark with the gathering clouds of battle. 'Now, today,' he told them, 'there is calm but it is a deceitful calm. On the horizon I see a cloud no bigger than a man's hand. But soon it will be overhead and will burst and flood us all.' His warriors cheered because they had not washed their spears since Cetshwayo had succeeded his father and the *inyangas* stirred their potions and drew their bones and said Cetshwayo was invincible and that *Imzimu*, the Spirit of the Kings, would guide him well. Soon, they said, it would be December when all the nation celebrated *Ukunyatela*, the four-day feast of First Fruition. Then, chanted the war doctors, the King and his regiments would discover their new strength.

Ukunyatela began with the King selecting the best and strongest regiment to fight with the strongest and fiercest black bull. For hours the men wrestled with it until, tired and wounded, it was finally thrown to the ground and its neck broken. Its limbs were torn from it and the dismembered beast was presented to the *inyangas* who smeared it with their potions as each part was roasted. Then, with ten thousand voices chanting and as many dancing in and around the Royal Kraal, the King led his warriors to the feast and as they ate, something of the beast's enormous strength and spirit entered them and stayed with them.

On the fourth and last day, after many more bulls had been killed and eaten, the King announced that his favourite regiment would be allowed to marry and wear the coveted *Isicoco* head ring. None of his warriors married without the King's approval, so the announcement was the signal for further celebrations. But not everyone rejoiced because the brides came from the girls' Ingcugce Regiment, twenty years junior to their husbands-to-be, and they had younger lovers of their own. Furious at the King's ruling, many silently withdrew from the kraal that night and ran south until they reached the Tugela and crossed into the safety of Natal.

But Cetshwayo sent after them and they were caught and dragged back and disembowelled and hung from gibbets on high hills as a warning.

Sir Bartle Freres, the British High Commissioner in Durban, was already incensed at a recent border violation by a Zulu raiding party led by the sons of Sihayo, one of Cetshwayo's favourite chiefs, chasing their father's unfaithful wives. And now this, a second crossing into Natal to kidnap and kill girls who had simply refused to marry! Sir Bartle reported these incidents to the British Colonial Secretary in London as major border violations which infringed on British Sovereignty, demanding that extra troops be sent to quell Cetshwayo, 'this monster in the north'. Sir Bartle had long been committed to a war against the Zulus. He had warned London many times of its imminence. Come what may, now he would ensure there was one.

He told Whitehall, 'Peace depends not on British designs, but upon the caprice of a bloodthirsty tyrant, committed to ritual mass killings: active steps must be taken to check his arrogance.'

Natal, he explained, could not be defended; the border was over a hundred miles of river with as many crossing-places and impossible to guard. Natal's only defence, he insisted, was the invasion of Zululand as soon as was practical.

Her Majesty's Colonial Secretary was not impressed and sent an answer advising moderation and diplomacy. But he was not optimistic. Without the telegraph his letter would take too long. Events in South Africa, he realized now, were no longer under his control and he prayed that if there was to be conflict it would be short and merciful.

In Ulundi, the Royal Kraal was quiet again. There was nothing to be seen of the celebrations. The regiments had dispersed to their separate garrisons across Zululand, charged by the feastings and the prospect of combat, however distant. Men, women and children followed the warriors' dust-trails across the broad sweeping hills of the Umfolongi, back to their farms and their cattle and the young grain already greening in their fields.

The rivers were brimming full with the new rains and the water snaked out further and further into the dust-dry land so that grain could be sown where there had not been corn in most men's memories. Soon the grain bins would be full and Cetshwayo was pleased. The drought was broken and the rains had come to Boerland as well as Zulu. Land was what made men fight. With their own pastures green again perhaps the Boers would return across the border back into the Transvaal. If they didn't he would appeal again to the British. They were still his friends and they would surely confirm his sovereignty and the Boers would face the combined wrath of two great armies if their plunder continued.

But then another message came from Durban summoning Cetshwayo to send his *indunas* to Natal. They were to go to a place called Lower Drift below a large white outcrop of rock on the steep grassy slopes of the Tugela where it flowed over a large sandbank before spreading into the Indian Ocean. The date was set for December 11th – in three days' time.

The sky was sagging and mists rolled off the sea so that

when the *indunas* and their supporting chieftains and warriors arrived they could see nothing of Natal on the far banks. The river was so full they were pulled across in rafts and when they stepped again onto land, they looked up to the bluff of white rock and saw through the greyness British sailors and marines and between them their Gatling guns.

The Zulus had come expecting to receive the authority to rule all the land they considered theirs and this they were given. But with it came an ultimatum and thirty days of grace to comply. The *indunas* sat and listened in astonishment, committing every word to memory, as the British demanded that their King should disband his army and renounce the traditional Zulu military system of rule. And to ensure that these conditions were met, a British Agent would be resident in Zululand. Six hundred of the King's prize cattle were to be sent to Durban as a penalty for border violations and Sihayo's sons were to be sent to Natal to be punished.

Inside the Royal Kraal, the *indunas* laid the letter of ultimatum at their King's feet, then stood back and watched as he ground the paper into the earth with his heel. The British knew him well enough to know he had no choice but to reject it. His kingdom was huge, his regiments scattered, and his rule, born of the great Shaka, was now deeply rooted in total obedience. He did not want war with his friends but they had now chosen to be his enemies and he did not know why.

Sir Bartle Freres did not have to wait his thirty days for the King's reply. Cetshwayo sent it on New Year's Eve, and it read: 'I am not King of the Zulus . . . I am a heap of dirt. I cannot be King until I have washed my spears.'

War between the two was not declared, yet the peace was over and soon, very soon, the fighting would begin.

The village was growing so fast now it was changing face by the month. More gold was being found across a wider area and many men had moved away from their river claims and were tunnelling into the side of the hills. There were as many diggers as ever working their own claims but a man called Nellmapius – Honest Jack reckoned he was a Hungarian count – had formed his own company and had bought land on Jubilee Hill and employed his own men, Africans as well as whites, to dig it for him. There was talk of a steam engine and a bridge being built and even a stagecoach coming from Lydenburg.

Shacks were replacing the tents and small, single-storey wooden houses were then built where the shacks had been. A small bank to replace Mr Phelan's scales had been opened by Cape Commercial, who offered British bank notes for his 'goodfurs' and safety boxes instead of jam jars.

A Belgian named Schou and an Englishman called Craddock opened a bottle and produce store further down the valley for those diggers who found it too far to walk to Honest Jack's. The two men brought with them a formidable range of drinks 'for cash only': seven brands of whisky, three gins, five sherries, draught and bottled ale, porter, Old Tom, Bavarian beer, still and sparkling hock, and Rough Pontac as well as products Mr Phelan would never allow in his store, like Amsterdam flour, Sperm candles, Liverpool and Windsor soap, pearl barley, white ginger and meerschaum pipes.

At Blyde River Drift a Mr Montague, recently from Pretoria, opened a small boarding-house with a notice above his door proclaiming it 'a great boon to arriving and departing Pilgrims'. A baker's and confectioner's opened next to him where tarts and ginger beer were always available during daylight hours and a Mr Slatter opened a butcher's shop near Macpherson's farm.

With the promise of even more developments to come, merchants and others from Lydenburg began to offer their services. Land surveyors, lawyers and auctioneers discovered they could earn more in a day's visit to the diggers than in a month among their own penny-pinching Boers.

Then a Mr Celliers, who said his father was one of the first trekkers and who for six months or more had been living on his savings and had not found enough gold dust to fill a thimble, decided to return to his first profession and published a newspaper. It was hand printed on two sheets and Mr Celliers was its chief cook and bottlewasher, gathering, printing and publishing his *Gold News* every day except Sunday. It was sold for a penny though he would frequently ask more from drunks and it was full of titbits, gossip, politics, scandals, beatings, suicides, and every libel and lie he could assemble as he rummaged up and down the goldfield.

Under his 'Local and General' column he reported the number of horses dying from sickness; that Mr Cecil Rhodes, the financier, had been seen in Bechuanaland; that yesterday's thunderstorm was more violent than the day before; and that Messrs Schou and Craddock had installed a soda-water machine.

He reported Major John's court proceedings: 'Johann, an Hottentot, charged with being drunk and disorderly, pleaded guilty and was jailed for a fortnight's hard labour. A kaffir was tried for assaulting a female servant. Case proved. Confined to prison and twenty-five lashes well laid on.'

But Mr Celliers' own favourite column was his 'European News'. It came to him via Cape Town, a month old. 'The Revenue of England showed an excess of two and a quarter million pounds beyond the budget estimate. Emperor William of Prussia is recovering from his illness. The Duke of Edinburgh has left Dover for Russia and great preparations are being made for his wedding in St Petersburg.'

With some of the money still saved in his chest the Reverend Makepeace paid for a single-storey house to be built on the slope above the church on the north side of the great church tree. He was a changed man, devoted to prayer and his daughter. Polly divided her days equally, the mornings spent watching her new home grow, helping and carrying, holding planks to be sawn, filling pouches with nails, sharpening chisels on pumice stone and when the roof was on, painting the inside walls with lime and colourwash. In the afternoons she would walk along the High Street to Mary's house to talk and cook and sew and with Jollie's silent instruction learnt to weave on the primitive loom Huw had built.

In their first month, Mr and Mrs Jenkins and their daughter Joanna stayed in the rooms Honest Jack had nailed to the side of his bar. He had now installed glass panes in the window frames and had hung properly joined doors with cast-iron hinges and a brass lock, so the family had more privacy than most in the village. But by the end of the month Mr Jenkins had spent all but eight of the gold sovereigns he had saved in his purse and with four of them he paid for timber and African labour to build a small shack with a corrugated-iron roof on the bare and stony site of a worked-out claim fifty yards up the slope from the river. It was a worthless spot that took the full heat of the afternoon sun and the swarms of insects that followed the river's flow at night. Nothing grew there, the topsoil had been worked over by anxious diggers too often and the scattered columns of yellow weed made the land seem even more desolate.

Mary and Mr Phelan, Honest Jack and the Reverend sent them bacon and vegetables, salt and candles, blankets and soap and Major John urged Huw to invite Mr Jenkins to work on the claims.

Mrs Jenkins, who had been such a bully in Oxford, who always knew what was good for her husband and what was not, and was never in doubt about her judgements of right and wrong, now no longer seemed to care about anything. She scrubbed her tiny shack cleaner every day and her husband's meal was always simmering in the pot on the stove and his table set by the time he came up from the diggings in the evenings. But she was long in bed by then. She would sleep until midnight and then get up and sit by the open door watching the river and its moving moonlit shadows. Mr Jenkins would lie awake and listen to her whisperings. She talked to herself and in such earnest conversations she was two people, a sane one and one not quite so. Mr Jenkins would pull the covers over his ears to hide as one told the other how the Zulus had attacked. But the blankets could not blot out the horrors the one Mrs Jenkins remembered in such detail or the horrible giggling as the other Mrs Jenkins listened.

For a month and a day she scrubbed the floor and walls so that the wood was never dry. That night, the moon was so bright he could see the colour of her eyes. She had washed her hair and brushed it and pinned it tight and she wore a pinafore over her nightdress so that she looked almost pretty again like the days when they were walking out. He watched her get up from her chair by the open door and walk down to the river but he did not follow. And when he could no longer hear her talk and her giggles, he went to sleep.

It was a sad but proper thing to do, Mr Jenkins said at the burial the day after and some thought they had misheard him. Others said he was simply upset. But neither he nor his eighteen-year-old daughter Joanna seemed much put out and they carried on as if none of it had happened and Mr Jenkins was even seen fishing the following Sunday at the spot where his wife was found floating among the reeds.

Joanna did nothing, Sundays or weekdays, but sit in the shade of Mary's verandah staring at the lowveld. She spoke only when she was spoken to and she found it hard to smile, which Mary thought was her way of mourning. But now she knew it was nothing of the kind and the girl irritated her. Day after day she lazed there as if the house was anybody's, helping herself to tea and cake when the village and the diggings were hard at work despite the heat and the flies that came with it.

'You'll not get rich staring at nothing,' Mary said to her one day.

'As rich as any fool out here, digging for nothing,' the girl answered back. The black curls spun as she tossed her head.

'Some will find gold,' Mary said.

'And most won't . . . my father among them. He never finds

anything and what he does he never keeps. He even gives the fish back to the river.'

'Your father's a kind man.'

'It's not enough to be kind and poor.'

'It is if there's no other way. Not for people like us.'

'I'm not people like us,' the girl said angrily. 'And I don't want to be. People like us are always working and have nothing to spend. If I thought that's how I'd be forever I'd throw myself in the river like mother.'

Mary flared. 'That's a silly and wicked thing to say. It comes from too much dreaming and too little doing. There's nothing wrong with people like us, Joanna.'

The girl turned and almost shouted, 'There's everything wrong. Everything! People like us sew buttons and hemstitch breakfast to suppertime. We stand up for our betters and thank them for it and curtsey when they make you take sixpence off the price because a stitch isn't straight and your fingers are red raw. But you daren't say no as they jingle the coin in their purses, threatening. I hate them. I hate them because they make people like us. But I'll be one of them one day. I will! I will be like those ladies I saw in Durban. I'll live in tall houses, with wide stairs and a fireplace in my bedroom. I'll wear flowered dresses so thin the sun shines through and I'll preen and pose the way they do, sitting under their parasols sipping tea all day waiting for their men to come home.'

She turned her back on Mary and looked out towards the peak, but she saw only the grand and dazzling white stucco of the new buildings along the Durban sea front and the rolling surf taller than a house, thundering across the sands. And she saw the handsome young English planters riding their horses waist-high through the sugar cane, with their white shirts open and strips of red silk around their necks and any one of them could have her if only they would make her one of them.

Mary leant down, took her hand and pulled her to her feet. 'If you've those ambitions, my girl, you'll not find them sitting here all day.'

'Then I'll sit somewhere else.'

'No you won't. You'll do as you're told and do something useful. From now on you can make your father's lunch box and Huw's as well. And you can take it down to them to make sure they stop their work to eat it.'

'I may not want to,' she said.

'Maybe not. But you will!'

And she did.

Huw paid Mr Jenkins the standard wage of an ounce of gold a week for his labour, equal to three pounds, twelve shillings and sixpence across the polished mahogany counter of the new bank. Mr Jenkins had kept his last four gold sovereigns and told Huw he intended to spend them on Joanna's wedding. And, talking as if the event were only days away, he said she would call her first daughter Victoria after the Queen to remind him of that green and pleasant land he had so carelessly left behind.

Mr Jenkins had the oddest habit of talking in riddles and rhymes which first confused Huw and then even began vaguely to irritate him. 'A little pot is soon hot,' he said when Huw remarked that his claims were probably too small to make a good profit. 'A hedge in between keeps friendships green,' was another, when Huw explained how the diggers kept themselves to themselves.

One morning when he was late for his work he said, 'Lose an hour in the morning and chase it all the afternoon.' So that Huw began to wonder if it was ever possible to have a normal conversation with him.

He was a thin and sad-looking man and so much like his wife they had often been taken as brother and sister. It was how he had always looked, though perhaps he was a little less sad and a little fatter in his tailor's shop in Oxford, which it had never been his intention to leave. It was the letter, forwarded by a London firm of solicitors, that had changed it all. It told him of a small inheritance from his half-brother, long forgotten and long disowned, who had died intestate, leaving a small farm, some stock and 'various parcels of land at a place called Umshlanga some miles north of Durban in the colony of Natal'. Mr Jenkins did not like tailoring, his business was too small, his customers too occasional and he was slowly going blind with the sewing. But he liked Oxford and the countryside surrounding it and most of all he liked its rivers and the fish in them.

Though his days, from breakfast to suppertime, were tied to hems and linings, buttonholes and fraying cuffs, he was all the while elsewhere, standing among the tall reeds, feeling the willow switch touch his neck, hearing the coot's call, the pike's splash, the line's tug and the distant flash of silver as it took the hook. Why should he want to go to Africa, whatever the gift? He did not want to own land so foreign, so far away.

Had he had his way he would have hidden the letter in its envelope behind the clock on the sideboard. But he seldom had his way and his wife and daughter went together to the solicitor's and made the arrangements to sell the shop to pay the fares. A date was set and the berths booked. Mr Jenkins' women were not prepared to be sad and ill-fed forever and they did not fish. The promise of a house with its various parcels of land by the sea in days of perpetual sunshine were all the dreams they had ever had come true together.

And so, long before Oxford's autumn was over, Mr Jenkins sold his last roll of grey worsted and his Singer sewing-machine and the cupboard full of paper patterns and his padded busts, all his drawers of pins and buttons and the rows of cotton thread on the shelf above the stove and on the Sunday evening before the Monday sailing he walked to his favourite stretch of his favourite river and cast his line for the last time. Then he sat with the water lapping his gumboots and watched the carp and bream jump around the float mockingly in the moonlight.

He sat there long after the fish had drifted down to their

own murky solitude, until the early-morning damp air chilled him and the church clock struck four o'clock. The London train left Oxford for Paddington at six sharp and the steamship *Edinburgh Castle* left the West-India Docks in East London at noon. Quickly he walked back along the river bank, following his shadow and with the moon bright on his back as unseen things ran noisily across his path. He found himself hurrying, which struck him as odd as he had never wanted to stay anywhere so much before. It was not until he turned the corner of his street and saw the sold sign above his shop that he realized he had left his rod and nets behind. But it did not seem to matter because that was where they belonged and now he had no use for them any more. He was not the kind of man to fish in the sea. Especially in Africa.

'What of Durban, then?' asked Huw. 'I've heard you a lot on Oxford but you haven't said why you left Natal.'

They sat under the shade of a tall bluegum tree eating their beef and pickles in half a loaf of Mary's freshly baked bread. As usual now, Joanna had brought it to them. She sat at the edge of the race, dangling her feet in the fast water, staring at Huw as she always did nowadays, following every movement he made, smiling quickly every time he looked up, her hands constantly moving, patting away a crease in her dress, brushing a fleck of dust from her arm, shooing a fly and combing her long black shiny hair with her fingernails.

Samson, whenever white men were with Huw, always sat some yards back but near enough to hear their conversation and able to repeat exactly word for word later what was said and discuss the topics with Huw at their own private communion.

Mr Jenkins wiped the sweat from his face with his forearm and knelt to soak his blistered hands in the water.

'Tinkers and crooked lawyers is why I left, Mr Huw,' he said. 'Lawyers who brought me and my women on a long journey to Africa only to find there was nothing at the end of it.'

'Nothing? The letter was a lie?'

'Oh no, the letter was right enough, leastways, it was when it left Africa. But it was worthless by the time it reached England, because in its travelling the stock had been sold to pay my brother's debts, and the farmhouse, if that's what they call such a hovel out here, had been taken by the lawyers to pay their fees.'

'So there was nothing for you?'

'There was something. A grandfather clock with no face and a mare that had lost her sight. So I sent one to the fire and the other to the knacker's yard. Serve me right, though, getting what I deserve and deserving what I got. I shouldn't have come chasing a dead brother's promises. That's how I remember him, if I remember him at all, always promising this or that, him who I hadn't seen in thirty years nor thought of more than once in all that time, either.'

Mr Jenkins struggled to stand upright again but pain seared his back and Huw moved to help him. 'You're finding the goldfields hard,' he said, 'but we all do at the start, and you mustn't despair.'

Mr Jenkins nodded wearily and held out his dripping hands with the blisters broken and raw across his white palm for Huw to see. 'But I mean to find it, Mr Huw,' he said. 'I've come this far and I'll not leave till I've enough dust in the jar to see me back to Oxford. I'll do that before I die and a bit of fishing, too.'

Joanna swung her legs so that the water caught her long skirt, lining the blue hem black. It clung wrinkled to her calves, showing her ankles which shone white. She was a heavily built girl, fleshy as her mother had been before Joanna was born, but well rounded. Her sulks had made her lips pout and her eyelids were heavy, and she had the habit of turning away abruptly from people who bored or angered her, as she did often with her father. But she was not bored with Huw and was careful not to show her moodiness to him. At nights, lying on her mattress at the foot of her father's bed, she imagined she could hear his voice and so exactly it was as if he were by her side. Then she would close her eyes and see him and she would lay her hands between the soft skin of her thighs and imagine they were his. As the weeks turned to months she persuaded herself she could love him and coax him to marry her. So she did not need any further urging by Mary to make the lunch and take it to the men and it was usually late afternoon before she dried her feet in the folds of her pinafore and left. It did not matter to her whether love was there or whether it was not; soon she planned to be his wife and as soon afterwards as nature allowed, to have his children. It did not need love to make them, she knew that already and no one seemed to care. Only one thing mattered now. When her father took her home again, as he must, away from this murderous filthy country, she would not go empty. She would take a husband and carry his children, in her arms or in her belly, it did not matter. But she would not go back to Oxford on her own, not to the barren empty spinster life, to sit and sew button-holes and stitch hems in the back room of a tailor's shop that stank of camphor and despair.

'Do you love her?'

'I don't know, mother.'

'Huw!'

'How should I feel? I love you, that's all I know of love.'

'God help us if you don't know the difference,' she said. 'Do you want to take her to bed?'

Huw blushed and turned and said to the wall, 'I've asked her to marry me.'

'You mean she asked you.'

'No, mother. It was a proper proposal. I know what I'm doing.'

'And what exactly is that?' asked Mary, folding her arms

and tossing her head. 'Asking a girl you've only known a few months and not exchanged a dozen words with in all that time as far as I know.' She heard her voice shrill and sly.

'I've got to know her,' he said.

'How? You haven't been out together. Or have you? Have you been meeting secretly in the woods? At least that would be encouraging.'

'Mother, I do . . .'

'Rubbish, Huw! You don't. You know nothing at all. What's her middle name? What star is she born under?'

He shrugged his shoulders. 'Does that matter?'

'Does it matter that you don't talk about the stars? And you say you're in love!'

'I didn't say that, mother.'

Mary did not know whether it was what he had meant to say. She waited for him to contradict it. Eventually she asked, 'Not even to her?'

'No. Not yet.'

'And you've already proposed? Don't you know what comes first? Have I cushioned you so long, suckled you longer than I should, that I have to tell you the order of things? Can't you see, you stupid fool? Can't you tell what she wants, what she's pretending?'

Huw swung round, his eyes dark and deep in his sunburnt face.

'No, mother,' he said hoarsely, 'be silent. I will not have you say such things about her. She is only young and has already suffered more than God ever intended. Her father will leave here one day, just as soon as he has enough in the jar, and she will go with him and I will not see anyone like her again in my lifetime, not here on the diggings. And mother, I must have children, a son, as a duty to father, to put down his roots here.'

Oh, how sad he looks, she thought. Like a big lost bear. And how cruel the girl must be to take him with such a trick.

'She told you that?' she asked. 'How she wants children and how both of you can grow to love each other and how your love will grow as your children grow? Is that how she is, Huw? Is that what she said to make you propose? Tell me . . . was it?'

He braced himself as if he was about to shout. But then he closed his eyes and let out a sigh. She waited, knowing she had said too much, not wrong things in themselves, but she was not used to being angry, least of all with him, and her words had come too sharp. But she couldn't let it happen without warning him, she was so certain of the girl's intentions. Huw was full of love but those who are unloved grow up to be unloving and Joanna was one.

God has such a barbed and prickly way of getting His own back she thought. Wasn't there such a girl, so many years ago, who had let herself be persuaded that love would grow as her child grew, knowing it not to be true but agreeing so she could save herself? Love of sorts and it served her right.

She knew that either way she could not win, but she would not lose him the way she lost Ianto. With Joanna he might stay in the valley, without her he would leave one day and look for someone like her. Let them marry without that love that sets a marriage firm and holds it tight, and who knows, by God's grace, it might come later equally to both or to only one. She knew that was all that could be expected, all that was really needed, the one who loves and the one who is loved. Hadn't she been heavy with Ianto and loved a man and been loved by another?

She went across the room and took Owen's lovespoon from its hook and hugged Huw from behind, lacing her arms around him and pressing her head into his shoulder.

'I'm sorry, my darling,' she whispered. 'Forgive me, a jealous mother so anxious not to lose her baby. All mothers are the same, Huw, dreading the day, knowing about it, preparing themselves inside and then bowled right over when it happens. They say you don't feel that way with a daughter, isn't that odd? But I think a son never really leaves his mother, does he, not really? He always leaves a little bit of himself behind, so I mustn't be selfish. Here, take the spoon, you needn't make your own. If you're going to plant young Llewellyns here, then use your father's spoon to stir in the happiness.'

He turned and she went on tiptoe to kiss him and he lowered his head to meet her lips. 'Forgive me, Huw – say you forgive your silly old mother.'

'No,' he said softly in her ear. 'It's you, mother, who must forgive me. I know well enough what I'm doing. I can't believe it's so wrong that God will not bless us, too.'

Joanna and Huw were married within two months, joined by the Reverend Makepeace in his tiny church, and Major John was best man. Mr Jenkins was dressed in a dark blue serge suit and a starched butterfly collar he hired for five shillings from an English digger called Billy Bean, who for the occasion and for no extra money bound Mr Jenkins' blistered hands with clean bandages. Mary and Jollie made Joanna's dress out of white cotton remnants left over by the Boer women and the white lace neck and cuffs had been sent up from Lydenburg specially by the stout Mrs de Wet, free and from kindness.

Mr Jenkins, suffering a long bout of coughing, was soothed just in time for the service by a potion brought by Mr Phelan from his Hottentot wife. People remembered that it also cured jaundice!

Early one morning, six weeks later, Mrs Joanna Llewellyn came to Mary's verandah, asking for a spoon of tea and to say that she had not bled since her marriage night.

It was William's eighteenth birthday and Major John gave him Walrus Baines' wagon. The canvas was in shreds and the dusselboom splintered but the axles were made of good *boeken-hout* and the hubs spun free and even on their spindles, caked in black fat. They stretched out the harness and reins which were torn in places but still shining and sticky with years of beeswax and when Huw steamed the driver's box apart to glue and reset it he found the initials WB and the date 1828, which, they guessed, made Walrus about twenty years old at the time.

Five of the sixteen oxen had died soon after pulling the wagon into the camp but the other eleven had survived and grown fat and healthy again, grazing in the deep, pink-topped oatgrass that swept down the slope from the ridge. Often it hid them so completely that when William or Tongo went out in the evening to herd them to their pens, they lay cunning and unseen, refusing to answer the names Walrus had given them long ago, and Tongo pounded their backs with his bare hands for their obstinacy when he found them.

But eleven oxen would not make a span, not one strong enough to pull such a wagon. It was Major John who suggested that instead, Huw should rebuild a smaller, sturdier one based on the design of the Cape Cart, using only one axle and pair of wheels but still with the central dusselboom. Five pairs of oxen could pull that and still follow the old wagon ruts. That way, he said, although William might only be able to carry half the normal load, he was more manoeuvrable and could take loads along tracks the four-wheelers could not possibly manage. They would keep the spare timbers and the rear wheels and axle so that, come better roads and bigger business, Walrus' old wagon could simply be put back together again. William thought it a grand idea and could almost see the old man puffing his pipe and nodding his head enthusiastically.

Major John said the routes east were closed and would be for a good deal longer. But there was plenty of business in timber, fruit and vegetables in Lydenburg and further south among the Boer farmers. The village itself was expanding fast and already he had had notice of more families, English and Dutch, travelling from the Cape to settle in the area. Some would surely find their way to Pilgrims Rest. It was all good for enterprise, he said; which seemed to set the seal on things!

During the cool weeks of May, William and Tongo, helped by Huw and Samson when they were not working the claims, dismantled the old wagon completely and laid out the timbers below Mary's garden fence, cutting out the rotten wood and matching with new, making new dowels and pegs, scraping and corking, smoothing and then finally painting. And at the forge by Darkes Gulley, Big Macpherson beat out new shackles and pins, studs and braces, applying his fire and his muscle, remembering his apprenticeship forty years back in the tiny north Devon port of Appledore. And so, on the day of its rechristening, which by clever hesitation and delays turned out to be William's birthday too, no one was in any doubt that the new wagon was stronger than the day the young Walrus had carved his name and that it would outlast William and possibly his children also.

That morning Tongo brought the oxen from their pens as Samson polished the harness for the fifth time in as many hours and when William was brought from his special birthday breakfast at Honest Jack's he had to walk no further than the horse-rail to see it below him, painted blue and gleaming. Jollie had tied straw dollies to the oxen's horns and Mr Jenkins had made cushions for the driver's box. But then came the biggest surprise.

Major John made them all stand in a line in front of the span, Mary with Tom, Huw, Joanna, Honest Jack, Jollie, Big Macpherson, Samson, Tongo and, by the lead ox, William. Then from the hotel parlour, having waited for the major's call, came a man dressed all in black with a three-legged stand and a large leather-covered box, which he proceeded to erect ten yards from them.

'A photographic camera,' shouted the major as he ran to join the line next to Mary and picked up Tom in his arms. 'So that our grandchildren will know how the great William Llewellyn transport empire began.' They waited ten minutes, burning in the sun, with Tongo wrestling to keep the oxen still until the white powder in the man's tray exploded. Then the animals pulled in all directions at once, nearly snapping the shaft in two, and careered off down the High Street with Tongo and William clinging to their necks, and Mary, Major John and the rest sitting in the dust cheering. The man in black said he had taken his picture and that within a month he would post it to them, complete with glass and a veneer walnut frame. The major thanked him and took him aside and gave him a gold sovereign, and after some rum and soup the man galloped away with his equipment tied across his back, on a horse as black as his hat.

William had grown tall suddenly: not yet – but nearly – a man and it astonished Mary, because only once since they had arrived in the valley had he been away for more than a few days. She had watched him become the camp's favourite. Somehow he knew instinctively how to place one digger from another so that he could be liked by men who did not like each other. He was able to listen to a sad soliloquy from someone who could not later remember being able to talk so freely to any other man before.

William had grown dark like Mary. His skin was the same honey brown and his shining black hair curled above his ears just like hers. It grew so fast that within a few days of a visit to Mr Hamilton the surgeon barber tentmaker he looked overdue for another.

He was never far behind, whatever he was learning, and then always ahead. He was not as tall as Huw nor as broad as Ianto had been, but there was no doubting where he had started his journey. When Mary watched him she saw her younger father, the kind of man he might have been had he been born anywhere but Bethesda, had he not grown old so soon, as grey as slate and as deep as the quarries. Too often now as she watched William she saw her father as he led a pony or raced the postboys, or swapped beer jugs that lined Honest Jack's verandah on a Saturday race day and then bet on the brawls that followed. She would remember Bangor Fair Day when her father had bought her a hot meat pie for sixpence, and how he had gambled his last ten shillings on a wrestling bout between two drunken Irish tinkers. And how he had sat on the wet sand that afternoon with the surf lapping his boots and she had paddled in the sea in her knickers.

William was too handsome to be good for him, they would say to her, but it was said with a smile. Nothing was ever said about him with malice nor did he ever exchange it. She felt what she had not felt with the other two, that as he had come of age her influence on him diminished as his on her grew. She could not, with Huw or Ianto, ever escape the burden of motherhood but as William had blossomed, she felt lighter and more able to cope. He had, suddenly and of his own making, become her ally. He had all but taken Owen's place.

So, on the evening of his birthday, after they had all celebrated with dinner and wine, when the house was asleep and the night quiet, she unhooked Owen's silver watch from its place by the mantelpiece and took it ever so carefully to him and laid it on the pillow by his face. And for a while she knelt by his bed listening to his breathing and the ticking of her gift to him.

Since the British government's annexation of the Transvaal the year before, a small company of British troops had been garrisoned on the outskirts of Lydenburg. It was only a gesture and generally thought a little absurd because the Boers who lived around were well armed and many of their farms were beginning to resemble ordnance dumps. There would be very little, in the event of disorder, the British soldiers dared do.

Colonel Anstruther, in command of the 94th Regiment, the Connaught Rangers, consoled himself with the belief that his value was not as a peacekeeper but as a monitor, keeping the Natal administration in touch with the Eastern Transvaal, providing intelligence about the Boers and the rebellion everyone was expecting sooner or later. But the Boers did not worry overmuch about that either and ridiculed the soldiers sniffling in the heat of their tents, ignoring advice not to scratch their mosquito bites which swelled and erupted into septic sores.

The Boers knew the soldiers were too cautious to leave their stockade and find out what was going on, and anyway if it came to stopping an army messenger leaving Lydenburg there were volunteers a hundred times over to do it.

All of which the colonel suspected, and which was why, when he saw the two-wheeled cart trundling into town and heard William's voice and accent, he caught his breath, thumped one fist hard into the other and sent his sergeant to invite the young Welshman into his tent to share a jug of cool lemon water.

At first they talked business. The colonel told William he needed to build a proper stockade and he offered a price far above what William would have quoted himself, to buy eight hundred staves, stripped of bark, sharpened and delivered in four loads, payment to be made in gold sovereigns.

The colonel pointed out that by trading with the British army William might be forfeiting trade with the Boers, but William shook his head and said he would not be told by one customer what he should not do or say to another.

'Then win over the women, William,' the colonel replied, laughing, 'and you'll not need to worry about the men. And with your curls you ought not to find that a hazard.'

He poured some more lemon water from the jug as the sergeant brought in a tray of bread and sausage.

'I was beginning to despair,' he said, 'of ever meeting a friendly face outside this camp again. Four months we've been here now and the jolliest thing I've seen is a frown! Mostly it's been a dose more severe!'

William nodded. 'The English are not very much liked here,' he said. The colonel beckoned William to the table to eat.

'They call us *verdompde Engelsmen* and *rooineks* – rednecks, you know – because of our sunburn,' he said.

'They call you *rooibaadjies* too. It means Redbacks. They like your red tunics.'

'Why?'

'They say men go blind with too much sun. They also say

only a blind man's bullet could miss you in those uniforms.'

Colonel Anstruther nodded. 'Yes, I suppose that's true,' he said. 'Not like the Boers, eh? You hardly see one until you're right on top of him.'

'They dress in the colours of the land,' said William.

'We could learn a lot from them, d'you think?'

'I'm not a soldier. It's no business of mine if they're saving up their bullets for you.'

'Is that what they're talking about, killing us?'

'The Boers are always talking about it. It cheers them up!'

'Do they hate us that much?'

William smiled. 'There's not a lot they do like, not even each other. Seems to me a Boer's only happy sitting on his own step, smoking his pipe and drinking his coffee and cursing the Devil if he can see his neighbour's chimney smoke.'

'And us too for hemming him in?'

'Perhaps,' said William.

The colonel gestured at the triangular opening in the tent and the view outside. 'They reckon that's all theirs out there, don't they?'

'They do.'

'Is that fair?'

'I wouldn't know. But our Gold Commissioner, who's an American, says that the British have blundered too often in their treatment of the Boers and that with kinder treatment they might never have left the Cape.'

He seemed to agree. 'And because of it,' he said, 'I and hundreds like me have had to come chasing up here to make them pay their taxes and stop them from kicking their kaffirs to death. And their dogs,' he added.

'Their dogs?'

'Yes. Didn't you know? Saw it soon after I came here. I've seen it many times since though I've been told to hold my tongue and temper. The Boers tie a puppy to a stake and get their blacks to kick and stone it near to death so that it grows up hating them and ready to tear them apart. Wonderful training for guard dogs but it's sickening to watch. I suppose they don't see their dogs the way we do.'

'We had English gamekeepers back home who set their dogs on men,' said William, 'just because they were snaring rabbits to feed their families. One man we knew lost his hand to a dog but still the magistrate punished him.'

'The law is a landowner, William, even in Wales.'

'Are the English as hard on their own?'

'Oh, yes indeed. As long as the men who make the laws and the men who administer them are landlords they'll put you down wherever you come from.'

'Then the laws should be changed.'

'Not by the landowners.'

'No,' said William, 'by the people.'

The colonel hesitated. 'Are you one of these union men?'

'No, but my father was.'

The sergeant came in with more lemon water. The colonel pointed at William. 'He's from Wales, Sergeant. Don't we have some Welsh with us?'

'Yes, sir, two. Hughes and Hughes.'

'Would you like to meet them?' the colonel asked William.

'No. Not especially. I've come here really so's to leave Wales behind.'

'Yes, of course. Silly of me. We English always imagine you're all brothers, one big clan, like the Scots. Or those bloody Boers out there. But why should you be? We're not. The English, I mean.'

'You seem to be,' said William. 'At least to us.'

The colonel laughed. 'Really? How odd. Well then, you can forgive me for thinking you'd have liked to see Hughes and Hughes. Brothers, are they, Sergeant?'

'No, sir,' the sergeant answered. 'Not in the least, sir.'

'It's a common name in Wales,' said William.

'So many of you and yet so few names, as if there aren't enough to go round.'

'The Welsh are very mean with themselves,' said William, smiling again. 'We're famous for it.'

The colonel smiled with him. 'Do you have brothers?' he asked.

William hesitated though he didn't know why. 'Yes, I have brothers – two and a little one.'

'And all up there in the hills?'

'Oh, yes. We came with our mother. I suppose you could say we came because of her.'

'How's that?'

'She wanted us out of Wales. There's a lot like us come here to Africa. Some have gone to South America too, I'm told.'

'There's a lot of Welsh in the army already here, you know, in Natal, most of them in the 24th Foot Regiment. Isn't that right, Sergeant?'

'Quite right, sir. Hard lads, too.'

'And they'll need to be. By the time this is all over they'll have wished they'd never left their valleys.'

William asked, 'Why is that?'

'War, William. A nasty, bloody war!'

'With the Boers?'

'Oh, no! Not yet, anyway. This one's against the Zulus.'

The word seemed to echo in the tent. William saw again the tiny Tongo bandaged in bed, whispering that single word over again, and that black fearful night, the small fire flickering where Walrus lay dying and in the morning the strangely contorted dancing people tinder black.

'They say it'll be weeks rather than months,' he heard the colonel saying. 'We're going to teach this King Cetshwayo a lesson. Seems he wants to be another Shaka, another black Napoleon, but we'll cut his tail off quick enough.'

'When do you suppose it will all start?' asked William quietly.

'We're a bit distant here,' he replied, 'but Cetshwayo has already ignored the British ultimatum and my bet is we're already on our way. Myself, I'm content to sit it out here and bide my time with the Boers. At least they'll fight by the rules, not like those bloody savages, by all accounts. Swamp you by sheer weight of numbers, tens of thousands of them, more men than we've bullets to knock them down with. That's what your Welshmen are up against, William. Believe me, you're well out of it unless you want to pay your debt to Queen and country?'

'I owe the English nothing,' William replied, picking up his whip ready to leave. 'But . . .' and he hesitated again.

'Yes?'

'I do owe something to a friend.'

'Well, if you go you'll find work enough for your wagon. They'll be moving up supplies and there's good commission and my bet is you'll be away from the bloodletting by the time it comes.'

'Thank you, Colonel,' he said. 'Maybe I will. But in the meantime I'll bring you your timber as we've arranged. Good-bye, and thank you for the sausage and lemon.'

Colonel Anstruther held William's hand firm. 'Just one last thing. Your name. Is it common in Wales too?'

'Yes,' he answered. 'Quite common. You'll not hear it as often as Hughes or Davies but there's plenty of us, north and south.'

The colonel let go. 'Are there many in the Transvaal, do you know?'

'I've no idea,' said William.

'You see,' the colonel went on, 'a fortnight ago I received a dispatch concerning a gang of renegade Boers, all youngsters who've taken it upon themselves to harass British supply routes. They've been setting fire to some of our wagons crossing from Natal and the Cape. Call themselves *ossewabrandwag*. I think it means the sentinels.'

William asked, 'Do you tell me this because you think they might attack me?'

'No. That's not likely. They're only after us. I'm telling you because there's a Welshman among them. Would you believe? Astonishing, the Boers taking on a foreigner like that. He's

Welsh, most certainly. One of our quartermasters heard him talk, no doubt about it. Now they've got hold of his name: Llewellyn. It was in a dispatch this morning. Then in you come and I think that's just about the strangest coincidence I've ever known.' He laughed. 'But you've no worries, William. A murderer doesn't come waltzing into a British camp to eat sausage and drink the army's lemon water.'

'A murderer?'

'That's right. A dozen wagons were ambushed just north of Utrecht a fortnight ago, had a cavalry blue with them who tried to ride off and raise the alarm. But they shot him – or rather this Welshman did. The report mentioned that specifically. The man we're after is a marksman. He hit the rider at over two hundred yards. Don't get many shots like that, which probably explains why the Boers took him on. Though it doesn't explain why he joined them. So, William, you'd be doing a service to your Queen if you keep your eyes and ears open. A marksman, and with your name. It'll be odd employment.'

'Yes,' said William, leaving. 'Odd indeed. But we hear very little up in the mountains, least of all what's going on down here.'

'Applying themselves to their fortune, eh? So they can all go home again, I shouldn't wonder.'

'Perhaps,' said William. 'Maybe that's what would be best for all of us. I mean, if we all went home.'

He climbed aboard his wagon as Tongo reined the oxen, but he didn't look back at the two men he knew were watching him. Nor did he dare to until Lydenburg had dipped out of sight.

It was his first view of the Drakensbergs from the lowveld. On the journey down, the tips had been covered in cloud: Walrus had called them their tablecloth. He halted the oxen on the lower slope of the escarpment where the powdery dust met the first outcrops of rock and waited for the heat to leave the sun.

Then they would begin the climb to Pilgrims Hill. Tongo lit a fire to boil a billy of tea and William walked to a solitary thorn tree and sat in its shade.

Swallows wheeled low over the grass, their beaks clicking as they snapped at insects. Above, he saw a hawk shimmering, its wingtips glistening, hovering in the stream of warm air, its head on one side watching a red rabbit move from its camouflage. There was a movement beyond it and William saw a small buck, what the Boers called *duikker*, come out slowly from the prickly scrub, curious to see who had stopped so close to its hiding place. Gingerly, it picked its way through the bushes, its spindly legs no thicker than the stems it trod over and all the time lifting its nose to the slight breeze to identify the scent of friend or foe.

The shadows of white clouds slid down the mountainside and spread like stains across the still flat land to the thin columns of smoke he knew came from Lydenburg. For a while at least his dreadful secret would stay there inside the army garrison. But only for a while, he knew, only for as long as it took another traveller passing through to bring the news up the mountain.

William cursed his brother's vengeance. The English had killed their father but he must be crying now in Heaven. And fearful, too.

'Oh, Dad,' he said aloud, 'I hope they'll leave us alone, not come and pester Mum and tell her what he's done.'

He went down on one knee and faced the mountains to pray to the only God he knew, the one who lived in dark chapels of black slate between vases of waxed chrysanthemums. The God who never forgave.

'Please don't let them tell. She says she sent him away but she didn't, no one did, really, he was only ever biding his time. He's always been wanting to go since they killed Dad, that's when he really left us, you know that. Please God, take him before the English do. So that she'll never need to know. Please God! Just this.'

He said his Amen and picked up his hat and went off to drink his tea. When he looked back, the buck had gone and he saw the hawk sitting in the topmost branch of the thorn tree, shining like metal in the evening sun, with the rabbit in its claws.

He sipped his tea and wondered. He had, for the first time in his life, prayed in English and it worried him that God might not have heard.

Throughout the mid-winter months of June and July, William and Tongo crossed and recrossed the shallow drifts of the Blyde River, driving their ox-wagon up and down the face of Pilgrims Hill, winding their way along the valley to the Ohrigstad River until the track dropped down to the water itself. Then they turned south towards Lydenburg where the going was straight and level until they reached the steep gorge of the Spekboom River. There, when the rains swelled the ford, they lashed tree trunks to the wheels and drifted across, sliding a little downstream, and Tongo spiked fish for dinner and had enough left to smoke them over the breakfast fire for lunch the second day.

At the beginning they ventured only as far as Lydenburg but within a fortnight a Boer farmer paid for twenty bushels of tomatoes to be transported to Middleburg and another sent them to Standerton with a wagon-load of sweet potatoes. Then a merchant offered cash on the knuckle for a trek even further south to Utrecht on the Buffalo River, to collect a steam pump.

By the end of July they had delivered the eight hundred staves to the British army garrison and Colonel Anstruther paid in gold sovereigns as he had promised. On each of the four deliveries he tried to persuade William to stay and talk as they had done on their first meeting but William firmly and politely refused. Then, at what was to be their last meeting, the colonel became impatient and asked William directly to supply information about the Boers, the movement of their commandos, their munitions, supplies and what they were saying about the British. He held out a leather pouch of sovereigns but William pushed it aside.

'In Wales,' he said, 'we would call that Judas money.'

'In England,' the colonel replied, 'we might call it patriotism. And good sense, William. We're not here to start a war but prevent one. They're the ones who want to fight. Remember that.'

'But you're in their country,' William replied.

'You'll not help, then?'

'No, I will not. It's not my fight. I've told you that before.'

The colonel suddenly turned on him angrily. 'Not your fight, be damned!' he shouted. 'You want it both ways, you bloody people. British when it suits you, Welsh when it doesn't. It's their country, is it? But you're digging their gold, Boer gold, which you sell in Natal because the English give you a better price for it there. Not your fight, damn you? Then who'll be yelling when the Boers start their tricks, who'll be waving the Union Jack and demanding safe passage out with an army escort? You tell your people up there that these staves are to keep the Bocrs out, not lo let the Welsh in. You tell them that, and anyone else who prefers Boer money to mine.'

William turned to leave and the colonel shouted after him. 'Sergeant, see this man off camp and be sure the sentries know not to let him in again. It seems the Welsh abroad are more foreign than they are at home.'

Later William learned that Colonel Anstruther had threatened he would let it be known among the Boers that William was in the army's pay. But it seemed he did not, because the farmers did not change their ways, and their wives spoke openly to him as they had grown accustomed to. Then William regretted the words he had used but it never occurred to him ever to return to the garrison. After all, if there were a war the British would be no protection. Not in a land of Boers.

* * *

As he did the rounds of the farms and shops, William had no difficulty in buying or selling. His problem was the sameness of the trading. Everyone, or so it seemed, grew only sweet potatoes, tomatoes and wheat and there was a limit to the number of profitable transactions he could make simply transferring vegetables from one end of the Transvaal to the other. Then he discovered that many of the farmers' wives grew small patches of other vegetables and fruit for their own dinner-tables: cabbages and pumpkins, carrots and beet, marrows and grapes and a fruit they called *stamvrug*, full of delicious pulp and a thick, sweet, red juice that ran like blood and made excellent brandy. So William set about persuading the wives to extend their patches and grow for profit, for cash, that being the most direct route to a Boer's heart. But their husbands were not so easily changed, nor would they be told by their wives what crops they should or should not grow.

So it was left to the widow Mrs de Wet, who wore Mary's dress on Sundays and had sent the lace for Joanna's wedding, to set the pace of agricultural change locally. She hired oxen and plough from her nearest neighbour, Mr Trichaerdts, and sent William to Botsabelo, north of Middleburg, for all kinds of seedlings. And she began to grow things that only the older Boers could remember eating in the days before the Great Trek.

She had been only a child of five then but her memory of the events was stark and vividly retold. She remembered the Boer women loading guns during the battle against the Zulu King Dingaan and the slaughter of Blood River which the trekkers prayed would be the last battle they would have to fight to obtain their peace and independence. Her memories of the Great Trek had been fondled so often over the years, she could never be certain now how much she had embellished with affection. But she remembered vividly the day she and her cousin, the same age, had played in the rushes by a river as their parents had outspanned under the shade of trees. She remembered how they had peered out from their hiding place when they had heard screams and shouting and guns firing and how they had lain flat on their stomachs not daring to move as black men climbed the wagons with their spears flaming, setting the wagons on fire and all the trees around them so that nobody escaped.

The two children did not move until hours after the blacks had gone and the fires were only smoking embers. They were hungry and looked about for food, not bothering with the bodies or noticing their ugliness. They did not even look for their mothers or fathers. Mrs de Wet could never remember how long they sat there, two little children, suddenly and grotesquely orphaned. But that evening, or maybe it was the next, white men came by on horses, men with long beards and tall floppy hats, and they picked them up in their arms and the men began to cry but the children did not. They silently ate the biscuits the men had in their pockets. Then the tallest of them picked her up on his horse and tied her to him with his belt and they rode away. Another man took her cousin and she never saw or heard from him again, though she always knew that like her, he had begun another life that day with a new family name.

William had long been Mrs de Wet's favourite, ever since the day he swapped her donkey Blom for the promise of the dress, machine-made by his mother. Whenever they stayed overnight in Lydenburg, William and Tongo slept on straw in her stable and ate *sosaties* and *bobotie* and potato dumplings in her kitchen. She lived in a small wattle-and-daub house with a thick black thatch and tiny square windows that shuttered from the inside. She had planted all kinds of flowers and climbing shrubs so that for three seasons of the lowveld year the lower part of the house was hidden completely by flame-thorn, wild currant, fuchsia, wallflower, sage, passion flower, canna and purple clematis.

Coming from the Cape, her ways were daintier than some of her neighbours', though, like them, she smeared the floors of her tiny farmhouse with cattle dung to keep the flies away.

But she chopped up wild flowers and herbs and pressed them for their juices and piled them into bowls so that there was always the smell of the outdoors even when the shutters were closed and bolted. When the flies were very bad she boiled blackberries and dipped twigs of bluegum into the sticky mixture and hung them from the rafters in between the smoked hams and biltong. When the twigs were thick with flies she shook them into a pillowcase and poured boiling water over them.

In the small parlour there was a ledge five feet high for her blue-patterned plates and her collection of bottles in all shapes and colours. A deal table stood in the centre of the room covered in a square of lace, held firm by four home-made chairs of heavy wood with seats of undressed leather. In the hearth was an iron rail three feet high with hooks for her cooking pots and a large kettle hung from one thick with soot, its lid never still as its steam curled with the woodsmoke up the wide inglenook. The light of a tallow candle, with its wick of twisted rag, did not reach the corners of the room so whenever she went for a plate or a knife she poked the fire to raise the flames. In the corner was a beautifully carved chest of *boekenhout* that had once been her stepfather's driving seat in the wagon that had brought them across the mountains. She sat on a high chair made out of yellow wood with her feet on a *stoof*, a handsome little footstool, under which was a bowl of burning charcoal. Like the fire, it was never allowed to go out and she always had a dozen different explanations whenever, especially in the heat of summer, she was asked why.

Because of an old habit, taken from her *voortrekking* days, she sewed tiny little parcels onto her petticoat. She would sew socks and slippers, handkerchiefs, belts, and even delicacies like boiled sugar-nuts and mint-drops and all hidden by her skirt. It made her look a yard wider but nobody ever guessed what was underneath.

In the evenings, long after the light had gone from her windows and the plates in the kitchen had been licked clean by the cats, William and Tongo sat on the floor by her *stoof* and she told them stories of the Boers, of how the *voortrekkers* were hustled and harried out of the Cape and then Natal, pushed further and further north as the British extended the boundary of their South African empire. She would tell how they were attacked all the way by the kaffir chiefs whenever there was the chance to kill and plunder. Yet she spoke of it all in such a gentle way, as if no one were to blame.

'When I was a child,' she would say, as the orange flames of the fire danced in her grey eyes, 'we seemed always to be on the move, always wandering, like vagrants and tinkers. The hardest part was our trek across the Drakensbergs. The men took off the rear wheels of our wagons and we children fetched branches to place under the axle and down they went with the hind part dragging along. Sometimes we used wheel drags to stop the front wheels turning, sometimes we emptied the wagons and then all our possessions had to be carried down the mountainside. Sometimes we even lowered our oxen and our cattle down on the end of a rope and pulley – hundreds of feet they went but we never lost one. No, it was by no means a simple business. It was a big affair.

'Our *predikants* – they're our preachers – would tell us we were like the wandering tribe of Israel looking for the promised land. We've been strongly impressed by our wanderings. Many of our habits and customs go back to then. Have you never seen, William, how much fuss we Boers make whenever we say our goodbyes, even though we may only be off on a day's ride to Ohrigstad? And then, when we return, how we are greeted and how we go about shaking the hand of everyone in the house? That's because all those years ago the people we met had often come from great dangers and those we said goodbye to we knew we might never meet again. The English are unkind about us and laugh at how we live, but the Boer, William, has had no time for easy English ways. We work hard through the day and eat before it's dark because our candles are made of coarse fat and rag and as the Lord told us not to be wasteful we pray in the dark. If our houses are crude it is because beams do not come dressed off trees and if we make bricks for our houses when we should be ploughing, there is less corn to eat and sow. We cannot have grand rooms and spreading roofs like the English, nor their slate or glass. We did not come here with money from the diamond fields. Nor have they fought like us and wandered like us, nor lost young husbands as I lost mine and all the children he never planted in me.

'When I married we had nothing but our faith and love. We slept together under a blanket on straw until he made me a four-poster bed. Then we lived in that under a covering of wagon canvas and he built the house around it. And when he'd finished – and it took him a year between the farming – he kept eight planks of the best hardwood, four for him and four for me, so that we'd be buried properly according to our church when the time came for us to go. And dear man, he went too soon. Much too soon. I've still got my planks though, ready to be made up.

'But we were happy. And if our preachers told us we were God's chosen people it was easy for us to believe it. We had game to hunt and eat; antelope and wildebeeste came so close at night they would cross my front porch. We kept skins and horns and sold them to traders for salt and coffee and linen. The land was good and rich and there was nothing we planted that did not grow abundantly.

'The English do not understand us. Perhaps that's why we left Europe at the beginning. Maybe we felt we were understood by nobody. If some of our men are slow and dull, we have others who are tall and blond and strong, and quicker than time. But they all share a love of liberty and are chivalrous and brave.'

When she was quiet, moving away with her memories, they would look at the fire and see pictures in her words and listen to the tapping of the kettle lid and the low hissing of the charcoal beneath her feet, waiting for her to come back.

She had many stories. Her favourite, and the one Tongo retold a hundred times to everyone he met on his travels, was of her Uncle Albrecht.

'He lived alone,' she said, 'on the far western stretch of the Orange River on the edge of the desert that's nothing but a wasteland. He hunted there, trading in animal skins, heads and claws in exchange for meat, brandy and ammunition. But one year the rains never came and Uncle Abe, as we called him, though he wasn't my real uncle, sat and waited for the big drought either to end or finally kill him. The country was so bone dry you could hear the grass crackle like tinder, and the wind come like a breath from a furnace, stirring up sand and dead snakes and lizards in the air, whipping the wool off dead sheep and sending their carcases spinning away naked. He hadn't eaten in a week and because the water in the river was black he would rise before the sun and lick the dew off the rocks. He was so hungry and thirsty, his stomach was clinging to his spine.

'His gun hung on the wall of his shack and on the table was one last shot and one full charge of powder in the horn. Every day for a week he'd taken the gun down and loaded the shot to look for meat but every evening he put it back up again. Then he got up one morning and decided it would be his last. If he was going to die he wouldn't let the drought take him. So he poured the powder down the barrel and rammed home the shot and went down to the stinking river to do it, not wanting to die on his own doorstep. He held the barrel towards him and hooked the trigger on the stick of a tree and was just about to pull when over the butt he saw . . . a buck!'

'A buck?' shouted William and Tongo together.

'A big buck,' she went on, 'sturdy and shining grey and with enough meat to last a man a month of careful living. So, sweating and trembling in case he hit the trigger, Uncle Abe unhooked the gun and turned it around. The buck stood proud and still, twenty paces off, but Uncle Abe couldn't stop shivering. Remember, one shot was all he had. But then, careful, so the sweat shouldn't dampen the powder, he sighted and fired. And the gun kicked him as flat as a pancake!'

'Did he miss?' shouted William.

'Did he, missus?' shouted Tongo.

Mrs de Wet paused and breathed in deep. 'No!' she said. 'He got him. And a ten-pound barbel too!'

'No!' the boys cried.

'And a brace of pheasants!'

'No!' they shouted.

'Then a hare!' she went on. 'And a porcupine!'

William stood up. 'Mrs de Wet,' he said solemnly, 'how could your uncle have got all those with one shot?'

'Well, I wasn't there,' she replied coyly, 'but according to Uncle Abe it went like this: when he pulled the trigger, the fish leapt out of the water and the shot passed right through it and killed the buck stone dead. When the gun flew out of his hands it knocked the hare unconscious and as Uncle Abe fell back he threw up his hands and caught two pheasants out of the bush!'

William and Tongo looked at her in silence, waiting, expecting some disclaimer. But the old lady pulled her shawl tighter around her shoulders and poked the fire in a matter-of-fact way.

Finally, William said, 'Mrs de Wet. What about the porcupine?'

'Well, it seems,' she said, 'and remember I wasn't there,' she repeated, 'that still holding the two birds, Uncle Abe sat down again. On the porcupine!'

The old lady became sad when she spoke of her younger days and one evening she wept when she remembered old Sarah.

'Sarah was an old black. It was hard to know how old, we never knew their ages. As time means nothing to them they seldom know it themselves. They are young or they are old and Sarah was old by our reckoning, well over seventy, because she said she remembered the Zulu King Shaka.

'We loved her and she was always kind to me. But she had a severe and unkind mistress and if father had had more money we would have bought her ourselves. She was beaten and so hard sometimes, the tears would trickle down her wrinkled cheeks.

'One day her mistress had been baking biscuits and sent Sarah to fetch some from the oven outside. The old girl was always honest but she had a sweet tooth and she thought it no great crime to take one. But her mistress was watching and she screamed and kicked her. "You have been flogged too many times," she shouted. "So instead I will tie you to a post and everyone can see what a thief you are."

'She took a long thin piece of leather cut from a dried hide and strapped old Sarah to a post loosely around the neck but tight enough to grip her and keep her from sitting down. Then she fastened her hands behind her back and made her stand there all day in the sun.

'The other native servants came to look and laugh and white men spat at her and their children threw mud. I waited until the excitement had gone and I crept up to her. The old girl sobbed, "I feel so ashamed, I want to die," she said. "Tell God I want to die."

'"I'm sorry," I whispered to her. "I'll go away. I'll not stare at you. I wish I could untie you."

'"No, no!" she cried. "You mustn't do that. But I love you. Please stay with me!"

'But I could not and I ran off crying myself. I wanted to go back to Sarah and I kept telling myself that I should but then I excused myself with this to do and that to do.

'Then there was a great commotion, women shrieking and men running, and when I got to the post old Sarah had kicked up her legs and hanged herself, choking on the strap. Her mistress came and took the strap but left her lying there all crumpled until she was carried away by her own people. And I was too afraid to help or even touch her goodbye. I've never forgiven myself. And nor will my God.'

William and Tongo left her by the fireside and went to the stable to sleep.

Sometimes Mr Trichaerdts, her nearest neighbour from the farm along the track, ate with them on those evenings whenever his ploughing brought him close to Mrs de Wet's farmhouse. He too had come with the *voortrekkers* though his family had been among the last to arrive. He worked the farm on his own, which meant that most of the thousand acres that were given to him as a settler were never touched by his cattle or his ploughshares. Once, he said, ten years back, he had been a successful farmer with his bins full of grain and his sheds full of cattle and sheep. But three years of drought had killed all his stock and locusts had eaten all his wheat. Locusts had always been a curse, he said, but no one had ever seen them like that before, coming like a thundercloud, making the sky black and devouring everything they landed on. He said farmers had sprayed their crops with soap and water and at sunset everyone brought out their oxen and cattle, sheep and horses to trample the locusts where they were eating. He had even paid the local chiefs to send for their witch doctor. When he came he ordered all those kraals with daughters to send them to him. Then he washed the girls all over with his magic potions and for a week he had them walking naked across the land, through the crops, squashing the locusts with their feet, from dawn to sunset. They were given blankets to sleep on but they cooked their own food and no one was allowed to speak to them. But it did no good and on the eighth day the witch doctor sent the girls home.

Early one morning, just as William and Tongo were about to leave, Mr Trichaerdts arrived at Mrs de Wet's riding an ox. One of his cattle, he said, had lung disease and he had just killed it. Now he had to inoculate the rest but he could not manage it on his own.

Within an hour William and Tongo had herded the thirty

cattle into the shed and tied them firmly by their necks to a rail and put a twist of rope around their rear hooves. Mr Trichaerdts then went down the line with a sharp knife and slit open their tails. William followed, carrying the sickly white and bloodied pus, which Trichaerdts called his 'serum', in a tobacco tin. As he slit the tail, William soaked a piece of rag in the serum and forced it into the wound. Trichaerdts told him that he had killed the diseased cow and had squeezed the pus from its lung. Once it had entered the live cattle's blood, he said, they would be safe.

They stayed and drank coffee while the old farmer sat with a pregnant cow in the stalls. They waited an hour but still he did not return so they dipped their mugs in a bucket of water and hung them on the hooks by the door and went to say their goodbyes. They found him, standing with his right arm sunk into her up to his shoulder, easing the calf out. Then he sat down, exhausted, and let his cats lick the afterbirth off his hands.

They were three miles beyond Lydenburg moving east for Pilgrims Hill when they saw it: a large white poster nailed to a tree, the writing vivid red. The army had named Ianto. He had killed again and the British Administrator of the Transvaal was offering one hundred gold sovereigns to anyone who helped in his capture or his killing.

It was December 28th, 1878. The recruiting sergeant had only managed to persuade eleven diggers in the valley to take the Queen's shilling and when he came up the garden path, Mary was waiting on her verandah to tell him he would not make his dozen there. She shouted at him loudly and for so long, Huw and Samson came running up from the river. But by the time they reached the brow the sergeant was already well away along the High Street in the wagon carrying his recruits en route to the

British army barracks in Natal via the Lydenburg stockade. Mary was white and shaking with anger and fear at suddenly knowing how close the English had brought their war.

'We threw mud at them when they came to Bethesda,' she said, 'and Meryl Davies hit one with a slate and bloodied his tunic. It's what I should have done too, just now, them bringing their shillings up here and asking us to provide them with men. If they want war then let them fight it with their own.'

They sat her down in her chair and Samson gently rocked it as Huw tapped her open palm as he always did to soothe her. He felt her trembling.

'He knew my name, all our names,' she said, bewildered. 'How would they know that, Huw? Tell me – all the way from Durban, yet he knew our names. How could he?'

Huw went down on one knee. 'Mother, maybe we are better known than we think. And why not? Walrus was there a long time and everyone must have known him. And he wrote us a letter so he must have told everybody about us, that's to be expected. There's nothing sinister about it, really.'

But Mary would not be soothed; not by Samson's rocking, nor Huw's caresses, nor Jollie's cups of tea, nor Polly's cakes. She knew that the red-coated sergeant, with his blond moustache and cold, grey, English eyes, had not come idly by. She had smelt brandy and heard him laugh about her strong Welsh lads who would not fight for their Queen to put down the impudent blacks. But he had only mentioned two of them. That was why she could not stop her trembling. The sergeant had known so much, he must know of Ianto. But he had not named him and she could not reason why.

William was about to take his wagon across a low waterdrift of the Ohrigstad River when he saw the scarlet uniform on the far side and the wagon preparing to cross. He recognized the diggers sitting in the back and at first he thought there had been trouble at the camp. Three he knew to be regular drunkards, a fourth had frequent fits and bit his tongue and had to be staked to the ground to stop him from tearing his own flesh. And he saw the young English digger they called Billy Bean who had hired Mr Jenkins his dark suit for Joanna's wedding and who was supposed to have been to an English public school.

Halfway across they sighted William and shouted that they were on their way to fight the Zulus. The sergeant stopped his cart opposite William and jumped down. His tunic was unbuttoned and the bare skin of his chest was wet and white. His face was red, his blond hair dark with sweat and when he spoke he smelt of drink.

'You're going the wrong way, my lad. There's nothing up there but cowardly diggers and frumpy widows. Come with us!'

'And which way is that?' asked William.

'To Zululand,' shouted another red-eyed digger, the one who had found a nugget in his first week and had lived on Mr Phelan's Cape rum ever since. 'We're going south to kill the kaffirs before they go to Natal and eat all the little white babies.'

The sergeant laughed and came closer. 'What have you there?' he asked, nodding at the wagon.

'Sisal rope and nails for the camp,' William answered.

'And lots of green fruit,' the sergeant added, lifting the tarpaulin cover.

'Yes, that's right; pears and apples and green tomatoes. I get the Boers to pick them early so that they ripen up in the village and not on the farms.'

'That's a clever boy,' the sergeant said, touching William's shoulder. 'But a cleverer one wouldn't waste it on such a crew, not when our quartermaster would pay him three times as much – four if you bargained well. Bring it along with us, lad, and your kaffir boy too. In a week we'll be with the regiment, the 2nd Foot, at the crossing at Rorke's Drift and we need transport riders, especially young ones and strong like you.' He let his hand drop from William's shoulder to his knee. 'And you mustn't worry about the Zulus, boy. They're just as easy to shoot as the rest of them.'

'I'm not worried about anything,' said William, 'but your war has nothing to do with me.'

The sergeant drew back. His eyes narrowed and he coughed and spat phlegm. 'Welsh, ain't you?'

William did not answer. Instead he beckoned to Tongo to move the oxen on. But the sergeant shouted, 'Stay put, nigger boy, or you'll have my whip across your head.' He looked back at William. 'I said, ain't you Welsh?'

'I am.'

'Course you are. There's a few like you round here, ain't there, calling it an English war.'

William saw the blood running fresh into the man's neck and cheeks. The sergeant spat again and swore, then he pulled himself up into the driving seat and lifted his rifle onto his knees.

'We're looking for a Welshie like you, and we'll have him soon, 'cos we know where he's going. And I'll tell you something else: we know where he's from. Oh, yes! He won't go running back to his mum – not with the price we're offering. There's not a Boer or kaffir or any one of those stinking diggers who won't sell him for a hundred pounds. You tell Mrs bloody Llewellyn that!'

William turned away quickly and fumbled with the reins. Then the sergeant shouted, 'What's your name, Welshie?'

William did not answer.

'I'm talking to you, Welshie bastard. Turn or I'll shoot your bloody liver out.'

Tongo stared terrified at William, knowing he would not lie. He heard the click of the gun. Suddenly Billy Bean spoke, loud and cheerful in his sharp high voice.

'Leave off, Sergeant. The boy's not too bright but he means no harm. He's just cussed like the rest of them. William's his name, Sergeant. Isn't that right, boys?'

The other diggers grunted. It could have meant yes. It was

not their business, but no man had the right to question another and demand an answer, especially a Limey in scarlet.

'Is that right, Welshie? Is that your name?'

William turned and faced him. 'Yes,' he said. 'William's my name.'

The sergeant spat again and watched the phlegm dribble down his oxen's flanks. Then he whipped them hard and the cart lurched forward and they were gone.

William looked at the sharp shallow ridges where the wheels had been and heard the crack of the sergeant's whip, but was afraid to look up, and hating himself for not finding Billy Bean's face to say goodbye.

'I can't go home, Tongo. But I haven't the courage not to. I've never lied to her. Never.'

Tongo nodded.

William said, 'She would know. She would see it.'

'Yes, master. Our mothers are inside us,' said Tongo, 'watching.'

They sat facing each other across the fire, the night breeze lifting the flames to their faces, then cowering and hiding them again. In the darkness William said, 'I am a coward, Tongo. What will I do?'

'You are alone,' said Tongo. 'There is no good thing to do.'

They did not speak again until the fire had died and the wet air chilled them.

'Tongo. The sky will break soon.'

'Yes, master, soon.'

'I want you to go to the village, to my mother.'

'I know.'

'I will write a letter telling her we've found some trade a long way south, I'll say Durban and that we'll earn a lot of money there. I'll say we'll be away for some months and that she mustn't worry. Will she believe me?'

'No, master. But you must tell her so.'

'Don't let her see you, Tongo. Slip it under her porch, then follow the Blyde and wait for me beyond the gorge. Remember, no one must see you. If they do they will keep you.'

'Are we going to Natal, master?'

'No, Tongo. We will go to the Buffalo River and follow the English to this Rorke's Drift. We'll make a profit from them, Tongo, and pray that God will settle things while we are gone.'

They hugged each other and went their opposite ways. The sun was still an hour coming. Soon the sky would turn pink and as Tongo climbed with the letter between his teeth, he could see the lowveld opening up below him and the cover of the mists breaking apart. Somewhere down there his young master was moving away in his wagon. Out of reach of Pilgrims Rest.

CHAPTER EIGHT

It never occurred to Mary that William would return. She read his scribbled note, folded it in four, creasing the edges sharp with her nail, and put it quickly into her Bible, pressing the covers hard together as if closing him there safe and forever.

Soon she found herself thinking of him as if he were already spent, remembering her ambitions for him as though they were already achieved. She began to doubt the future, suddenly suspicious of Africa. The land had suddenly turned sour.

Jollie knew but Mary hid it from the rest. How could they know as certainly she had lost two sons, one searched for by the English army, and now the second, her beautiful William, gone? She had lost them too soon, all this way from Wales.

'If fatness constitutes beauty, then they are beautiful. Most of them, after their first child, became very, very fat indeed with large hanging dairies and great bellies with navels so thoroughly surrounded with flesh that a swallow, given a little labour, might make a comfortable nest in one! Mind you, their men are formidable and we'd be wise not to mess with them. They are the greatest single army in Africa and believe they are guided by their Gods to rule it. It's not for nothing that they call themselves Zulu. It means the children of Heaven.'

Their talk was of the Zulus because that morning British forces had crossed the Buffalo River from Natal into Zululand under their commander, Lord Chelmsford. The war against

King Cetshwayo had begun. Mary knew now why William had left, and where he had gone to.

The Reverend Makepeace was holding forth at Mary's supper table, having eaten second helpings of pheasant, sweet potato, pumpkin and greens and three helpings of Jollie's steamed sultana pudding with cornflour sauce. It had been a long dinner. They had sat down at six, just before the last of the evening light had left the windows, and it was now past ten. Major John was there and so was Honest Jack.

Huw had stayed only long enough to eat his meal and then ran quickly back to his wife's bedside, because that afternoon, a little after two, Joanna Llewellyn had given birth to twins a fortnight premature, a boy and a girl, the valley's first white babies. Mary had delivered them with Jollie as a helper and Polly running back and forth from Honest Jack's kitchen carrying armfuls of clean white flannel, tailed by his girls struggling with huge jugs of steaming water.

They were fine babies, dark like their parents and looking even darker because of their fresh blue eyes which, Mary said, would turn brown all too soon. The boy was heavy and long-limbed and came out with his eyes wide open so that Mary said he knew where he was going. His sister, who arrived ten minutes later, was smaller and wrinkled and covered so thick in the wax of birth she looked grey and almost mummified. But Jollie smacked her botton and she spat out mucus and cried louder than her brother and soon they washed her pink and when they held her to Joanna they said she was smiling, though they knew it was nothing of the kind.

That evening they celebrated and Huw left ten pounds with Honest Jack so that diggers might toast the health and long life of Owen his son and his little daughter, who was to be called Victoria, after the Queen.

The evening was warm, so when the Reverend had finally stopped eating they took their jugs of wine out onto the verandah. Honest Jack sent for another bottle of Cape brandy and Mary brought out a basket of granadillas. The Reverend pretended to be shocked at the sight of them.

'Granadillas you may call them, Mary, but I recognize them as passion fruit – the favourite of venomous snakes – and "the fruit of that forbidden tree whose mortal taste brought death into this world". I'll have two!' he said and they laughed.

The clouds that had carried rain to Natal and Zululand seemed to have emptied themselves there and now only covered the earth with shadows. The breeze purled up from the river, spreading all the scents of Mary's garden, and it pleased her. The crickets buzzed near and far, coming and going like surf on the sand, as they always did when the air was heavy. Major John ventured it would rain but Honest Jack sniffed the night like a beagle and said no, the weather had spent itself. The Reverend stretched himself flat on the floor, stared at the sky, the jug of wine balanced on his chest, and said he could not care one way or the other. Then he changed his mind and said he hoped it might rain because his grandfather had always taught him as a child that God came down in the rain to make things grow, and God was long overdue here!

'My grandfather,' he said, rubbing his hands together as if to warm up his memories, 'used to adore thunderstorms, the way some people are fascinated by fires. He was one of the odder Makepeaces in a family of very odd people indeed. There were the long-headed Makepeaces and the round-headed, depending on which side of the family you came from. This grandfather was a longhead! He wore knee breeches, pink silk stockings, buckled shoes and a white choker round his neck to keep his tonsils warm. He had a turret at the end of the lawn, the start of a castle he'd intended to build. It looked like a madman's folly. Whenever there was a storm he ran like a crippled hare down the lawn in the rain, pulling the choker over his head like an old fisherwoman, climbed to the top of his turret and stood there exalted as the lightning flashed around him.

'He said it was electric messages from the door of Heaven and he was well over eighty when he received his last; it sent him to bed with a sneeze and he left it in a shroud. Unknown to us he'd married his housekeeper a couple of years before, though I don't think she ever let him get his breeches off. A cunning little vixen – and dreadfully disappointed in her expectations because when his will was read out the estate belonged to the creditors. Eventually the poor soul emigrated to Sydney, which rather serves her right!'

They laughed and Mary asked, 'Is that all true, Reverend?'

'As true as the world is round, Mary.'

'And well remembered,' said Honest Jack.

But the Reverend replied, 'I'm cursed with a good memory, Jack. Believe me, there are things I'd sooner forget but they remain to taunt me. D'you know, I envy the man who forgets easily.'

'And so do I!' answered Honest Jack. And then they all remembered and the Reverend leant over and held his arm. 'I'm sorry, Jack – that was clumsy. Forgive me.'

'It's all right, Reverend. I can't forget them – nor will I either. Not if I ever mean to have them back.' On Saturday, Honest Jack had received the weekly letters from his wife in Lydenburg and for the first time they included some sketches of his daughters. He had kept in his room three days and nights, taking only soup from his girls and ignoring their pleas. It was only the news of Joanna's babies that brought him out.

Mary peeled a peach for him and cut it in quarters. 'Tell us about the Zulus, Honest Jack.'

He hesitated and took more brandy, so Major John answered instead. 'The first I saw of them was in Durban: well-built fellows, none under six feet and it seemed they went out of their way to avoid the other kaffirs there. By law they were obliged to wear clothes in town so they covered themselves in anything they could steal or borrow – old military tunics, stewards' jackets, topcoats, I even saw one in an undertaker's frock coat. They all wore bangles round their arms and ankles, twisted copper or brass wire. And some of them had holes in their ears to carry snuffboxes and pipes. Even saw a cowhorn in one!'

'That's for his dagga,' said Honest Jack. 'Though I don't think, Major, that what you saw were Zulus as I remember them. Mind you, put any kaffir in a town and he'll lose his way and dignity soon enough.'

He took another sip of brandy. 'The first I saw of them was a good twenty years back, long before Cetshwayo . . . must have been in Dingaan's days. We were taking some wagons up from Pietermaritzburg to Dundee, and we'd had to go east a bit to drop off some stuff at Elandskraal, not far from the Zulu border. We came across four of them looking very sorry. They'd been in a scrap, though we didn't speak the lingo then so we never did find out what had happened. One had been speared through his lung and was coughing up blood, catching it in his hands and drinking it again; another had half his leg shorn away and the third had the top of his skull almost sliced through. It was like a lid kept together by a hinge of skin and when we lifted it we saw his brain inside pumping away like a great big white heart. Heavens knows how long they'd been there or how far they'd walked, but we loaded them aboard and took them into Dundee and left them at the hospital.'

'What about the other one?' asked Major John. 'You said there were four.'

'I did indeed, and that's really what my story's about, because when we were next up there – oh, it must have been another few months on – they'd gone, all recovered, even the one with half a head, gone back to Zululand. All except the fourth. And that's the rub, because all he had wrong with him was a torn ear-lobe. It seems the doctor just cut it off and when he saw what they'd done to him he died of shame. You see, he was no longer beautiful and he willed himself to death.'

'That's astonishing,' said Mary.

'God strike me if it isn't true.'

'Oh, I'll vouch for it,' said the Reverend. 'They're a brave tough people, live and die by their dignity and strength. Only the fittest survive in Zululand, the weak perish. Mind you, so do the disobedient and the schemers. The first King Shaka slaughtered over two million kaffirs he considered unfit or unwilling to join his children of Heaven. And what of this new Cetshwayo? He's supposed to have killed twenty thousand of his own people in the fight for the throne, though I suppose our Tudor kings were just as ruthless and they did it a good deal later in British history than the Zulus have in theirs.'

He lifted his head, sipped more wine, and said, 'They were my first sight of Africa. I went from Durban to St Paul's, just beyond Eshowe, to make them Christians. What arrogance! Mind you, had they been, I should have had a very busy first day because when I arrived there was a funeral and a wedding taking place together. The old Zulus wailed at one and some very pretty young girls danced at the other. I remember how they all wore tiny blue-and-white aprons no bigger than a man's palm, but no matter how they danced, or how they sat, the little thing hid all it was intended to hide!'

'Tell us about the burial,' said Mary.

The Reverend pushed away the bottle Honest Jack offered. 'No, Jack, thank you. Brandy doesn't stoke the memory, it stifles it and addles the retelling.' Instead he took another sip of his wine and went on.

'I'd watched the dead man's wives sit all night by the open grave, spitting on the ground in turn and drawing signs with their forefingers in the mud they'd made with their spittle and tears. They'd piled stones inside the grave like a chair and sat the corpse on it. His shield and assegai were placed by his side with a bowl of food and a jug of water and all his little bits and pieces laid neatly around him, ready for the journey into the next land. They put a large flat stone on his head so his spirit wouldn't wander at night and wrapped a soft cowhide over his shoulders to protect him. Then, just about dawn, they filled up the hole and when they'd finished they planted a tree so that no one would ever walk over the spot again. The old man had been a chief so the mourners went to a small river a mile away, the women one side and the men on the other, and they washed themselves all over, again and again until they considered themselves clean. And only then did they stop their weeping and wailing.'

'And they call these people savage?' said Mary.

'Oh, they can be savage enough,' said Honest Jack. 'Nothing's more terrible in all Africa than Zulus ready to wash their spears in blood. Their name is enough. Say Zulu to any kaffir here and see the terror in his eyes, and we're a long way from the border. That's how they rule, Mary, that's how they've become so powerful. When I was a young man and new, I rode with Walrus Baines from the Orange River north, and every day was a fright to me, every day we had some kind of a tussle with the Basutos, the Sekekune, the Swazis and any other kaffir chief who thought he could take an easy pick at us. But I never knew what terror was until we went into Zululand! I don't think Walrus had been there often because it shook him too and it was a long time before he ever went there again.

'We were along a ridge, being high, you see, was about all the protection you could expect, though Walrus was never fond of high ground. We saw a thousand of them coming on a village, advancing in the shape of a crescent, that's how they spread out when they attack. But this village was well stockaded and they couldn't get in, so finally they tied balls of dry grass to their knobkerries and set fire to them and threw them at the thatch huts. The whole village went up like gunpowder. It was like smoking out a warren of rabbits. The poor devils came out choking and half dead, some of them already on fire, women hugging their babies and dragging the older children. Over the roar of the flames we could hear them screaming and above that the Zulus' "*Usutu! Usutu!* Kill! Kill!" They stamped out the lot of them – every single one, babies on the end of spears, ripping open their stomachs as they danced and sang to the terrible screams of the old hags burning inside. Some of the old people did crawl out but the Zulus picked them up and threw them over the fence back into the fire again. That's how they do it. Those few who've witnessed it, like me, and the fewer who've survived it, spread those kind of stories across all of Africa. That's why the Zulu legend is so terrible, even here.'

For a while no one spoke and Honest Jack took more brandy. Then Mary asked, 'Is it why the English are afraid?'

'No, Mary,' said Major John. 'They're not afraid. Only worried the Zulus will spread over into Natal. They're a frightening war machine and there's no knowing where they'd stop or how you'd stop them if they began to move south or west.'

'If you ask me,' said Honest Jack, 'it's the Boers who're urging this war on. They'd like to see the Zulus put down, then all the pasturelands right up to the Umfolozi would be theirs. They hate the Zulus. They'll never forget Retief.'

'What's that?' asked Mary.

'Retief was one of the early Boers,' the major answered, 'one of the Great Trek leaders. He took a party of men to King Dingaan to ask for grazing rights. Dingaan welcomed them and when a deal was agreed, he invited them to stay and eat and watch the dancing. But as they fed he had them slaughtered, every one. Soon after the Boers killed three thousand of them in revenge. The river was running thick and red with corpses and it's been called the Battle of Blood River ever since. So you see, the Boers are very happy the English have gone over the Buffalo after them today.'

'The war won't be that easy,' said Honest Jack. 'Not at this time of the year, with so much rain that way.'

'War is an option of difficulties,' said the Reverend. 'A famous British general said that once – Wolfe, I believe. Mind you, knowing the type, Lord Chelmsford possibly thinks it'll be just a pleasant little promenade. But he and the other fools in Durban want a war and a war will be had. They all want to believe it is a civilizing war against barbarity. It is one of the great irritations of the English, how readily they believe their own myths.'

'Why?' asked Mary. 'Surely the Zulus have a right to live in their own land as they choose? Why can't the Queen order the government to settle it without war?'

'My dear Mary,' said the Reverend, laughing, 'if you laid out every British politician head to toe in a line, you'd still not reach a sensible conclusion. This Prime Minister, Disraeli – Beaconsfield – call him what you like, is a prize fool with as much grasp of affairs here in Africa as a man climbing a greasy pole. I'm afraid, Mary, bloody though it will be, and whether it's to do with Boer or Zulu, the affairs of Africa will be settled in Africa and nowhere else. But Disraeli's being pushed into this one and he's sending freshers out from London, hastily raised. He'll pay the price for it, too.'

'Why don't you get God to settle it, Reverend?' asked Honest Jack.

'He's not averse to a little war, Jack, here and there,' he answered with a smile. 'Indeed, I often wonder if He doesn't cause them simply for a little diversion. The Book of Exodus says, "The Lord is a Man of War". You'd be surprised how full the Bible is in its praise of death and destruction, though I suppose that's only to be expected from a wandering tribe of sheep stealers. "Thy right hand, O Lord, is become glorious in power and hath dashed Thine enemies in pieces. Thy greatness hath overthrown them that rose against Thee and Thy wrath has consumed them as stubble. The beauty of Israel is slain upon high places; how are the mighty fallen." Wonderful, isn't it? Wouldn't surprise me if there isn't a Bible in every general's knapsack.' He paused, then went on, 'And I most sincerely pray Chelmsford has one too because he and the poor devils he leads will have precious little else to help them.'

'And Amen to that!' said the major and Honest Jack together.

* * *

It was past midnight and Mary said she would walk to Huw's house. Polly and Jollie were sleeping there by Joanna's bed. But the Reverend told her to stay and said he would call on them on his way back to the church and Honest Jack struggled to his feet and brushed the driblets of brandy from his chin and said he would walk with him as far as the hotel. After they had gone Major John came and sat on the floor by Mary.

'So we shall have a christening,' he said.

'Two. Owen and Victoria.'

'I think Huw would rather she was Mary.'

'So I believe, but Victoria is her name.'

'Two new Pilgrims.'

'Two new South Africans.'

'I wonder,' he said, 'I wonder if it will come together as it should – all of us from the Cape and Natal and all the Boers too, from the Transvaal and the Free State.'

'Only the whites, John?'

'Of course. Even that would be a miracle.'

'What will become of the blacks?'

'Mary, I'm talking of nationhood.'

'So am I.'

'Then you're a dreamer. Only the Zulus have a nation. And maybe their cousins, the Matabele across the Limpopo. The other tribes are just too small and too weak on their own. They'll have to be content to live under us, under our protection. It can only be that way.'

Mary sighed. 'Isn't there enough room for everyone? No one is born to be a servant forever and the land is so big.'

He did not answer. For a while he held Mary's chair with his left hand and rocked it back and forth. Then he said, 'It is big. When I first came to Africa I thought it was too big. Wherever I went I had the oddest feeling that I was seeing it for the first and last time, like a visitor passing through who knows his home will always be someplace else. D'you know it would madden me so much, sometimes I'd go and stand hip-high in a river just to feel it around me. And often I'd bury my hands in the earth and grind the grit between my fingers so I could feel it biting me.'

She took his hand and smoothed her fingers across his and said softly, 'The land has a way of making you feel a stranger if it doesn't want you.'

'That's unkind,' he said.

'I was thinking of myself, John.'

'In Wales?'

'Wales and here.'

'No, Mary, not here. This is where you belong, you said so the very first day I sat with you, under the church tree. You said it was like returning.'

'You remember that?'

He kissed her fingertips and nodded. 'Of course.' Then he said, 'I'm sorry we haven't cheered you up. We were hoping we could, with the wine and talk and the babies and all.'

For a moment the moon broke the clouds and lit the small clusters of bougainvillaea William had planted.

'They're purple and he thought they'd be red,' she said.

He looked out across the verandah to the moving finger of light. 'He'll bring you more, Mary.'

'I only want him.'

'And so you will.'

'Not if there's a war.'

'Wars are for soldiers.'

'Not always.'

He hesitated. 'He'll come back, too.' But he knew that was not true. Ianto could not come home again, not if what the sergeant said was true. When they caught him, murderer or traitor, it didn't matter, they would kill him. He would face the firing squad or the hangman's noose and they would not even send her the body. They would bury it in lime in an unmarked hole with not a parson or mourner to see him covered. And how would she know? Who would tell her? 'Please, Mary,' he said, 'you must not be so sad. Not today.'

She nodded. 'And tomorrow's always Sunday! That's what

my father used to say to me whenever I cried. Though he couldn't have known how few he had left when he said it.'

'You loved him?'

'For as long as I could. But he left us and went south to work. He's buried in a coal shaft near Merthyr and they've never reopened it. He deserved better than that, I think.'

'I'm sorry, Mary.'

She laughed but there was no humour in it. 'I'm sorry too. I've lost men all my life. And good men, too. Why is that, John? So many bad people in my village live to old age when the good die so young.'

'Before they could become bad?'

'No! Not my father. Nor my Owen. They lived good lives.'

'We live many lives, Mary, not one but many. I know. I'm a family of brothers and I don't suppose one has really ever got on with another.'

'Did you have a favourite?'

'Oh, yes. The first.'

'Children are good.'

He said, 'He couldn't bear the world as he saw it. There was no love in it, no father love, no mother love. No love anywhere. So another brother took my place, just as gentle, I remember, but determined to save me from brutal things. And then as the world opened up and he saw what was there he kept himself from it, until eventually he found himself marooned.'

'On a little island?'

'All by himself.'

'He could have come back if he'd tried.'

'But he didn't, you see. He despaired and then another more stubborn brother took his place.'

'All these years, John?'

'Yes, Mary. All these years. In America I had some very black years. I got drunk often, the bottle was about my only company. I hated the taste but it provided the oblivion.'

'Ianto was like that,' she said, 'though he never ever drank more than a glass of ruby wine. Sometimes his moods would last weeks, even a month, dreadful black moods. And when they'd finished I'd see how thin and hollow he was, as if it had eaten some of him away. He never belonged.'

'Not to you?'

'He was mine. For a while.'

'What sent him away, Mary?'

She kissed his fingertips but she would not tell. She had no need to now. She had lived with it long enough and there was only one other to share it with and now he was gone. All these years she had feared the moment, knowing he would leave, but never, never did she think that God would send him off first. It was unkind if this was His vengeance.

'God sent him away,' she said at last. 'It's unfair but all my life I've been taught not to question Him. Though I wonder if He doesn't sometimes take the Devil's road to get what He wants.'

He suddenly turned and faced her and wrapped his arms around her ankles. 'If that is true,' he said, 'then maybe I should go the Devil's way to get what I want too.'

She felt his hands on her legs. 'No,' she whispered, 'I'm not as strong-willed as you.'

'I wish that were true.'

'It is, almost.'

'Will you?'

'No.'

'What if I were patient and a gentleman?'

'But you are.'

'Will you marry me?'

'I don't think so.'

'Why not?'

'You're young enough to be my small brother.'

'Does it matter?'

'It might in another ten years.'

'I'd love you more.'

'You'd love me less.'

'How can you know?'

'I've loved before. And married, too.'

He looked surprised. 'Why did you say that?'

'Because that's how it was.'

'Two men?'

She hesitated. 'Yes.'

'Tell me!' But she did not answer.

'You can love again, Mary. And marry, too.'

'Yes, I could do both, though it's not something I've thought much of. I have my little Tom and Huw and my memories. My boys are all sides of me, you see.'

He rested his chin in her lap and she caressed his face. 'It's not fair, is it, John? I grow older and watch my sons grow up. Then there's nothing left but to remember how it was and how they were. I often think I would like to have been pregnant every year until I was too old to be; then I'd have my children around me all the time and the last would just be fully grown by the time I was ready for the grave.'

He looked up at her. 'Have my children,' he said.

'Perhaps.'

'Soon?'

'Perhaps, but not yet.'

'When shall I know? How will you?'

She smiled and she had not done so for weeks. She leant down and kissed his hair. 'It was some years ago for me, John, and I was very unhappy with love then. But I don't think I shall ever forget the feeling of it or wanting to find it again.'

He stroked her legs and kissed her palms.

'I feel delicious,' she said.

'But I must wait?'

'Oh, yes, please wait! Wait for me, John!'

And she bent forward and let her lips rest on his.

The Royal Kraal at Ondini stood in the centre of Zululand scooped out of a hill on the Ulundi Plains. Two vast circles of spiked palings, three miles round, one inside the other, protected it and a thousand mud and thatch huts sat protected between them. The palings encircling the King's great thatched dome were decorated with branches of trees hanging with red and purple blossoms.

For two days now, those who lived within the great kraal, the King's bodyguards, his plumed warriors, his favourites, the lesser chiefs, the wise *indunas*, the mischievous war doctors, the clowns, magicians, the cooks and butchers, the carvers and smiths, the herdsmen and goatherds and all their families had sat by their fires awaiting the royal summons.

It came at last, early on January 17th, 1879. Without waiting for the sun to burn off the morning mist, King Cetshwayo emerged from his sleeping-rooms, first stooping under the low entrance and then slowly standing high and broad. His body attendants fussed about him, arranging the shiny leopard skins around his shoulders, straightening the heavy necklace of gold wire that carried eight lions' teeth each longer than a man's forefinger. They held out bowls of lotions for him to freshen his face and jars of sweet-smelling ointments for his body. He was a big and heavy man with a tight ring of *imbongi* on his head and a neat trimmed beard around a small mouth. His subjects formed one vast circle, forty deep, as the *izaunsi*, the chief witch doctor, kindled a fire with tribal firesticks and mixed the protective charms for the King's *inkatha*, the coil of python skin he sat on to fortify him against evil. And all the time the King's *imbongi* danced and leapt around him wildly, bowing and weaving and shrieking their praises.

The *izaunsi* stood before him and held up to the King's lips a jug of special potions, thick and brown like stale blood. Then the thousands watching and seeing everything held their breath as the King filled his mouth, and, turning to the rising sun, spat it out in a spray so that the tiny crystals in the liquid cascaded in an arc and sparkled like a thousand tiny diamonds. Three times he filled his mouth, three times he blew out his magic, three times he thrust his assegai at the red sun rising above the Makosini Valley, birthplace of the Zulu nation, and three times all within that great kraal roared: '*Bayete! Bayete!*' in royal salute. The King was now ordained by the spirits of his ancestors, Shaka and Dingaan and his own father, M'Pande. The Zulus were ready for war.

Cetshwayo's scouts had returned early with their reports. The British plan, they said, was to attack Ulundi in five columns: from Luneburg and Utrecht in the north; from Eshowe and Kranskop in the south and at Rorke's Drift in the west. They had already crossed the Buffalo at the Drift and were now only thirty miles away, but they were a slow and heavy army, pulling wagons and guns across land where oxen sank to their knees in the rain. So Cetshwayo decided he would not wait for them to come to him. He would send his regiments to meet them and cripple them, for there was nowhere for them to hide.

That afternoon he summoned his regiments to assemble at Nodwengu some miles from the Royal Kraal: the Undi Corps, the Thulwana, Unokneke, Ngobamakosi and Umbonambi, the Umcityuuve and Udhloko, in all over twenty-five thousand warriors, eager to wash their spears against the invaders, the red-coated army, fabled rulers of the world.

The British advance column under Colonel Pulleine of the 24th Foot Regiment numbered just over two thousand regular troops and their native contingents. They had marched from Helpmakaar ten miles inside the Natal border and had camped at the foot of a mountain named on the map as Isandhlwana. It resembled a sphynx, its rocky head jutting south, its rump north. The British troops had arrived exhausted after days of pushing and humping the wagons and gun carriages.

But their fatigue had nothing to do with the decision not to entrench. Despite reports of the movement of Zulus behind the Mabaso in the Swabeni Valley and along the Nqutu Plateau, a few miles to the north, and despite the scouts' warning of activity in the Mangweni Gorge to the south, no preparation was made for defence, no laager of wagons made, not a trench was dug, not a spade lifted. So confident was the commander-in-chief, the Hon. Frederic Thesiger, Second Baron Chelmsford, that he wrote in his diary that evening:

> 'I do not believe these reports of a large force of Zulu. Some people are alarmed here but they are not able to appreciate what an army can and cannot do. No enemy, kaffir or Boer, could withstand the discipline and firepower of the British Army. Really! People see danger where there is none.'

So under grey, forbidding Isandhlwana, the shining white bell-tents faced east across the plain towards Ulundi, exactly pegged out, precisely in line and vulnerable.

Little more than a telescope's sighting away, the Zulus, hidden from Isandhlwana in the folds and gorges of Nqutu and Mangweni, waited for the new moon, for they did nothing of importance until the old one had died. That night, the clouds parted and the full round moon in its dying hours lit up the plateau and the plains and the two armies lying so close to each other. Tomorrow a new moon would be born. The Zulus prepared for battle.

The witch doctors began their sprinkling ceremonies, smearing the faces of each of the regimental commanders with potions and powders, waving flaming torches over the heads and bodies to evoke the war spirits. Each warrior drank from a jug which made him retch and empty both his stomach and his bowels so that come morning, he would be clean and light. Around their necks they hung the red roots of the *umabope* plant which they would snap off and chew to make them feel even lighter and braver. They watched the *isangomas*, the evil wizards, weaving among them, carrying their calabashes pierced with holes streaming magic water, which divined whether a warrior lived or died.

They brushed their great black and white shields of hardened cowhide, sharpened the blades of their assegais with stones and polished the heads of their knobkerries with oil from their hair. Some wore the *Isicoco* head ring, showing they were married men, others carried the mark of the King's favoured regiment.

The weather had not lifted. The morning clouds drooped grey and heavy and the wind swept the drizzle across the plains from the east to the waiting Redcoats. Lord Chelmsford had now left them, for despite the advice of men who had lived among the Zulus and knew their ways, he had gone off with a large escort to reconnoitre elsewhere, leaving the main camp in the charge of Colonel Pulleine who despite his years of service had never heard a shot fired in battle and did not know how he would react if he did.

But Lord Chelmsford had gone to search the wrong place, and a little after midday ten thousand Zulus appeared on the ridge of the Nqutu Plateau in a line four miles long. Slowly they began to advance, stamping the ground in unison and buzzing like a million bees, swarming closer and closer. The British in their brilliant red tunics and sparkling white helmets held up a hand to protect their eyes from the wet wind and gasped, for no sooner had the 'chest' appeared, when either side of it rose the 'horns', ten thousand more warriors on the run and at such a speed no men of any British regiment could have kept their ranks and intervals so perfectly. Then with the crescent complete, they came as a single army thundering down the slope, roaring out their battlecry: '*Usutu! Usutu!* Kill! Kill!' towards the shallow red line below them.

The men of the 24th stood steady, shoulder to shoulder. They knew the odds: every rifle must bring down ten Zulus if they were to survive the day. But as each man raised his gun to aim at his first, he knew he would be dead long before he had a chance to fire at the tenth.

* * *

William sat astride Flansman and watched it all from the top of Stony Hill. The track had brought him from Rorke's Drift that morning. Tired of waiting for new orders, he had ridden out to see the camp at Isandhlwana for himself.

For three weeks now he had, with another two hundred wagoners, transported food and ammunition from Helpmakaar to the crossing on the Buffalo River they called Rorke's Drift. It had been slow work. Not every wagon was as strong as his, nor all the oxen as fit, and there had been many accidents and long delays. Every day it became harder and more dangerous, because it was now the rainy season with sudden fierce thunderstorms and cloudbursts that turned a dry *spruit* into a raging torrent twelve feet deep within an hour. The tracks became quagmires, and oxen slipped and sank into craters of soft mud and broke their legs and necks and were shot and butchered for the soldiers' daily meat rations. Mules and horses that could not or would not pull the smaller carts because of the mud clinging to the wheels were shot too. Transport riders who threatened to leave were shown the butt of a rifle, some even the bullet. It seemed to William that Africa had joined forces with the weather in the defence of Zululand, and that the British army was already half beaten by it. But he did not question his paymasters; with every load safely arrived at Rorke's Drift he was five sovereigns better off and the biscuit tin in his saddlebag was now heavy with coin.

William looked down and heard the crack of two thousand rifles echo across the plain and saw the rockets explode into the mountainside; he saw the balls of white smoke rise above the gun carriages and heard their muffled booms; he watched mounted troops separated from the main camp and desperate to reach it, cut down and slaughtered a thousand yards from the British lines. The seven-pounders exploded, sending their searing shrapnel into a hundred black bodies but the bombardiers could not load brass fast enough and soon they went under too. The cry was heard, 'Save the guns!' but the Zulus threw them and their gunners into the gorge and watched them smash together on the rocks below.

The warriors swept down, for there was no fire that could stop them. Their first line fell but the one behind trampled the bodies or picked them up and carried them as shields. The British infantrymen did not pause to aim but every shot killed in the moving wall of black, the rifles cracking like machine-guns so that as the Zulus came forward they left behind a carpet of dead. Then they were upon them and the tunics and helmets began to sink beneath the welter of savage fury, a sea of black overwhelming tiny islands of imperial red.

Consumed by victory, thirst and hunger the Zulus crossed the camp, ripping down tents, ransacking the supply wagons, spearing the oxen, tearing raw meat off them, and drinking from the brandy casks and the medicines in the hospital chests. They stripped the British dead of their red tunics and put them on, whooping and dancing as others tore trinkets from the bodies and cut off fingers for their gold and silver rings. They sought out the wounded who had dragged themselves into a ditch or a shallow stream and tore out their stomachs and raised their dripping assegais to the sky. If their own wounded could not walk they too were killed with a spear thrust deep into the left armpit.

The few British soldiers to escape were ignorant of the country and ran or rode the wrong way and were soon overtaken and hacked down. Some riders did reach the Buffalo, but at the wrong crossing; the river was in full flood, the walls sheer and the torrent forty feet wide. Some men whipped their horses to jump but none surfaced and they drowned with their riders or were swept away into the race where any living thing was battered to death against the stones.

But one rider had a single mission. Lieutenant Melvill had

been ordered to save the colours and snatching the pole he rode for the river and the crossing, using his sword and pistol to fight his way through Zulu ranks. There, ready to cross, was his friend Lieutenant Coghill who quickly reined his horse into the water with him. But Melvill's horse slipped and shied and the lieutenant, clutching at the flag, was swept away. Coghill turned again to save him but by now the Zulus had reached the river bank and shot his horse from under him. Still Coghill would not leave Melvill and clung to him and, tossed and whipped by the currents, dragged him back to the bank. But the Zulus had crossed the stepping-stones and, exhausted, the two young men sat down back to back and waited. They emptied their guns on the first to reach them. Then they too were killed and their bellies opened for their spirits to be released.

The battle of Isandhlwana had lasted less than three hours but four thousand Zulu dead now lay scattered across the slopes. Of the one thousand four hundred British regulars less than eighty survived and only because they were on horseback and had left the battlefield early. Soon, before the sun set, Africa's mightiest army would be gone; gone beyond the plains, beyond the hills and gorges and into the black night. On Isandhlwana nothing moved except the flames that lit up the charnel. And no sound was heard except the crackle of the fires and the hiss of the rain on the cinders.

Rorke's Drift is six miles south of Isandhlwana as the crow flies. There the Buffalo River is more than a hundred yards wide, fifteen feet deep and fast-flowing. In both directions it is strewn with rocks, some showing, most hidden, but at the Drift the bottom runs smooth from bank to bank and provides a passable ford.

Twenty-five years before, a trader called Jim Rorke had built a store on the Natal side with his verandah facing the setting sun and had cut a passage down to the water so that wagons might cross easily. The Zulus called it Kwa-Jimu, the place of Jim, and the hill behind is Shiyane, though this had been changed since Rorke's death by a Swedish missionary, Otto Witt, who had renamed the hill Oscarberg after his king. Now the mission station had changed its purpose and its face again. For ten days since the British invasion had begun, Rorke's Drift had been the transit base for all wagon and foot traffic across the Buffalo. The Royal Engineers, under Lieutenant John Chard, had constructed two large flat-bottomed pontoons carrying eighty men each, which had helped to speed up the flow, and in the past ten days over five thousand men with their thousand tons of supplies had passed across the Drift into Zululand.

Since mid-morning, Chard and the other officer present, Lieutenant Gonville Bromhead, had heard the sounds of distant gunfire coming from Isandhlwana but they had already been told to expect some Zulu scouting in the area and assumed it was nothing more than minor skirmishes. Some firing from the east was only to be expected.

Not that Bromhead would have heard it clearly, or possibly at all, because although he was only thirty-three he was so deaf he often missed orders on parade. But no one could doubt his dedication to the service or his pedigree. He came from a long line of soldiers. His great-grandfather had died at Falkirk one hundred and thirty years before, and his grandfather had been captured at Saratoga. His father had fought for Wellington at Waterloo and a cousin had routed the French in an uphill charge at El Bodon. One of his brothers had fought in the Crimea and a second had distinguished himself in the Ashanti Campaign.

Here, he was in charge of 'B' Company 2nd Battalion 24th Foot Regiment, sometimes known as the 2nd Warwickshires and soon to be renamed the South Wales Borderers.

There was also a chaplain, an enormous barrel-chested man with a large red beard, called Smith, and Major Surgeon Reynolds, not a regular, therefore junior to both Chard and Bromhead, who looked after thirty-four patients in the makeshift hospital. Fifteen of them, walking convalescents, were that day helping Private Henry Hook in the kitchens. He came from Gloucestershire and felt the foreigner in such a Welsh company. There were so many Jones and Williams, Davies and Hughes that when the sergeants shouted an order at any one of them they suffixed his last name with the initials of his first, and if that were the same, as often it was – there were five Jones with the initial I and four Williams with J – a man might lose the use of his name altogether and be known only, as was Private David Jones, as '356'.

No traffic was expected at Rorke's Drift that day. All of Lord Chelmsford's columns had now gone through and only a few wagons, delayed by accidents, were overdue. The men relaxed; the midday slaughter of two bullocks for fresh meat was the only expected entertainment of the day. Chard and Bromhead took an early lunch under the shade of the trees in missionary Witts' tiny orchard and they ordered the men to do the same.

At two o'clock, the two lieutenants did their rounds, beginning with the commissariat store and ending at the hospital across the yard. The patients, in small rooms that led off the verandah, lay on straw-stuffed pallets raised a few inches off the floor by a platform of hard mud to keep them from ants, beetles and scorpions. There was Corporal Myers and Corporal Connolly and a giant blond Swiss, Corporal Frederich Schiess, all recovering from leg wounds from an earlier skirmish. Some men were suffering from snakebites, others had been injured in wagon accidents or thrown from their horses. Sergeant Maxfield was delirious with fever, and Privates Green and Hunter were both paralysed with rheumatism.

The lieutenants came back to their tent pleased that in the hour since they had heard the first gunfire it had come no closer. Routine sentries had been posted some way up Oscarberg and Private Hitch had been sent to sit on the hospital roof. And when Lieutenant Bromhead said he would ride off a mile or so for a look around, Chard was left to muse on how he could defend his tiny garrison in such an unlikely event. After twenty minutes of inspection he concluded he could not. The perimeter was spread too far and the only two secure buildings, the store and the hospital, were on either side of the yard forty yards apart. Both were thatched and vulnerable to fire and overlooked by Oscarberg behind. The hospital was anyway too constricted to be useful; the tiny rooms had no connecting doors and to move from one to the other could only be done by going out onto the verandah. So he decided that if the alarm were sounded he would use the two wagons in the yard and transfer Surgeon Reynolds' patients and all his own men to Helpmakaar, ten miles and a three-hour journey southwest.

But Chard never did finish his plans for evacuation. As he was crossing to the store there was a shout from the sentries on Oscarberg and when he ran to the track, he saw, coming across the plains from Isandhlwana, the boy he knew as William Llewellyn, the transport rider from the Drakensbergs. His horse splashed across the river and as they ran towards him he shouted at them. But it was not until he had fallen from his saddle into their arms that they understood his words. He had seen the main camp overrun and a large force of Zulu, four thousand or more, were now on the move, coming west to Natal and the crossing at Rorke's Drift.

They carried him to the store and Private Hook brought him soup mixed with a little brandy and William told them that by his reckoning they had less than an hour.

Chard's first impulse was still to evacuate but with the main camp overrun the ammunition supplies in his charge would now be critical to Lord Chelmsford's other columns and he could not abandon them now. Anyway, the wagons were too slow-moving and the Zulus would overtake them long before they even sighted Helpmakaar.

Quickly he shouted his orders for the tents to be pulled down to give the rifles a clear line of fire and then set about building his fortifications.

'Take out the mealie bags, Sergeant. Stack them four high, loophole and barricade from the hospital to the store. And bring the wagons to the corner facing the hill. Pack solidly, Sergeant, I don't want to see daylight through them. And have them take the water cart to the river and fill it. And everyone runs, Sergeant! Whatever they're doing, they run at it or this'll be the last we'll ever see of each other.'

Helped by Commissionary Dalton he paced out the perimeter. It was over four hundred yards round – too long, they agreed, for the one hundred and nine rifles of 'B' Company to defend. So they built a second and last line, taking in only the small yard and the store: a wall of biscuit boxes was laid from the store to the road.

Mealie bags were wedged into the windows and doors of the hospital and six men were sent there to defend it. Private Hook was among them. So was William.

The sun, which had not shone on Isandhlwana, was bright here now and the men stripped to work, humping the bags of mealie and boxes of biscuits from the stores out onto the defence perimeter, stopping only to drink from their water-bottles. The lieutenants and the commissionary, together with the red-bearded Chaplain Smith, moved among them – directing, finding a hole that had not been filled or part of the wall of bags that needed further reinforcing. Men were sent out to cut down scrub within a fifty-yard range to deny the Zulus cover and others cut branches from the trees in the mission orchard.

The wall was finished in less than an hour, every hole blocked, every weak point strengthened. The little garrison was now completely enclosed. Then Chard, Bromhead and their sergeants placed each man in his firing position, allocating areas of command to the corporals, inspecting rifles and bayonets. Water-bottles were refilled, ammunition boxes opened and placed at ten-yard intervals along the line; cartridge pouches were stuffed full and the first few dozen laid out in a line by each man's right hand to save him fumbling. Finally, when every man was in place, Bromhead with his sword drawn gave the order: 'Fix bayonets!' and the three-sided blade, two feet long, was snapped onto the muzzles. Then Bromhead told them to sit and rest. He had little enough experience, he said, but enough to know panting men did not take good aim.

In the hospital Private Hook picked at a splinter in his hand with the tip of his bayonet and smiled at William standing at the next window. He was a broad and powerfully built man with a kind face and a large drooping moustache. 'Now we wait for dusk, young man,' he said. 'Or the Zulus – whichever comes first. Mind you, if they come together, God help us 'cos there's nothing more we can do on our own.' As he stopped speaking there was a sudden shout above them, and Private Hitch, who had been sitting his sentry duty astride the roof, came sliding down tearing at the thatch to break his fall. 'Here they come,' he shouted, 'black as Hell and thick as grass!' It was exactly five o'clock. Soon it would be dusk.

The first came, as Chard and Bromhead guessed they would, over the top of Oscarberg: from that height, Dabulamanzi their commander could see the layout of the post and judge its weakest points. Three more regiments, the Uthulwana, Udloko and the Indluyengene, then appeared from the north. Dabulamanzi knew, as did his four thousand warriors, that by crossing into Natal they had disobeyed the orders of King Cetshwayo. But they had been denied the battle at Isandhlwana, denied the washing of their spears and their chance to return home glorious. Dabulamanzi knew that to excuse his disobedience and appease his king, victory here must be total.

Inside the hospital William remembered Isandhlwana and the buzzing of bees and the terrible roar as they swarmed, but all he heard was 'B' Company's sudden fire like the slamming of many doors and the clatter as the first assegais hit the walls.

The men stood shoulder to shoulder firing as fast as they could load, twelve rounds a minute, their red tunics and white helmets bright targets in the low evening light. If a man did not bring his rifle back quickly to reload, Zulus grabbed the muzzle to wrench it away. All along the line the attackers tried to climb the mealie wall but were shot or bayoneted and fell back, staining the bags red; before one rush was over another joined it and dozens were crushed in the stampede. Still the wall held firm and so did the Redcoats behind it.

Chaplain Smith hung a haversack around his neck filled with loose cartridges and went along the lines scooping them out to the riflemen, sometimes running, sometimes crawling on his hands and knees, exhorting them at the top of his voice with messages from the Bible, reproving them for every blasphemy they shouted back at him. Zulus were firing from Oscarberg with rifles they had captured at Isandhlwana and Commissionary Dalton protecting the wall in front of the hospital fell back with a bullet in the right shoulder. Still directing the fire of the men in his section he handed his rifle to the assistant store-keeper, Byrne, who with Corporal Scammell turned their fire on the hill.

The giant Corporal Schiess had hopped from the hospital as soon as the 'Stand to!' was sounded, strapping his injured leg tightly with his belt so that he could join the fight. In a raging fury, he pulled himself up onto the wall to fire, but a spear split open his boot and tore away his instep, and as he hesitated a Zulu with a captured rifle fired at him and the blast blew his hat off. Schiess plunged his bayonet into the Zulu's face and then jumped to retrieve it. Then as Corporal Scammell stretched over the bags to pull him up again he was shot in the back by the snipers, and fell back groaning. Chard picked up Scammell's rifle, and pulled him across the yard, firing with one hand as the corporal fed him with cartridges from his pouch. Schiess clambered back again but then the man next to him fell across him dead with an assegai through his throat and his helmet hit Schiess and broke his nose and he watched blood flood the breech and run down the barrel of his gun. Spears split open the mealie bags and the flour billowed into the air like clouds of white steam hiding attacker and defender from each other.

Surgeon Reynolds was treating the wounded on the verandah of the store, pulling out spears and resetting broken arms and legs as best he could. As soon as they were treated, those who could walk went back to their rifles. Corporal Allen, whose right shoulder had been shattered into thirty-six pieces, stuffed his wrist under his belt to support it and used his good arm to help Chaplain Smith distribute the ammunition. Used cartridge cases littered the ground so that it was impossible to move from one firing position to another without slipping and sliding.

The men protecting the front of the hospital could hold out no longer. It was dusk and they were wasting fire on the shadows, above and below them, so Chard pulled them back into the yard. That shortened the perimeter but it was still too extended and Chard knew he would have to reduce it further and bring everyone into the last redoubt, the wall encircling the store. That meant he would have to abandon the hospital and all the men inside it.

Hook and William and a third man, Private Joseph Williams, were trapped. The Zulus were rushing and flattening themselves against the building, grabbing the rifles at the loopholes and thrusting their assegais at the red tunics behind as others hurled themselves at the barricaded door, smashing it with heavy stones. Hook shouted as it splintered, and as arms reached round, William blew the first apart and stabbed the next. But as the black body fell away, there were two to replace it and as the centre plank of the door split open William loaded and fired through the gap into the chest of the warrior facing him.

Then all three men smelt it – the acrid smoke of gunpowder mixed with something new. They looked up and saw flames tonguing under the thatch between the rafters.

'God help us!' shouted Hook. 'They've bloody well set us on fire!' Then he turned and pointed to a small axe that was used for shaping mud bricks. 'Grab it, lad,' he shouted to William. 'Grab it and break a hole through to the next room. And hurry, lad, hurry, otherwise we'll be butchered or burnt!'

William ran with the axe to the side of the delirious Sergeant

Maxfield's bed and crouched beside him. He swung at the mud wall, but it was thirty years old and had dried like stone. Chips flew into his face and he grazed and tore his knuckles, and soon the handle was slippery with blood. So he tore the ticking off Maxfield's pillow and wrapped it round the handle. Inch by inch he broke it open until it was two feet wide. Then he pulled the patients from their beds, dragged them across the floor and pushed them through. Hook fired through the loop-holes, and Private Williams stood with his back to the wall facing the splintered door, firing and reloading, and when he could not reload in time, ran forward bayoneting as they tried to twist themselves through the gap. But then it broke from its hinges and crashed onto the floor with Zulus sprawling behind it. Private Williams fired again and plunged with his bayonet for the last time as a dozen arms pulled him down. They tore off his tunic, exposed his stomach and ripped him open. Then, furious at his stand against them, they cut his body apart.

Hook ran to the hole and pushed Corporal Connolly, the last struggling patient, through, then clambered after him as the Zulus reached Sergeant Maxfield and he began his terrible screaming.

It was a smaller room with a door, bolted and barred and with a window that looked out over the yard towards the store. On the far side William could see the men of 'B' Company fighting from behind their mealie bags. Even if he could get the patients out of the window there was still thirty yards of open ground to cross. But the fire, like the Zulus, was following them, and he remembered Hook's words: 'Butchered or burnt,' and smashed the window open with his rifle butt.

Hook was firing at the door now as it bulged with the weight of men behind it, but he came too close and an assegai knocked off his helmet and grazed his temple and blood trickled into his eye. He shook his head and with a roar he began firing with two rifles, Connolly sitting on the floor reloading for him.

One by one William lifted the men up to the window and

they pulled themselves through. The flames from the roof lit up the yard and when the riflemen saw them drop, some turned their fire at new targets as Zulus tried to climb the wall by the verandah to cut off the escape.

William carried the first patient the thirty yards and then ran back for more, and Hook, on his third run with Connolly on his back, was just clear when the hospital roof collapsed with a roar and a shower of flames.

Lieutenants Chard and Bromhead knew they could retreat no further. If the last wall of bags was breached it would be over and there would be no survivors. The flames from the hospital had helped them, exposing the Zulus as they manoeuvred into new positions ready for a new rush. But Chard could not risk a second fire at the store so he sent six men up to the roof to beat out the flaming spears.

It was now past ten o'clock; the Zulus had begun their attack at five. Every man had fired many hundreds of rounds each, the barrels of their rifles glowed red-hot and their hands were scorched and blistered. The heat softened the brass cartridges in the breeches so that some guns were misfiring as the shells jammed. Some would not fire at all and men were fighting with their bayonets. Their shoulders were black with bruising from the kick of the guns, their faces sore with gunpowder burns; their throats were parched and their stomachs empty and men turned away from the wall to retch and splash their boots with bile.

The water-cart had been abandoned in the outer yard but now the men at the wall and the wounded on the ground were desperate, so just after midnight, Lieutenant Chard led a charge over the top, firing as he ran, his men bayoneting and clubbing with their rifles as others grabbed the dusselboom and pulled the cart to the wall and threw the hose over it.

There was now no sense of time, there had been too many charges and too many volleys. Men were deaf with the din and their eyes saw nothing else but the rush of black and the sudden spray of blood that turned the night red. Faces rose up to their guns, danced briefly in the light of the muzzle flashes and with a scream were gone again. But the nearness of dying did not kill 'B' Company's will to live, and hour on hour, thumbs pressed cartridges home and fingers pressed the triggers. The eye did not need to aim, there was nothing to miss; only too many to kill.

When Lieutenant Bromhead took out his watch again it was after two and the attacks had begun to falter. There were fewer spears and longer intervals between the rushes. But they were still out there, the glowing timbers of the hospital roof still lit them well, hiding behind every tree and bush, crouching in every ditch, spread flat against the wall and behind the pyramids of their own dead and dying. Every so often they began their chant but they did not move. Then at four the hospital fire flickered and died and there was nothing but the black menace beyond. And there was still an hour to sunrise.

Chard and Bromhead went on their rounds again. They counted fifteen of their own dead and two more dying. Twenty-five of the wounded could still stand and fire a rifle but when Allen and Hitch brought the count of ammunition it confirmed what everyone had already guessed. The Zulus need only come once more to win. So 'B' Company waited for the first light of morning, wondering if that was all the Zulus were waiting for too. Little by little the night lifted and dawn seeped in. In the greyness behind them they could make out the shadow of Oscarberg but the mists of morning stayed close to the ground and they could not see what they hid. Their eyes were red and sore and tears trickled down their cheeks, washing thin white lines in the grease of the gunpowder smoke that masked their faces. It seemed as if all the colour had been washed from them and everything around them. The air was thick with dew, it muted every sound and slowed every movement and men who had lived by a city's river suddenly remembered it.

They became aware of the sweet and sickly scent of death. It filled their nostrils and made them forget the smells of fire and gunpowder Then, as the mists slowly lifted waist-high, they saw the dead and the half-dead. A black body rolled in its agony, another twitched in the last spasm of life, an arm was raised, a hand seemed to beckon then it fell to the earth again and was still as a rifle cracked from the wall. Lieutenant Chard stood every second man down. Zulu bodies were dragged away from the cookhouse and a fire was lit and water put on for tea. But it was still a long way off boiling when the sentry looking north shouted the alarm again and for the second time the cry went up: 'Stand to!' And there, two hundred yards away, they saw them spaced perfectly in line, shuffling slowly forward. The weary men of 'B' Company raised their rifles again, slipped in their cartridges and said their prayers, some silently, some out loud, some in English and some in Welsh, watching and waiting as Lieutenant Chard stood by, ready to give the order to fire. But he did not. Nor would he need to. For the Zulus, having come only fifty yards closer, suddenly crouched, and resting their shields and assegais against their knees, took snuff.

Their fight was over. They had not eaten or rested in four days and they would go only one way now. They would turn about and march due east, passing below Isandhlwana until they reached the Umfolozi River. There they would wash and rest before returning to Ulundi, to their kraals and homes, to their families and cattle, and to their King Cetshwayo. They had washed their spears, they had protected their motherland from the foreign white invader. There was nothing left to do here now.

Suddenly, like a thousand flocks of wild birds together, they rose and without an order being heard or any signal seen, they bowed their heads at the red-coated enemy who had fought them so bravely and so fiercely and they raised their assegais to the sun in salute. Then they turned and trotted silently away.

The reek of death grew stronger the longer the sun burnt. They counted three hundred and seventy bodies beneath the wall, on the slopes of Oscarberg, and on the verandah. Inside the charred ruins of the hospital they found the hardly recognizable shapes of those who had been burnt alive in the flaming thatch, fused together. As the burial parties moved further out they came across hundreds more who had been carried away during the night and thrown into ditches and shallow ravines, and for weeks to come floating corpses would jostle along the banks where the river ran slow or were smashed and drained of blood against the rocks in the stony drifts downstream.

At midday the men lined up and a cask of rum was brought out of its hiding place in the Quartermaster's Store and Colour Sergeant Bourne issued every man a generous noggin. In the queue was Private Hook, a life-long teetotaller.

'What are you doing here?' they asked.

'Well, I reckon I'll be forgiven just this once,' he replied with a grin. 'I think maybe I deserve a bit of a treat!'

That afternoon, with men scouting carefully ahead, Chard sent ten men with Chaplain Smith and Surgeon Major Reynolds in William's wagon to Isandhlwana to see for themselves. They followed the track across the lower slopes of Stony Hill until they reached the eastern side of the battlefield.

The breeze carried the stench, and they tied handkerchieves around their faces and those who did not have them held dried grass to their noses. Hyenas skulked among the thousands of corpses, gorging on the flesh; vultures screeched and ran, too full and too heavy to fly. The breeze took the scent of slaughter up to the top of the mountain and set the jackals howling. At the side of one wagon two little drummer boys hung from butcher's hooks that had been jabbed under their chins, and some men lay staring at the sky with their lower jaws torn away: men who had had their beards carried off by the Zulus as trophies.

For a while they stayed in the wagon, too shocked and too

afraid to step down for fear they might tumble and fall among the gore. Nothing and no one was whole. Oxen, cattle, horses, mules and infantrymen, all split open by the assegai; and the Zulu regiments decimated by the riflemen's volleys and the gunners' shells. Isandhlwana, an ugly mountain on a beautiful plain, had become the graveyard of Africa's two great imperial armies.

The men congregated by the side of the wagon and went down on their knees as Chaplain Smith said his prayers. Further up the slopes jackals barked and eagles spiralled high above their nests in the grey-white peak. The chaplain finished and they murmured their Amens and when he turned to them they saw his wide red beard was wet with tears.

'How are the mighty fallen,' he said in a whisper, 'and the weapons of war perished.'

For an hour they loaded the wagon with boxes of ammunition and took good rifles from dead men's hands. Surgeon Reynolds piled together the remaining medicines and collected the maps and papers that were blowing about the tents. Seeing they were ready to leave, Tongo pulled the oxen round on a long rein and William closed his eyes as they trod and burst the swollen bodies.

Then he saw him, fifteen yards away, grinning as he remembered him, his blond hair moving in the breeze across his face as it had always done. He remembered the dark suit at the wedding and how he had gently bound Mr Jenkins' swollen hands before the service and he heard again the cocky voice that had no obvious English home. The man he had not had the courage to say goodbye to, now stared at him with an assegai through his heart, his killer clinging to him like a lover, and Billy Bean's bullet through his.

They separated them from their death clasp and as Tongo dragged the Zulu away, William found a shallow hole and curled Billy Bean into it, surprised now how little afraid he was of the dead. He pushed the blond hair to one side, closed the lids to hide the blue eyes, and the lips to hide his smile and placed his hands across his chest the way he had seen them do in Bethesda to men in coffins. Then he covered him gently in a canopy of dried grass and ferns and laid a lattice of twigs and brushwood over it.

Finally he piled stone on stone in a cairn above him so that Billy Bean was well protected and would not be pestered by eagle or jackal, vulture or hyena or any other thing of Africa ever again.

The mail steamer *Dunrobin Castle* was ordered to leave Cape Town a day ahead of schedule to hurry Lord Chelmsford's report home. She reached the cable head on the Cape Verde Islands on the tenth of February and when the news reached London, the massacre of Isandhlwana became a sensation and a national humiliation, a disaster without parallel since the retreat from Kabul nearly forty years before. Disraeli would have ordered the defeated Chelmsford home had not the Queen pre-empted him by publishing the telegrams she had quickly sent the British commander expressing her regrets and support. So the stunned Disraeli lamented, 'Who are these Zulus? Who are these remarkable people who defeat our generals and convert our bishops and have put an end to a great dynasty?' Then quickly, using every bit of his showman's cunning, he engineered the disgrace of Isandhlwana out of public sight and mind and, keenly assisted by the Queen, turned Rorke's Drift into a triumphant legend the same day. Together they made it a second Waterloo, encouraging the hurrahs as if all Natal had been saved from a Zulu massacre when they knew it was nothing of the kind.

Parliament voted its thanks to Lieutenants Chard and Bromhead, and Queen Victoria invited them to Balmoral and bestowed on them and nine others the Victoria Cross, making the defence of the once-obscure tiny garrison on the Buffalo River the most highly decorated battle in British military history.

William Llewellyn, listed among the awards Gazetted in

London that month, was given the Albert Medal and when th
Queen learnt where he was from she issued two command
ments: first that a bronze plaque be cast and delivered to th
chapel elders in Bethesda with the royal order that it be hun
there to mark the birthplace of now its most famous son; an
second, that the medal be sent post-haste in the Royal Ma
bag to Cape Town for its journey to the Drakensbergs. And s
the Battle of Rorke's Drift became of epic proportions and i
would be said much, much later that its defenders got mor
praise than they might have expected. But it was never, neve
said that they got more than they deserved.

Mary saw the dust tailing up. There was no mistaking it. I
was a wagon a long way off, a wagon trundling slowly acros
the lowveld, its image shimmering in the heat of the hottes
day. She knew it could easily have been one of a score c
transport riders taking the Lydenburg road east. It was only
spiral of dust, but not for a moment did she doubt it wa
anyone else but him, and she thanked God she had not had t
wait long. Before the day was over, William would be home
to Pilgrims Rest.

CHAPTER NINE

The rains that had crippled the British in Zululand now turned around. The weather came west. Those who said they knew promised it wouldn't stray above the Orange River, but it did. Then they said they had never known it at this season go further than the Vaal but it did that too. So those who said they knew became quiet and others who knew better were alarmed. Soon they said it would be the first day of winter and the Transvaal skies should be blue and cloudless and the air sharp and thin. No one could remember such black and heavy days and tomorrow was the first of May.

It began to rain on the third, a dull steady drizzle and the clouds settled so low over the village that day seemed to be night and it was possible to stand on Mary's porch and not see the end of her garden or the Royal Hotel from the church porch. At first the diggers put up with it, working and sleeping in a sea of mud because reservoirs quickly formed on their workings and provided a free and steady flow of water for their races. They found they could work at twice the speed and settle for twice the weight of gold every evening and, they told each other, the water coming off the mountains had been known to bring down gold nuggets the size of a fist.

But within a week, as the water-table rose, the small reservoirs became lakes, making work almost impossible and instead of nuggets, the water cascading off the peaks sent down only landslides of mud and bouncing boulders that could shatter a man's skull. After a fortnight, with the rain still straight and steady and the days the same unchanging grey, the river suddenly rose five feet and ever so slightly began to change course, ignoring its old meanders, forcing out new and dangerous channels. The diggers took the measurements of the new levels but obstinately continued working and built barricades of mud around their tents. Only a few noticed that the villagers had left their kraal and had moved further up the slopes to higher, drier, safer ground.

Huw did not know how much longer he could risk working so close to the river, but Mr Jenkins appeared not at all worried by it. 'As long as a river can find its way unhindered to the sea,' he said, 'it'll do no harm.' For three days now they had been working around a large boulder twice Mr Jenkins' height, digging a pit on one side to topple it.

Diggers thought themselves lucky to have one as they were famous for hiding nuggets. Mr Jenkins would have had it down anyway. He said it haunted him, reminding him of a fat round carp, as he stroked its smooth glistening black belly. He said it even had a mouth, open to the sky, full of water, waiting for a fly. In the evenings, when work was over he would look back from the higher slopes and see it silhouetted against the river, big and monstrous, curling up from the Blyde, snapping at invisible bait. He called it God's own sculpture, put there to remind him of what he had lost and left behind in Oxfordshire and of all the fish he would never catch again. But, he told Huw, he would catch this one, this fat stony carp, nuggets or no nuggets.

That morning Huw shouted to him above the noise of the gushing river. 'I'm going for some timber. We're sinking too deep and there's no knowing in this wet when it'll fall. Stay clear until I'm back and we'll work it from a platform.'

But Mr Jenkins could not wait and the fish seemed already to have left the earth, only its tail now was submerged in the muddy pool. He touched its sides and, squeezing the water from his eyes, he bent down and plunged his hands under to feel for its tail. But the rock fish would not wait either and it began to tremble, he could feel the tremor in his fingertips and it began to turn as he held it, as if he was a wizard and his touch had filled it with magic life. He looked up into the rain and saw it huge above him and he put out a hand to catch its belly, but with a final violent shudder its tail skidded away and it came toppling down. Then only a little of Mr Jenkins' face showed beneath it, a nostril and a contorted mouth to give him air, and one eye barely above the yellow water, watching for Huw's return.

The cushion of mud saved Mr Jenkins but he would never walk on his own again, or fish. The boulder had broken his legs and buckled his right shoulder, wrenching the upper arm out of its socket and crushing the blade. The splinters had torn through the flesh of his back and stuck out like four white brittle fingers.

They took him to Mary's house and washed him clean and fed him soup and brandy through his broken lips. Mr Hamilton, the surgeon barber and tentmaker, left his workshop and sewed Mr Jenkins together again with the twine he used for his tents and the smallest sack needle he could find. The Reverend watched him and poured drops of morphine directly into Mr Jenkins' open mouth to keep him unaware of the mess and pain.

Mr Jenkins had left his trousers and shoes behind and as there was nothing Huw could do to help, he went back to recover them. The boulder did not look like a fish any more, more of a whale, humped and blue-grey, beached on its shallow yellow sea. He waded towards it with the water flapping his knees, then crouched and felt the underside, searching with his fingers. He found one shoe but then he touched something new, something as hard as a stone but not a stone, something as smooth as the boulder but not part of it. He knelt lower until the water covered his back and began to prise it away, but it was encased in hard clay and loath to leave its hiding place. He clawed and twisted, his body shaking with the strain. Then with a final frantic tug it came free. He fell backwards under the water and when he came up again and opened his eyes he was holding a nugget larger than an orange, heavier than slate and becoming brighter and brighter as the rain washed it clean.

All work in the valley stopped for the rest of that day and the following one too, as the diggers queued outside Major John's office, shivering and soaking, waiting for their first glance and touch. It weighed two hundred and eighteen ounces on the Gold Commissioner's scales and was worth more than a digger might expect to earn in five years' hard graft.

Once the last man in the queue had held it in his hand and kissed it, as they all had, the valley started work again and any claim with any boulder on it doubled its price overnight, and the rain and the mud were ignored as teams of men worked furiously to move them, large or small, to get to the small fortune they were certain they were hiding.

Mr Jenkins woke from his nightmares of black and bouncing fish that had, in his half-conscious days and nights, barged their way into his river banks, crushing rods and shrubs and trees and then himself. In his world of pain he listened to the clanging rain on the corrugated roof and knew it was not his roof; he sniffed at the garden-scented sheets covering him and knew it was not his bed. He felt the pain and yet it seemed apart from him as if he were two people lying side by side. He listened again to the voice that sometimes spoke to him but there was no comfort in the words. As much as he tried, he could not ask if he were whole and the longer he delayed the more certain he was, he was not.

A week later they showed him the nugget and said he could now go back to Oxford and fish and cast his lines and feed his bait. But Mr Jenkins did not want to fish again. As they nursed him and dressed his wounds, washed and shaved him and brushed his hair, he thought about his new situation, and decided he would not go now or ever. Not to grim, grey, complaining England. He had come to Africa with the promise of wealth. Now Africa had given him a little so he would stay and spend his share here and enjoy as much of Africa as there was time left and then, on the day there was none, they could cover him in Africa's earth.

But Joanna Jenkins told Huw they should leave for Durban as soon as her father was well enough to travel and with that in mind, she prayed his convalescence would not be a long one. She said they should go as soon as the roads were passable again: and the rains could not last the whole winter – everyone knew that. With their half share in the nugget, she said, they could buy a house close to the sea and they would have gas lights and servants and a coal-burning stove and hot water and a fence around the garden and a nanny for the twins. Huw could make his furniture and even sell it if he wanted, though Heaven knew there was no need to now. They would put their money into a bank and it would earn them interest. Just as soon as the rains stopped.

'When will you leave, Huw?'

'I'm not leaving, mother.'

'You must.'

He did not answer.

'Huw, this is not a life for children.'

'You brought yours.'

'I had no choice. Now you have.'

'But I don't. I love this valley and all the things in it. I have no longing to be anywhere else now, this is my home, our home, Joanna knows that. We can build a proper place here and she can have all the nice things she wants from Durban. But I'll not go there for them, mother. Never. I'm my own man now and my mind's made up. I shall find her all the things she wants to make her happy and then I'll build what I want here.'

'Build, Huw? Build what?'

He walked towards her, smiling. 'A school, mother. A church school. I've spoken to the Reverend about it and he'll show me how and what books to buy and help me with the lessons and so will Polly. She'll help with the children, she wants to. She said so.'

'Huw, what children? There's only little Tom here.'

'African children, mother, the Mapulani. My school will be for them. I want to teach them our ways, our good ways. Not all the children, not at first, we couldn't cope. But Samson and I have already selected the first, the ones who come regularly to listen, the ones who remember the scriptures and sing our hymns. Mother, in the villages we go to they are already speaking to us in English. They've learnt it just from the stories and songs we sing. Isn't that marvellous?' He glowed and put his arms around her.

'It's God's will that I should do it,' he said. 'You know it is. He gave me the nugget.' His eyes seemed on fire, scorching his tanned face darker, as he told her of his plans: where the schoolhouse would be built on the little plateau that nestled on the slopes of Jubilee Hill; how the children, possibly twenty to begin with, would live there, going home only at Easter and Christmas; how the children he taught would grow up and go back to their people taking God's word with them. Then Mary knew she could not dissuade him, even had she wanted to. But she also knew that Joanna would go and take her babies with her. She was not made to be a preacher's wife.

It was late, so they said their prayers together and Huw left the house. Mary shook her head as she watched him go. Such cussed holy plans, she thought, Heaven made; that he should save Africa's children and lose his own.

She went to bed and tucked the covers tight under her chin, listening to the rain on the roof, the doubts nagging inside her. God had provided for Huw's good and holy work. But God, she knew, was full of promises and hopelessly short on guarantees.

Mary hoped the stagecoach would bring it, but the swollen rivers and the slowly moving lakes of mud had turned the village into an island and only the bravest rider and a braver horse would attempt the journey from Lydenburg. Before the weather had closed in the road had been so improved that instead of the postboy's run and William's trundling wagon, it was planned that a stagecoach would do the journey to Lydenburg and Ohrigstad and come up Pilgrims Hill. A bridge of neatly dressed red stone now spanned the river especially for it and Mary was hoping that on its first ceremonial run, it would be carrying William's medal from Queen Victoria, sent by special royal messenger all the way from Durban.

But an army officer and his escort, riding from Pietermaritzburg, brought it instead. Honest Jack fed them and took them up to Major John's where the officer read out the citation and the Reverend Makepeace led three cheers.

The medal was gold and oval-shaped with a ring through the royal crown and the A for Prince Albert intertwined with Victoria's V. Around it were the words '*For gallantry in saving life on land*'. The officer pinned it to William's coat by a crimson-and-white-striped silk ribbon and they waited for William to make a speech but he would only say how proud he was to have fought with the men of 'B' Company and prouder still they were Welshmen, even though, he said, most of them seemed to have come from Birmingham!

They drank wine and Honest Jack made two drums of Cape Smoke for the diggers, though he agreed at Mary's request to put in less cayenne pepper than usual and more brandy so that the men might toast Will longer and louder and not lose the linings of their throats.

Jollie and the serving girls baked a hundred and more buns filled with roast buck and forcemeats and Mr Phelan, determined to help in the celebrations, brought Polly a five-pound tin of West African cocoa powder which she made into a chocolate cake and the grocer reckoned it weighed twenty pounds or more.

Despite the drizzle it was warm and the diggers sang and jigged in the High Street to the crippled Teddy's concertina. Mary watched them and thought of another time and such a party when two Cornishmen made out they were a horse and everyone had joined their tail and hollered their way around the houses until Walrus' white horse with Tongo clinging to his mane stopped it all. She felt suddenly anxious and despite the moment, the music and William and Polly's laughter, the feeling would not leave her. And then she saw on the bough of the church tree a large solitary bird, sleek and white, a sharp image in the drizzle, almost shining against the black and grey day. She went to the end of the verandah to see it better. Tongo was waiting.

'You see *impandulu*, Mrs Mary?'

'Yes, Tongo, I see it.'

The young army officer came from under the eaves. 'What is it, ma'am?' he asked.

'Oh! Only a bird,' she replied. 'It's called a hammerkop but the Africans think it's magic and carries messages from their spirits.'

'What did your boy call it?'

'*Impandulu*,' she answered, 'the lightning bird. They say it's always followed by storms.'

The officer looked out beyond the escarpment where the low sky was the strangest mixture of colour, yellow and purple, and saw the first fork of lightning hit the ground.

William and Tongo brought the horses and soon the soldiers were on their way across the Blyde going south. The air became very still and for the first time since the rains began the diggers pulled up their pegs, rolled up their tents with their bedrolls inside and trudged through the mire to the higher, drier ground above the hotel.

Without being called, William's goat and Jollie's heifer came down off the slopes where they were grazing and nuzzled the doors of their pens. In great commotion, geese and ducks slid into Big Macpherson's farmyard looking for shelter and the family of baboons that jostled and snapped at each other in the bluegum tree by Mary's house left for the caves high up on Black Rock Hill.

At three o'clock Mary heard the thunder. It was still a long way off but she told Jollie to light the fire and William and Tongo tied extra stone weights to the corrugated-iron roof. At four o'clock the flashes of lightning were so near, there was barely a second to spare before the thunderclaps followed. Then a solid blanket of water hit the roof and the rain fell like glass rods, hitting the ground with such force the earth seemed to be exploding from within.

At five o'clock hail ripped open the diggers' tents and bruised and cut their skin so that they scrambled blind to the shelter between the wooden piles under the hotel. A digger named Memphis refused to leave his claim, shouting he'd seen much worse in the Yukon. But as they watched they saw lightning strike the sieve in his hands and saw the trickle of light run up his arm to his neck, and when they got to him he was lying on his back, his dead eyes staring at the sky, the charred sieve melted in his hands and his tongue blue and swollen to the size of a small pumpkin, forced out between his black and broken teeth.

It was six o'clock as they dragged him clear but they left him when they saw the mud oozing down Jubilee Hill, and over the plateau where Huw had planned his school.

In three hours the river rose fifteen feet and spread as many yards on either bank, taking everything with it, diggers' shacks, their races, boulders that ten men had failed to shift in a week's work, and tearing up trees, tossing them end over end.

Huw had built his little house at the last bend of the river, a hundred yards from where it turned and dropped down through the forests, ravines and waterfalls to the lowveld below. He had built it hastily, waiting for the summer to come and the land to dry out so he could ram the poles into firm ground. It was a pretty place, with a natural screen of trees to protect them from the winter winds and the scorching sun in summer. But now the river was less than forty yards away and coming closer every minute, threatening to break its course and run both ways, and turn his half acre into an island.

Throughout the day Joanna had refused to leave the house for safer ground at Mary's. That morning she had given Huw the choice of going to Durban with her and the babies, or staying on his own without them. All that afternoon they had sat in their parlour with the curtains drawn, hiding from the rains and other people; Huw desperately searching for a middle way, between bouts of anger and despair, until he was deaf to her, ignoring her pleading, coaxing and ranting, unable to reason with her until at last she cursed God out loud for sending her to such a place and mating her with such a man.

For an hour they sat in silence, facing each other with the twins wrapped in a blanket on the floor between them. Then she went to the bedroom and slammed the door hard behind her. Huw closed his eyes and rocked the babies with his stockinged feet. He may have been dozing or praying, but the fire was almost dead when he heard her scream and she was in the room.

'The river, Huw!' she screamed. 'The river! It's at my bed!' And he looked, and saw the yellow water curling behind her like a snake.

He scooped up the babies and kicked open the door to let the night in and saw the house had broken from the bank and was moving, ever so slowly, away . . .

From the peaks to the valley the night was bright with lightning. Mary saw them, a hundred yards off, Huw on the porch holding the babies, and Joanna behind him with her arms tight around his waist and the river lapping their knees. Mary screamed out their names but the wind brought them back. No human sound could be heard above the thunder and the terrible roar of the water.

William and Tongo brought the oxen down and looped a rope around their necks, and men tied the other end to a tree. They whipped the animals in and the spinning currents tugged at them as they lurched deeper. They had not gone more than thirty yards, with the oxen's heads barely above water, when William stood on the back of his and waved his hands across his face, shouting.

Only Big Macpherson understood. 'Bring 'em back, Major,' he bellowed. 'Bring 'em back. They're sinking in the mud and they'll topple over and we'll lose the boys as well.' He ran to the rope pulling others with him and slowly they heaved the oxen back. When they were clear he cut the rope and winding it around his middle he waded upstream and began swimming out.

There was no break in the storm now, and the earth shook so much men wondered if the world was coming apart. A hundred or more of them lined the river's edge, some standing with the water over their waists, so they might be closer to see better, watching the giant man swimming and drifting nearer to the house.

There was no land to be seen around it. The river was at the windows and things came floating out, a chair, the kitchen table, a cot, all caught up in the brown frothy river and swept away, as Huw and Joanna clung desperately to the porch posts like a crew in a drowning ship.

Major John held Mary tight in his arms but she would not be turned away. She whispered their names over and over, Huw and Joanna, Victoria and Owen, as she watched the black bobbing head of Big Macpherson. The men cheered and she saw him clinging to the window frames with the rope now piled around his shoulders. Little by little he inched his way forwards to the front of the house as the timbers tore away under his weight. Then the men cheered again and in the storm's light they saw him fling himself around the posts and Huw, holding the bundle of babies in one arm, caught him with the other. Joanna followed the big man's instructions and pinned Huw to the posts and Macpherson held up his right arm as Huw tied the babies to it with his belt.

They were ready to loop the rope around themselves and the men watching took up the strain ready to pull. But the vengeance of the night was not yet over and suddenly the house seemed to explode as the fork of lightning touched it. It blew open the roof and blew open the drum of cooking oil in the kitchen and before the thunder had time to follow, the little house was ablaze and Huw, Joanna and Big Macpherson with the babies tied to him, stood on their floating inferno, half in water, half in fire, until they were lost in both.

Mary turned and buried her head in the blackness of Major John's coat. When she looked again there was only the river and already it had taken them away. She tried to scream her despair but there was only the rush of the wind and water and the fury above her and Major John caught her as she sank down.

William stood on the ox's back at the edge of the water, Tongo sitting beneath him holding him firm. Suddenly he pointed downstream with both hands and men standing back from him caught his words before he had need to shout them again and they were quickly passed from man to man. 'Pull, pull! Big Macpherson's still there holding on! For God's sake, pull!' A hundred pairs of arms heaved and strained and the rhythm grew faster and stronger and then they saw him, his giant body tossed like a tiny cork, his head barely showing, but his right arm as straight as a pole above him, with the bundles still strapped to it.

It took them five more minutes to pull him in. They cut the babies from his arm and Mary and Jollie ran with them to the house. His left hand was locked so tight around the rope they had to prise the fingers apart with a pickaxe prong and he was so full and heavy with water it took ten men to lift him. The Reverend Makepeace walked and prayed by his side, stumbling and slipping in the mud with the bearers, watching the face in the torches' light. When the men stopped for breath he leant over and stroked his forehead and cheeks, shielding the rain from the open unblinking eyes and whispering all kinds of praise, prayers and holy promises. But Big Macpherson was dead before they came to the High Street and the Reverend gently stroked the eyelids closed before they laid him down under the lamp on Honest Jack's floor.

The rain stopped early the next morning and before noon the clouds lifted and began to move from the ridge for the first time in three weeks. They found Huw's body caught in rushes little more than a mile downstream, though they never found Joanna's. They carried his coffin from Mary's house to the church, William, Major John, the Reverend, Honest Jack, Mr Hamilton the surgeon, and Mr Phelan. Polly hung black ribbon from the trees along the way and every digger came, and waited hatless to watch him pass.

Samson made a bier of flower petals and the coloured feathers of singing birds and after the Reverend Makepeace had read the prayers Mary went on her knees and kissed the coffin and as it was lowered they let Samson sing his own lament. Then, one by one, one after the other, they left the tiny cemetery, their heads wet from the dripping church tree and their faces damp with tears.

Mary waited to be alone, and knelt by the small headstone of black rock they had pressed into the soft earth. On it was chiselled in bold letters:

HUW LLEWELLYN
1854–1880

WAITING WITH GOD
IN PILGRIMS REST

Samson brought African women to wetnurse the babies, Owen and Victoria, but he never left them. Mary agreed that they should sleep in the Reverend Makepeace's house so that Polly could care for them and Samson sat with them throughout the days and slept on a straw pallet outside their room at night, and at any murmur or tiny stir he would lift his head and wait, listening until they had settled again. Sometimes Polly heard him speaking softly to them in his own tongue and she fetched one of Honest Jack's servant girls to translate. She said he was telling the babies about their father, about his work with Samson, what they had done together, where they had travelled and all they had planned to do. He told them about Huw's Africa and his patience and gentle persuasions, and how the village people wanted to believe in Huw's God because they believed in him. The girl told Polly the babies would remember the stories, because babies could listen and understand long before they could speak. And Samson must already have carried some of their father's spirit to them, because she said, nodding as if there was not the slightest doubt, they already understood Samson's words.

Mrs de Wet told William he ought not to come again until it was all over. She said there had been trouble with the British soldiers from the Lydenburg Fort, some drunkenness and a merchant had been wounded in the leg when he caught them stealing. And then a week ago, they had surrounded a farmhouse six miles out. One of the men wanted for attacking army wagons, a local boy with a wild head, had returned to spend the night with his wife. But the English never captured him. The wife released the cattle from the house and in the confusion the man escaped. The soldiers shot six of the cattle dead but refused to pay for them, so the farmers dragged the rotting carcases and dumped them outside the army gates. The soldiers doused them with lighting oil and burnt them but they still refused to pay a penny. The Boers were now very angry and the soldiers dared not leave their fort, except to fetch water and only then under armed escort. It was being said that they forced their blacks to taste it first in case the Boers had poisoned the supply.

'So,' she said to William, 'you see why you should stay away. Boers don't trust anyone but their own. Best go until it's all over,' she said again.

'What's all over?' he asked.

And she answered, 'The war, William, the war! Between you and us. The men are already planning for it and there are a lot more guns here now. It frightens me to think who will die but I can't see it being settled any other way.'

'Settled?' he asked, puzzled. 'What should be settled? What is there to settle?'

And she told him that the Boers wanted their republic back. They wanted to govern themselves again under their own flag, paying taxes to their own Volksraad and not to the English. 'These men, these Boers of mine, William, they're slow of thought and they're slow in their speech but they're determined and unforgetting. All this time they've been biding their time. They've come a long way from their first African home in the Cape and they were here a long time before the English. These men and their women, like my mother and father, chose the spear and the lion, the hyena and vulture, disease and hunger rather than live under the cruelty of British rule, and we know something of their cruelty. They have not been kind governors.

'Your people will not have heard of Slachter's Nek but every Transvaaler's son and daughter knows the story by heart. It happened when I was still a child. Five of our men were sentenced to hang by the English, accused of a treason they never even had the chance to commit. It all started over some fool farmer kicking his Hottentot and ended with the English shooting him dead. His family thought of shooting the English back but before they even took their guns down they were convicted of treason and strung up. The English made their families – the women and even the little children – come and watch. But as they stood at the scaffold it collapsed and the men fell to the ground unhurt. The famiies ran forward, crying out, "It is the finger of God! They are saved." But they were not! The English repaired the scaffold and strung them up again and with their necks broken, the women and children were forced to stand by their swinging feet.

'And the English say they came to Africa to civilize it,

William! But things are different now. They say that our Paul Kruger has ridden the length and breadth of the country, from the Vaal to the Limpopo, from Zeerust to Hamilton and everyone cheers him, everyone's with him and it was never like that with the old President Burgers. My people have changed and it's the English who've changed them. All of a sudden we've come together. It was having a republic, our own Transvaal, and then seeing the English take it away. It made us understand what it was we'd lost. Before we were just Boers, coming together only when it suited us, paying our taxes only when we felt like it. I think the only thing we shared were our prayers and only that because they were free.

'But not now, William, not now. I think the English have saved us. Even our people on the other side of the Orange River are helping now and d'you see what that means? We're not just Boers, not just Transvaalers. We're becoming one people – Afrikaners – our motherland is all South Africa, and we must thank the English for it, this love we have, what we call our *heinwee*, our *verlange*.'

'In Welsh,' said William, 'we call it *hiraeth* – a kind of longing.'

'And that,' she said, 'is why our men are getting ready with their guns.'

He asked more questions but she would not answer them. She could not, dared not; she knew well enough the punishment now for talking too freely. She knew of the black servant boy who had whispered to the English sergeant in the fort and was hanging from a tree with his tongue split in two soon after the soldiers had surrounded the farmhouse. So she gave William more of his favourite milk custard pie and packed him a box full of granadillas for his mother.

Bewildered that another war promised to come so soon after the other, he asked her, 'Do the English want all the lands of all the people?'

And she answered, 'All they can get, William. All they can get.' She hugged him tight and kissed his cheeks.

'*Pas my seun goed op.* Take care, my son, my favourite boy. Keep away from the war and may the Lord look after you.'

'And you, Mrs de Wet,' he said. He hugged her back and knew he would not see her again.

It was Prime Minister Gladstone's fault. The Reverend Makepeace said so and no one argued with him though there were a few who sometimes puzzled over the words he used.

'He promises the Boers one thing when he's out of office and then threatens them with the opposite when he's in. The man's a fool, a liberalizing fool, with two tongues, and a coward to boot!'

That day Mr Celliers, publisher of the *Gold News*, had reprinted Gladstone's speeches to Parliament which had so excited and angered the Reverend Makepeace that he spent the entire morning stamping around the camp and village reading them out aloud to everyone and no one in particular, ignoring even Polly's pleadings to come indoors. At midday he stood on Honest Jack's verandah haranguing like a soapbox revolutionary.

'First he delights the Boers by telling them he'll end annexation and return the Transvaal to them. He even denounces Disraeli as being dishonourable for taking it in the first place. And then what does he say?'

He held the newspaper out at arm's length so that no one below could doubt they were the Prime Minister's words.

'"To repudiate annexation is one thing but to abandon it is quite another."

'That's what he said. Can you believe it? He plays with words, this man, the way a Jew juggles his abacus, to his own best interest and damn the correctness of it.' He quoted again:

'"The Transvaal will stay British for as long as the sun shines."' He slapped the newspaper angrily across the verandah rail. 'Facts are stubborn things. Mr Gladstone says: "and it is a fact the British are in the Transvaal and an undoubted fact we shall stay there." That's what the old fool said from his dispatch box and the silly louts cheered him for it!

'But they know nothing, none of them, nothing about the places they govern and the people like us who live at the Empire's frontiers. Just keep the Transvaal, they say, because British rule is best and everyone deserves it. Poppycock! Humbug! Twaddle! The Boers will teach Mr Gladstone what stubbornness is all about and we'll all of us go down when they do it.'

The Boers despaired but it was the words uttered in a private conversation between two British gentlemen in a drawing-room in Pretoria that finally outraged them, the words of Sir William Owen Lanyon, the colony's newest knight and youngest administrator, and they crossed the country quicker than telegraph.

'The Boers,' he said, 'these bloody immigrants from the Cape, are like children who have yet to be taught a lesson in obedience.'

By the beginning of December 1880 the bloody immigrants under their newly formed triumvirate, Kruger, Joubert and Pretorius, had met and agreed their plan of campaign in the tiny village of Paardekraal south of Pretoria and soon after, six thousand mounted Boers were on the move under arms with the orange, white and blue Vierkleur, the flag of their Republic, flying at the head of their columns.

Every evening now after supper, Mary went to the little cemetery and sat by the grave. As soon as the earth had settled she had sown gousblom seedlings, what the diggers called African daisies, inside the rectangle of stones, and on every visit she brought a can to water them and a hoe to keep down the weeds. She had also taken a corm of belladonna lily from her garden that Huw had planted five years before and set it by the stone.

The sky was clear as she stepped from her verandah, the garden choked with the mix of perfumes. She saw the diggers' tents on the slopes, across Jubilee Hill, tiny golden pyramids lit by the lanterns inside. Men were still noisy in Honest Jack's bar and the lamps were alight inside the Reverend Makepeace's house where William had gone for supper with Polly. She knew the Reverend Makepeace was in his church but tonight, for once, she did not want his company, so she passed his porch carefully, watching his shadow weaving in and out of the yellow light of the altar candles. Above her she heard the giant church tree and higher up the slopes the chatter and bark of the family of baboons who had decided that the cave behind the ironwood tree was a safer, more private place than her bluegum.

She opened the church gate that led into the graveyard, lifting it on its hinges to stop its squeak, and kept on the grass, climbing past the headstones and long mounds of earth hiding the known and the anonymous dead. Then she turned right, where the paths crossed, and she gasped. Directly ahead was Huw's grave and kneeling over it was a man in a black cloak and a large slouch hat, and before the breeze could carry his Welsh prayers to her she ran, whispering, 'Ianto! Ianto!'

They hugged but did not speak, their arms locked around each other, caressing and kissing. She felt a trickle on her neck, warm and sticky. 'You're bleeding!'

'Yes, mother. An English bullet. But it'll not kill me and I'll have them back for it.'

She would not let him speak more. The Reverend Makepeace was in his church still and diggers were passing below, stumbling and singing their way to their beds. She led him higher up the hill, beyond the church ground, beyond the highest pitched tents and then dropped back again by the side of the spring below the ridge of black rock and the pastureland that led down to the pens. She sat him in the straw by the heifer and went away on tiptoe for hot water and dressings, praying that the house was asleep. She washed and bound his arm.

The bullet had chipped the bone but had passed out the other side of the muscle.

'What happened, Ianto?'

'We stopped the English, mother. They were on their way to kill us.'

'Us, Ianto?'

'I've found new friends.'

'You've only one family.'

He did not answer.

'Now the English want you.'

'They have for some time, mother.'

'Yes. I've supposed so ever since a sergeant came here with questions.'

'They've been everywhere,' he said.

'And everyone knew, except me.'

'You have new friends too, mother.'

'What will they do when they catch you?'

'They'll not catch me.'

'What will they do?'

He shrugged and shook his head. She saw the faint red stain spreading slowly across the dressing, rising through the layers of lint until it touched the four sides. She wound more bandage around it.

'I suppose they'd string me up like a Boer,' he said, 'or shoot me as one of their own.'

'My God!' she whispered.

'I'm with the Boers, mother. It's their country. This is Boerland and they'll not let the English take it the way they took ours. That's why I fight with my new friends.'

'And kill.'

'Oh, yes.'

She closed her eyes. 'Dear Lord, forgive him.'

'Don't pray, mother,' he said. 'Not that way. If God is fair He'll have heard us, too, the Boers know their Bible as well. Don't worry, mother, they'll not catch me. We're always ahead of them.'

She made a loop in the bandage and tied a double knot and tucked the ends back inside. The bleeding did not show any more, though the black and blue bruising was swelling either side. She gave him a clean shirt, folded and pressed and smelling of dry grass.

'Huw's?'

She nodded.

'The English killed him, too,' he said.

She did not answer.

'Just as sure as they killed father.'

She closed her eyes again and slowly shook her head.

He leant forward. 'Huw would never have come here but for them. They sent him all this way – you know they did.'

She looked up. 'You're a fool to think that, Ianto. If anyone killed him, I did. I brought him here, not the English. And he was happy here, happier than he could ever have been in Bethesda. There was nothing there for him any more.'

'Not after they buried father.'

'Nor before,' she said. 'Nor ever. I've found it here, too, something that's not in Wales. That's what Huw had and he wouldn't have swapped a lifetime there for the few years he had here.'

'Then he's as much of a traitor as they say I am, throwing up his bloodline like some bad meat. He was Welsh, he owed it to Wales, but when the English pushed us out they squashed him just as certain as their wagon broke father's back.'

She buttoned up his shirt, and tore a strip off his old one to make a sling. Then in a voice he had never heard before, she asked, 'All this because they killed your father?'

She looked towards the house. 'And yet asleep over there is my son who fought with them; for them. And hanging over his bed is a medal their Queen gave him for it.'

'I know that too, mother.'

'But there's so much you don't know, so much. And I wonder, I wonder whether if you knew more, it might stop you from hating them and killing them.'

'Why do you use that voice, mother? What should I know?'

She went on as if she hadn't heard him. 'I wonder if it would save you yet?'

He reached out and gripped her arm so tight it hurt. She could feel the throbbing of her pulse beneath his fingers.

'Tell me what? What should I know?'

'The English did not kill your father, Ianto,' she said.

'They killed him, they . . .'

'Killed Owen Llewellyn. But he was not your father. You are my son, you came from me, you were my first, but your father was . . . he was my only other lover, Ianto, and he lies buried by my father's side in a pit shaft near Merthyr. They died together, when I was already five months gone with you. We were to have married within the fortnight, that's why he'd gone south to dig coal, just as my father did, to earn more money than they could ever have done with slate. Your father left before I even knew I was pregnant and I never wrote to him. There was no need, was there? We'd have been married before you came and I didn't want him back before he'd saved his money for the house.

'They told me later there was a fire in the shaft where he and Dad were working, and to save the others further up the tunnel the order was given to flood. Just the two of them there but they reckoned it saved forty. It was in the newspapers and they said there'd be a plaque for them, but there never was. I suppose you can't expect that every time someone dies in the pits, can you? They said it was the only thing to do – two men for forty – and I think that was right. So would they. They would have done it themselves if they'd had to. The order was given by a Welshman, the manager, he came from Brecon. They told me that only a Welshman could have done it, killing his own like that. The English would have dallied, worried that if they had ordered it, the men would have . . .

'And so I married Owen Llewellyn the day I should have married your father. Owen knew about you coming. I told him before he asked me, but I think he'd guessed anyway. Four months later everyone thought you were Owen's and they said I'd been playing with two men and they never forgave me. Owen never forgave them, but I had no complaint, really. I knew I was the luckiest girl, to have loved two fine men and kept one of them much, much longer than I ever expected. And he gave me more happiness than perhaps I deserved.'

The hand that held her had long stopped trembling, and now it relaxed and slid into her lap. She held it between hers but she was uncertain. There was no anger in his face any more but there was nothing in his eyes to help her.

'I've carried it all these years, Ianto, this secret, afraid to tell you, waiting until you were a man before I dared and then not daring once you were. Do you understand? I kept it to myself to protect you and me because I couldn't risk you going. You're mine, Ianto. You belong to me just as much as the others – more, perhaps, because of what you carry inside you, a little of him. Tell me you understand, Ianto. Tell me it's easier now, not harder – that it helps you.'

Still he said nothing but the longer she waited the more sure she was he was still hers.

'There's still time to save yourself,' she said. 'If there's to be a war it will help you to escape because both sides will think you're dead. You can ride south to Cape Town, you'll not be known there and then you can go anywhere, back to Wales, America, Australia. I've money enough saved here for your ticket. Go anywhere, Ianto, but leave Africa!'

She felt the pull of his hand and she let go. He stood up. His face was lit by the moon. He pulled on his cloak and hat.

'What will you do?' she asked.

He looked down and he smiled. 'I'll do as I'm told, mother, as I've always done. Go south to the Cape.'

'I'll get the money.'

'No, mother. Not yours. I've enough for what I need and I'll find more if I haven't.'

'For Wales?'

'No. Not there. Not now. Perhaps South America. I met a

man from Cardiff who was going there. Argentina, he said. It sounds a nice word. Argentina.'

'Oh, Ianto!'

'Don't cry, mother. You kept your secret well and for the best. Don't cry, now. I'll not do any more fighting, I promise you. Here, I'll leave my gun. I can't do more, can I? Do what you want with it, bury it or save it for baby Tom. He'll have a good eye, you see. He'll hunt well. He's an African now.'

He leant down and picked her up in one arm as if she were a child. 'It's a silly state of things, mother, a grown man and nowhere to go. In the middle of the world and nowhere to go!' He kissed her softly on the lips, then let her slip gently to her feet.

'I'll get some food,' she said.

'No, I've plenty in the saddlebag.'

'Where's your horse?'

'Safe, a mile away along the river.'

'Will you manage?'

'I'll have to. I've enough years ahead so I'd better.'

'Will you send a letter?'

'Yes. So I can tell you when I'm coming to see you.'

'Ianto!'

'Oh, a long way ahead, mother. When this is all over and the English have gone home. Then I'll come.'

'God bless you, my sweetheart son. Take care.'

They kissed again and held each other tight. He pushed her away.

'What was his name?'

'Richard,' she said softly. 'Richard Morgan Thomas.'

'I shall take it for myself,' he said. 'So he lives on.'

'So you both will.'

'Yes.'

'Goodbye, then.'

'Goodbye, mother.'

* * *

He made a wide circle of the house and dropped down between the trees to the path that led to the ruins of Big Macpherson's farm. Then he crossed the new bridge and kept to the river bank until it moved off south in its wide meander. His horse was tethered still a half-mile further on but the moon was still bright and the earth firm beneath him. He felt strangely light as if a heavy pack on his back had been suddenly cut away. His arm and shoulder throbbed but the sharp pain, like the pricks of a thousand needles, had gone. He stopped to tie another knot in the sling to raise his arm.

Across the silver river he could see the light of the single lantern hanging on Honest Jack's verandah and beyond it the dark shape of his mother's house and the shining white bark of the tall bluegum trees that lined the east side of her garden. He remembered standing on such a spot on such a night not so many years back with his rifle still warm in his hands. He remembered the burning kraal consuming the bleeding and naked body of the witch doctor and the column of lamps as the diggers and Major John brought the girl safely home.

Now he was leaving again but in a different mood and for other reasons. And with a new name.

He heard his horse whinny and he buttoned his cloak tighter under his neck as he walked the last few yards. She stood by the tree as he had left her, with just enough halter to graze. He would water her and then be a long way off before dawn. She whinnied again. He knew it was to warn him but it was too late.

'Stand still, Ianto Llewellyn!' shouted a voice he knew. 'I have a gun and you have not. Stand still or I'll blast you to Hell where you belong.'

He was hidden by the tree but the barrel of his gun stood out like a stiff black eel above the mare's nose.

'Stand still, curse you!' he shouted. 'I've shot a man before!'

'I am still, Honest Jack. And I'm going nowhere particular.'

'Wrong you are, boy. You're going straight to the Devil whose servant you are, serving him just as you serve the Boer swine, killing for them, the same Dutch bastards who've been slowly killing me.'

'You've had more letters?'

'Rot you if I have then!' he shouted back and he came from his cover, stumbling but holding the muzzle straight at Ianto's chest. He stopped six feet away and the warm night air spread the smell of brandy.

'I'm sorry,' said Ianto.

'Sorry for me with a crippled leg, full of Boer lead and a wife and children so close I can feel them tugging? Sorry for the English boys you murdered, no older than your brother? Sorry for their mothers who won't be able to sit and clean their wounds as yours did tonight? They won't even know what they've lost until a month's time and Africa will have eaten their babies up by then. You traitor, boy! That's what you are, a traitor and a disgrace to your dead brother's memory and your mother's love.'

He spat and a little carried to Ianto's face. He went to wipe it off.

'Still, boy, still!' shouted Honest Jack, waving the gun. 'Your hand won't save your face and it's your face I'm aiming at 'cos you haven't a heart!'

'Then kill me.'

'I will, lad, I will. If I'd the nerve I'd take you to the army myself and claim the sovereigns they're offering. I should let them do it their way with a dozen bullets for my one, but I've no nerve left in me, not even the brandy gives it me any more.'

He raised his gun and pulled it into his shoulder. The mare behind him shook her head and snorted and somewhere beyond the gorge on the slopes to the lowveld, a lone jackal called but nothing answered. The night seemed suddenly hollow and the two of them like echoes bouncing off each other, he and the drunken, emptied man. Ianto felt as if he were already dead.

'Do it, Honest Jack,' he said softly, 'here and now. Let the river take me away. But if you have any love left in you for good and decent things, don't tell my mother how I went. Let her think

I've gone south. That's what she wants to believe whatever else she supposes. Will you do that for her?' And he looked into the small black circle of the muzzle and closed his eyes.

'Damn you, damn you, and damn the God that made you!' Honest Jack began sobbing and he slowly sank to his knees, burying the end of the barrel into the soft earth in front of him.

'I would have shot myself soon after,' he said. 'I brought two shells for it, one each.'

'How did you know?'

'I saw you with your mother come down off the hill behind my place. I never sleep when I have the letters and they came today. I followed you both and saw her mend you. And I saw you leave your gun behind.'

They knelt opposite each other a yard apart, the rifle sticking out of the ground like a broken sapling.

'I couldn't have killed you, Ianto, not your mother's son, not even full of brandy. But you'll be caught, you know that. With so much money on your head, some greedy Boer will turn you in. Then you'll be hanged as a traitor. And you are, Ianto. Whatever else I may have said, you *are* that! Seeing you there with your mother tore at my innards, you with her, she and her children, hugging, kissing them, knowing them. But not me and mine, and with the two loveliest angels only a half day's ride away, forbidden to see them, touch them, me, their father.' He wept again and covered his eyes with his hands. Ianto sat back and turned his head away.

Presently he said, 'I'll get you your family, Honest Jack. I know where they are, I know the farm.'

Honest Jack wiped his face with his sleeve. Then using the rifle as a crutch, pushed himself up. Ianto stood with him. 'I'll get them back,' he said again.

'If you had said that when I had you in the gun,' said Honest Jack, 'I would have pulled the trigger.'

'I know that,' said Ianto.

'Who are they with?'

'The Bezuidenhouts.'

'Where's their farm?'

'Breitenbach, just north of Krugers Post.'

'You do know, then. Ianto, how can you be sure they'll let them go? Bezuidenhout's a hating man.'

'He owes me. I've been riding with them for a long time now. They're with the Lydenburg Commando and the sons have been with me lately on the Ossewabrandwag attacks. I pulled them out of an ambush two months ago. Old man Bezuidenhout knows he'd have no sons now if I hadn't. He knows I gave him his family back. He'll give me yours.'

Honest Jack said nothing for a minute or more, but seemed content to tidy himself, doing up the few buttons on his waistcoat and patting the dust from his jacket and trousers. Then he wiped his face dry with a handkerchief that had been tied around his neck.

'God bless you, Ianto,' he said, nodding his head but not looking.

Ianto smiled. 'I was the Devil's servant a while back.'

'Oh, no. This isn't his work. If it is real, it's not his. What must I do?'

'Meet us halfway. I can't come back again. I'll bring them along the Ohrigstad road; watch from Pilgrims Hill. When you see us, come riding down and we should meet before the road crosses the stream a few miles north of Krugers Post.'

'I know the place, Ianto, but be careful. The English patrols are everywhere now and they want you more than any Boer.'

'I'll be careful, especially now. I want you to have your wife and children, Honest Jack. All my life I've seen families coming apart, always losing someone, someone leaving or dying. You'll have yours again, I promise.'

'When, Ianto?'

'Tomorrow. Be on the hill from noon, and we'll be there long before the light goes. I vouch you'll have them home for suppertime.'

Honest Jack held out his hand. Ianto hesitated.

'With a traitor?' he asked.

'With your mother's son.'

'Yes,' said Ianto. 'I'm that, at least!'

They shook hands and Honest Jack helped him into the saddle, untied the halter and gave him the reins.

'You'll not take my gun?' he asked.

'No,' said Ianto.

'Tomorrow, then?'

'We'll be there.' Ianto smiled down at him. 'Don't forget now, will you!'

He kicked the mare and turned her round and Honest Jack stood by the tree in the white light of the moon and listened to them thudding away faster and faster, further and further into the night.

It was a little after daybreak when Major John hurried from his office, almost running the last few hundred yards to Mary's house, the dispatch in his hand. The Reverend Makepeace saw and ran after him.

'They've hoisted their flag over Heidelberg,' Major John said, waving the paper at them as they sat around the breakfast table. 'And one of their commandos, three thousand men or more, have galloped into Potchefstroom. There's been a dreadful fight and the Royal Scots Fusiliers have surrendered. The rest are holed up in the fort under siege. They've also attacked Standerton and Wakkerstroom. They're sweeping across the entire Transvaal.'

Mary pulled him to a chair and gave him coffee.

'They've declared their republic under Kruger,' he went on, still waving the paper, 'and they've sent the British administrator an ultimatum. God knows what'll happen now!'

'Mrs de Wet said it was coming,' William said. 'She said there'd be a war.'

'Well, the British certainly didn't know about it,' said Major

John. 'They haven't enough men to cope. I don't suppose there are more than two thousand troops in all the Transvaal.'

'What will they do?' asked Mary.

'Send for more.'

'Have the Boers formally declared war?' asked the Reverend.

'Not yet, but after putting up the flag and killing a few dozen Fusiliers I don't see they need to! The ultimatum's as good as one, anyway. The British have no intention of complying. They're used to sending threats, not receiving them. My guess is they'll ignore it and when it expires the Boers will take every British garrison the next day.'

'That Lanyon's a fool,' the Reverend Makepeace said. 'Only a week ago he was saying the Boers were cowards. What did he say: "Anything they do will just be a spark in a pan." And he got his knighthood with foresight like that!'

Major John turned to Mary. 'You must leave here, all of you. I'm arranging for you to go to Pretoria; you'll be safe there, it's a strong garrison, they'll not attack it. If there's going to be war this is not the place to be.'

'The Boers won't touch us here, surely,' she said.

'Boers or English, who knows what they'll do, especially if it drags on into the summer. This is a strategic position, Mary, good for either side, especially the English with their artillery. My mind's made up. You must pack. Polly will go too and take the babies. She'll agree to that, Reverend?'

He nodded. 'She'll agree.'

'William, you'll take your wagon with Tongo. I'll persuade Honest Jack to ride with you. I've sent a runner to Colonel Anstruther at the Lydenburg fort, he has orders to evacuate tomorrow morning and he'll take you all in his column. There are a lot of wagons going and you'll be safe with his men around you. I'll keep Flansman here. We may need the horses.'

He reached out and held Mary's hand across the table. 'You will go, won't you?'

She smiled. 'I don't think I'd budge for any other man or for any other reason.'

'You'll be back soon,' he said. 'Somebody must come to their senses, though Lord knows who it'll be. Now start packing – food, blankets, water, and William, bring the goat and heifer.'

That evening, Mary wrote in her diary:

> 'Tomorrow Wednesday 16th December 1880 we leave Pilgrims Rest and may be away some months. There is to be a war and John thinks it might last until the summer. The Boers are fighting for what is obviously theirs but the English are too. The wagon is packed tight but it is mostly clothes and bedding so it is not heavy. The goat and heifer are tied behind. Polly is coming too with the babies who I think will soon be hers, but the Reverend is staying because the diggers refuse to leave and he says it would not be right. Honest Jack also will not go and says he has his own reasons for staying though I can't think what they are unless it's his brandy. But he is a good man and he must take care of himself. I pray that Ianto is now a long way south and I pray too that God will look after our little home while we're gone.'

Two hundred and sixty-four officers and men of the 94th Regiment, the Connaught Rangers, were lined up and waiting inside the fort when William brought the wagon into Lydenburg. As soon as he braked outside the gates, Colonel Anstruther gave the order to move and line by line, six abreast, they marched out following the band, led by a drummer and a boy bugler. The men's white helmets were dazzling in the strong sunlight and their blancoed webbing and pouches shone sharp against their bright red tunics. All, without exception, had moustaches, and some had beards and Mary was astonished how young the faces were behind them. The drummer tapped out the step and the boy bugler at his side and only half as tall winked at Polly as he passed. She was so surprised, she blushed and the soldiers cheered.

The Boers were waiting on the outskirts of the small town, farmers, merchants and their families lining either side of the road. As the first lines of soldiers passed, they were surly and silent but then one shouted abuse and it was quickly taken up by the others. The old ones waved their fists and shouted: '*Verdompde Engelsman. Maak Gou,*' and the younger ones shouted in English, 'Get out and hurry up, you rednecks.' Then, as the bugler, walking by the side of his colonel's horse, turned south at the fork in the road, they saw ahead of them, silhouetted against the sky, a scaffold and hanging from it were five dummies made of straw. They were all wearing the white helmets and bright red tunics of the 94th.

'It's Slachter's Nek, mother,' William whispered. 'It's what we did to them a long while ago.'

The Boers following a little distance behind began cheering. The colour sergeant ran forward to the colonel.

'Shall I have them cut down, sir?' But the colonel shook his head. 'No, Sergeant, let them swing. Our friends must have their laugh.'

And William remembered Mrs de Wet's words. 'We're a determined people. And unforgetting!'

It was a cloudless day and hot, with no shade across the treeless veld, so Colonel Anstruther relaxed discipline, allowing the men to put their rifles in the wagons. They sang as the band played 'Kiss me, Mother'. It seemed to Mary most unlike a war.

Presently the colonel fell back from the head of the column and rode alongside, and Mary gave him a cup of water. He seemed a pleasant man, genuinely sad at what was happening.

'Why have you left your fort, Colonel,' she asked, 'if there's a war going on?'

'Orders, ma'am,' he replied, smiling and handing back the empty cup.

'Yes, but why? There must be a reason behind an order?'

'I'm sure there is, ma'am, but it's not often one is accompanied by the other, at least not in the British army. I've been told to proceed to Pretoria, so proceeding we are. And on a fine day, too.'

'Your men seem happy to be going.'

'Oh, yes. They've been cooped up for too long. Not many have been out of that stockade in six months or more, only those on patrols, which, given the circumstances, has become a very dangerous promenade indeed. I've still got one out, though. They'll follow later. We're looking for someone, have been for some time now. Our supply wagons have been attacked again and again – and long before this present mess started. Call themselves the *Ossewabrandwag* – fire-raisers, madmen.'

'And you've not caught any yet?'

'We're after one in particular and with respect, ma'am, one of your own people – Welsh, I mean – and with your name, which I've always thought the oddest thing.'

'Not so odd, Colonel,' she said with a smile. 'We've a dreadful shortage of names in Wales. If you're not a Llewellyn, you're a Jones or a Hughes or a Williams. We're very mean with ourselves.'

The colonel looked across at William by her side and nodded. Seems we've had much the same conversation ourselves?' And William nodded back.

The colonel went on. 'To be honest, ma'am, and now that we're all riding together, I must tell you we were very suspicious of you at first. In fact at one time we were convinced the man we're after was your son. Isn't that right, William?' But William did not nod again. 'Damn certain we were, ma'am, and you came very close, all of you, to arrest. But when the Gold Commissioner up there, your Major Carpenter, told us all your sons were working the claims – well, we had to look elsewhere. And anyway we can't think bad things now, can we, not with a Zulu campaigner and an Albert Medal in the family.' And with that he saluted and cantered back to the head of the marching men.

William asked her, 'When did you know, mother, about anto and everything?'

'Oh, a long time after everyone else. And it seems Major John knew before all of us, and lied for us, too.' Then in a whisper she told him how Ianto had returned to the graveyard on his brother's birthday, and given his gun to her.

'But mother! Without a gun – and the patrol are out looking for him now!'

'Shush! William, shush!' she said, soothingly, patting his hand. 'Ianto has nothing to fear from them now. He's a long, long way away, beginning again. Oh, a long way south, my darling!'

It was a minute past four o'clock when Honest Jack looked up from his watch and saw them, two specks a long way down, two horses slowly jogging along the dusty Ohrigstad road. Six hours he had been waiting in the shadows on Pilgrims Hill and he had cursed the day's heat and the sweat that stained his clean white shirt, cursed the stiff and sharp white collar that chafed his neck red raw. He had shaved twice over and had splashed the razor burns with witch-hazel so that now his face felt on fire. The brilliantine that flattened his hair trickled down his temples and stung his eyes and his swelling feet threatened to burst the seams of the black polished high boots he was wearing for the first time in two years.

All day he had been racked with the growing, gnawing suspicion that Ianto had lied, that even with the gun buried at his feet he had contrived a new torture with promises so earnestly made. And at exactly four o'clock, with the shadow of his horse spreading longer across the ground he was near despair. Home by suppertime, Ianto had said, but already the sun was sinking.

Then, in that sixty seconds, Honest Jack's world turned around. There was Ianto, there was his wife, and there, sitting in front of them both, one on each saddle, were his daughters Honest Jack went down on one knee, crossed himself, closed his eyes and made his silent promises. Then quickly he mounted his horse and began the trek down to the place where the roads crossed.

Had he paused a moment longer, had he prayed for a few seconds more, had he stopped to loosen his collar or kick off a boot, he would have seen the others before they saw Ianto. But he did not see them going forward, crouching below the line of rocks that edged the road, hiding them, fifteen Redcoats with their rifles at the ready and their bayonets glistening like long, thin and deadly shafts of glass.

They could have shot him there and then but their orders had been to take Ianto alive and that was what Sergeant Mackay wanted most of all. Six weeks before, a young trooper of the 94th had been driving a wagon to Natal for supplies. An empty wagon and an unconcerned, unarmed soldier suddenly ambushed by masked Boers and another whose mask could not hide his Welsh voice as the few who survived remembered it. Even the bones were charred when they were brought to Sergeant Mackay's quarters in the Lydenburg fort but he knew it was his son. The steel bracelet he'd given him for his seventeenth birthday was still around the wrist.

The sergeant had ordered his men to track the riders to a gorge a mile ahead. There they would block both ends and trap the Welsh traitor and murderer.

Ianto knew before he heard the shout. An eagle suddenly flew angrily from its eyrie among the rocks and only a man could do that.

'We have you, Welshie! Leave your horse and your girl-friend too. Jump down and walk to the middle. Put the babes on the ground and leave them.'

But Ianto reined quickly and the horses almost shied. He grabbed the other's halter and kicked and together they galloped away from the booming, echoing voice. Sergeant Mackay shouted again: 'Don't fire, men – hold your fire. Hold, hold, hold! There's no way out for them!'

But Sergeant Mackay, for all his planning, did not know the gorge as well as Ianto. The walls were not regular and two hundred yards short of the far end, the rock face broke open into a smaller ravine twenty yards across with an overhanging lip. It was like a nest, protected on all sides but one. Ianto jumped down and pulled the horses through.

'Don't be afraid,' he said to the woman. 'You've a long way to go – it's not over yet. They'll not have us that easily. Indeed, they'll not have you at all!' He helped the young woman down and then the children and they sat in the corner.

He knew they did not have long. Honest Jack had seen them and would already be halfway down and if they were not at the crossroads, for sure he would be tempted to jog further this way. Then they would shoot him.

Sergeant Mackay shouted again. 'Come out, Welshie. You're trapped like a rabbit in a hole and I'm the bloody ferret. I'll have you out of there, dead or alive, take your choice. You're going to die, Welshie, but I'd rather it wasn't here. I want a little bit of ceremony with a lot of 'em watching. My lads would put you down now, but I says no! He knows he's going to die, I says, so let him do it slowly, thinking about it all the way from here to the limepit. I says, give him a chest full of bullets, one for every poor Englishman he's killed. Ain't that right, Welshie, ain't that how it ought to be?'

For a while there was silence. Then Ianto heard the sound of an axe. They were going to smoke them out.

Ianto cupped his hands and shouted: 'That's the clever thing to do, soldier, light a fire, lots of smoke, let my friends know I'm here. They'll see it from Lydenburg well enough. You may take me but they'll take you too, and you've no friends left now – they've all gone. I watched them leave this morning.'

A bullet pinged a yard above Ianto's head. Then another, closer, and splinters of rock dropped onto his sleeve.

He shouted again: 'Don't show yourselves. I've only one arm but I can still shoot better than any of you. And you know how well I aim. But I've a better idea, soldier. A tooth for a tooth.'

'Got a bargain, Welshie?'

Ianto saw how the shadows were lengthening into the cave.

Soon it would be dark and they could light their fire and no one would see the smoke.

'If you want me, Englishman, listen. I've a mother here, a Boer mother and her two children. They are not mine. I was taking them to their farm in Ohrigstad.'

Another bullet shattered a hanging spindle of rock within reach of his arm.

'Let them go,' he shouted. 'Let them ride away. I'll see them when they're higher up, I'll see them from here. When they're safe away I'll come out. I'll throw my gun out and come after it.'

'Is that your bargain, Welshie?'

'Yes. And you haven't much time, soldier, if you want to catch up with your colonel. He's a long way off by now.'

He waited. The girls began to cry and the mother held them tighter. Then Sergeant Mackay answered.

'We don't want the woman, Welshie. Or the babes. Send them out.'

Ianto shouted back, 'I'll kill at least two of you if you're lying.'

'Send her out,' said the sergeant.

Ianto hesitated then nodded to the mother. He lifted her up into the saddle and then gave her her children.

'Now don't hurry,' he said. 'Trot. He'll meet you where we planned and as soon as you do, go as fast as you can.' He smiled at her. 'I promised Honest Jack you'd all be home by suppertime.' The three of them stared at him wide-eyed. He slapped the mare's flanks and pushed it towards the opening.

'They're coming!' he shouted.

'We're waiting,' came the answer.

She held the mare and turned in her saddle. A shaft of evening light touched her and he saw suddenly how pretty she was.

'*Danke*,' she whispered. '*Danke, meneer.*'

'Goodbye,' he said, 'and home by suppertime, in Pilgrims Rest.'

CHAPTER TEN

It was midsummer and Christmas was only five days away. Soon they would be safe and protected among the English in Pretoria.

Colonel Anstruther's men of the 94th and their column of supply wagons had journeyed well, the men ambling at the oxen's pace, singing with the band. There were thirty-five wagons in all with William's the last, and stretched so casually, half a mile separated the first from the last, and as the road dipped and turned across the plains the Boers had once called Nazareth, the tail lost sight of the head.

Mary had enjoyed the trek and the outspans. It had been hot but the breezes made the days tolerable and the nights pleasantly cool. Major John had prepared them well for the journey, making it more like a treat than evacuation. It was a chance to see some new country, he had said, more of Boerland, and at the end of it, Pretoria, where she and the girls could spend some of their gold money shopping. There were dresses from Durban and shoes from Cape Town, rugs and heavy weaves from Zululand and baskets from the sugar plantations in Natal. And there was a silversmith recently arrived from Bristol who made his own jewellery, his bangles, earrings and necklaces heavy with all of Africa's precious stones: topaz and emeralds, tourmalines and red jasper, tiger's eye, amethyst, serpentine and jade.

She had been so excited by it all that it was only now, near to the end of her journey, that she wondered if she had not said goodbye to him too cheerfully and whether her kisses had been too light and too hastily given.

There had been only one delay some miles out of Middleburg. Two messengers had ridden out, coming and going within an hour of each other. They had spoken to the colonel with serious faces, pointing westwards, but the colonel had shaken his head and laughed and the messengers had ridden away despairing. The sergeants told the men that the horsemen had come to warn the colonel of a large armed Boer patrol in the area but he had scorned their warnings, saying he would bang the big drum and frighten them off. And the men of the 94th had laughed too.

But William and the other civilian wagon masters and their Africans who had lived among the Boers did not laugh and they went together to the colonel and urged him to send his own patrol ahead and put out scouts on their flanks.

'Gentlemen,' he told them, wagging a finger, 'I fear you worry too much. This is Sunday 20 December and if you know your Boers as well as you say you do then you'll know it's the only day of the week when they won't work or fight. Now, come, no fretting. It's a fine Sunday and tonight we'll drink Bavarian beer at Fleischmann's and enjoy some of Pretoria's best roast buck.' And he cantered away, humming to the band.

Thirty-eight miles from Pretoria the road is crossed by a small clear running stream known as Bronkerspruit, the Boer name for the 'watercress stream'. The road winds its way down through grassy bumpy hillocks and meets the stream at the bottom of a shallow valley. To the left, looking west, is a hill, broader than any nearby and higher, with clusters of young leafy thorn trees spread up and over the brow, thick and green.

At one o'clock on the Sunday the band stopped playing midway through their refrain of 'Kiss me, Mother' and the men stopped singing and halted abruptly. The wagons jostled and braked behind them. Ahead and above them, five hundred Boers rode out of their hiding places between the trees and moving swiftly across the hills on either side of the valley were five hundred more.

A horseman came sideways down the slope from the trees

carrying the white flag of truce and when he reached the road he reined and cantered towards them. The colonel rode to meet him.

When they were side by side, a yard apart, the Boer touched his cap. 'Good day, meneer. I have a letter from my commandant.' He held it out but the colonel did not take it. Instead he said, 'Is it in English, my friend?'

'It is, meneer,' the Boer answered.

'And you can read English?'

'I can read English and Afrikaans, meneer.'

'Then I suggest you read it out to me in English, and quickly too, so as to keep my delay here to a minimum.'

The Boer nodded his head and unrolled the paper

'It says, meneer, that we have proclaimed our republic and that the new government of the Transvaal requires you do not proceed to Pretoria. You are to turn about and go back to your fort in Lydenburg. It is signed by my Commandant Franz Joubert. These are my orders.'

The colonel turned his horse around to face his column. 'You may well have your orders, my friend,' he said. 'But I too have mine, and as they have yet to be countermanded I shall obey them. I am not aware that any war between us has been declared so I shall consider you either insurrectionists or common bandits and I order you to stand aside and let my column pass. You will see we are not prepared for war. My men are mostly without their arms. Now take your letter back to Mr Joubert and tell him *my* orders are to proceed to Pretoria and proceed I damned well will!'

He kicked his mare and cantered away. The Boer did the same and the band began to play 'God Save the Queen'. But Colonel Anstruther was still twenty yards from the drummer when the first bullet ripped into his back and sent him hurtling to the ground.

The Boers opened fire on all sides at once and as the colonel pulled and crawled his way towards his men he knew he had been tricked. The Boers had moved into firing positions and marked each man, using a letter and the white flag of truce.

The men of the 94th ran in all directions in their panic, searching for cover and screaming for their rifles. But there was no place to hide, no trees, no shrubs, not a trench to crawl into, not a stone to crouch behind. So they lay in the road covering their heads with their hands but it did not slow the bullets down. Those close enough to a wagon went for a rifle but the fire was so intense they ran into a wall of lead and some were cut in half across the waist. A dozen or more bullets hit a single man and spun him round like a wooden top.

Oxen at the front stampeded and the wagons overturned and rifles and ammunition pouches spilled and scattered across the road but men were dead or crippled before they could reach them. Now the Boers were on three sides above them and running down the slopes for closer aim. The 94th hid themselves behind the wagons but the Boer snipers aimed between the wheels and took away their legs.

Hardly a shot was returned and men shrieked out for orders but no orders were given because the Boers had aimed their opening shots at the officers and had killed all but one with their first bullets. Colonel Anstruther had now been hit five times and the drummer and boy bugler had dragged him between a pile of his own dead, the red cloth of his tunic mangled in his gaping wounds. He pulled the boy towards him and tried to speak but blood filled his mouth so he spat and tried again: 'Stop it, bugler. Sound the ceasefire . . . we must leave a few to tell the story.'

The boy stood up and the drummer stood with him as the bugle sounded the surrender. When the firing had stopped, he looked down to his colonel but he was already dying by a torn and bloodied drum and the drummer face down in the stream, the crystal water turning crimson.

Slowly, carefully, some on foot, some on their horses, the Boers came down to count the British dead. Slowly, carefully, they stepped between the pools of blood in the white dust road, turning over bodies with the toe of their boot, kicking a rifle or a helmet aside. The older men took off their hats and shook their heads, unable to believe what they had done. The young ones, proud of their marksmanship, shouted to each other. How many had hit the heart? How many the brain?

When all but one of the Boers had reached the road, the last rode out from his cover in the thorn trees, a tall man with a thin grey lined face wearing a waistcoat and a top hat and a belt of cartridges across his chest. And around his waist he had wrapped the orange, white and blue flag of his republic. He came to Colonel Anstruther's body and stopped. He, like the other older men, seemed surprised at what they had done, as if they had been elsewhere and were seeing it for the first time.

He ordered his men to open the medical chests and the young marksmen were ordered to stop their boasting and help with the wounded. He said brandy should be given to men who asked for it and the eyes of those who needed nothing more should be closed.

He was given a count of the British casualties. In the ten minutes of the attack, fifty-seven had been killed, another hundred wounded; thirty oxen and sixteen mules were dead, six wagons overturned. A civilian wagon master had been hit in the arm with shrapnel, another grazed in the head. Five British soldiers had gone crazy and had stolen bottles of brandy and were now fighting each other half-naked in the stream.

A half mile back, William heard the firing and the screaming and then the bugle that finally stopped it. He had hidden Mary, Tom, the girls and the babies, making them lie flat along the bottom of his wagon. The side boards were two inches thick, of the hardest wood, and although he counted four hits, none of the bullets had sunk deeper than an inch. Mary and the girls were tearing dresses into strips for bandages and compresses.

William unhitched his front ox and rode down the line. He was within twenty yards of Joubert when they stopped him, crossing their rifles in front of him.

He shouted, 'Let me ride to Pretoria for help. We must have doctors!'

Joubert shook his head and waved him away. A large Boer, wider and taller even than Ianto, took hold of the ox's horns and twisted them, turning its head. It groaned with the pain and he twisted it further and it went down on its knees, throwing William off. The Boer held out his hands and twisted them again, threatening to break William's neck. But William ignored him and shouted again.

'You have slaughtered unarmed men. You have damned yourselves and your republic. But don't damn the men still living. You've killed too many.'

The commandant was already talking to other men about other things, preparing to leave, preparing to take the 94th's rifles and ammunition boxes, and collecting the fittest survivors as prisoners.

'My name is Llewellyn,' William shouted again. 'You know my brother Ianto. You must know him!'

Joubert stopped talking. He turned in his saddle and then beckoned William, speaking to the men in their own language to let him through. He leant down from his horse and spoke softly so that no one near to them should hear.

'You are his brother?'

'I am,' replied William. 'From the goldfields.'

'You are . . .'

'William.'

'But there is another?'

'He is dead. His name was Huw.'

Joubert sat up again. Then he said, 'Yes, I do know your brother.'

'Then you'll let me go?'

Joubert rubbed his eyes. 'We owe a debt. A large debt. But I cannot risk the safety of my men by letting you ride into an English garrison.'

'Then let me walk!'

'It is forty miles.'

William grabbed his stirrup. 'I don't care. They must have help here. You can't let them die!'

Joubert looked at him, his eyes were grey and watery. At last he said, 'Then walk. This road will give you no more interruptions. You can be in Pretoria in eleven hours. Now off! I owe you no more.'

Mary packed him meat and he tied it to his belt with the water-bottle. He was about to leave when a sergeant, his foot shattered and bleeding, dragged himself to the wagon.

'Please, governor,' he said in a whisper, 'take this for us, wrap it round you, under your shirt, they'll not look. Please! For the regiment and the dead colonel. We can't let them take it now, not after this.'

Then he fell in a dead faint into William's arms and Mary helped pull him under the wagon out of sight of the sun and the Boers. They saw he was clutching the colours of the 94th.

William stumbled, exhausted and bleeding, into Pretoria at half past three the following morning, Monday the twenty-first. They rang bells to wake people. Doctors gathered their medicines and horses were harnessed to the ambulances and Father Mayer from the convent rode out with the first. News of the massacre was immediately telegraphed to Pietermaritzburg and onwards to Durban, an hour before the Boers cut the lines. At midday, martial law was declared. The war had formally begun.

The ambulance brought the wounded survivors into Pretoria that afternoon. The drunk soldiers were bound hand and foot and bleeding from the whippings the Boers had given them. The dead had been buried in a mass grave where the stream and road met. There was no time to build a cross and the ceremony was brief. Father Mayer could not find words to hide his distress and anger so he only uttered the few necessary to the service.

But what he saw at Bronkerspruit would never leave him. And those who went with him to help, those who knew more about war than he, were numbed by its new dimension, shocked by the Boers' cold-blooded planning.

But the single, most dreadful suspicion that remained in all men's minds that day came from the twenty bodies they found a mile away. They were together, all had minor wounds except for a bullet-hole in their right temple. No man who saw them ever managed to persuade himself that they had not been shot where they lay, looking west along the Pretoria road, waiting for help.

Come the spring, and travellers along that road would stop and inspect the hump of earth, like a large molehill at the side of the stream, and puzzle at the dozens of young shoots pushing their way through the new grass. Some would identify them as peach seedlings but wonder how they came to be in such a desolate spot. Then they would remember the massacre and know they were standing at the grave of the 94th, where men had been buried in their uniforms with their knapsacks on their backs and the ripe peaches still inside them.

That evening in their camps, the Boers were jubilant. The war was only hours old but already they had seen their first victory and across the Transvaal they knelt in the dust by their fires, bowing their heads and nodding at their preacher's praise. 'Almighty God, thy chosen people thank thee, who had stood by us and with so many of our enemy dead, allowed only one of ours to be killed.'

* * *

After the massacre Mary decided they should turn back. The other wagons had followed the ambulances south and Mary might well have done the same had she not watched the hundred British prisoners, bloodied, shocked and herded together and harnessed, like oxen, to the wagons for the journey to Heidelberg. The war was in the south, she thought, and it would be wiser and safer to go back north to Lydenburg and home.

But four nights later as they had outspanned on the foothills of Bothasberg they were surrounded by a Boer patrol. They took Jollie's heifer and laughed at her speechless tearful protest as she clung to its neck. They would have taken the goat too if Polly had not shown them the twins, and told them the children would starve without the goat's milk, which was true. But the Boers still turned them around, and the next morning they saw William riding to meet them.

It was New Year's Day when William brought the wagon into Pretoria. They had expected bustle and a busy town but when they came over the brow and looked down at the wide weeping willow road that ran to the square, they saw it was deserted and the shops and houses empty.

In the twelve days since martial law had been declared the midsummer sun and rain had already begun to claw the town back to the bush. Water cascaded over drainpipes cluttered with leaves and other debris; vines and creepers fingered their way across walls and windows and waist-high grass had already buried garden fences. Curtains, torn and stained, flapped from windows that had jumped their catches and birds nested in the chimney cowls.

A kitten sat on a porch and Polly ran to fetch it. William ran after her and together they followed it through the open door into the front parlour.

Polly said, 'Everything is set for dinner. There's coal in the stove, the kettle's full on the hob and there's potato and pumpkin in the sink.'

She coaxed the kitten to them and William put it in his coat pocket and kept a hand on its thin trembling little body to keep it still. Tongo kept pace with them as they went along the road looking in through other doors and windows. Every home had been left just as suddenly. The little town had been abandoned.

'It's as if the war has already come here,' William said.

'And already moved on,' she answered.

They waited as a pack of dogs turned a corner fifty yards away following a giant grey wolfhound with a squirrel in its jaws.

Families of baboons wandered from store to store, from the butcher's to the baker's, from the hat shop to the post office, scratching at the windows and pounding the doors with their fists, like customers irate at a merchant's late opening. Tame meerkats ran wild with rats and black and grey and tabby cats stalked the roofs and parapets.

William stopped by the bank. A large notice, hastily printed in red letters on a white board, was nailed to the door. He shouted out the words.

'It says: "Danger: these buildings are dynamited and detonator traps are concealed".'

A Royal Engineers major had scrawled his signature with the tip of the paintbrush: 'Le Mesurier'.

Another had been nailed to the door of the town hall. On the courthouse was a third but with a different message:

BOERS BE WARNED!
IF YOU ENTER THIS TOWN
BRITISH GUNS WILL SHELL YOU.
PRETORIA WILL BE SAVED FROM YOUR
OCCUPATION EVEN IF IT MUST
FIRST BE DESTROYED.

Major Le Mesurier had signed that too.

A rifle was fired and William came running to the wagon. Five more shots followed quickly. Across the street came the wolfhound and behind it three British soldiers. They fired again and the dog leapt and howled and fell dead, blood oozing from its back and yellow froth from its mouth.

The corporal saw them and shouted angrily, waving his gun: 'What's your bloody business?'

'We're from Lydenburg,' said William.

'You Boers, then?'

'No. We're Welsh. From the goldfields. We've come here to get away from the war.'

The corporal laughed. The men with him laughed too, longer and louder, mocking.

The corporal eyed Mary and Polly. 'So you've come here to get away from all the nasties, eh, my little darlings? Well, what you've done, my dears, is to jump from the frying-pan into the bloody fire as they say. You see, we're under siege. Trapped like a fox in a hole. The Boers are gathering around us threatening to take us street by street, though God help them if they try, 'cos we'll blow them apart with our heavies.' He came closer and Mary smelt the tobacco on his breath.

'Now then,' he said, spitting the words, 'if you're with the Boers I'll help you on your way with a bit of Birmingham brass up your backsides. But if you're really with us you'll get yourself up to the civilian camp. But not you, sunshine,' he said, catching Tongo by the neck. 'You come with us – the kaffirs are kept with us. You'll have to work for your stay, nigger-boy, and work bloody hard, too!'

Then he turned to William again. 'Take what you want from your wagon and leave the oxen by the gates. We'll take them inside to our own pens. Now get going – up there where the flag is – and double quick, military fashion.'

They turned and behind them on a hill a few hundred yards away they saw a limp and tattered Union Jack and Mary remembered Major John's parting words: 'If there's a war, Pretoria is the safest place to be.' She closed her eyes and thought of her valley and her little house safe above the clouds and she wondered what mischief God was up to now.

* * *

The British army had turned Pretoria's prison and Loreto convent next to it into a refugee camp. Already they were desperate and overflowing and people were jealous of their tiny plots. The first to come had taken the driest, safest corners though many had since sold them for a sovereign to later, wealthier arrivals thinking, as so many did at the start, that nothing would last long and the nonsense would soon be over. But now they sheltered from the rain and heat under stinking tarpaulins or torn and flimsy canvas and had spent their sovereigns on a bag of flour or a small sack of potatoes and the siege was nearly a fortnight old.

William with Jollie's help stripped the wagon of its hoops and canvas and carried them into the convent yard and erected it just below the nuns' cells. During their first nights, in the pauses between the snipers' fire, they could hear the sisters in prayer and the hum of their litanies. Mary thought of Huw and Samson and she brought out her Bible and read aloud every evening by the light of a single candle.

Then the British military commander, Colonel Bellairs, ordered the nuns into the chapel when it was discovered the windows of their cells overlooked the slopes of the Maghaliesberg Mountains where the Boers had set up their main camp. Now the narrow windows had been sandbagged and loopholed and British rifles rested on the ledges where crucifixes had been, and instead of psalms there was the coarse cackle of soldiers' laughter.

Little by little, in the days and nights that followed, Mary and Jollie, William and Polly settled themselves, making a little manger as a cot for the babies and coaxing them not to cry. Baby Tom became suddenly very strong-minded and talkative, never ever far from Jollie, carrying for her and always her spokesman, never shy to explain to strangers why she could not speak and able to say what she could not quickly and fluently without, it seemed, any signal from her. He was her tongue and a third arm.

One day he said to Mary, 'Why do you call me baby Tom?

I'm nearly seven.' Jollie smiled and Mary answered, 'Mothers always think of their youngest son as their baby. Always, no matter how old they are.'

'Did you call William "baby William"?'

'For a while.'

'But you stopped when I came?'

'Yes.'

'Why can't you have another baby?'

Jollie pulled Tom into her arms and pressed him against her and Mary kissed the back of his neck and said, 'No! No more, my darling. But I promise never to call you "baby" ever again.'

Once it was known in the camp that they had travelled from the north, men and women came visiting, anxious to know what was happening outside in the Transvaal. They shook their heads and wept when Mary told them. Some brushed the rain from themselves and cut the mud from their boots and sat on Mary's floor and ate her biscuits and told her how suddenly the war had come to them: how that Monday women had been cooking lunch, expecting their men from work and their children from the school, sweeping another storm's water from their porches, when a bugle was blown in the square and soldiers rode through the streets shouting out that war had been declared and the Boers were running wild.

They were summoned into the market square, over four thousand men, women and children, and told by the administrator, Sir William Lanyon, that he was handing over Pretoria for safe keeping to the military and that from now on every person, man or woman, married or single, was under the strict code of military discipline. Then he called for volunteers to fortify the garrison and volunteers to defend it. He said the town was too straggling to be properly protected so it would have to be abandoned and everyone confined to two laagers: the military camp on the hill, and the jail and the convent. People, he said, should not be afraid and there must be no panic. Soon the relief column of reinforcements under General Sir George Colley would arrive from Natal and the Boers would then get a thorough beating and everyone could settle down again peacefully under British rule. One of the sergeants had made a Union Jack from the lining of his tunic and as it was hauled up the flagpole people cheered and threw their hats in the air and Sir William led three hurrahs for the Queen. But then the flag was hit by a hail of Boer bullets and Sir William could not stop the panic that followed.

Soon the streets leading out of town to the camps were ankle deep in mud and packed with people afraid of being left behind: ox-wagons and pack mules, women dragging crying children and pushing handcarts piled high with clothes and food; some carried wall clocks, ivory statues and rugs and any valuable thing they dreaded leaving behind in their empty houses, but at the gates of the camps the soldiers stopped them and everything but food and clothes was dropped in the mud to warp and rot in the rain. Africans toured the streets with other carts filled with rifles and ammunition pouches and corporals handed them out to anyone who looked as if they might be capable of firing one. Those civilians too old or incapable of firing a gun were delegated other duties. The high court judge had become the chief dispenser of rations, a leading lawyer was responsible for the supply of dried cured meat; the Wesleyan minister became the sanitary inspector and the town clerk was in charge of bedding.

Sir William Lanyon organized his own brigade, eight of the most senior councillors, whom he armed with knives and double-barrelled shotguns. They were quickly ridiculed, sworn as they were to defend their council chamber stores to the last sweet biscuit and glass of sherry.

For as long as she could Mary fed the family on the food they had brought with them. But the damp turned much of the flour sour and suddenly there were weevils in the biscuits. So on the third Monday she sent Jollie to queue at the quarter-master's store for the daily rations and Tom went to help her.

But there was so little, he carried it back easily on his own. Jollie had written it all down. Every man registered in the camp was allowed a pound of bread a day, two-thirds of an ounce of tea, two ounces of sugar, one and a quarter pounds of dried meat and a half-ounce of salt. Women got half rations, children a quarter.

'We shan't survive on this,' Polly said to Mary that evening as they made the stew.

'We shan't survive without,' she answered.

'They say it'll be over soon,' Polly said. 'One of the sentries told me they'd seen flares last night, in the east. They say it's General Colley coming.'

'Then he'd better come quick about it,' said William, 'or there'll be precious few of us left.'

He remembered another English general and the death and disaster that followed the faith people had had in him. And he wondered whether it would not be more sensible to surrender to the Boers than wait on the promises of another of the army's aristocrats.

'They're beginning to kill the oxen for meat,' he said. 'They'll have ours soon, you'll see. I've told them they're all we have and we shan't get home without them, but they've put everyone's in the same pen and the butchers are killing the two nearest the gate every day.'

'We can't live without meat,' said Mary. 'There's nothing else but bread. We'll take what's left of the best of them when this is all over.'

'But ours are the fittest and the best,' he protested. 'And they're Walrus's.'

'I know that well enough,' she answered, raising her voice. 'But do you suppose Walrus would have us starve so's the beasts can live?'

Polly touched William's arm. 'The volunteers are getting extra rations,' she said quietly.

'I'm not fighting for the English. At least, not against the Boers.'

'The other young men are.'

'For their own reasons, too. But they're not mine. I've done my fighting for the English.'

She linked her arm through his. 'I think you should join them,' she said again. 'It'll mean a little more food for us and the babies and who knows, when the Boers see how well we're fighting back, they may give us a bit more space and move away. Then your oxen will live to take us home again.'

His anger left him quickly. He smiled at her and then Mary. 'Well, anyway,' he said, 'for another pound and a half of bread and meat I'd fight for Lord Penrhyn right now. And who knows, I might pick up a fowl or two while I'm peppering some Boer's backside!'

The next morning William took his rifle and enlisted in the mounted volunteers called D'Arcy's Horse, after the captain who led them.

The Boers now kept up a constant fire, their snipers on the hills waiting and watching for anyone who showed themselves above the sandbag barricades. People huddled in the gloom of their tents as bullets tore through the canvas and shattered poles, showering them with splinters. More often now they sat the long evenings in the dark because a lantern gave the Boers an easy sight and their shadow a target.

In the first weeks, Mary and Jollie wound up bandages of strips torn from calico sheets and sewed sandbags out of canvas and tarpaulins. Then they were told to work in the hospitals. There were two, one in the convent, the other in the army camp and they were both run by two civilian doctors who had left a profitable surgery in town. But within a fortnight the two demanded to be paid for their work, so the military discharged them and patients jeered and spat sickly phlegm in their faces as they left.

A young Scot took on their work. He had arrived in Pretoria the day before martial law was declared and had only qualified as a doctor in Edinburgh three months before. His name was Simon Ferguson.

Soon, Mary and Jollie were working with him most of their days and many of their nights too. At first there were only six patients in the convent hospital, but when a cooking fire overturned and set a tent on fire, it lit up the camp and the snipers killed a man and his daughter, and wounded another seven people. There was no more room for beds in the convent's hall, so Mary and Jollie pushed straw into palliasses and laid them side by side on the floor. Soon, though, the weather added more ills to injuries and it became too cramped for Dr Simon to operate there. So the army gave him a bell-tent, a trestle table, a drum of carbolic and a box of a hundred candles and he did his cutting and sewing under canvas.

Then the Boer snipers began using telescopes and their marksmen became too accurate so Dr Simon shortened the trestle legs with the saw he used to cut bones and did his operations kneeling as bullets ripped through the tent above him and let in the rain.

Jollie became his constant assistant. She vomited at the start of the first operations but she did not flinch again and put the sponge of chloroform to frightened faces, and held the flesh and swabbed away the blood and pus. She even carried the amputated limbs wrapped in canvas for the soldiers to burn or bury.

Early in February Colonel Bellairs ordered a well to be dug. Since the siege had started he had worried about the camp's water supply. It came from a river three miles away in a furrow that passed close to the Boers' camp and he was certain they would poison it. They dug for five days and found water at thirty feet but the well gave barely nine gallons a day, and people who had queued hours at the quartermaster's for their food rations refused to queue again for water and took it where they found it, despite the risk. Then a woman and her child were brought to Dr Simon's tent with a fever and when he saw the blood in their stools he said they had dysentery. Mary stayed with them for a day and a night, whispering to the mother whenever she opened her eyes and singing quietly to the little daughter who never closed hers. The mother died first and the child a few hours afterwards and Dr Simon told Jollie to burn their clothes and even the rag doll the little girl had tied to her wrist so as not to lose it.

Dr Simon demanded that Colonel Bellairs close the well but he argued against it, saying there was no proof. It was even possible, he said, that the Boers had begun to poison the stream and the woman and her child were its first casualties. But when the father came to take away the bodies he said his wife had been the first to drink from the well and had not taken water from the stream since.

Still the colonel waited until the two were buried before he ordered the well to be filled in.

It was now the middle season where summer turns to autumn. Men looked to the mountains and to the sky but there was no respite from either. The days should have been mild and the evenings fresh, but they were not. They were grey and full of rain and the nights hot and heavy. Everywhere, there was the dreadful noise and stench of people's suffering. The ground was slimy and foul and the air thick with the smell of rotting mealie bags and the brimming waste pits. And now the graves outside the sandbag wall were lined two deep.

As she became more weary Mary found it harder to sleep. Despite the heat of night she was tormented by mosquitoes which forced her to hide under the blanket until she was wet with sweat. She would listen to the howls of wandering dogs down in the town and the barks of baboons angry at some interruption. Sometimes she could hear the Boer snipers calling from their hideaways up in the Maghaliesbergs, distant tiny voices, the echoes so jumbled she could not tell whether they were shouting in English or not. But strident or coaxing, she knew they were mocking and cruel and laughing at all the misery they saw. It was then she felt the jab of despair, a finger prodding her stomach, and she remembered things she hoped had gone from her forever, things of Wales, things of Bethesda, nagging and hopeless, they all came tumbling back when she had been so sure they never would again. They grew suddenly, giant and awful in the dark, and for her first time in Africa she began to wonder whether she would survive the weeks and months of the siege with the will to endure any more African years; whether she might not, after all she had done and said and seen, go back that long, wasteful, wearying way to Wales.

But then, in the worst lonely moments, she saw Pilgrims Rest and the velvet lawn of pink-topped oatgrass that stretched away behind her house to the ridge of shining black rock; she saw her garden of wisteria and fuchsias, white arum, and montbretia and the red and purple billowing bougainvillaea. She heard the sound of humming birds and smelt the wood-smoke and saw Major John, laughing as he came to her, and the creak of her rocking-chair on the porch and the feel of his hands around her and her kiss on him. And she knew she would not leave him or Africa, ever.

In the third week of February on a thundery night they brought a girl of nineteen to Dr Simon and Mary helped them lay her on the trestle table. She told the family to go, but they stood outside in the storm until lightning suddenly lit up the camp and a sniper's bullet hit the convent wall a yard above their heads and they ran off, crouching below the sandbags.

Mary and Jollie stripped the girl and washed her body, which was covered in red spots. Dr Simon took a swab of her saliva and listened to her heart.

'Is it dysentery again?' Mary whispered to him. 'She's very hot.'

He shook his head. 'It's one of two things, Mary. And I'm praying it's measles.'

'If it's not?'

'Then it's typhoid, though I can't be sure; I've never seen a rash like it before, except in my books. We must keep her cool and wait. You sleep, Mary, and Jollie, put her clothes in a pit and burn them when it's light.'

But Mary did not sleep. She covered the restless girl in a wet blanket and in the dim candlelight watched the rash slowly crawl across her face, each tiny spot joining the next until the clusters were larger than a penny.

The army bugler sounded the start of another day as he always did half an hour before it was light, but the girl was already dead and the rashes had turned pale blue when Dr Simon gently pulled the blanket over her face.

They sewed her up in the blanket doused in carbolic and they called the family so that she could be buried quickly. But the news of her death somehow got out to the Boers who knew the family well and had thought of her as a favourite. And so, just before breakfast-time, six of them came walking up towards the camp, following the line of the water furrow, waving a white flag and carrying a coffin between them.

Colonel Bellairs ordered his sentries to let them come closer and a Boer shouted out that they had brought the coffin for the girl and that if the British agreed there would be an armistice so the family could carry her to the cemetery in town and bury her properly. It was agreed and the British sentries pulled the coffin across the trenches. And when they opened it they found the Boers' wives had lined it with flowers and strips of pink satin.

It was the first kindness in nearly two months of bitterness and Mary was among the many who stood in the muddy avenues between the tents as the family carried her away, people mourning yet astonished at their cheerfulness and relief at being able to stand again in the daylight out in the open and see the town and some even their homes in the distance.

The armistice was ended too abruptly. As the family came back that afternoon the Boers fired over their heads to remind them that the business of war had resumed and the women shrieked and the men cursed loudly as they clambered through the mud over the sandbags and ran for the cover of their tent again.

But the kindnesses were not yet over. Three days later tw young Boers, coming too close to the British lookouts, wer wounded in no-man's-land and the white flag was raised again Dr Simon, with the colonel's approval, sent out stretchers s the Boers could carry the two back to their own lines. An later when the stretchers were returned they were laden wit fruit and tobacco.

The volunteers of D'Arcy's Horse could not patrol far. The were expected to stop the Boers crossing and occupying th circle of no-man's-land. And none did, possibly because the had heard that the Royal Engineers' Major Le Mesurier ha buried mines out there, though whenever there was an ex plosion, day or night, the army simply said it was their ow artillery.

Then one of Captain D'Arcy's men was unseated when hi horse reared at a rabbit and dragged him by his stirrup int no-man's-land and after the explosion there was nothing to b seen of horse or rider. No one again believed the gunners coul have fired on one of their own side by mistake or so accurately It was the beginning of much bitterness between the Volunteer and the army which came to a head on the first day of March the beginning of the third month of the siege.

Twenty of D'Arcy's horsemen, William among them, wer patrolling the east side of the camp, with the slopes of th Maghaliesberg Mountains rising before them and the tips c the Boers' tents just showing beyond the nearest brow. A littl after midday the patrol heard shots and an army rider came t them breathless, saying that a company of British troops, on hundred men in all, were pinned down by Boers firing fror the cover of an abandoned farm called Red House Kraa William's patrol rode to them, their rifles cocked at their hips but as soon as the British Redcoats saw them coming they gc up from their hiding places and left the horsemen to fight alon

William reined his horse round and cantered in front

them, shouting to them to turn back and fight. He saw one stop and raise his rifle and William felt the wind and whistle of the bullet. He turned his horse again and whipped the men but he saw another muzzle flash and heard the Boers suddenly firing behind him as a second bullet tore into his back and he went down under his horse with his body exploding.

He felt as if he had been drained of blood and every breath tore the parched and cracking skin.

There was the faintest familiar smell of carbolic which reminded him of the doctor's tent and his mother.

'Don't move, my darling,' he heard her whisper. She wiped his face with a wet flannel and squeezed water through his broken lips from a sponge.

'How am I?' he whispered.

'Lucky as always,' she answered. 'Your horse fell on you but you were cushioned in a dip. You've broken ribs and some nasty bruises.'

'My back feels strange.'

'Dr Simon has taken out the bullet. It's chipped a little bit of bone but he says you'll be up soon.'

'Damn the Boers!' he said.

She blew on a spoonful of broth and he sipped it.

'I can't feel a thing,' he said. 'Not really. No pain, nothing. Why is that, mother?'

'Dr Simon says it's shock. He says the bullet touched a little nerve and it will take a bit of time to sort out.'

He turned his head. 'Mother.'

'You must rest, my darling.'

'Mother,' he said, 'am I moving my legs?'

She ran her hand along the covers to his knees. 'Yes.'

'Isn't that odd?' he said. 'I can't feel that I am. Only that I want to.'

She sat and stroked his hair and soon he was asleep. She went outside. It had stopped raining but there was no break in the grey clouds and she thought of the day she had last seen the lightning bird before the floods took Huw away. Why was it that rain and sickness and death seemed always to come together?

'You mustn't worry. He'll walk again.'

Dr Simon was standing by her. 'You said you couldn't be certain,' she said.

'I can't. But healing has much to do with believing. Even doctors say so.'

'If only believing made it so,' she said. 'When will you know?'

'I can't say. There's blessed little damage and I was very careful. But we know nothing yet about the nerves, Mary. We can chop and sew a body together but what the brain decides to do is God's domain.'

'Oh dear,' she said softly, putting her hands to her lips. 'And I am so losing faith in Him.'

He put his arm around her shoulder and waited until she had stopped crying. Then he said, 'I took the bullet to Captain D'Arcy.'

'Why?'

'Because it wasn't like anything I'd seen before. I didn't think it was Boer.'

'Is that what he thought too?'

'He said it came from a British rifle.'

She sighed. 'And he was only trying to make them fight like soldiers.'

'They shot him for it, Mary. D'Arcy said it was bound to happen. He said the Redcoats left William and the others to fight alone but it wasn't the first time. They're afraid to fight, he said. They're coming back from patrols with their ammunition pouches unopened and their rifles cold.'

She turned to go back into the tent. 'Tell me,' she said, 'whose side ought we to be on?'

That evening Captain D'Arcy rode alone into the army camp and dismounted outside the adjutant's quarters. The British soldiers watched him and left their tents and fires carrying their billycans of tea to see and hear better.

The major came out buttoning up his tunic. 'Good evening, Captain,' he said. 'Unannounced but not unexpected. What can I do for you?'

D'Arcy stepped forward, pulling his horse with him.

'Your men are deserters, sir,' he said loudly so that everyone might hear. 'Worse than deserters because they shot one of my men who was trying to make them do their duty as soldiers.'

'You do not whip soldiers to make them fight, Captain. Leastways, not Englishmen.'

'No, Major, you're quite right. When they desert you are obliged by army law to shoot them dead.'

The major fastened the last button at the collar and pulled his tunic straight. 'Captain,' he said, 'you can be assured we will conduct our own enquiry according to those laws and will punish accordingly if it's found necessary.'

'Your men are cowards, sir!'

'Be careful, Captain. Colonel Bellairs has forbidden such talk.'

'You'll hear it from me! My men are veterans of campaigns from the Sekekune to the Zulus and they know what should and should not be done in war. They know who the cowards are and who are dead because of them and no military man whatever his rank or threats will stop us from saying so.'

'Is that all, Captain?'

Captain D'Arcy turned and from his saddlebag pulled out a white chicken. Its neck had been pulled. He held it high so that all the men around could see. Then he offered it to the major. 'This is from me and my men to you and yours. You will find there are enough white feathers on it for all of you!'

And the major stood perfectly still as Captain D'Arcy dropped the dead bird at his feet, mounted and trotted away.

Later that evening, before the Boer snipers began their sporadic night fire, the military commander, Colonel Bellairs, came to Dr Simon's tent and spoke with Mary. He brought her a bar of soap scented with herbs. His wife, he said, had packed it for him many thousands of miles away, though she could not have expected him to use it. At other times in another place, he said, he would have brought her flowers. He apologized for not coming sooner. It was not until he had judged the court martial proceedings that afternoon that he had known how seriously William was wounded.

Mary made him tea and they talked of the siege and listened to the sniper fire. He kissed her hand and bent over and held William's. 'I have had many sad days in my life,' he said, almost whispering, 'far too many. But I could never have expected to see a hero of Rorke's Drift shot down by British soldiers. And by my own. Yes, God help me. By two of my own!'

The rain began to patter on the tent as he went out and she heard the short burst of a Gatling gun as the British sent a flare into the sky over the mountains. 'It's nothing to worry about,' he said. 'Nothing stirs but stagnation.'

She slept by William's side until the bugler woke her just before dawn, and it was still barely light when she heard the quick burst of rifle fire from the army camp and she knew it had been done. Later they told her Colonel Bellairs had witnessed the execution by firing-squad himself and had ordered the bodies to be thrown into a pit of lime and the grave left unmarked.

Those who kept calendars ticked off the days . . . seventy now . . . and how far away was Easter? How much longer now, they asked each other, and who will come first, General Colley and his Gordon Highlanders or Joubert and his Boers? Some still talked as if the relief column was just over the hills. Some still said they saw signals flashing from the east at night though in the morning they knew it was only the Boers' mischief.

Late one evening a woman came running to Dr Simon's tent saying the sentries could hear bagpipes and the doctor ran with her up the hill to hear better and the tents emptied as others followed after them to join in the cheering. But they were soon back silent and shaking their heads and all that night Mary lay by William's bed, thinking she could hear bagpipes too but it was only the wind. Colley would not come.

Sir George Pomeroy Colley was the most brilliant general in he British army. But he was soon to find out that Africa was he great leveller, with no respect for a man's achievements or ambitions. His tenure was to be short and disastrous and all because he listened to bad advice from an ignorant man, Sir William Owen Lanyon, administrator of the Transvaal.

Sir George already knew Sir William's famous description of the Boers as 'hardly more intelligent than the kaffirs, bloody immigrants . . . who need to be taught a lesson'. On a winter vening they had been drinking port in Sir William's elegant drawing-room. Sir George had eaten well and he considered himself very fortunate indeed to be briefed so early in his African career by a man of Sir William's calibre with such a depth and breadth of knowledge about the country and people he governed.

'There are some good Boers; they have lights as well as shades,' Sir William had said. 'Equal to any Englishman, sometimes better, inasmuch as they add to our virtues a great hospitality. But you know, a good Boer is as clannish as a bad one and just as able to close his eyes to the evil things his brothers and cousins do. Mark my words, George, this clannishness, this trumped-up notion they call Afrikanerdom, gives them an exaggerated concept of who they are and what they're capable of doing. We must knock it on the head, George, remind them that there's only room for one government in South Africa. We don't want a war, eh? But by jingo, if we do!' They both laughed and raised their glasses.

'I hear they're formidable shots,' said Sir George.

'They are – they are. Few of our riflemen can hold a candle to a Boer – they're the greatest shots in the world. I've heard it said they're taught from the age of three, and they'll often boast they'll have an enemy dead on the ground for every cartridge in their magazine within twenty seconds. But remember, George, our soldiers are only permitted to practise in one year with the number of cartridges a Boer will use in a normal day's hunting. But they've got courage. I was once told of a Boer who lost half his hand using a bad cartridge and got his friend to shape his fingers with a hammer and chisel. But they've nothing to touch our infantryman in line. They prefer to fight, of course, on the defensive. It gives them a religious excuse. They can also bet on taking fewer casualties! You've nothing to fear, George. Nothing. We'll give them a pasting if we're asked to.'

'And what if we are asked to?' asked the ever-cautious general. 'That is, what if you were to ask me? How would I come?'

Sir William stood and beckoned to his friend and with their glasses replenished the two knights walked away from the fire to the far side of the drawing-room where a pair of silver candelabra lit a map behind them. Sir William pulled the candles closer and with a long fingernail scratched a cross into the soft canvas where the Transvaal, Natal and the Free State met.

'This is your place, George, just here. It's the only gap in the entire wall of the Drakensbergs an army could march through.'

'And its name?'

'The Boers call it Laings Nek. It's a little way down from the Ingogo River about eight miles from Newcastle.'

'And what's this?' asked Sir George, peering closer and tapping a spot on the canvas. 'Odd-shaped thing. Looks rather like a sugar loaf.'

'It's an old volcano,' replied Sir William. 'Overlooks the Nek. The Boers call it Majuba. The Zulu name for it is Amajuba. It means "the Hill of Doves".'

* * *

And so fate decided in that moment of wicked mischief that Sir George would be defeated in that order: at Laings Nek, the Ingogo River and last and bloodiest of all, Majuba.

General Colley marched out from Durban with as queer a mixture of British soldiers as had ever been brought together. Among them were the Gordon Highlanders, recently arrived from Afghanistan. It was the first time anyone in Natal had seen a kilted regiment, and thousands cheered them on their way as they marched along the seafront with their pipes playing 'The Bluebells of Scotland'.

Watching them go was a young war correspondent, Winston Churchill, who wrote in his dispatch to London, 'They are a splendid bunch, and looking forward to a frolic with these Dutch rebels. It is not to be dreamt of that a parcel of Boers should stand against such fine soldiers.'

And so Colley's little army began their journey for Laings Nek below Majuba and the two thousand Boers waiting for them there.

The Boers had placed themselves well at the Nek through which the Redcoats hoped to pass on their way into the Transvaal to relieve the siege of Pretoria. But Sir George, so certain the Boers would run, sent only half his army and the Boers quickly shot them to pieces. The soldiers tried to rush the Boer positions, running uphill, but after a hundred yards they were too exhausted to hold their rifles steady and when it was over nearly two hundred men were left behind on the grassy slopes, dead or dying. When the Boers went looking for their casualties, there were none.

The brilliant Colley survived but was deaf to caution or common sense and when his scouts told him of a large Boer patrol beyond the Ingogo River, he ate his lunch, took his sword and went after them. By the evening he had led five more companies to the second slaughter.

They were ambushed as they crossed the river, their horses

shot from under them. They fought bravely into the night with the rain coming down in torrents and the cold wind chilling and killing the wounded quicker. The battle was lit by the broken gleams of an uncertain moon but by midnight the clouds completely covered the sky so the battlefield was lit only by the lightning and muzzle flashes and men could not tell thunder from cannon. Two weeks, two battles, two defeats and half his army killed or wounded. It was, as one of Colley's subalterns wrote in his diary: '. . . only to be expected in an army where bravery is more esteemed than strategy and good sense.'

But worse was to come. The Boers were now jubilant and hundreds more were coming flooding across the Vaal from the Free State to fight alongside the Transvaalers, knowing now that the British did not have enough force to defeat them. Bypassing Colley, they invaded Natal and rampaged through the countryside, cutting telegraph wires, looting abandoned English farms, burning wagons, killing oxen and stealing cattle and horses. The small English towns became refugee camps crammed full and no man slept without a gun by his hand and his horse saddled ready. The English along the Natal border and in the besieged towns of the Transvaal began to believe their army had deserted them.

Then, on February 26th, a Saturday, Sir George did the most desperate and foolish thing of all. After a long and pleasant dinner in the mess he called his officers to him and told them that he was going to climb Majuba! He would take all he had left of his little army, four hundred and ninety soldiers and sixty-four sailors and lead them up the steep face of the mountain and catch the Boers napping!

With the moon skirting the peak, he took off his boots and put on a pair of carpet slippers so that he could climb better. Then he shook the hands of his two young subalterns from the Gordon Highlanders at his side, Lieutenants MacDonald and Hamilton, both delighted and excited by their extraordinary general and his daring enterprise!

For seven hours they groped and heaved themselves up the

face of Majuba, each man carrying his rifle, seventy rounds of ammunition and three days' rations on his back, men who had never climbed in their lives before. But when finally they reached the top, exhausted, their hands and knees cut and bleeding, they looked down the other side and saw the Boers' fires two and a half thousand feet beneath them.

Soon after daybreak and despite orders to stay concealed, the men began shouting abuse and shaking their fists and the Boers fired back at them. But their bullets fell a long way short and Sir George was pleased. 'Let them waste their ammunition,' he said. 'This is all very comfortable indeed. We could stay here forever.'

The kilted Gordons were excited. Majuba, with its stony crags and purple heather, could have been any part of their beloved Highlands. They shouted down to the Boers, 'Come up here, you beggars!' The Boers did not hear but they came all the same.

At nine thirty they began inspanning their wagons and the men cheered, thinking they were about to pull out. But at ten the Boers separated into groups and Lieutenant Hamilton urged Sir George to entrench because it seemed the enemy was not in retreat; they were simply angry the British were fighting on a Sunday. And as the young lieutenant watched he saw the Boers preparing for an assault up the face of Majuba themselves. One hundred and eighty of the youngest and strongest were selected and at a few minutes past eleven on that bleak February morning they divided into two and began their climb.

Hamilton ran to Sir George's tent with the news. 'The Boers are advancing, General. Will you let us have a charge? I hope you do not think it presumption on my part to come up and ask?'

'No presumption, Mr Hamilton,' the general replied, forking the last slice of meat from his breakfast plate. 'But we'll wait until the Boers advance further and then we'll give them a volley *and* a charge.'

'Sir!' says Hamilton. 'But shouldn't we entrench? With defences we might keep the entire Boer army away. At present the men have nothing to hide behind.'

'Hide, Mr Hamilton?' said Sir George, wiping his lips clean. 'You speak of hiding? Good hidings is our business, sir! And a British officer stands up front to do it. You'll do well to keep that in mind! Remember, "If the trumpet gives an uncertain call, who will prepare himself for battle?" Saint Paul, Mr Hamilton, Saint Paul, who knew something of duress.'

Lieutenant Hamilton said no more. He saluted and turned about and Sir George stretched in his chair and went to sleep.

The young Boers came up firing so accurately the British soldiers had little heart for a volley and then none at all for a charge. Soon they could see the Boers' faces and they shouted to their officers: 'Permission to fix bayonets, sir,' and the shout came back: 'No! We're not fighting bloody savages.'

The first over the edge was a twelve-year-old farm boy but others were soon behind, coming now on three sides, and the British suddenly realized they did not have the men to cope. They began firing wildly, breaking ranks and running from one side of the mountain's flat top to the other, looking for somewhere safe to tuck themselves. As men broke away near him Lieutenant MacDonald ran in front of them pointing his revolver and shouting: 'Fight, curse you, fight! They're only children coming at us!'

But they pushed past him and ran, throwing their guns away. The men who stayed were doomed. No Boer bullet was wasted. Thirteen of the eighteen who stood by Hamilton were killed and his kilt and tunic were torn to shreds. For a while MacDonald held the west side and then tried to pull his men back to a humped ridge at the edge, but with every yard they retreated another man dropped, and by the time he reached the ridge only one, a private, was still with him.

Woken by the commotion, Sir George came running out of his tent, shouting orders at the top of his voice, wild-eyed like a man waking from a nightmare. He ran forward of his men still in his slippers, firing his revolver at the nearest Boers twenty yards away. But his bullets went high over their heads and a young boy came forward and, carefully aiming his rifle, hit Colley over his right eye. The bullet entered his brain and made a gaping hole as it left the back of his head. The impact lifted him off the ground and he fell, face up, into a thorn bush.

The British lines gave way; but they would not, could not rally, and instead ran between the Boers to the small field hospital set up in a small depression on the lowest part of the plateau. But Boer fire followed them, and hit the doctors and attendants and many of the wounded were hit a second and a third time. One of the orderlies, Lance Corporal Farmer, held up a white handkerchief but they shot him through the elbow. He held it up with the other arm but they shot that too. So the soldiers carried on down the steep slopes, throwing off knapsacks and pouches, webbing and bayonets as they fled.

Hamilton was now the only officer left alive on the ridge and seeing his general killed, he too turned and ran. But a bullet chased him and grazed him and knocked him down and when he came to, young Boers were emptying his pockets and tearing off his belt and badges, and towering above them a giant of a man with a pipe in his mouth and the Hamiltons' ancestral claymore in his hands. They stripped him nearly naked and kicked him downhill and he wandered half-conscious and bleeding, not knowing whether he was nearing friends or foe until he was found by a British patrol and carried to camp.

The Boers stripped the bodies, leaving only a man's socks on. The Highlanders' kilts and sporrans were the greatest trophies, and many a Boer daughter would soon be seen wearing them on Sundays to commemorate the victory. Colley's body was laid out like the effigy of a cathedral knight, his eyes still staring at the grey sky over Majuba, until an old Boer knelt and closed them. Then they began chanting their hymns of thanksgiving, shouting, 'Thank you, General Jesus, for beating the English today.' The next morning the Boers let the English come to take their general away, and formed a silent avenue as he was carried down the mountainside. When he was buried at the military cemetery at nearby Mount Prospect, none of the mourners mentioned his failure, nor would they. He would remain their champion and men who should have known better said 'Amen' to the verse:

> 'He needs no tears,
> Who in the forefront of the fight,
> Met death as should a gentleman
> Upon Majuba's height.'

A little battle in a little war, but another two hundred and thirty were killed and wounded. The Imperial army had been disgraced and humbled and no British regiment was ever to carry its colours into battle again.

A little war and a little battle, but for years to come men would mention the name and shake their heads, or point their finger at the square-topped mountain and say: 'There the British Empire began to crumble; there it happened, on a February Sunday afternoon, when British soldiers fled from Boer farm boys and threw down their rifles, running helter skelter down Majuba.'

The treaties and conventions of the surrender had still to be signed but every Englishman in the Transvaal knew that his day was over.

Soon the Boers left their snipers' nests and their tents on the Maghaliesbergs and came riding triumphantly into Pretoria. They tore down Major Le Mesurier's warnings of British shells and the mines and sent one of their youngest to the top of the town hall roof to raise the orange, white and green flag of their victorious republic. Then they turned into the square and rode six abreast across the wide street up the hill to the fort.

Men, women and their children stood on the sandbagged barricades and watched in silence as they trotted by, led by a man with a bandolier of cartridges over his shoulder, a man with a tall black hat and a thin grey face, the man who had led the massacre of the 94th at Bronkerspruit, Commandant Frans Joubert. The regiment's bugles and drums hung from their saddles, souvenirs of that day, and their saddlecloths were stitched together from the scarlet and blue uniforms they had stripped from the British dead.

Joubert stopped on the rise that overlooked the refugee camp, in the shadow of the battlements, and read out the terms of the victory. 'Self-government and independence has been restored,' he said, 'and whatever else has been preached in London or the Cape or Durban these past months, the Transvaal has been returned to us the Boers. Afrikanerdom has triumphed!'

His men cheered and fired their rifles at the sky. Children were startled and cried but no one else moved. They were waiting for Colonel Bellairs to come to the battlements and open the gate and call Joubert a liar; to deny that the British government had agreed to any such thing, that the ceasefire and armistice were simply to enable peace and British rule to return as before. But the gates did not open and neither the colonel nor any British soldier showed his face.

Joubert waited for a moment, then turned and led his horsemen back down the hill towards the town again and when they had gone, men and their women sat down on the sandbags and wept openly and their children sat by them, wondering why. For three months they had survived the days of Boer bullets and the long, long nights of death and despair, believing that with the Union Jack flying the British would see them through.

In their fury, the young men of D'Arcy's Horse smashed their rifles against the walls of the fort and cursed England's name and older men, who had worn their medals from other campaigns throughout the siege, tore them off and heeled them into the ground. Someone climbed the flagpole and brought down the Union Jack and trailed it through the mud and people who the day before might have risked their lives to keep it flying, watched in silence. An effigy of Prime Minister Gladstone was hung from a gibbet and burnt and children danced and cheered as the wax melted. Their fathers and their brothers ran to the sandbag walls shouting that they were Englishmen no longer. One old man who had lost his three sons in the fighting caught Mary's arm. 'I would rather have stayed here another ten years living on rats and dogs,' he said, 'than go free this way.'

The army released the African servants from the fort and within the hour Tongo found Mary. She took him to William and he squatted by his bed for the rest of the day chatting. But William only stared at the ceiling, his body so still it might have been dead. He must not worry, Tongo told him. The wagon was still together, and even though one of the oxen had been shot for meat the others were well and with a week of good grass they would pull again. Just as soon as William said so he would bring them harnessed and ready and they could all leave for their home in the mountains again.

Mary was desperate to go but she dared not. Three times a day now Dr Simon left his other patients and rolled William onto his stomach to inspect the swelling between his shoulder blades. It felt like a tight bubble of air but he knew it was liquid, like white blood, he said. He would not pierce it, though, because he was sure nature had put it there to protect the damaged nerve.

'I think William's body is fighting for itself,' he told her. 'Sometimes the swelling is warm, almost hot, as if the fight is right there beneath it. I believe, Mary, that until the day it goes away William will not walk from Pretoria.'

As other patients recovered and their families came to take them to their homes in town, Dr Simon moved his surgery back into the convent and William was put into a bed for the first time. Mary and Polly took it in turns to nurse him, one in the day, the other at night, waiting for the swelling to go down. And Tongo stayed by him watching for the legs to move again.

* * *

News of the British surrender spread through the Transvaal and across the borders into the Tribal lands quicker than any horse could have carried it. And when they heard, the Great Chiefs Sechele, Montisiwe, Mankoroane and Khama hung their heads and called their counsellors and there was silence in the kraals and villages.

Paramount Chief Mapoch left his kraal long before his wives had stirred and walked on his own through the mists and wet grass to a giant balancing rock on the rim of a wide bowl scooped out of the earth. The air was thin and sharp and as he waited he pulled his cloak around him and rubbed his cold nose with cold fingers.

As the sun lifted they gradually came to him, one by one, not together as villagers or families but purposely alone to pay separate homage to their great chief who had lived so long, it was said, their fathers were only children when he was already a man and a warrior.

He watched them come and sit below him as the sun rose. It warmed their backs and he opened his cloak so that his old thin body might feel its life as well. For two hours he stood there, perfectly still, a tall grey statue on a ball of reddening granite.

Then his *indunas*, his counsellors, sitting beneath him and close by, began clapping and those behind them clapped too and so it spread back and across the bowl until thousands of pairs of hands, large and small, young and old, were beating together, harder and harder, louder and louder, until suddenly, without any order or signal, it stopped, completely and together, as if all sound had in that instant left the world. Mapoch stood like a cross with his arms outstretched and boomed across the listening obedient heads.

'We have been deserted, we who carried their shells and hauled their heavy guns and gave their soldiers food and water. The English have gone and they have delivered us to the Boers like so many herds. They who promised us great harvests have sown nothing and we will reap nothing. We will eat only the bitter bread they leave behind. They have given us away and soon the Boers will come on their horses for revenge. They will come into our lands as they please and plunder, stealing our cattle and our children and burning our villages. They will take what we have today and all we might have had tomorrow. They will spread north beyond us and east and west until they reach the oceans each side so that nothing will be ours and we will have no inheritance.

'I am Mapoch and my ancestors are witness to my good promises and faith. But today the English have buried their honour and for all time on their heads will rest the blood of the tribes they have abandoned.'

He gathered his cloak, turned and walked out of their sight down the granite slope of the giant rock, back along the path to wait for the horsemen to come.

Once the British marksmen had left, the nuns returned to their cells and scrubbed them clean with Dr Simon's carbolic. They hung their Christs and Madonnas on the walls and placed their crucifixes on the window-ledges so that the sun and the moon would take it in turn to light His head again.

Mary sat by the convent door and listened to their morning prayers. She could see Pretoria below and hear the occasional sounds of hammers and saws, as houses and shops were put properly together again. But she could not see men working and there were no other sounds, none of the bustle of a town coming back to life. No children played in the gardens or on the porches, no horses or oxen were on the streets, no women hung out their washing. The great wide square remained empty. The town was muted, like some hot summer afternoon when even the flies settle in the shade and wait for the cool breezes of evening.

Some miles distant she saw that the Boers had returned to their tents on the Maghaliesbergs. She could see their fires and their horses grazing. It was as if everyone on both sides were now waiting, expecting to be told what to do next, who was to go where and when. It was as if all of a sudden, everyone had lost.

Captain D'Arcy came to see William and say his goodbyes but William heard nothing and saw only tiny lizards cross the ceiling. Dr Simon showed the captain the swelling between the blades and placed his finger on it to feel the heat and the captain shook his head.

He offered six of his men to escort Mary and the wagon north but Mary said no. When she finally left Pretoria, she said, she would leave the war behind. But the captain shook his head again and said the war had been everywhere and it would be with them all the way home. Come to Natal, he urged her, to Pietermaritzburg or Durban. 'There's no reason to stay here any longer, ma'am,' he said. 'There's no more room for us in the Transvaal. This is all Boerland now, right the way across the Vaal into the Free State. We'll hang on to Natal and the Cape but that's how this country has been divided, at least for the time being.

'After this miserable little fight the Boers reckon they're a match for us but we've really been beaten by the British government and its treachery. The price of this so-called peace will be paid . . . not now . . . not by me or my men . . . but in time when other Englishmen are sent out to settle the score. I tell you, ma'am, the British taxpayer has not heard the last of this country and its little wars.

'Gladstone has given the Boers with guns in their hands what he refused to give them in peace time, and that's a fatal thing to do to men with domination over so much land and so many ignorant races.

'What's happened here, ma'am, is just a punctuation mark in a history book . . . a comma, not a full stop. This hasn't been a war, it's been too short to settle anything. The Boers have won too quickly and the English too easily humbled and they'll not put up with it for long. They'll come back. God knows when, but God help us when they do.

'The curtains have been drawn on this South Africa of mine but it'll be raised again and when it is there'll be such confusion. New Irelands will rise here – mark my words, they will. Then heaven help us and our children and their children, too!'

He went to William's bed and took his hand. 'When he is well again, ma'am, give him my thanks for the honour he brought to me. There isn't one among us who hasn't done more than his bit of praying for him. If prayers are heard any more.'

He stepped back from the bed and saluted and Mary watched him walk out into the sunlight and heard his horse carry him away. But she did not move to see him go.

The weather had broken at last and Polly sat her night watch outside under the stars. She turned up the wick of the oil lamp so she could see to darn the tears in William's shirts.

Except for the first few words after his operation he had not spoken in the three weeks since. Nor had he moved so they feared nothing in him would ever move again. All he could swallow was milk or broth and the swelling now seemed larger than a man's fist, red and sore with fever. Dr Simon's words never left Polly. 'Until it goes he will not walk from Pretoria.' Now she feared it going. Better not to know than to be certain he was trapped and living in a dead man's shell, until he died inside it. How unfairly are the good and the brave repaid! They were her father's words and she had heard them often as a child. God is capable of the most monstrous injustices, he would say, testing a man's loyalty and racking him with doubts with His absurd and wicked judgements.

But still she and Mary began and ended each day or night watch on their knees in prayer even though they guessed He did not feel obliged to help. Their faith was reduced with every day of William's silence but they had to pray. There was no one else.

Her eyes began to tire so she broke the thread and rolled up the shirts and went inside to William. The doctor had propped him on his side to ease the pressure on the swelling and she could see it throbbing, the only moving thing in the still body, as if only it had life and the power to take it away.

Then she gasped and fell back against the door. At the top of William's bed a yard from his head and almost hidden in the gloom she saw Tongo. He was standing perfectly still and though his eyes were wide he was not awake. His arms were stretched out in front of him, the tips of his long fingers barely touching William's temples and moving ever so slightly, shivering like blades of dry winter grass in the wind.

But his arms and chest were taut, every muscle hard and glistening with sweat, bulging as if the black shining fabric was about to burst open.

'Tongo,' she whispered but he did not hear. Then he began to move his lips but when she heard the voice she sank to her knees. It was the voice of an old man, broken and frail, coming from a hundred years away, speaking in a language she had never heard before, shrill, then sinking to a whisper, booming and then hoarse, angry then pleading, on and on, endless and unbroken, coming from Tongo's mouth.

As she watched, his body began to shake and then the muscles began to cavort as if they were bearing some enormous weight, stiff and straining, turning and twisting as if there was a larger, stronger body inside, powerful and desperate to escape. The voice coaxed and cajoled, as Tongo stared above him, his eyes wide and yellow in the lamplight, spittle flecking from his lips and dripping onto his chest. And all the time the fingers caressed and danced on the limp unconscious body, transmitting their magic.

Then suddenly he screamed and roared as if two voices had come inside one and he flung his head violently from side to side. The fingers stiffened and the hands clasped William's head like a vice, squeezing and boring into the scalp so that tiny streams of blood trickled across the nails and the voices roared again as if they were winning and had almost won.

'Tongo!' Polly screamed. 'Tongo . . . Tongo.' Then there was silence and everything was still. Tongo closed his eyes and his hands slid from William's head as he fell to the floor.

She crawled forward to the bed and pulled herself level with William as Mary and Jollie came running in.

'Polly, Polly, what is it? What happened?'

But Polly only pointed at William's back, at the smooth white skin between his shoulder blades.

'It's gone,' she whispered. 'It's gone!'

And the three women knelt together and cupped their hands to their lips in prayer as William opened his eyes, turned his head and held his arm out to touch them.

They were ready to leave within three days and William walked to the wagon, though Dr Simon said he did not know how.

'Mother Nature normally won't be hurried,' he told Mary as they watched.

'Maybe it was God's work,' she said.

'Or the Devil's.'

'In Africa, Simon, God and the Devil are the same.'

He picked up the last of the parcels of food and clothes she had wrapped together and walked with her away from the convent, helping her across the broken sprawling sandbags.

'Does Tongo remember nothing?' he asked.

'No, nothing . . . at least, nothing he thinks concerns us.'

He looked puzzled. She held his arm in hers.

'An old good friend, who first brought me into Africa,' she said, 'told me we can overestimate the Africans or underestimate them, value them or not, treat them well or not, just as long as we don't discover what they hide.'

'And they have much?' he asked.

'Oh, yes,' she said. 'More than we know. They have kept something our fathers lost.'

Dr Simon and Tongo helped lift William onto the driver's

box and with Jollie and Polly cuddling the babies inside, Mary climbed alongside him and took the reins.

'I can stop being a nurse now,' she said, smiling down at Dr Simon. Then she asked, 'Will you go to Natal with the others?'

'No,' he said. 'Too many English there. At least, too many better-qualified English doctors and I think I'd starve. No. I think I'll go further south. I've heard there's been some discoveries only a few hours from here. They've found more gold at a place called Witwatersrand – I think it means white water reef – and there's a new settlement forming up, with diggers and businessmen coming in. The Boers already have a name for it: they're calling it Johannesburg. Maybe I'll find enough sickness there to make a living.'

'Come and see us if you can,' she said, holding out her hand.

'I will, Mary. I will. And if your gold runs out . . . maybe you'll come south to see me. And you, William? You can make your fortune there and I'll keep you fit to do it.'

As they reached the corner they turned for their last look, and Dr Simon was still on the sandbags, waving.

As far as they could see, the road was lined with the English going south: ox wagons, mule carts and African drovers whipping the herds ahead of them. Furniture and farm tools were arranged in neat piles outside every house and abandoned dogs ran wild. The English were leaving and what they could not take with them they were burning. Columns of smoke rose up into the still autumn sky as they put a match to their barns, their timber stores, their grain bins and tobacco kilns, scorching the earth rather than leave the Boers a pennyworth more: abandoning their farms where a portrait of the Queen and her Albert had once hung over every mantelpiece.

Men shouted abuse at them in English, thinking they were Boers. Women spat and their children threw stones at the oxen and a young horseman used his whip on Tongo's back but cantered away before Mary could reach for William's rifle.

The scars of the war followed the road just as the cumbersome British army had done in the months before, trailing their heavy lumbering supply wagons behind them until they were overtaken and overwhelmed by the faster, lighter Boer commando. Houses along the road had been ripped open by the sweep of bullets from a British Gatling gun and the cornfields were cratered by their artillery. Every rock and boulder seemed to have been grazed and chipped in some battle lost and won, and everywhere there were bloated cattle waiting for the vultures.

They were north of Middleburg near a kraal called Botsabelo when Mary held up her hand and pointed. A few hundred yards on their right they saw a fort, its earth defences rising like the sides of a dyke, and fluttering limp from the mast in its centre, the shreds of a Union Jack. Further to the right, in a line from its splintered gate, Mary saw what looked like a small plantation of young saplings with mounds of bright chalk between them. She helped William down but Polly shook her head and Jollie turned away.

The bleached bones of the horses' skeletons lay perfectly in order, spread across the ground like exhibits in a museum, picked immaculate and clean by a thousand tiny scavengers. Their harnesses and saddles were still in place, their leathers and brasses polished and shining. They were like resting phantoms preparing to fly again.

The Boers had buried the English riders where they had fallen and instead of crosses, a bayonet or a rifle had been rammed into the earth to mark the graves.

Mary and William stepped carefully between the markers like visitors to a strange or foreign cemetery. There was no other sound but theirs and no other movement, not a whisper of a breeze, not a cloud's shadow. She remembered a rhyme, her father's words, and she recited them out loud wondering if more than just the two of them might hear.

> 'Oh why do people waste their breath
> Devising dainty names for death?

If they should ask you why we died
Tell them because our fathers lied.'

She looked at the monument and its flag in tatters.

'Do you suppose,' she asked, 'that God has a special place for the boys who died here? Somewhere just for them? It would be dreadful if He housed them with stockbrokers and grocers.'

William said nothing. They held hands and walked slowly to the wagon and did not look back.

They were coming to the foothills of the Steenkamp Mountains just south of Lydenburg when they saw a line of people spread out across the slopes walking towards them. They looked as if they were sowing corn but as they came closer Mary saw their heads were bowed, men, women and older children searching the ground. Behind them four women held the corners of an open blanket.

They passed within twenty yards of the wagon but they did not look up. Then there was a shriek and a woman fell to her knees and began sobbing. Others rushed to her and they also fell down and began weeping and shouting prayers and the men behind took off their hats and sang psalms. When they had done, the first woman stood and those with the blanket came forward and she threw a human skull into it. Mary understood. This had been another battlefield and the widows and their families, their brothers and sisters, their uncles and cousins had come to collect enough bones to fill a coffin. But the lion and the hyena, the jackal and the vulture had come early and had broken and scattered the skeletons across the lonely veld.

The line was reformed and they went on again until someone found a shin bone or a hand or a rib and then they sobbed and sang and prayed again until they disappeared over the hill.

The Lydenburg garrison had been burnt to the ground. Nothing was left but charred timbers and a large circle of ash.

A dozen Boers blocked the road, their rifles across their shoulders. The tallest walked towards them and William recognized him as the youngest Bezuidenhout son. He pushed Tongo away and took the reins, turning the oxen around.

'This is the way for you, Engelsman,' he said in his surly Boer way. 'South . . . to Natal, where you and all the other rooinecks belong. This is Boerland now . . . *maak gou!*'

'We are going to the goldfields,' said Mary, pulling on the reins. 'We're stopping at Mrs de Wet's.'

Bezuidenhout laughed. 'No one goes to the goldfields,' he said, 'or leaves them unless our Paul Kruger says so. And you've a long way to find the old lady. She's dead. Now off, before I put a bullet up your tail!'

Mary reined back again. The Boer pulled his hat hard over his forehead and the others brought their guns off their shoulders.

Then William shouted, 'Stop! I am Llewellyn, the brother of Ianto.'

Bezuidenhout came forward slowly, slapping the flanks of each oxen as he passed and laid his rifle across the last one's back. He looked closely at William. Then he said, 'That's right, so you are. The sun is low. I can't see properly your face.' He touched his hat to Mary and shouted to the men at the barricade, and they lowered their guns.

Then he said, 'We are to keep this road closed but we can't stop you, not the brother of the Welshman.' He turned and shouted to Tongo, 'Here, boy . . . take it again.'

William said, 'You said Mrs de Wet was dead.'

'That's right. The day the English went. They left a patrol behind to do some work but our own Wenkommando caught them up and chased them to the old lady's house. They fought well, mind you, three hours it took until they were dead. Their sergeant was the last, and my, did he fight well, that man! But as we went to fetch them the roof fell in and the whole place went up in fire. Next day, when it was cool, we found them all joined together, melted, the way fire does. And that's how we buried them. Except the one, the one they killed. The one they left outside.'

'And who was that?' asked Mary.

But already the Boer was walking away, shouting to Tongo, 'Now move, kaffir, move! On your way!'

There was little to see now of the farmhouse. The mud and stone walls were only a yard high and the timbers that had held the thatch were sticks of charcoal no thicker than a pole. In the corner, where the old lady had kept her dresser, was a naked old black, skinny and wrinkled, crouching among some chickens, smoking dagga out of a cow's horn with a reed. He nodded and giggled and threw dust at the fowls.

'It was such a pretty place,' said William. 'She always had a fire going and a kettle on the boil. It was like a gingerbread house, cosy and always smelling as if there was something nice for supper. She kept the dress you made her on the wall here with a bag of herbs by it.' He leant his head against the wall but Mary could not help him. 'She made milk custard pies,' he said, 'and her Uncle Abe shot a buck and a fish and some pheasants too, all with one shot. And a porcupine.' But it was only a whisper and the old naked man giggled again and began picking at scabs on his legs.

They outspanned that night on the banks of the Speekboom some miles from Krugers Post. Tomorrow, they would rise early, before the sun came up, ready for the long climb up Pilgrims Hill.

They lit two fires and Jollie made a stew as Polly put Tom and the twins to bed. The cocks scratched and shuffled in their cages beneath the wheels and the goat lay beside them, his head resting on his forelegs like a dog on a rug.

Tongo let the oxen out on a long rein to graze but shortly afterwards they heard lion a mile or two away and William said he would sit a while with his rifle and pull the oxen in once they had had their hour of grass.

Mary sat close to the fire even though the night was warm. She felt weary, tired and tiring, but she did not want to sleep. She wanted the night to go away quickly so it would be day and they could start for home. More than anything now she wanted that, to see the house, and her own furniture, to pick at the weeds between her flowers and smell the woodsmoke from her grate. She wanted most of all to sit in her rocking-chair on the verandah and look out to the lowveld and know at last what it was, after so many years of wondering: dummies in army tunics hanging from a scaffold, men in scarlet staining the road red and a stream that bled a drummer boy dry. The lowveld was a hundred nights of gangrene and diarrhoea and bullets that let in the rain. It was a girl as young as Polly in a coffin of flowers and men as old as grandfathers crying like babies on a weary March morning. The lowveld was a tiny copse of dead men's rifles and sunbleached horses and peach trees growing from knapsacks; burning corn and the long queue south, and wandering, wailing widows taking back from the fields what was theirs in a blanket.

From her mountain top she had always thought of it as one huge green and tan land stretching its thousands of miles to the seas, changeless and secure. But now she knew it was not one land but many, all being torn and clawed at by as many separate people, jealous and hating and fearing each other, British and Boer, black and white and in such confusion. There was no peace now, nor would there be. South Africa was too large and the people in it too small to cope. God should never have made countries so big that people lost them.

The lions called again and she heard William moving in the long grass, and it came back to her, that night she had first heard them, sitting by such a fire, listening to Walrus Baines and marvelling at it all.

How short is a year, and now she had seen seven here. She felt she had caught Africa on the tilt, and so delicately balanced was it between the old and the changing, between the changeless and the new, that their arrival, just a few like them, had been enough to tip the scales and everything was now tumbling into a new order, making new patterns. Was that why the lions were calling? Angry at what they were losing?

She looked up from the flames as William and Tongo came in pulling the oxen behind them.

'Is their hour up already?' she asked.

'No, mother, but the lions seem closer, at least they're louder. Something's worrying them. Tongo thinks someone's disturbed them.'

'Someone?'

'Yes,' said Tongo. 'They are eating but they are moving again. Only man can do that.' He brought more wood and stoked the fires, but he did not sit with them. He stood half in and half out of the light, listening.

Mary asked, 'Shall I heat some soup?'

But Tongo hissed, 'Listen! Listen!'

Mary could hear nothing but she went to the driver's box and pulled out Jacob's panga and William dropped spare cartridges into his pocket. The only sound was the breeze flapping the wagon's canvas. Then Tongo hissed again and held up his hand, his eyes wide, staring out into the black. Then he whispered, 'Horse coming . . . man on horse.'

Mary went and stood by him . . . the boy Tongo, now a young man sturdy and tall. He could hear what they could not, could guess what they could not.

'What is it?' she whispered but he did not reply. His eyes narrowed and he raised his face to the night. William put the rifle to his shoulder and pointed the barrel into the blackness. Then suddenly Tongo was smiling and ran forward.

'It *is* a horse, Mrs Mary,' he said, clapping his hands. 'It is Flansman and Major John.'

And Mary understood. He had ridden through the night, ignoring the lion and the Boer's curfew, to tell her something she already knew. Then he would take her home.

* * *

The white ashes of the dying fire took on the colour of the sun as it bled into the morning sky. She stood and stretched and watched a herd of buck come out of the cover of the mists and browse across the slopes of Pilgrims Hill. It was a crisp new day and soon she would be home, with Ianto already there.

Major John had spoken of it in whispers as they sat together through the night. 'He was the bravest of all, Mary. Honest Jack will tell you, and his wife too. He could have ridden off on his own, he knew the bush well enough. He could have escaped, she said so. But he saved the family and Honest Jack's life as well. The Redcoats would have shot him too, he knew that.

'The soldiers were taking him to Pretoria for execution but they only got as far as Lydenburg. Then they shot him before the Boers shot them. The brothers came up to us with his coffin and made the strangest request. They said he was an *uitlander*, an outsider, and they told the Reverend that his grave should be dug at right angles to the others to show he did not belong: not to them, nor the English, nor Africa. And that's how he lies, Mary. On his own.'

She reached out to him. He turned her hand and kissed her palm.

They drank tea and William and Tongo inspanned, ready for the climb. The sun had burnt the mists away, as it does every African morning, shrinking the dew and turning the damp back to dust as nature's tiny things scuttle to the shade. The sky turns silver at the edge and a shimmering haze melts the horizon so that Africa has no beginning and the searching eye no end.

Geoffrey Jenkins

Geoffrey Jenkins writes of adventure on land and at sea in some of the most exciting thrillers ever written.

'Geoffrey Jenkins has the touch that creates villains and heroes – and even icy heroines – with a few vivid words.' *Liverpool Post*

'A style which combines the best of Nevile Shute and Ian Fleming.' *Books and Bookmen*

SOUTHTRAP
A BRIDGE OF MAGPIES
FIREPRINT
HUNTER-KILLER
A RAVEL OF WATERS
THE UNRIPE GOLD
A GRUE OF ICE
THE WATERING PLACE OF GOOD PEACE
THE RIVER OF DIAMONDS

FONTANA PAPERBACKS

It was too late.

She'd seen him. For the first time since she'd walked out of his hospital room. Twenty-six months ago. That had been the last time the world had seen Leonid, too. He'd dropped off the radar completely.

But he was back. Everywhere Kassandra turned there'd been news of him. She'd managed not to look. Until now.

Now her retinas burned with the image of him striding out of his Fifth Avenue headquarters. In spite of herself, she'd strained to see how much of the Leonid she'd known had survived.

The man she'd known had crackled with irrepressible vitality, a smile of whimsy and assurance always hovering on his lips and sparking in his eyes.

The man who'd filled the screen had appeared totally detached, as if he didn't consider himself part of the world anymore. Or as if it was beneath his notice.

And the stalking swagger was gone. In its place was a deliberate, menacing prowl. Whether or not the changes were by-products of the impact of his accident, it had been clear, even in those fleeting moments on-screen:

This wasn't the man she'd known.

* * *

Twin Heirs to His Throne
is part of Mills & Boon Desire's No. 1 bestselling
ser